Caroline Ande ... is the mind of a butte... ...s been a nurse, a secretary, a teacher, has run her own soft-furnishing business, and is now settled on writing. She says, "I was looking for that elusive something. I finally realised it was variety, and now I have it in abundance. Every book brings new horizons and new friends, and in between writing books I have learned to be a juggler. My teacher husband John and I have two beautiful and talented daughters, Sarah and Hannah, umpteen pets and several acres of Suffolk that nature tries to reclaim every time we turn our backs!"

Award-winning author **Jessica Hart** was born in West Africa, and has suffered from itchy feet ever since—travelling and working around the world in a wide variety of interesting but very lowly jobs, all of which have provided inspiration to draw from when it comes to the settings and plots of her stories. Now she lives a rather more settled existence in York, where she has been able to pursue her interest in history, although she still yearns sometimes for wider horizons. If you'd like to know more about Jessica, visit her website www.jessicahart.co.uk

National bestselling author **Jules Bennett** has penned over forty contemporary romance novels. She lives in the Midwest with her high-school-sweetheart husband and their two kids. Jules can often be found on Twitter chatting with readers, and you can also connect with her via her website, julesbennett.com

The Single Dads
COLLECTION

July 2019

August 2019

September 2019

October 2019

November 2019

December 2019

Falling for the Single Dad

CAROLINE ANDERSON

JESSICA HART

JULES BENNETT

MILLS & BOON

First Published in Great Britain 2019
By Mills & Boon, an imprint of HarperCollins*Publishers*
1 London Bridge Street, London, SE1 9GF

FALLING FOR THE SINGLE DAD
© 2019 Harlequin Books S.A.

Caring for His Baby © Caroline Anderson 2007
Barefoot Bride © Jessica Hart 2007
The Cowboy's Second-Chance Family © Jules Bennett 2017

ISBN: 978-0-263-27617-6

1019

MIX
Paper from
responsible sources
FSC
www.fsc.org
FSC™ C007454

This book is produced from independently certified FSC™ paper to ensure responsible forest management.

For more information visit: www.harpercollins.co.uk/green

Printed and bound in Spain
by CPI, Barcelona

CARING FOR HIS BABY

CAROLINE ANDERSON

PROLOGUE

CRISIS in night. Please contact us ASAP.

Harry Kavenagh stared at the message handed to him by the hotel receptionist, and felt a cold chill run through him. No. Not now. He wasn't ready.

He'd never be ready—not for this.

Still staring at the words, he rammed the fingers of his other hand through his hair, rumpling the dusty, sweaty strands even further. So what now? He turned the paper over, looking for more information, but there was nothing.

'When did they call?' he asked.

'This morning, sir. Just after you went out.'

Fingers suddenly unsteady and his heart thudding in his throat, he called the number from his room. Five minutes later he was in a car on the way to the airport, his mind still reeling.

He couldn't believe it was actually happening. Stupid. He ought to be able to. It had been his idea, after all. They'd wanted to turn off the machine weeks ago, with his agreement, but he'd seen enough loss of life. Too much. So he'd begged them to reconsider—exhausted, perhaps a little drunk and stunned by what they'd told him, he'd haggled them into submission.

They'd kept their side of the bargain. And now he had to keep his.

He swallowed, staring out of the window, not seeing the bombed-out buildings, the shattered lives all around him. A shell exploded a few streets away, but he barely noticed. It all seemed suddenly terribly remote and curiously irrelevant, because in the space of the next few hours, his whole life would change for ever.

She was tiny.

So small, so fragile looking, her fingers so fine they were almost transparent under the special light. She needed the light because she was yellow. Jaundiced, apparently. Quite common in slightly prem babies. Nothing to worry about.

But Harry worried about it. He worried about all of it. How on earth was he supposed to look after her? She was just a little dot of a thing, so dainty, no bigger than a doll. Small for dates, they'd said. No wonder, under the circumstances.

He didn't want to think about that, about how he'd failed her mother. How he'd brought her here to London to keep her safe and then failed her anyway.

'How are you doing?'

He looked up at the nurse and tried to smile. 'OK. She was screwing her face up a minute ago. I think she might have a nappy problem.'

'Want to change it?'

He felt his blood run cold. No. His hands were too big. He'd hurt her...

'She won't break, you know,' the nurse teased gently. 'You'll be fine. I'll help you.'

So he changed her nappy—extraordinarily complicated

for something so ordinary—and by the end of the day and a few more goes he'd mastered it, even managing to grip those tiny little ankles between his fingers without snapping her legs when he lifted her up to swap the nappies over or wipe her unbelievably tiny bottom.

Such soft skin. Such astonishing perfection, all those little fingers and toes, the nails so small he could hardly see them. She was a little miracle, and he was awed beyond belief.

And terrified.

The nurse—Sue, her name was, according to her badge—brought him a bottle and helped him feed her again, and she brought it all up all over him. Panic threatened to choke him, but Sue just laughed and cleaned her up, lent him a fresh scrub top and handed her back.

'Make her slow down. She's feeding too fast—tip the bottle up a bit more so she doesn't get so much air. And wind her in between.'

In between what? And wind her? How? He'd never winded a baby in his life, and he was damned if he knew where to start.

With that, or with any of it.

He felt faintly hysterical, but that was probably lack of sleep and shock. He stifled the urge to laugh, but then his eyes prickled and he felt the panic rise again.

What on earth had he done?

The old Chinese proverb rang hollow in his ears. *If you save a life, it belongs to you.*

He stared down at her, this tiny girl who apparently was his, her transparent fingers wrapped around his little finger with incredible strength, and the panic receded a little, replaced by wonder.

She was amazing. Beautiful. Scary as hell, but astonishing.

And his.

Officially registered this morning as his daughter, in the presence of the registrar of births, marriages and deaths just round the corner from the hospital.

He'd registered her mother's death at the same time, armed with more forms and certificates from the hospital, and then he'd gone back there and asked to see Carmen's body, so frail, so young, but finally at peace. And he'd told her about the baby, and promised her he'd do for the baby what he'd failed to do for her—to keep her safe. So now, in every way that mattered, she was his.

'Get out of that, Kavenagh,' he murmured, but strangely he didn't want to. He couldn't imagine walking away from her. Just the thought of abandoning her to fate made him feel so fiercely protective it scared him.

Together with everything else today.

God, he was knackered. Maybe if he just propped her up on his chest and leant back...

'Harry?'

He opened his eyes a crack, blinking at the light, and Sue's face came into focus. 'Why don't you go and have a lie-down? There's a room here for parents—nothing flashy, just a few beds and a separate area with a TV and little kitchen, but you could sleep for a while.'

Sleep. Oh, yes. Please. He had to get some sleep. It had been weeks since he'd slept properly, with the constant shelling and rocket fire going on all night, but this had tired him more than any of that.

He nodded, realising that the baby was back in her crib under the light and that everything was being taken care of.

'Will she be all right?' he asked, as if his presence actually made a blind bit of difference, but the nurse just smiled and nodded.

'Sure. I'll look after her for you, I'm on till nine, and I'll hand her over to the night staff before I go. Come on, I'll show you the parents' room.'

A bed. Crisp white sheets, a slightly crackly pillow and almost instant oblivion…

'You'll be OK.'

He stared down at Sue, wishing he could believe her. She'd spent the last few days telling him he could cope, showing him not just how to change nappies and hold feeding bottles, but bath and dress and simply cuddle his tiny daughter, and he'd begun to believe that maybe—just maybe—he'd manage. Till now.

She was so small, his little doll, but she was tough, like her mother—fierce and determined, and for something so tiny she had a blood-curling scream. He'd become almost confident, in the safe environment of the special care baby unit, surrounded by the bleeps and clicks of the equipment, the hurried footsteps, the laughter and the tears. But now…

'We're always here if you have a problem. You can ring at any time. You will cope, Harry,' Sue said again, as if by repeating it she could make it true, and stretching up on tiptoe, she kissed his cheek and went back inside, leaving him on the outside of the doors, stranded.

What was he supposed to do now? Where could he go? His flat? It was nothing more than a crash pad, really, and it didn't feel like his any longer, but stupidly until now he hadn't even thought about where he'd take the baby. Just not there. It didn't seem right. But where?

He looked down at his tiny girl in the shockingly expensive baby carrier he'd bought that morning, and his heart squeezed. She was staring up at him intently, her almost black eyes fixed on his face, and he found himself suddenly calmer.

He knew what to do, and it was more than time he did it. He should have done it years ago.

'Come on, my little Kizzy,' he murmured softly. 'We're going home.'

CHAPTER ONE

SOMEONE was moving in.

It had been weeks since the last tenants had left, but there was a car on the drive and the lights were on.

Emily craned her neck and tried to catch a glimpse of the people, but she couldn't see through the trees. Not clearly enough, anyway. The branches kept drifting softly in the light breeze and blocking her view, and every time she shifted, so did the leaves.

And she was turning into a curtain twitcher, for heaven's sake!

She snapped the curtain shut and turned her back on the window, tucking up Freddie and smiling down at him. Gorgeous. He was just gorgeous, and she wanted to scoop him up and snuggle him.

Except he'd wake in a foul mood and the sweet little cherub would turn into a howling, raging tyrant. The terrible twos were well named, and he wasn't even there yet, not for five months!

She grinned and tiptoed out, blowing him a kiss and pulling the door to, just a little, before checking on his big sister. Beth was lying on her back, one foot stuck out the side, her tousled dark hair wisping across her face.

Emily eased the strand away from her eyes and feathered a kiss over her brow, then left her to sleep. There was a film on television starting in a few minutes that she'd been meaning to watch. If she could get the washing-up stacked in the dishwasher, she might even get to see it.

Or not.

She hadn't even stepped off the last stair before she saw a shadow fall across the front door and a hand lift to tap lightly on the glass.

Her new neighbours?

She sighed inwardly and reached for the latch. She'd have to be polite. It wasn't in her to be anything else, but just for tonight it would have been nice to curl up in front of the television and be utterly self-indulgent. She'd even bought a tub of Belgian chocolate ice cream...

'Em?'

'Harry?'

Her hand flew to her mouth, stifling the gasp, and then her eyes dropped, dragging away from his to focus on...

A baby?

She blinked and looked again. Yes, definitely a baby. A tiny baby—very tiny, hardly old enough to be born, held securely against the broad chest she'd laid her head against so many times all those years ago.

'Oh, Harry!' She reached out and drew him in, going up on tiptoe to kiss his cheek and somehow resisting the urge to howl, because if there was a baby, then there was a woman, and if there was a woman...

She let him go before she did something silly. 'Gosh,

it's been so long—how are you?' she asked, her voice not quite her own, her eyes scanning his face eagerly.

'Oh—you know.'

No, she didn't, despite seeing him on the television almost on a daily basis. She didn't have the slightest idea, but his mouth was twisting in a parody of a smile and he looked exhausted.

Actually, he looked a great deal more than exhausted. He looked fantastic. Tall, bronzed, his striking pale blue eyes crinkled at the corners from screwing them up in the sun in all the godforsaken trouble spots he spent his life in. He needed a shave, and his hair was overdue for a cut, the dark strands a little wild. Her fingers itched to touch them, to feel if they were still as soft as she remembered, but she couldn't. She didn't have the right. Apparently, while she hadn't been looking, he'd given that to some other woman.

He turned a fraction, so his head was blocking out the light and she could no longer see his eyes, so she glanced down and her heart jerked against her chest. The tiny babe was all but lost inside the big, square hands that cradled it so protectively, the little head with wild black hair sticking out from under the edges of the minuscule hat cupped securely by long, strong fingers.

Such a powerful image. Advertising had recognised the power of it decades ago, but here it was now, standing in her hallway, and she felt her knees weaken.

Her resolve was turning to mush, as well.

'You're back,' she said eventually, when she could get her brain to work. 'I saw the lights on. I didn't think it would be you.' Not after all these years. Not after last time… 'Are you alone?'

'Yes. Just me and the baby.'

Just? *Just?* She nearly laughed out loud. There was nothing *just* about a baby, most especially not one that tiny. She wondered how long it would be before his wife joined them and rescued him. Later tonight? Tomorrow? Although she hadn't heard that he was married, but then he hadn't stayed in touch with her or her brother Dan, and she didn't keep her ear that close to the ground.

Liar! her conscience shrieked. *Weekly checks on the Internet, avid scanning of the news, hanging on every word of his news reports…*

'So where's the baby's mother? Does she trust you?' she asked, just because she couldn't stand the suspense another minute.

His smile twisted, and there was a little flicker of what could have been panic, but his eyes were sombre and there was something in them she just couldn't read. 'No mother,' he said expressionlessly. 'It's just us—me and the baby.'

Hope leapt in her chest, and she squashed it ruthlessly. Quite apart from the fact that there was a story here he wasn't telling her, another go-round with Harry Kavenagh was absolutely the last thing she needed for her peace of mind, but his reply answered why he was here, anyway, and there was no way she was getting suckered into that one! He could cope with the baby on his own, thank you very much!

She pulled back, both physically and emotionally, trying to distance herself from him so she didn't get drawn in, but then the baby started to fuss, and a flicker of what was definitely panic ran over his face, and she had to steel herself against him.

'So—what can I do for you?' she asked, trying not to

sound too brisk but giving him very little encouragement
at the same time.

He looked a little taken aback—perhaps she'd been too
brisk after all—but his shoulders lifted and he smiled a
little tiredly. 'Nothing. I'm staying here for a bit, so I just
came to see who was here, to introduce myself—say hello
to your parents if they were still here. I wasn't sure...'

Was it a question? She answered it anyway, her mind
still stalled on his words. *I'm staying here for a bit...*

'They're in Portugal. They live there part of the year.
Mum was homesick, and my grandmother's not very well.'

'So you're house-sitting for them?'

'No. I live here,' she told him. And then wished she'd
said 'we' and not 'I', so he didn't feel she was single and
available. Because although she might be single again, she
was very far from being available to Harry Kavenagh.

Ever again.

The baby's fussing got louder, and he jiggled her a bit,
but he wasn't doing it right and she looked tense and
insecure. Emily's hands itched to take the little mite and
cradle her securely against her breast, but that was ridiculous. She had to get rid of him before her stupid, stupid
hands reached out.

She edged towards the door. 'Sounds hungry. You'd
better go and feed her—her?' she added, not sure if the
baby was a girl, but he nodded.

'Yes.'

Yes, what? Yes, she's a girl, or, yes, he'd better feed
her/him/it? She opened the door anyway, and smiled
without quite meeting his eyes. 'I hope you settle in OK.
Give me a call if you need anything.'

He nodded again, and with a flicker of a smile he went out into the night and she closed the door.

Damn. Guilt was a dreadful thing.

She walked resolutely down the hall, got the ice cream out of the freezer, contemplated a bowl and thought better of it, picked up a spoon and the tub and went into the sitting room, put on the television and settled down cross-legged on the sofa to watch her film.

Except, of course, it had started and she'd missed the point, and anyway her mind kept straying to Harry and the baby, so tiny in his hands, and guilt tortured her.

Guilt and a million questions.

What was he doing on his own with a baby? Was she his? Or a tiny orphan, perhaps, rescued from the rubble of a bombed out building...

And now she was being completely ridiculous. The baby was days old, no more, and the paperwork to get a baby out of a war-torn country would be monumental, surely? There was always the most almighty fuss if a celebrity tried to adopt a baby, and she was pretty sure he counted as a celebrity.

Unless he'd kidnapped her?

No. He had the slightly desperate air of a man who'd had a baby dumped on him—one of his girlfriends, perhaps, sick of his nonsense and fed up with trying to compete with the more exciting world he inhabited? Maybe she'd thought he needed a dose of reality?

Or perhaps she was dead, had died in childbirth...

'Oh, for goodness' sake!'

She put the ice cream back in the freezer, hardly touched, and stood at the kitchen window, staring out at the house next door.

She could hear the baby screaming, and the mother in her was heading down the hall and out of the door, a cuddle at the ready. Fortunately the pragmatist in her stayed rooted to the spot, wishing she had defective hearing and wasn't so horribly tuned in to the sound of a crying child.

She made herself a drink, went back to the sitting room and had another try at the television. Maybe another programme, something less dependent on her not having missed a huge chunk. She flicked though the channels.

A cookery programme, yet another make-over show, a soap she'd never watched and a documentary on one of the many messy wars that seemed to be going on all over the world.

Which took her straight back to Harry Kavenagh and the tiny crying baby next door...

'Hush, little one,' he pleaded, jostling her gently. 'Have a drink, sweetheart, you must be hungry. Is it too cold? Too hot?'

Hell, how was he supposed to know? He liked his coffee scalding hot and his beer ice-cold. Somewhere in between was just alien to him.

He stared in desperation at the house next door, the lights just visible through the screen of trees.

No. He couldn't go round there. She'd hardly greeted him with open arms, after all.

'Well, what the hell did you expect?' he muttered, swapping the baby to his other arm and trying a different angle with the bottle. 'You drop out of her life for years and then stroll back in with a baby in your arms—she probably thought you were going to dump the baby on her!'

He tightened his grip on his precious burden and the crying changed in pitch. Instantly he slackened his grip, shifted her to his shoulder and rubbed her back, walking helplessly up and down, up and down, staring at Emily's house as he passed the window.

The lights were out now, only the lovely stained-glass window on the stairs illuminated by the landing light. Strange. He didn't remember her being afraid of the dark. Maybe it was because she was alone in the house...

'Stop thinking about her,' he growled softly, and the baby started to fuss again. 'Shh,' he murmured, rubbing her back again and going into the bathroom. 'How about a nice warm bath?'

Except she pooed in it, and he had to change the water in the basin one-handed without dropping her, and then it was too hot and he had to put more cold in, and then it was too full, and by the time he got her back in it she was screaming in earnest again and he gave up.

He could feel his eyes prickling with despair and inadequacy. Damn. He wasn't used to feeling inadequate. 'Oh, Gran, where are you?' he sighed a little unsteadily. 'You'd know what to do—you always knew what to do about everything.'

He dried the baby, dressed her in fresh clothes and tried to put her in the baby-carrier, but she wasn't having any. The only way she'd settle at all was if he held her against his heart and walked with her, so he did exactly that.

He pulled his soft fleecy car rug round his shoulders, wrapped it across her and went out into the mild summer night. He walked to the cliff top and then down through the quiet residential roads to the prom, strolling along next to the beach and listening to the sound of the sea while the baby slept peacefully against his heart, and then when he could walk no more and his eyes were burning with exhaustion and he just wanted to lie down and cry, he took her home and sat down in the awful chair that the tenants had left and fell asleep.

Not for long.

Not nearly long enough. The baby woke, slowly at first, tiny whimpers turning gradually to a proper cry and then ultimately a full-blown blood-curdling yell by the time he'd found her bottle in the fridge and warmed it and tested it and cooled it down again by running it under the tap because of course he'd overheated it, and by the time he could give it to her she'd worked herself up to such a frenzy she wouldn't take it.

He stared down at her in desperation, his eyes filling. 'Oh, Kizzy, please, just take it,' he begged, and finally she did, hiccupping and sobbing so she took in air and then started to scream and pull her legs up, and he thought, What made me think I could do this? I must have been mad. No wonder women get postnatal depression.

He wondered if it was possible for men to get it. Clumsy, inadequately prepared fathers who'd never been meant to be mothers to their children—men whose wives had died in a bomb blast or an earthquake and left them unexpectedly holding the baby. Or men widowed when their wives died in childbirth. Or even men who'd taken the decision to be the house-husband and main carer of the children. How did they cope?

How did anyone cope?

He changed her, then changed her again when she was

sick down her front, then gave her another little try with the bottle and finally put her down in the carrier, shut the door and went upstairs to the bedroom he'd used as a child, leaving her screaming.

He had to get some sleep if he was going to be any good to her.

But the only furniture in the room was a bare, stained mattress, and he couldn't bring himself to lie on it even if he could ignore the baby's cries for long enough to get to sleep.

He looked around him critically, taking in the state of the place properly for the first time, and realised that if he was going to live in it, it was going to need a team of decorators to come in and blitz it, new carpets and furniture throughout and probably a new kitchen.

And in the meantime he'd be living there with the baby?

He must have been insane.

He should have let the doctors throw the switch all those weeks ago instead of interfering.

Acid burned his stomach and he shook his head.

No.

Whatever came next, what he'd done so far had been exactly the right thing. The only thing. And it would get easier. It had to. He'd learn to cope. And right now he was going back downstairs, and he'd lift her out of the carrier and lie down on the grubby chair and cuddle her on his chest until they both went to sleep. The rest he could deal with tomorrow…

'I'm going to get you!'

Emily ran after her giggling son, chasing him down the garden and scooping him up, and straightened to find Harry standing on the other side of the fence staring at her and Freddie in astonishment.

'Um—hi,' he said. She smiled back and said, 'Hi, yourself. How's the baby?'

Freddie looked at him with the baby on his shoulder, gave his lovely beaming smile and said, 'Baby!' in his sing-song little voice and clapped his chubby hands in delight.

Now she'd had time to register it, Emily was too busy searching Harry's exhausted face to worry about the baby. There were deep black smudges under his eyes, and his jaw was shadowed with stubble. She ached to hold him, to stroke that stubbled chin and soothe the tired eyes with gentle fingers—'Are you OK?' she asked, trying to stick to the plot, and his eyes creased with weary humour.

'I'm not sure. I'm so tired I can't see straight at the moment. We had a bit of a problem in the night.'

'I heard,' she said, feeling guiltier still for her less-than-enthusiastic welcome the evening before. 'Um—look, why don't you come round and have a coffee? We're not doing anything, are we, Freddie? And we've got an hour before we have to pick up Beth.'

'Beth?' he said.

'My daughter.'

She wondered if he'd notice the use of 'my' and not 'our'. Maybe. Not that it mattered. If he was going to be living next to her for longer than ten minutes, he'd work out that she was alone. Anyway, she didn't think he was worrying about that at the moment. He was busy looking slightly stunned, and she wondered if she'd looked like that last night when she'd seen *his* baby for the first time.

Probably. She'd been shocked, because the last time

they'd met, they'd both been single and free, and now, clearly, he wasn't. And as for her—well, she was single again, but far from free, and maybe it was just as much of a shock to him to know she was a parent as it had been to her to realise he was.

Because, of course, if she knew nothing about his private life for the last umpteen years, it was even more likely that he knew nothing about hers.

Or the lack of it.

He gave her a cautious smile. 'Coffee would be good. Thanks.'

Coffee? She collected herself and tried for an answering smile. 'Great. Come through the fence—the gate's still here.'

She opened it, struggling a little because the path was a bit mossy there and the gate stuck, and he grabbed it and lifted it slightly and shifted it, creaking, out of the way.

'The creaking gate,' he said, and added, with that cheeky grin that unravelled her insides, 'It always did that. I used to know just how far to open it before it would rat on me.'

And she felt the colour run up her cheeks, because she remembered, too—remembered how he'd sneak through the gate and meet her at the end of the garden in the summerhouse, late at night after everyone was asleep, and they'd cuddle and kiss until he'd drag himself away, sending her back to bed aching for something she hadn't really understood but had longed for anyway.

'We were kids,' she said, unable to meet his eyes, and he laughed softly.

'Were we? Didn't always feel like it. And the last time—'

He broke off, and she took advantage of his silence to walk away from the incriminating gate and back up the garden to the house, Freddie on her hip swivelling wildly round and giggling and shrieking, 'Baby!' all excitedly.

She really didn't want to think about the last time! It should never have happened, and there was no way it was happening again.

She scooped up the runner beans from the step, shoved open the back door with her hip and went in, smiling at him over Freddie's head.

'Welcome back,' she said, without really meaning to, but she was glad she had because the weariness in his eyes was suddenly replaced by something rather lovely that reminded her of their childhood, of the many times she'd led him in through her parents' back door and into the welcome of their kitchen.

'Thanks.' He reached out and ruffled Freddie's bright blond curls. 'I didn't know you had kids.'

There was something in his voice—regret? She shot him a quick look, filed that one for future analysis and put the kettle on. 'Yup. Beth's three, nearly four, and Freddie's nineteen months. Real or instant?'

'Have you got tea? I daren't have too much caffeine. I had so little sleep last night I want to be able to grab every second of it that's offered!'

She laughed and reached for the teapot, lifting it down from the cupboard and putting Freddie on the floor. 'Darling, go and find your cup,' she instructed, and he trundled off, humming happily to himself.

'He's cute.'

'He is. He can be a complete monster, if it suits him, but most of the time he's gorgeous.'

Harry gave a strangled laugh. 'I wish I could say the same for this one, eh, Mini-Dot?'

'Mini-Dot?' she said, spluttering with laughter, and he chuckled.

'Well, she's so tiny. It's not her real name. Her real name's Carmen Grace—Kizzy for short.'

'Oh, that's pretty. Unusual.'

'Grace is for my grandmother.'

'And Carmen?'

His face went still. 'For her mother,' he said softly, and there was an edge to his voice that hinted at something she couldn't even begin to guess at. Maybe he would tell her later. She hoped so, because she didn't feel she could ask. Not now.

She would have done, years ago, but they'd spent every waking minute together in those halcyon days of their youth and there had been nothing they hadn't shared.

But now—now she didn't know him at all, and she didn't know how much he was going to give her, and how much she wanted to give back.

So she said nothing, just made them tea and found a few chocolate biscuits and put them on a plate. Then Freddie came back with his cup trailing a dribble of orange juice behind him, and she refilled it and mopped up the floor and hugged him, just because he was so sweetly oblivious and she loved him so much it hurt.

He giggled and squirmed out of her arms and ran out into the garden, and they followed him, she with the tray, Harry with the baby—Mini-Dot, for goodness' sake!— and she led him to the swinging seat under the apple tree.

'Is this the same one?' he asked in wonder, but she laughed and shook her head.

'No, it fell to bits. Dad bought a new one a few years ago, so you don't have to sit down so carefully any more.'

He chuckled and eased himself down onto the seat, leaning back and resting his head against the high back and closing his eyes. 'Oh, bliss. This is gorgeous.'

'Bit of a change from your usual life,' she said without meaning to, and he cocked an eye open and gave a rusty little laugh.

'You could say that.' For a moment he was silent, then he sighed and opened his other eye and turned his head towards her. 'It takes a bit of getting used to—the quiet, the birdsong, the normal everyday sounds of people going about their daily lives. Crazy things that you wouldn't think about, like the sound of a lawnmower—when I can hear it over the baby, that is,' he added, his mouth kicking up in a rueful grin.

She answered him with a smile, then felt her curiosity rise. No. She wouldn't go there...

'What happened, Harry?' she asked softly, despite her best intentions.

His smile faded, and for a moment she didn't think he was going to answer, but then he started to speak, his voice soft and a little roughened by emotion. 'I found her—Carmen—sitting by the side of the road, begging. Every day I walked past her on my way from the hotel and gave her money. Then after four days she wasn't there. The next time I saw her, she'd been beaten up. Her mouth was split, one eye was swollen shut and the other one was dull with pain and despair. She wasn't expecting anything—a few coins, perhaps, nothing more—but I took her to a café and bought her breakfast, and talked to her. And it was only then that I realised she was pregnant.'

Emily clicked her tongue in sympathy. 'Poor girl.'

He nodded. 'She'd been raped, she told me. She didn't know the father of her child, it could have been any one of several men—soldiers. She'd didn't know which side they were on. It didn't really matter. She was a gypsy. They aren't highly regarded in Eastern European countries—liars, thieves, lazy—you name it. And two nights before she'd been raped and beaten again. But she was just a girl, Emily, and she was terrified, and she'd lost her entire family.'

'So you took her under your wing,' she said, knowing that he would have done so, because he'd always been like that.

He gave a tiny hollow laugh. 'In a manner of speaking. I moved her into my hotel room, fed her, got a doctor for her, and while I was in the shower she stole my wallet and ran away. So I tracked her down and asked her why. Eventually she told me she was waiting for me to rape her.'

Emily asked again. 'So what did you do?'

'I married her,' he said quietly. 'To keep her safe. Ironic, really. I brought her home to London and installed her in my flat. I gave her an allowance, paid all the bills and saw her whenever I could. And gradually she learnt to trust me, but she was lonely. Then she started going out and meeting up with people from her country and she was much happier. She was learning English, too, at evening classes, and starting to make friends.'

He fell silent, and she waited, watching him, knowing he would carry on when he'd found the words.

'She was mugged. She was seven and a half months pregnant and someone mugged her on the way home from college one night. She ran away and crossed the road without looking and was hit by a car. She was taken to hospital, but she had a brain injury, and by the time they got hold of me she was on life support and they were doing brain-stem tests. So much for keeping her safe.'

The horror of it was sickening, and she put her hand over her mouth to hold back the cry. 'Oh, Harry, I'm so sorry,' she whispered.

'Yeah.' He swallowed. 'They didn't know whether to switch off the machine. They'd scanned the baby and it was fine, but they didn't know how I'd feel. I'd just flown in from an earthquake, I hadn't slept in days and I was exhausted. I didn't know what to say. I just knew I couldn't give up on the baby—not after everything we'd been through. She hadn't done anything wrong. She hadn't asked for this, and I've seen so many children die, Em, and not been able to do anything about it. And here was one I could do something about. I couldn't let her go. So I asked them to keep Carmen alive, long enough to give the baby a chance. And last week she ran out of time. Her organs started to fail, and they delivered the baby and turned off the machine. I got there just too late to say goodbye.'

He stared down at the baby on his lap, her mouth slack in sleep, her lashes black crescents against her olive cheeks, and Emily's vision blurred. She felt the hot splash of tears on her hands, and brushed them away.

'Harry, I'm so sorry,' she said again, and he looked up, his eyes haunted, and then looked down again at the precious bundle in his arms.

'Don't be. Not for me. I know it's hell at the moment and I feel such a muppet—I'm not used to being so phenomenally incompetent and out of my depth, but it will get better. I'll learn, and she's amazing. So lovely. So much perfection out of so much tragedy and despair. And I'm all she's got.'

Emily wanted to cry. Wanted to go into a corner somewhere and howl her eyes out for him, and for the baby's poor young mother, and for little Carmen Grace, orphaned almost before her birth.

'So that's us,' he said, his voice artificially bright. 'What about you?'

'Me?' she said, her eyes still misting. 'I'm, ah—I'm fine. I'm a garden designer—fitting it in around the children, which can be tricky, but I manage more or less. Get through a lot of midnight oil, but I don't have to pay for my accommodation at the moment.'

Although if her parents did sell their house, as they were considering doing, that would all change, of course.

'And their father?'

She gave a tiny grunt of laughter. 'Not around. He didn't want me to keep Beth. Freddie was the last straw.'

Harry frowned. 'So what did he do?'

'He walked—well, ran, actually. I haven't seen lightning move so fast. I was four months pregnant.'

'So he's been gone—what?'

'Two years.'

Two difficult, frightening years that she would have struggled to get through without the help of her parents and her friends, but they'd all been wonderful and life now was better than it had ever been.

'I'm sorry.'

She smiled. 'Don't be. Things are good. Hang in there, Harry. It really does get better.'

He looked down at the baby and gave a twisted little smile. 'I hope so,' he said wryly. 'It needs to.'

'It will,' she promised, and just hoped that she was right...

CHAPTER TWO

FREDDIE'S CUP landed in her lap, dribbling orange on her, and she absently righted it and brushed away the drips.

Finally she looked back at him. 'So—aren't the legal ramifications vast? Nationality and so on?'

He shrugged. 'Apparently not. I was Carmen's husband, I'm down on the baby's birth certificate as her father. That makes her British.'

'But you're not. Her father, I mean. Couldn't that land you in trouble, if they ever found out?'

'How? Are you going to tell them? Because I'm not. I know it'll be hell, but I won't be the first father to bring up a child alone, and I doubt I'll be the last. And if not me, then who? The legalities are the least of my worries. I owe her this. It's the least I can do.'

The least he could do? Devoting his life to her? He was either even more amazing than she'd remembered, or utterly deluded.

Probably both. Rash and foolhardy, his grandfather used to say affectionately. But kind. Endlessly kind. He reached for his cup, the baby held against his shoulder by one large, firm hand, but her head lolled a little and his grip tightened and she started to cry again.

'Let me—just while you drink your tea,' she said, and reaching out, she lifted the tiny little girl into her arms.

'Oh—she's so small! I'd forgotten! They grow so quickly—not that Freddie was ever this small. Beth was dainty, but even she—'

She broke off, the baby's fussing growing louder, and she walked down the garden a few steps, turning the baby against her breast instinctively.

And with the same instinct, little Carmen Grace nuzzled her, then cried again. Oh, poor lamb. She needed her mother!

'She's hungry,' she said, her voice uneven, and he got up and reached for her, but Emily shook her head, curiously reluctant to let the baby go.

'Bring the bottle. I'll hold her while you get it, it's all right.'

He hesitated for a second, then went, squeezing through the gate and returning a few moments later with a bottle. 'I don't know if it's the right temperature,' he said, handing it over, and Emily tested it on the inside of her wrist and frowned.

'It's too cold. I'll go and warm it. Keep an eye on Freddie for me.'

She went into the kitchen, gave the bottle a few seconds in the microwave, shook it vigorously and tested it again, then slipped the teat into the baby's mouth, silencing her cries instantly.

Good.

She went back down the garden and found Harry on his knees with Freddie, playing in the sandpit. As she walked down the garden he sat back on his heels and looked up at her with a relieved smile.

'Sounds peaceful.'

She laughed and settled herself on the bench, watching them and trying not to let her stupid thoughts run away with her.

'Did you love her?' she asked, then wanted to bite her tongue off, but he just sat back again and stared at her as if she was crazy.

'She was a child, Em. I married her for her own protection. Yes, I grew to love her, but not in the way you mean. It was just a legal formality, nothing more. I never touched her.'

She felt a knot of something letting go inside her, but she didn't want to think about the significance of that. She turned her attention back to the tiny scrap in her arms. The bottle was almost empty, the tiny amount she'd drunk surely not enough to keep her alive, but she was so small, her stomach must be the size of a walnut. Smaller.

She lifted her against her shoulder and rubbed her back, waiting for the burp and watching Harry as he piled sand into the bucket with Freddie and helped him turn it out.

'Mummy, castle!' Freddie shrieked, and the baby bobbed her head against Emily's shoulder, her whole body stiffening in shock. She soothed her with a stroking hand, rocking her and smiling at Freddie.

'I can see,' she said softly.

'How about a moat?'

'Wasa moat?' he asked, and Harry chuckled.

'It's like a big ditch full of water that goes all round the outside—here, like this,' he said, scraping out a hollow ring around the slightly wonky castle.

'You made one on the beach with Dickon and Maya last week,' Emily pointed out, and Freddie nodded and scrambled to his feet.

'Mummy, water!' he demanded, running to her with his cup, but Harry got up and grinned and ruffled his hair.

'Let her sit there for a minute. We'll get the water. Come with me and show me where the tap is,' he said, and held out his hand.

Freddie, normally the last person to allow such a familiarity, slid his hand trustingly into Harry's and trotted happily beside him, chattering all the way to the kitchen.

Emily glanced down at the baby, sleeping again, her tiny face snuggled into the crook of her neck so that she could feel the soft skin, the warm huff of her breath, the damp little mouth, and the ache in her chest grew until she had to swallow hard to shift it.

'Poor baby,' she crooned, cradling her head with a protective hand. 'Don't worry, darling. We'll look after you.'

She didn't even think about the words. They came straight from her heart, bypassing her common sense, and as she rocked the baby in her arms, she felt a sense of rightness that should have rung alarm bells, but the bells were switched off, and the warning went unheeded.

Freddie was delicious.

Bright and bubbly, his fair hair sticking up on one side as if he'd slept on it. It was soft and unruly, much like Harry's own, and it felt just right under his hand.

''Nough?' Freddie asked, and Harry nodded, looking at the jug he'd found.

'I think it's enough.'

But, of course, it sank straight into the sand, and Freddie's excitement turned to disappointment.

'Mummy!' he wailed, running to her and throwing himself at her knees, and Harry felt racked with guilt because he'd suggested it and it had failed and now the boy was upset. Damn. Could he do nothing right?

Em looked up at him with an apologetic smile. 'There's a cake ring in the drawer under the oven,' she told him. 'It should just about fit over the castle. You could use that and fill it with water.'

So they went back up to the kitchen, and found the cake ring, and with a bit of adjustment they fitted it over the sandcastle and filled it with water, and even found a stick to make a drawbridge and floated a leaf in it as a boat.

And the look on Freddie's face was priceless. 'Boat!' he said, and ran to his mother yet again, his eyes alight. 'Mummy, boat! 'Ook!'

Emily looked, admired it dutifully and threw Harry a smile over Freddie's head, then stood up. 'I have to get Beth,' she said, 'and I think this little one needs her daddy's attention.'

There was a spreading stain below her nappy, and Harry's heart sank. He wasn't sure if there was a washing machine in the house, and she'd only got a few clothes. Clearly, at this rate he was going to have to buy a whole lot more!

'Fancy company? If I change her quickly, could I come, too? And afterwards, if you were feeling really kind, you could point me in the direction of the nearest supermarket or baby shop so I can buy her more stuff.'

'Sure. I was going to walk, but we can take the car. I'll give Georgie a ring and warn her we might be late.'

He nodded, took the baby from her gingerly and went through the fence. She was starting to fuss, but she settled once he'd changed her and put her in the carrier, and he met Emily on the drive just as she was putting Freddie into his seat.

'Can we squeeze this in?'

'This?' she said with a chuckle, taking the carrier from him. 'Poor baby, what a way to talk about you! He's a bad daddy.'

She hoisted it into the car and strapped it in, then got behind the wheel. He slid in beside her, shifting so he could watch her. 'So where are we going?'

'A friend's—actually, Georgie Cauldwell. Do you remember her? Her father's a builder—we used to go and crawl around on the building sites when we were kids.'

He nodded. 'I remember her—small but fiery. Brown hair, green eyes, lots of personality?'

She shot him a look. 'You do remember her. Very well. Did you have a thing about her, Harry?'

He laughed softly. 'Hardly. You were more than enough trouble for me.' He looked away. 'So what's she doing now?'

'She's married to a guy from London with pots of money. He's a darling. They've got three kids that were his sister's, but she was killed on the way home from hospital when she had the last one. It was awful. Anyway, they've adopted them and Georgie's pregnant now, so it's just as well they've got this big house.'

She swung into the drive of a huge Victorian villa overlooking the sea and cut the engine. Two boys came running over with a little girl he knew instantly must be Beth. She was every inch her mother's daughter, from the soft dark curls that tumbled round her shoulders to the twinkling, mischievous eyes that reminded him so much of Em when he'd first met her.

And behind them came Georgie, older of course but still essentially the same, a baby in her arms. He unfolded himself from the seat and stood up, and with a little cry of welcome she hugged him with her free arm, her smile open and friendly.

'Harry! Emily said you were back—oh, it's so good to see you again. Welcome back to Yoxburgh. Come on in and meet Nick—Oh, and this is the baby!' she added, peering into the car. 'Oh, Harry, she's lovely!'

The baby in her arms was pretty gorgeous, too, and when she burrowed her head in her mother's shoulder and then peeped at him and giggled, he couldn't help responding. 'So who's this?' he asked after a moment or two of pee-boo-ing and giggles.

'Maya,' Georgie said. 'Aren't you? She can say her name now. Tell Harry who you are.'

'Harry,' the baby said, swivelling round and pointing, and burrowed into her shoulder again. Still smiling, he followed the direction she'd pointed in and met a challenging stare.

'You've got my name,' the boy said, his head tilting to one side. 'I'm Harry.'

Harry grinned. 'Is that right?'

He nodded.

'Well, in that case I think you must have my name, since I had it about twenty something years before you needed it, but hey, that's cool, I don't mind sharing. It's a good name, it would be mean to keep it to myself.'

They swapped grins, and then he was introduced to Dickon, Harry's younger brother, and Em's daughter Beth.

So many children—and now it was his turn. He got the carrier out of the car, turned it towards them all and said with a curious feeling of rightness, 'This is Kizzy. She's my daughter.'

'Is Emily her mummy?' Dickon asked, puzzled, and Harry shook his head.

Should he say this? Hell, these kids had lost their mother only a year or so ago. Was it really fair to dredge it all up?

Yes. Because life wasn't fair, and the truth would come out at some point, he was sure, so he shook his head again and said gently, 'Her mother died.'

'Our mummy's dead,' Dickon said matter-of-factly. 'Georgie's our new mummy. Is Emily going to be Kizzy's new mummy?'

Emily laughed, the sound a little strained to his ears, and started towards the house. 'Heavens, no! I've got enough on my plate with Beth and Freddie, haven't I, darling?'

Beth slipped her hand into her mother's and snuggled closer. 'Babies are nice, though. Georgie's having a baby.'

'Well, I'm not,' Em said firmly. Too firmly? He didn't know. All he knew was that all this blatant fecundity should have sent him running—and it didn't. And the idea of Emily being Kizzy's new mummy was suddenly extraordinarily appealing…

'Lovely house.'

Nick looked around and smiled the smile of a supremely contented man. 'It is, isn't it? Georgie and her father did the work for us, and we love it. I thought it was ridiculously big at first, but with all the kids and another on the way and my mother living with us and working here, and me working from home at first, frankly if it was any smaller it wouldn't be big enough.'

For a man who'd evidently been a bachelor a little more than a year ago, he seemed extraordinarily happy with the way things had turned out. They were in the garden, sitting in the shade of a big old tree and looking out over the sea, and every few seconds his eyes would stray to his family, an indulgent smile touching his mouth.

Harry could understand that. His own eyes kept straying to Em and her children, her revelation about their father still ringing in his ears.

He walked—well, ran, actually. I haven't seen lightning move so fast.

Bastard. Fancy leaving them. Although maybe it had been better to leave them with Emily who clearly adored them than to stay and make them feel unloved and unwanted, and then at the first opportunity pack them off to boarding school and to their grandparents in the holidays...

'So where are you staying? Georgie said something about your grandmother's house.'

He wrenched himself back to the present and gave a rueful smile. 'Well, that was the idea, but it's had tenants since she died ten years ago and I haven't been back since the funeral. To be honest, it was a bit of a shock, seeing it. The agents told me it needed some cosmetic attention, but I think they were erring on the kind side. It needs gutting, frankly, so I think we'll have to rent something.'

Georgie lifted her head and frowned at him. 'Is it really that bad?'

'It needs total redecoration, and if I'm going to live there long term it'll need a new kitchen and bathroom at least, but for now a lick of paint and some clean carpets would work wonders. I don't suppose your father knows anyone reliable?'

Her eyes flicked to her husband's. 'We could send in the A-team.'

Nick chuckled. 'Indeed. We've got a whole range of trades,' he explained. 'They're used to working together, they do a good job, their prices are reasonable and at the moment they're not busy because there's been a hold-up on a development. So—yeah, if you want, we could send them along to give you a quote.'

'Fantastic. That would be great.'

And if they could do half at a time, he could stay there. It was summer, after all, and he and the baby could spend most of their time in the garden.

He didn't let himself think too much about why it seemed so important to stay there rather than rent another house— one that wouldn't be next to Em. After all, she'd already made it clear she wasn't interested in being Kizzy's new mummy.

Not that he was about to ask her, or had even really thought about it for more than a moment, but he thought about it now—couldn't think about anything else, in fact, however foolish he knew it was. If he had any sense he'd keep well out of her way and not indulge the foolish fantasy that they, too, could have a fairy tale ending like Georgie and Nick…

Emily was stunned.

If I'm going to live there long term?

He was considering it? Really?

She'd thought he was back for a few days—just a quick visit to sort out the house ready for the next tenants. It had never occurred to her that he might be coming back for any length of time—or maybe even for good!

But if he *was* back for good—no. She couldn't let herself think about it. Daren't let herself think about it, because her heart couldn't take any more. She'd been stupid over Harry Kavenagh once too often, and she wasn't going to do it again.

'So when can you start?'

'Tomorrow? We'll strip all the wallpaper and rip out the old floorcoverings, decorate throughout and then you'll be ready for the new carpets. Should take a week at the most with the team on it.'

'A week?'

'Uh-huh. Some of the windows need quite a bit of work, unless you're going to replace them?'

'Um—I hadn't intended to. I was hoping to live here while you do it.'

'With the baby?' The foreman shook his head. 'No. Sorry, I really wouldn't recommend it. Not with all the old lead paint. It's OK when it's left alone, but when it's disturbed it can be harmful to children, and she's so tiny.' His face softened as he looked down at the baby in Harry's arms, and Harry's eyes followed his gaze and his eyes locked with Kizzy's.

Wide and trusting, fixed on him.

'No, you're right,' he said, wondering what on earth he did now. 'Come tomorrow. I'll find somewhere to go. It's not like there's much here to worry about in the way of furnishings. I'll get carpets and stuff organised for when it's done, so it won't be for long.'

He waved them off, hesitated on the doorstep and then went round to Emily's house and rang the doorbell.

'Oh. It's you,' she said, wondering if there would ever come a time when her heart didn't hiccup at the sight of him. 'I thought you would have come through the fence and knocked on the back door.'

He smiled a little awkwardly. 'I don't want to take advantage.'

'You aren't taking advantage.' She opened the door a little wider. 'Come on in. I was just about to have coffee. Join me.'

'Thanks.' He followed her down the hall and into the kitchen, perching on the stool awkwardly with Kizzy snuggled against his chest, and watched her while she made their drinks.

'Still off coffee?' she asked with a smile, and he shook his head, his mouth kicking up in an answering smile.

'No. I need caffeine today. I've just had the decorator round. He's coming tomorrow, but they're going to hit the whole house at once and strip it all right out. I need to find a hotel for us for a week. I wondered if you'd got any ideas or recommendations?'

'A hotel?' she said, and then, knowing she was going to do it and utterly unable to stop her mouth making the words, she said, 'Don't be silly. You can stay here. It's only a week. You'll be no trouble.'

No trouble? Was she out of her mind? And what was she thinking, *only* a week? That was seven nights! Well, five if she was lucky and he was talking working weeks, but it was Monday now, and if they'd said it would take a week then there'd be a weekend in between and so it would be properly a week before the decorators left, and then the carpets would have to be fitted and the furniture delivered. So, next Wednesday at the earliest. Oh, rats. Still, the house was plenty big enough and there were three bathrooms. They wouldn't be tripping over each other at least.

Besides, it was too late, because he was accepting, hesitantly, reluctantly, but still accepting, and only a real bitch would say, 'Actually, no, I've changed my mind, I didn't mean it at all!'

Or a woman whose life was complicated enough, whose heart was finding it altogether too difficult to be so close to the person who'd held that heart in the palm of his hand for so very many years...

'I've found my old baby sling,' she told him, putting the coffee down in front of him and lifting the sling off the end of the worktop where she'd put it ready to give him.

'Baby sling?'

She smiled and handed it to him. 'You put it round your shoulders and over your back, and the baby lies against your front, without you having to hold her all the time, so she can hear your heart beat and you have your hands free. They're wonderful.'

He studied the little heap of soft stretchy cotton fabric with interest. 'I've seen things like this all over the world—women tying their babies to them so they can work, either on their fronts so they can feed them easily, or on their backs.'

She nodded. 'The so-called civilised West has just cottoned on. It's a big thing now. They call it baby-wearing, as if they'd just invented it, but since you seem to be doing it anyway I thought you might like to borrow that to make it easier.'

'Thanks. You'll have to give me lessons,' he said, putting it down again with a defeated laugh. 'It looks like a loop of fabric to me.'

'It is. Here.'

And just because it was easier to show him than to put it on him with the baby still in his arms, she looped it round herself, adjusted it, took the baby from him and snuggled her inside it, close against her heart.

Kizzy shifted, sighed and snuggled closer, relaxing back into sleep without a murmur. 'See? Then you get your hands free.'

He gave a cheeky, crooked grin. 'Or I could let you carry her, since you seem to be the expert.'

She laughed, sat down and sipped her coffee, relishing the feel of the little one against her, warm and curiously reassuring. No. She mustn't let herself get too used to it. It was much, much too dangerous. Her heart had already been broken by this man, and there was no way she was going to let his daughter do the same thing.

'I don't suppose you want to come carpet shopping with me?'

She met his eyes over her cup. 'Can't you cope?' she asked, desperately trying to create a little distance, and then could have kicked herself because she would have loved to go carpet shopping with him.

He shrugged dismissively. 'Of course I can cope. I just thought it might be more fun.'

'What, with Freddie in tow and Mini-Dot here yelling the place down? I don't think so.'

'She's not yelling now,' he pointed out. 'Maybe she's stopped that.'

Foolish, foolish man.

The baby began to stir almost before he'd finished speaking, and within seconds she was bawling her tiny lungs out.

'I'll get her bottle,' he said, standing up, but Emily got up, too, extracted Kizzy from the sling and handed her to him.

'I've got a better idea. You take her and deal with her, and when she's settled, you can take her carpet shopping. And I can get on with my work.'

A fleeting frown crossed his brow. 'I'm sorry. I didn't realise you were working,' he said, and took Kizzy from her arms. 'We'll get out of your way. And don't worry about having us to stay. We'll find a hotel.'

'Harry, no!' she said, angry with herself for upsetting him.

'No, really,' he said, his voice a little gruff. 'I'm sorry. I can't just come back here after all these years and expect you to welcome me with open arms.'

Oh, Harry, if you only knew, she thought, and her hand came out and curled over his wrist, holding him there with her. 'I didn't mean it like that. It's just—I do have work to do, and Freddie is having a nap and it's my one chance. Please, come and stay. I can't let you go to a hotel. Not with the baby. Anyway, Freddie and Beth will love having her here. Please?'

His eyes were serious, searching hers for an endless moment, and then, finally satisfied, he nodded briefly. 'OK. But we'll try and keep out of your way so we don't stop you working.'

She felt the tension go out of her like air out of a balloon. 'Still want help with the carpet shopping?' she said with a smile.

CHAPTER THREE

HE HADN'T realised just what an expedition it would be, shopping with three children.

Kizzy was more than enough trouble, but by the time he'd got her fed and settled and Freddie had woken up, Beth had come back from playing with a friend, so they were all going together.

And then, of course, because she was so tiny and seemed to be hungry every three minutes or so, he needed to take feeds for Kizzy, and because she was just like a straw he'd need nappies, and because he was so rubbish at putting the nappies on she'd need a total change of clothes...

He bet they took less equipment on an Arctic expedition.

'You OK there?'

He gave Emily what he hoped was a smile and nodded. 'Sure. I'm fine. I've got everything, I think.'

She eyed the bulging bag dubiously. 'Got wipes?'

Of course not.

He found them and put them in, then straightened up, baby carrier in hand. 'Will I need the sling? Because I still don't think I know how to put it on.'

'I'll help you. Bring it,' she instructed, and so he

followed her out—to her car, not his, because it was set up with baby seats for her two. Beth and Freddie were already strapped in, reaching across and poking each other and giggling, and they looked up and beamed a welcome at him and Kizzy that made him feel—just for a second, until he reminded himself that he wasn't—as if he was a part of their family.

As if he belonged.

And the pain hit him in the chest like a sledgehammer.

He sucked in a breath. 'Hi, kids,' he said, leaning over Freddie to put the baby carrier in the middle, and Freddie reached up and grabbed his face and planted a wet, sticky kiss on his cheek.

'Harry!' he said happily, and Harry straightened up and ruffled Freddie's hair and swallowed hard.

No. They weren't his kids. He wasn't going to get involved. Look what had happened the last time he'd got involved in someone's life…

'All set?'

He clipped on his seat belt and nodded. Emily started the car and headed for town.

It was a good job he had her in tow, she thought.

He was fingering a lovely pale pure wool carpet with a thoughtful look on his face.

'Imagine it with baby sick and play-dough on it,' she advised sagely, and he wrinkled his nose and sighed heavily.

'So what would you suggest?'

'Something a little darker? Something scrubbable? There are some you can pour bleach on. Maybe a tiny pattern, just to break it up? Or a heather mix, so it's not a flat, plain colour.'

He was glazing over, she could tell. Poor baby. For the first time in his life he was up against having to consider something other than his own taste. And he didn't like it.

'I want wood, really. I'd like to strip the boards, or put down an oak strip floor, perhaps. I've got solid walnut in my flat and it's gorgeous. And you can wipe it clean.'

'Hard to fall on, and it can be a bit cold. Anyway, they probably couldn't do a really nice floor that fast.'

'Oh, damn,' he said, ramming his hands through his hair and grinning ruefully. 'I tell you what, you choose. You've had more experience than I have. So long as it covers the floor and I can have it next Tuesday, I don't care.'

So she chose—a soft pale coffee mix that would stand children running in and out—and then wondered what on earth she was thinking about because the only child running in and out would be Kizzy and she was less than two weeks old! He'd probably replace the carpet before she was walking.

'Next?'

'Furniture? I haven't got any.'

So she took him to a place that sold beds and sofas and dining furniture, and he ordered the best compromise between what he wanted and what was available at short notice, and then right on cue Kizzy started up.

Freddie was wriggling around in the buggy, wanting to get out, and Beth was hanging on her hand and needed the loo.

'How about lunch?' she suggested. 'Then we can tackle curtains and bedding—a bit more retail therapy for you.'

'Retail therapy?' He gave a snort. 'Not in this lifetime—but lunch sounds good,' he said, the air of hunted desperation easing slightly at the suggestion of reprieve, and she nearly laughed out loud.

Poor Harry. Anyone less in touch with their feminine side she had yet to meet, but she had to hand it to him. He was taking it on the chin and giving it his best shot, and she felt a strangely proprietorial sense of pride in him.

Swallowing a lump in her throat, Emily tucked her arm through his and steered him into the little café next door, sat him and Beth down, found a high chair for Freddie and took Kizzy from the sling on Harry's chest, rocking her while the waitress heated the bottle. Then she fed her while her children played with their bendy straws and Harry sat back and closed his eyes and inhaled a double espresso with the air of a condemned man taking his last meal.

It was all she could do not to laugh.

'Well, that was painless.'

'Painless?' He cracked an eye open and studied her for signs of lunacy. 'I thought we'd never get them settled. I'm exhausted.'

'You'll get used to it,' she promised. 'I did.'

'You're a woman. You have hormones.'

'Yes—and usually they're a hazard,' she said with a chuckle in her voice, and he opened the other eye and sat up a little.

They were in her sitting room, all three children sound asleep, and his few possessions were now installed in Dan's bedroom, which just happened to be next to hers. Unfortunately. He could have done with being at the other end of the hall, or downstairs, or even at the end of the garden—

No. He couldn't afford to think about the summerhouse. Not now, when he was alone with her for the first time in years, and there was soft music flowing all around them and all he wanted to do was take her in his arms and carry on where they'd left off...

'Are you OK?'

'Sure. Why?'

'You're scowling.'

He tried to iron out the muscles in his face and struggled for a smile. 'Sorry. Thanks for today. I don't suppose you enjoyed it any more than I did,' he said, and then realised it was actually a lie, because in some bizarre way he had enjoyed it, all of it. And because he couldn't lie to her, because he never had, he shook his head and smiled again, properly this time. 'Actually, it was fun, in a strange way,' he admitted, and she smiled back, her eyes soft with understanding.

'You'll get used to it, Harry. It's not so bad after a while.'

'Because it's so long since you've done anything for yourself that you forget to miss it?' he suggested, and she gave a wry chuckle.

'Got it in one. And the kids are lovely. They give you back all that love in spades.'

He studied her, wondering about her love life, if it consisted solely of cuddles with her adorable children or if there was a man somewhere.

'You're scowling again.'

He laughed. 'Sorry. Tell me about your garden design business. Did you do your parents' garden? I noticed it was different—better.'

'Do you like it? I did it years ago. It was one of my first projects. The swing seat had broken, and the garden needed a thorough overhaul. My father asked me if I wanted to do it as my first commission, when I was finishing my course.

I would have done it anyway, but he insisted on paying me—said I had to live and he was sick of supporting me!'

Harry laughed with her, picturing her father, gruff and loving, always supportive, and her mother, warm and motherly and generous to a fault, like a younger version of his grandmother Grace.

'You're very lucky to have such loving parents,' he said, his own voice a little gruff, and she nodded, her eyes searching his face and missing nothing, he was sure. He looked away. 'So how's business now?'

'Good,' she said. 'I've done quite a bit for Nick and Georgie, both in their garden and in the development behind their house, and Nick's got some other projects under way that I'm drawing up some ideas for, and I've done a few other domestic jobs around the area.'

'Enough to live on?'

'I manage,' she said, but there was something in her voice that made him wonder how tight it was and how dependent she was on her parents for accommodation, or if it simply suited them all. He wondered if the rat who'd fathered her children and then legged it made any kind of contribution, and thought probably not.

'No, he doesn't,' she said, and his head jerked up.

'Did I say that out loud?' he said guiltily, but she shook her head, her smile wry.

'No. You didn't have to. You were scowling again.'

'Ah.' He pressed his lips together, but the words came out anyway. 'Tell me about him.'

She shrugged. 'Nothing to tell. I met him at a party— no surprises there. He's always been a party animal. We lived together for a year, and I became pregnant with Beth.

He wanted me to get rid of her, as he put it, but I wouldn't. I told him it was too late, and I really thought he'd come to love her, but he was pretty indifferent to her.'

'So why didn't you leave him?'

Her laugh was humourless and a little bitter. 'I had nothing to live on. I didn't think it was fair to come home to my parents. They were enjoying being free of responsibility, and they were taking all the holidays they couldn't afford while Dan and I were at home. So I stayed with Pete, and two years later I was pregnant again.'

'And he left you.'

'Mmm. I told him on Saturday morning, and on Saturday afternoon he packed up and moved out while I was at the supermarket. He left me with the flat, the rent was due and I had no money for food. He'd stopped my card so I couldn't use it at the supermarket, and when I got home with no food after an embarrassing fiasco at the checkout, he was gone.'

'So what did you do?'

'I came home. My father collected us and brought us home, my mother looked after Beth so I could go back to work until I had Freddie, and they've been fantastic. I don't know what I would have done without them.'

Her voice was soft and matter-of-fact, but underneath he could sense a wealth of pain and he ached for her. He knew what it was to be unwanted, knew how it felt to be an unwanted child, and having heard her story he was more than ever sure that Beth and Freddie were better off without their father.

'You don't need him,' he said, and she smiled.

'I know. And you don't have to sound so cross. He did

me a favour, really. Without him I wouldn't have had my children, and at least he had the decency to go off and leave us alone, instead of hanging around and being cruel…'

He felt his legs bunch. 'He hit you?'

She laughed and shook her head, leaning over to push him back onto the sofa. 'Relax. There are other ways of being cruel.'

Oh, yes. And he'd met many of them in his time. He relaxed back against the sofa and sighed, then patted the cushion beside him. 'Come here.'

She hesitated a second, then she sat beside him, snuggling against his side as she'd done so very many times before. 'I've missed you,' she said softly. 'I see you on the telly and wonder how you are, if you'll ever come back to Suffolk…'

'And I have.'

'Mmm. With Kizzy. I might have known you'd find a waif and rescue her. You were always a softie.'

He thought of Carmen, how she'd looked after she'd been attacked, and how she'd looked in the chapel at the mortuary, her young face finally at peace.

'I don't think I did her any favours,' he said gruffly. 'Maybe if I'd left her there, or handed her over to the aid agencies…'

'Then what? She would have had a child and no way of supporting it except prostitution. Would you want that for her?'

He shook his head. 'But she didn't deserve to die.'

'Of course not, but life's a bitch, Harry. You gave her hope, gave her a home—and you've given her baby a home and a father, safety and security for the rest of her life.'

'We have yet to survive it, of course,' he said wryly. 'Only time will tell.'

'You'll survive it.' She tipped up her face and smiled at him, her hand coming up to cradle his jaw with gentle fingers. 'You'll be a wonderful father, Harry. Give yourself time.'

He nodded slightly, not sure if he could believe her but no longer really thinking about it, because her eyes were tender, her mouth was full and soft and, oh, so close, and without thinking, without giving himself time to analyse or argue or reason, he lowered his head and touched his lips to hers.

Oh, dear heaven, she tasted the same. All these years and he could remember her taste, her scent, the feel of her lips under his, the soft stroke of her tongue against his, the tiny sigh, the warmth of her breath, the frantic beating of her heart against his fingertips as his hand glided down over the hollow of her throat and settled against a soft, full breast, fuller than before, her body a woman's now, lush and generous, the curves just right for his hand.

And he wanted her as he had never wanted her before, as an adult, a man who knew all the joys in store instead of a hormonal youth who simply hoped to find out. And the knowledge was almost enough to destroy his self-control, to push him over the edge.

But then, just as he was about to let her go, when his mind was already pulling back even as his hand curled against her breast, she lifted her head away, her eyes confused, and said, 'Kizzy.'

Kizzy? What had Kizzy to do with it?

And then he heard her crying, her screams getting louder by the second.

He jerked himself to his feet, strode towards the door and

bounded upstairs, his heart racing and his body clamouring to turn round and go back and finish what they'd started...

Emily sagged back against the cushions and lifted her hand to her lips. Had it really always felt that good? And if so, how on earth had they ever stopped?

She closed her eyes and waited for her heart to slow, listening to his voice, a soft rumble on the stairs as he carried Kizzy down. Her cries subsided for the moment, a cuddle enough to comfort her for now.

Emily nearly laughed aloud. A cuddle from Kizzy's father was nothing like enough to comfort her. She wanted more—much more—but she'd be insane to let this crazy situation go any further, because whatever else she knew about Harry, she knew that Yoxburgh wouldn't be enough to satisfy him for long.

He'd always talked about seeing the world—a result of his restless upbringing, trailing round the globe in the wake of his parents who had been too busy to pay attention to their little son. So although he'd never had their love, he'd had experiences in spades, and the wanderlust that was a part of his father's make up was part of his also.

And so he'd go—maybe not now, maybe not for a while, but eventually, when it all got too dull and easy and the world beckoned. And she'd be left, broken-hearted as Pete could never have left her, because although she'd thought she'd loved Pete, she knew full well that an affair with Harry had the potential to bring her far more joy and far more sorrow than Pete could ever have done, because he'd never had that unerring capacity to touch her soul.

So she simply wasn't going to go there, not now, not

ever. And if they'd got scarily close on the night of his grandmother's funeral, they weren't getting that close again. No way. It was far too dangerous.

She could hear him in the kitchen, hear Kizzy starting up again, and taking a deep breath to steady her, she got to her feet and went through. 'Want a hand?'

'I'm OK,' he said, his back to her and his voice tight.

Damn.

'I'm going to do some work, then,' she said, and went into the study and shut the door a little more firmly than was quite necessary, just to be on the safe side.

'Oh, Kizzy, what did I go and do that for?' he murmured, staring down at his tiny daughter with regret. 'We were getting on so well, and now I've gone and screwed everything up, but she was just there, you know, and I just wanted to kiss her. Nothing else. What a silly daddy.'

He took the bottle out of her mouth and propped her up against his shoulder, rubbing her back until she burped gloriously in his ear, then he gave her the rest of the bottle, cuddled her for a minute and then took her back up, changed her and put her down in the travel cot Em had found in the loft.

Kizzy went out like a light, without a murmur, which left him nothing to do but go back downstairs and sit and watch the study door and wonder if Emily was mad with him.

He paused in Freddie's doorway, staring down at the sleeping boy. He was huge compared to Kizzy, but he was still a baby really, his steps sometimes unsteady, his chin only too ready to wobble if things went wrong. Beth wasn't that much older, either, but quite different, bright and beautiful and full of mischief, her sparkling eyes just like Em's.

Beth was lying sprawled across the bed, too close to the edge, and he shifted her back and covered her again before heading downstairs with all the enthusiasm of a French aristo going to the guillotine.

He owed Em an apology, and he wasn't sure if he dared be in the room with her long enough to make it. At least not without a table between them to keep them apart.

He went into the kitchen, made some tea and tapped on the study door. 'Em?'

'Come in,' she said, turning towards him with a wary look in her eyes as he pushed the door open and went in, tray in hand.

'I've brought you tea.'

'Thanks.'

He hung on to the tray, because if it was in his hands he couldn't do anything else with them. 'My pleasure. And we haven't eaten. Want me to cook something?'

She swivelled her chair a little farther and reached for the tea. 'What can you cook?'

He laughed. 'Probably nothing English. What have you got to work with?'

'All sorts. I did a big shop the other day. Go and have a look. I just want to finish this off and I'll come and give you a hand.'

He nodded and went out, sighing with relief that the awkwardness seemed to have gone and their friendship was back on track.

Unless he poisoned her! He opened the fridge and studied the contents. Peppers, chicken breast, onions, tiny cherry tomatoes, salad, apples in the fruit bowl, couscous in the larder cupboard and spices in the rack next to the hob.

Excellent.

'Smells good.'

He jumped, turning towards her with a laugh lighting up his eyes and the knife pointing towards her threateningly, but she didn't feel threatened. 'Do you have to creep up on me?'

'Sorry.' She grinned without remorse and perched on the stool at the breakfast bar. 'Found all you need?'

'I think so. Did you get your drawing done?'

'Yes. I was just making a few changes to the planting. So what are you cooking?'

'Moroccan chicken and couscous. I wasn't sure if you liked things spicy, so I haven't made it too hot, but it's fruity so it takes the edge off it. Here—try a bit.'

And he held out a fork with a little pile of couscous on for her to taste. She leant forward, closed her lips around the fork and wondered if he'd been tasting it, if his lips had closed on the prongs of the fork, too, if he'd…

'Wow! That's gorgeous!'

'Not too hot for you?'

She shook her head, putting her hormones back in their box and concentrating on the food. 'No, it's lovely.'

'Good. I'll just finish off the chicken and I'll be done.'

'Want a hand?'

'No. Just stay there and keep me company.'

So she sat there, watching him work, her eyes drawn to the muscles in his shoulders flexing as he stirred and flipped the chicken in the pan, his buttocks taut when he shifted from foot to foot, crouching to lift out the plates from the oven and then straightening, thighs working…

Damn. She was going to drool in a minute.

He threw the chicken into the couscous, scraped the juices into the mixture and stirred it through then piled it into the bowls and set them down on the breakfast bar in front of her, hooking his foot round a stool and drawing it closer before sitting opposite her.

Their knees brushed and she pulled away, just as he did, and he apologised automatically and then he met her eyes and smiled wryly. 'Actually, I'm sorry for all of it. For landing on you like this—for kissing you.' Then he shook his head and laughed softly under his breath. 'No, that's a lie. I'm not sorry. I'm sorry I'm not sorry, if you see what I mean. I didn't mean to kiss you, and I shouldn't have done, but I can't be sorry I did. Not unless it gets in the way of our friendship, because that means too much to me to mess with it. Ah, that was the most garbled speech in the world, but—I guess what I'm trying to say is, forgive me?'

Forgive him? For kissing her so tenderly, so beautifully, so skillfully?

'There's nothing to forgive,' she said, her voice a little unsteady, and picking up her fork, she turned her attention to the food before she said or did anything she'd regret…

CHAPTER FOUR

'Can I ask you an enormous favour?'

Emily lifted her eyes from the baby's face and met Harry's clear blue gaze. Maybe one day she'd be immune to watching him with the baby in his arms as he fed her, but not today or any time soon.

'Sure,' she said, wondering if her voice was as husky as she suspected.

'I need to go to London. I didn't really give them much warning that I was going to be taking time off. I'll go on the train, I think it's the quickest, and I shouldn't be gone more than five hours—six, tops. I'll leave all the feeds ready for you—the made-up packets are a doddle, even I can manage them, and with any luck she'll sleep for most of it, but I need to go and talk to my boss, and I can't really take her with me.'

'Why not?' she suggested, just to see what he said and to find out if he'd thought it through. 'It might be quite useful—you know, make the point of how tiny she is and all that.'

He shook his head, his mouth kicking up in a wry smile. 'No. My boss is a woman. There's no way she'd be impressed by that. She'd expect a woman to get child care to cover a meeting. She won't make an exception for me. And

I know it's a pain, and I promise I won't make a habit of it. It's really just this once. And, yes, I could take her and dump her on a secretary or something on the way in, but it isn't really fair on the secretary and it certainly isn't fair on Kizzy. I've already thought about doing it, and if I didn't have to ask you, I wouldn't. I know you've got more than enough to do, and I'll make it up to you—babysit yours so you can get some work done or something. Look after them while you get a massage. Whatever you like.'

She put him out of his misery. 'Done. You can babysit for me while I work, *and* I'll have a massage. And you can pay for it,' she added, waiting for him to renege, but he didn't, he just nodded and looked relieved.

'Thanks, Em. I owe you.'

'I know. The meter's running.'

He chuckled and lifted the baby against his shoulder, burping her. Hell, he was getting good at it. Those big strong hands cradled her with a tenderness that made Emily want to weep, and now he was relaxing into the role, Kizzy obviously felt safe. Emily envied her. She'd give her eye teeth to be cradled in his arms with him staring adoringly down at her like that.

She shot to her feet. 'More tea?'

He shook his head. 'No, I'm going to turn in. I'm shattered. So—is that OK for the morning, then?'

'Tomorrow?' she said, startled, and he nodded.

'Sorry—didn't I mention that? Is tomorrow a problem?'

'No,' she said, mentally scanning her diary. 'Except the decorators are starting.'

'Hell,' he said softly. 'Could you keep an eye on them? Make sure they're OK and don't do anything silly?'

'Have you agreed colours?'

'Colours?' He looked suddenly overwhelmed, and she took pity on him. He'd had a hard day, and the learning curve must seem to him as steep as Everest.

'Don't worry. I expect they'll be doing preparation for a day or two. I'll pick up some colour charts for you, or they might have some. If all else fails I'll decide for you—but don't blame me if you come back and find the hall sore-throat pink!'

'You wouldn't,' he said, his eyes filled with panic, and she chuckled.

'Don't push your luck. Go on, go to bed and we'll sort the rest out in the morning.'

He nodded and stood up, the baby asleep in the crook of his arm, and he paused beside her and looked down into her eyes. The light was behind him so she couldn't read his expression, but his voice was gruff.

'You're a star, Em. I don't know what I would have done without you.'

And without warning he bent his head and brushed his lips lightly against hers, then with a murmured, 'Good night.' He went upstairs and left her there, still reeling from his touch...

The overhead lines were down.

He couldn't believe it. He'd had the day from hell. His boss had grilled him like a kipper about when he was going to be able to return to work, he'd had his contract terms pointed out to him in words of one syllable, his mobile phone battery had died and now this.

The train had come to a shuddering halt midway between stations, and there was nothing they could do but wait for the lines to be repaired. And in the meantime the air-conditioning was out of action because the train wasn't running, and the staff were wandering up and down, handing out bottled water and reassurance while the entire world got on the phone and told their loved ones what was going on.

Except him. Because his battery was flat, because with everything else he'd had to do he'd forgotten to put it on charge. And now Em wouldn't know where he was or be able to get hold of him, and some woman next to him had recognised him and was hell-bent on making conversation. He would have borrowed her mobile and phoned Em, but her number was in his phone so he couldn't get it and besides he didn't want the number registered on the woman's call log, because there was just something persistent about her that rang alarm bells.

So he sat, stripped down to his shirtsleeves and wondering if it would be rude to take off his shoes and socks, and endured her conversation in the sweltering heat and worried about Kizzy and whether Em was coping, until he could have screamed.

Where *was* he?

She looked at her watch again, and tried his mobile once more, just in case, but either he was stuck in the underground, it was switched off or the battery was dead.

And Kizzy was refusing her feeds. She'd been sick, she'd spent most of the afternoon with her legs bent up, screaming, and finally Em had got Freddie and Beth off to bed and was pacing up and down, Kizzy in her arms turned against her front for comfort, and she was grizzling and hiccupping and it was tearing Emily apart.

She shifted her from one arm to the other because she was getting cramp, but as she settled her on the other side her breast brushed Kizzy's cheek and she turned her little head, instinctively rooting for the nipple.

And with her maternal instinct kicking in, Emily's nipples started to prickle and bead with milk, even though it had been months since she'd given up feeding Freddie.

Months and months, but as far as her body was concerned it could have been yesterday, and she pressed the heel of her hand against the other breast and bit her lips to hold back a whimper.

Oh, she ached to feed her. The instinct was overwhelming, and Kizzy felt it, too, nuzzling her and sobbing, and in the end it was more than she could bear.

How could it hurt? Wetnursing had been around for ever—for as long as mothers had died in childbirth, other women had fed their babies for them, and no one had thought twice about it. It was only now, in this sanitised age where bottle-feeding was an accepted option that anyone would even blink at the idea.

And anyway, she didn't need food, she needed comfort, poor motherless little scrap, and if Emily could provide comfort for this tragic infant, then who was she to deny it?

She sat down in the middle of the sofa, unfastened her bra and lifted it out of the way, then turned the baby to her nipple, brushing it against her cheek, and as if she'd been doing it all her life, Kizzy turned to her, opened her mouth and latched on.

There. Just like that, peace was restored. The hiccupping sobs faded to nothing, the only sound in the room was the rhythmic suckling of the baby, and cradling her close,

Emily stroked the back of the tiny starfish hand pressed against her breast and closed her eyes.

Poor baby. She should have done it hours ago, but she'd thought Harry would be back.

She glanced at her watch, concerned for him. The decorators had been and gone, leaving colour charts behind, and she'd made them tea and chatted over the fence in between feeds and Freddie's tantrums and Beth's persistent demands for attention, and somehow the day had disappeared.

Now it was night, almost eight-thirty, and it was getting dark outside.

She was just about to phone him again when she heard a key in the door. She felt a sudden flutter of panic, and glanced down at Kizzy. What if he was angry? What if he didn't understand? She thought of prising the baby off and reassembling her clothes, but there wasn't time, and anyway, she couldn't lie to him. She'd have to tell him, whatever, and she'd just have to hope he could understand.

'Em, I'm so sorry—the wires were down…'

He trailed to a halt, staring in amazement. She was *suckling* her! Breastfeeding Kizzy, as if it was the most natural thing in the world, and he felt a huge lump clog his throat.

For a moment he couldn't move, but then his legs kicked in again, and crossing over to her, he hunkered down and reached out a finger, stroking the baby's head, then looked up into Emily's stricken eyes. 'You're feeding her,' he said hoarsely.

'I'm sorry. She wouldn't settle—she's been crying for hours, and it seemed the only sensible thing to do. I'm really sorry, it's the only time—'

'Sorry?' He stared at her in astonishment. 'For giving her what her poor mother was unable to give her? Emily, no. Don't be sorry. She had donated milk in SCBU, just to start her off, but of course I couldn't keep it up. Don't have the equipment.' He smiled, and then his smile wobbled a bit and he frowned. 'I just— It was the one thing I couldn't do for her, the one thing I've felt so really bad about, and I never thought for a moment, never dreamt—'

He broke off, choked, and rested a trembling hand on Kizzy's head, watching as her damp little mouth worked at Em's nipple, and a surge of emotion washed over him, so strong it would have taken the legs out from under him if he hadn't already been down there.

'You couldn't get me a drink, could you?' she said, her voice soft, and he nodded and cleared his throat.

'Yeah. Sure. Of course. What do you want?'

'Tea? I'd better not have juice, it might upset her.'

He stood up, his legs a little unsteady, and went out to the kitchen, put the kettle on and leant his head against the wall cupboard while the world shifted back gradually onto an even keel.

He'd fantasised about this.

For the past two days, whenever she'd been carrying the baby or holding her like that, turned in to her body, he'd fantasised about her breastfeeding his child.

Not that Kizzy was his, except he couldn't imagine her being any more important to him whatever her parentage, and Em certainly wasn't his to fantasise over, but that hadn't stopped him, and now she'd brought his fantasy to life.

Only the once, he reminded himself. She'd probably never do it again, and why should she, really? It was a hell of a tie, and Kizzy was nothing to do with her. Anybody else would have shut her in a bedroom and left her to cry herself to sleep.

But not Em. His Emily had always been fiercely protective of children, breaking up squabbles on the beach when she was only ten, leading crying toddlers back to their distraught parents—he couldn't remember a time when she hadn't mothered something, be it a child or an animal.

That was the first time he'd been in the summerhouse, when she'd shown him a hedgehog with a damaged leg. She'd put it in a box in the summerhouse, and she had been feeding it on cat food bought out of her pocket money. He'd helped her look after it, and they'd both ended up with fleas.

He laughed softly at the thought, and her voice behind him caught him by surprise.

'Penny for them.'

He turned with a smile. 'I was remembering the fleas from the hedgehog you rescued. And here you've got another little stray.'

'Hopefully not with fleas.' She chuckled and handed him the baby. 'Anyway, she's your little stray and she needs her nappy changed. I'll make the tea—or do you want something else?'

A large bottle of Scotch? Nothing else would blot out the hellish day—but Emily had, with her gentle smile and her loving kindness to his daughter.

'Tea would be lovely,' he said, his voice suddenly rough, and took the baby upstairs to change her and put her in her cot. He checked the others, went back downstairs and found Em in the sitting room, the mugs on the table in front of her. She was sitting on the chair, not one of the two sofas, retreating, he imagined, to a place of safety, a place where it wouldn't be so easy for him to sit beside her, draw her into his arms and kiss her senseless.

For a second he was tempted to scoop her up out of the chair and sit down in it with her on his lap, but then common sense prevailed—better late than never—and he dropped into a corner of one of the sofas, facing her.

'Bad day?'

'Probably nearly as bad as yours,' he confessed with a wry smile.

'So how was your boss?'

His laugh sounded humourless, probably because it was. 'Let's just say she could have been more accommodating. I've taken a month's unpaid leave to give me time to sort things out. Let's just hope it's long enough.' He picked up his tea and cradled the mug in his hand, his head resting back against the cushion and his eyes closed. 'Oh, bliss. It's good to be home,' he said, and then almost stopped breathing, because that was exactly what it had felt like—coming home.

For the first time in his adult life.

He straightened up and turned his attention to the tea. 'So how did the decorators get on?' he asked, once he was sure he could trust his voice.

'OK. They've stripped out all the old carpets and put them in a skip, and they've started work on the windows. Here, colour charts.'

She pushed a pile of charts towards him on the table, and he put down his tea and picked them up, thumbing through them. 'What do you think?'

'I have no idea. I don't know what your taste is, Harry.

I haven't seen you since you were twenty one, at your grandmother's funeral. Our minds weren't on décor.'

No. They'd been on other things entirely, he remembered, and wished she hadn't brought it up, because he was straight back to the summerhouse, scene of many a moonlit tryst in their teens, stolen moments together on a voyage of discovery that now seemed so innocent and then had seemed so daring, so clandestine. Except that night, after he'd buried his grandmother, when things had got just that bit closer.

'Neutral,' he said, dragging his mind back from the brink. 'Or should children have bright primary colours to stimulate them?'

She shrugged. 'I don't know. I go with instinct, and my instinct is earth colours, unless you're talking about toys, but they can be put away and leave the place calm.'

'Calm, then.'

'I think so.'

He nodded and tried to pay attention to the colour charts, but all he could think of was their first kiss and their last—until last night, that was, only twenty-four hours ago, and still much too fresh in his mind. Coupled with coming home—there he went again—and finding Emily feeding Kizzy, he was having a hard time keeping his mind off sex and on the subject.

No. Not sex.

Emily. Emily in his arms, Emily's lips on his, Emily holding the baby, suckling her, the image still so powerful it was going to blow his mind.

He threw the colour charts down. 'I'll look at them tomorrow. See them in context. I can't even remember what colour sofas I chose now.'

She laughed, reaching for her tea and curling back up in the chair, her legs folded so that her feet were tucked up under that lovely curve of her bottom. 'Brown,' she told him. 'Bitter chocolate in that thick, bumpy leather—the tough stuff.'

'Right.' Concentrate on the sofas. 'So shoe buckles and toys don't scratch them. I remember. So we probably don't want to paint the walls black, then.'

She laughed again, and he felt it ripple right through him. 'Probably not. So, tell me about your boss.'

He shook his head. 'She was tough—tougher than the leather. I knew she would be. Don't worry, I can deal with her. It was the journey home that was so awful. There was a woman on the train who recognised me, and I was trapped with her for hours. I was getting ready to strangle her. She was creepy. I got the feeling that if the sun set I wouldn't have been safe.'

Em spluttered with laughter. 'Was she after you, Harry?'

'I think she might have been,' he confessed drily. 'Then again it might just be paranoia.'

'Or your ego.'

'Or my ego,' he conceded with a grin. 'Yeah, she was probably just a nice woman who was bored as hell and thought she could tell me her life story because she knew me. That's the trouble with spending your evenings in everybody's living rooms—they think they know you, and I suppose to a certain extent they do. Depends how much you give away to the camera.'

She tipped her head on one side, studying him. 'How much do you give away?'

He shrugged, trying to be casual because he knew the

answer was that he gave away too much of himself, even if it didn't show on camera. 'Depends. As little as possible, but sometimes things really get to you—like the earthquakes and the mudslides and things. Hideous. You can't keep that under wraps. Not if you're human. And then there are the fantastic moments when they pull a child out alive days later—I can't just tell it deadpan, but you have to bear in mind you're reporting the news and not making a social commentary. That's not my job, and if I have feelings or allegiances, I have to ignore them. It's all about being impartial, about giving people the facts and letting them make their own minds up. So I try not to give my own feelings away, but sometimes—well, sometimes I fail.'

He laughed softly and put his mug down on the table. 'Sorry—getting a bit heavy here. Tell me about your day.'

She studied him thoughtfully for a moment, then smiled, allowing him to change the subject. 'Well—let's just say I've had better. Freddie was a nightmare, Beth decided it was going to be one of those days when she wanted to make things with her mummy and so wanted my undivided attention, Kizzy was miserable and the decorators wanted tea.'

'Just another peachy day in suburbia, then,' he said with a suppressed smile, and she chuckled.

'Absolutely.'

'So you didn't get a lot of work done.'

'Not so you'd notice.'

He nodded, feeling the prickle of guilt for the umpteenth time that day. 'Sorry. That's my fault. How about I have the kids for you tomorrow so you can rest and do a bit of work and get your head together?'

'That would be fantastic. I've got a roof terrace design

to deliver to Georgie and Nick—the one I was working on last night—and if you could bear it, I'd like to take it over to them in the morning and discuss it. It's up to you.'

'That's fine. You do that. I'll cope, I'm sure.'

Except it didn't quite work like that.

Kizzy had other ideas. She woke at eleven, and he fed her, but she didn't seem to want her feed, and then she woke again just after twelve, and he was trying to get her to take the bottle when Em appeared in the kitchen, her eyes tormented.

'Harry?' she said softly.

'She just won't take it.'

'Want me to try?'

He shrugged and handed her the baby and the bottle, but she spat it out and turned to Em, nuzzling her.

And Em turned those tormented eyes on him and said, 'Oh, Harry, I have to…'

She was going to feed her. Again. Bare her breast and put the baby to it, and he was standing there in the kitchen in his boxers and it was all just too much.

He swallowed hard and nodded. 'Sure. Go on up to bed with her and I'll bring you tea,' he said, and the moment she was up there, he ran up, found a long T-shirt and pulled it on to give his emotions a little privacy. Then he went back down, made two mugs of tea and carried them up to her room, putting hers down on the bedside table.

'Call me when you're finished, I'll change her,' he said, and was heading for the door when her quiet voice stopped him.

'Stay and keep me company?'

'Don't you mind?'

She shook her head. 'It's not like it's anything you haven't seen before, is it? The places you go in the world, women do it all the time in public.'

But not her. Not his Em, feeding his child. But she was right, it was nothing he hadn't seen before, and so he sat down on the other side of the bed, propping himself up against the headboard and trying not to stare at the little puckered rosebud lips around her nipple.

'I don't think I've got enough milk for her,' Em said regretfully after a few minutes.

'Is that going to be a problem?'

She shook her head. 'No, not really. I'll be able to give her comfort, if nothing else, and she can get her feeds from you.'

Except she wouldn't. Not then, not later, not in the morning. It seemed she was a baby of discernment, and she'd decided only Emily would do.

Well, she'd made a rod for her own back with that one, Emily thought, and wondered where they went from there.

At best, she was feeding every three hours. At worst, it was more like one and a half or two hours. And, OK, at the moment Harry was living there, but once the decorators had finished and gone and he moved back, was he going to come through the gate in the fence every two or three hours through the night to bring the baby to her to feed?

Or, worse, leave the baby with her?

No way.

She loved Kizzy, wouldn't harm a hair of her fuzzy little head, but she wasn't hers, she hadn't asked for this and there was no way she was taking on responsibility for her. And she was in no doubt that Harry would put up a token fight and then give in and let her if she so much as hinted that she was willing.

She needed an exit strategy and, frankly, until she could convince Kizzy to take the bottle again, she wasn't going to have one. And another thing. How would she explain it to her children? Sure, they'd accept it, but would they then go and tell the world? Kids were so open. OK, not Freddie, although he might be jealous and start wanting to feed again, as well, but Beth might very well say something at playgroup or to Georgie or the boys.

She closed her eyes and stared sightlessly down at the little scrap busy making herself at home with her adopted milk bar. 'Oh, Kizzy,' she murmured. 'Why me?'

But she knew why her. Because nobody else would have been rash enough. They would have let her yell and handed her straight back to her father the minute he walked through the door.

It was her own fault, and she was going to have to deal with the consequences.

Just until she could talk Kizzy out of it. And in the meantime, she was supposed to be going to a business meeting with Georgie and Nick, and how the hell was she going to explain this to them? She'd just have to time it exactly right...

Damn.

Kizzy was yelling again, Freddie wanted to make another sandcastle with a moat and couldn't make the sand pile up because it was too dry, Beth wouldn't help him get water because she was busy pestering Harry for help with putting stickers on a book, and he was ready to rip his hair out.

How on earth would Em cope?

He took a deep breath, thought about it and went into the kitchen, stuck a bottle in the microwave—just for a quick blast on low—filled the plastic jug with water and took it to Freddie, helped Beth line up two stickers down the edge of the book and went back and grabbed the bottle.

Slick.

Except she wouldn't take it, Freddie spilt the water and Beth wasn't happy with just two stickers, she wanted more and she wanted him to help her stick them on.

Great. Fantastic. Where the hell was Emily? He glanced at his watch and was stunned. She'd only been gone three quarters of an hour!

'Are you OK? You look really tired.'

She gave Georgie a weak smile and flannelled. 'Harry and the baby are staying with me at the moment, and the baby was up a lot in the night.'

Georgie tipped her head on one side and studied her thoughtfully. Too thoughtfully. 'You've still got a thing for him, haven't you?' she said softly. 'And he's staying with you? Is that wise?'

Not in the least, but she wasn't telling Georgie that!

'It's fine,' she lied, 'but I really ought to get back.'

'Rubbish. He can cope. It does them good—they find hidden strengths. Look at Nick. Fifteen months ago he didn't have a clue about children. Now he's an expert. It's just practice.'

'Well, I don't need him practising on my children,' Emily said firmly, and scooped up her bag and keys. 'Are you sure about the design? Quite happy with it?'

'Absolutely. You've seen the place in London, you know what Nick likes and you've come up with a design that works for him and for the site. What's not to be happy with?'

Emily nodded. 'OK. Great. Thanks. And I haven't forgotten the bit round the back you want looked at. I will get round to it. It's just that at the moment with Nick's commercial stuff and with Harry and the baby…'

'It's fine. It'll keep. We won't do anything with it till the autumn anyway, so relax. And go back to him, if you have to. I must say if I were you and there was a hunk like that waiting for me, I wouldn't want to hang around having coffee with a chum!'

'But I do,' she said, meaning it. 'I'd love to have time with you, talk to you…' She trailed off, and Georgie's eyes sharpened.

'Em, are you sure everything's OK?'

For a moment she hesitated, wondering whether to say anything, but Georgie probably wouldn't understand. This was her first pregnancy, she'd never fed a baby—she might be horrified. 'I'm sure,' she lied again, and, kissing Georgie's cheek, she bent to touch Maya's head and smile at her, then headed home.

And just in the nick of time.

She could hear Kizzy as she turned onto the drive, and her let-down reflex was working overtime. She squashed her nipples with the heels of her hands and ran into the house, dumped her bag and went out into the garden, to find Freddie yelling and throwing sand out of the sandpit, Beth sulking over her stickers and Harry pacing helplessly with the flailing baby in his arms.

The look of relief on his face was comical.

'You're back,' he said needlessly, and without a word she took Kizzy and the bottle, went down to the seat under the apple tree and tried to fool her. Not easy, with Freddie climbing up her legs and Beth hanging round her neck from behind and Kizzy busy spitting out the teat.

'Hey, kids, how about some juice and biscuits?' she suggested, and looked up at Harry pleadingly.

'Good idea,' he said, picking up on it immediately. 'Come into the kitchen and we'll see what we can find. And you'd better wash your hands first. Come on, young man, let's go and find that biscuit tin,' he added, prising Freddie off her legs and setting him on his feet, then herding him towards the kitchen.

Now, then. She tried again with the bottle, but it was futile, so she hitched up her vest top, unclipped her bra— a front-fastener, dug out of the bottom of her underwear drawer—and plugged the baby in.

Peace. And with any luck she'd get enough food inside her before her children came back out and saw what she was doing. Not that she had any problems with them knowing, it was the rest of the world, and since she didn't intend to let this become a long-term thing—like, more than today, if possible!—there didn't seem any point in them finding out.

All she had to do was convince Kizzy that the bottle was just as good.

She tried sneaking the teat of the bottle in beside her nipple, but Kizzy was smarter than that. She spat it straight out and went back to the real thing.

So much for Plan A.

CHAPTER FIVE

'HOUSTON, we have a problem.'

It was the evening, and she'd spent the day dodging her children every time she'd fed the baby, while he'd struggled to keep them entertained and out of mischief.

Which, to give him credit, he'd managed very well, but it was getting silly, and she'd had a lot of time to think about it.

He cocked an eyebrow at her. 'Want to elaborate?'

'This feeding thing. It's not going to work. Not long term. I shouldn't have started it, it's my own fault, but now I have, I have to find the way out.'

'So what do you suggest?' he asked, his eyes troubled. 'Any ideas?'

'I'm going to see if I can get hold of a breast pump. I've used one before, when I had Freddie, because I had tons of milk and they were desperate in our local special care baby unit.'

He nodded, and she realised he would have known about it from his time there with Kizzy. His next words confirmed it. 'They had one in our SCBU,' he said, smiling crookedly. 'That's where Kizzy's milk came from—they called the thing Daisy. I doubt if you'd get one like that, though.'

'Oh, no, but I'm sure there's one I can get to use at home, but I don't know where from. I'm going to talk to the health visitor in the morning. I know her—she'll sort it if she can. But once your house is decorated, you'll be moving back, and we're going to have a problem if she still wants me. We have to wean her off me, Harry—and fast.'

He was frowning. 'So what's the plan? Give her bottles with your milk in until she gets used to the bottle again, then switch back to formula?'

She nodded. 'That's the idea.'

He pressed his lips together, ran a hand through his hair and nodded agreement. 'Yeah. Well, it makes sense. I can't expect you to do it for ever. Or at all.'

She sensed there was something he wasn't saying, but she didn't push it because she didn't want to be talked out of it. Wouldn't be talked out of it. No matter how sorry she felt for Kizzy.

'Can I borrow your computer and go online?' he asked abruptly.

'Sure.'

She watched him leave the room, and dropped her head back with a sigh. How on earth had she got herself in this mess?

Five minutes later he stuck his head round the door. 'Come and see,' he said, and she got up and followed him to her study.

'Breast pumps,' he said, pointing at the computer with the air of a magician. 'Manual, electric, single, double—tons of stuff. Bras to hold them in place so you can work while you do it—whatever. Order what you want—and get the works. It comes next-day delivery and I'll pay. It's the least I can do.'

* * *

The stuff turned up the following afternoon, and she disappeared with it to experiment. He tried not to think about it. He was getting fixated, and it was ridiculous.

'Hey, Freddie, come here, little man. Let's put some more suncream on you and you need that hat on.'

'No!' he screamed, throwing himself over backwards and flailing. 'Not hat! Not cream! Go 'way!'

A window flew open upstairs and Em leant out, clutching a towel to her chest. 'Is he OK?'

'He's fine. He doesn't want sunblock.'

'Bribe him,' she advised, and shut the window.

Huh? Bribe him? A nineteen-month-old baby? With what?

'He likes bananas,' Beth said softly in his ear, and giggled. 'So do I. And biscuits. 'Specially chocolate ones.'

'Is that right?' he said, slinging an arm round her skinny little shoulders and hugging her. 'And I suppose you want one, too?'

'Course,' she said, wriggling free and grabbing his hand. 'C'mon. Freddie, let's get a biscuit.'

'No! Want Mummy!' Freddie yelled, and Beth just shrugged and headed up the path to the kitchen, towing Harry in her wake.

'No biscuit if you don't come. Or banana. Come on, Harry. Let's have a tea party. We'll make some for Mummy, too.'

So he went with her—no choice, really, unless he let go of her hand, which he was curiously reluctant to do—and they made tea and put biscuits and fruit out on plates while he watched Freddie out of the window to make sure he didn't come to any harm.

He'd rolled onto his front, and he was still sobbing,

but at least now he was in the shade and he wouldn't come to any harm.

'What's Mummy doing?' Beth asked while she was arranging the biscuits for the fourth time.

'Um—feeding Kizzy, I think,' he said, hoping she wouldn't go upstairs, but she just carried on arranging the biscuits until she was satisfied.

'There. Shall we take them in the garden and wait for Mummy?'

'Good idea,' he said. 'Have you got a picnic blanket?'

Her eyes lit up. 'So we can have a picnic under the tree! Um—Mummy has—it's upstairs, I'll get it,' she said, and before he could stop her, she was gone.

He groaned inwardly, but there was no point going after her and, anyway, he couldn't take his eyes off Freddie that long. Hopefully Emily would have finished by now…

'What are you doing?'

Emily looked up at Beth, standing in the doorway swinging on the doorhandle and watching her, and gave up.

'Kizzy needs milk, but she doesn't like the milk from the shops, and she hasn't got a mummy.'

'So are you giving her your milk?'

'Yes. Like I did when Freddie was small, and I went to the hospital and gave them milk for the tiny babies so they could have it in their bottles.'

'Because Kizzy's tiny, isn't she?'

Emily nodded.

'So why don't you just feed her like Freddie?' she asked, looking puzzled.

Why not, indeed? Except that she wasn't her child, and

cradling her that close, suckling her, was going to make it all the harder when Harry took her away.

'Because I can't. Harry needs to move back to his house when it's decorated, and I've got to work. And I don't want to be up all night, I'm tired.'

'Oh. Won't she mind?'

Probably, but it was tough. 'She'll be fine,' she said firmly, hoping it was true. 'Did you come upstairs for anything in particular?'

'Picnic blanket. Harry and me made biscuits and bananas and tea and juice—oh, and strawberries. We're having a picnic in the garden. Are you coming, Mummy?'

Made biscuits? She would have smelt it. Probably just poetic licence. 'In a minute,' she said, eyeing the reservoir and wondering if it would be enough. 'Take the blanket down and I'll be down soon.'

Although not that soon. She filled a bottle, then washed out the machine, put the parts into fresh sterilising solution and right on cue, Kizzy started to cry.

The acid test, she thought, and, scooping the baby up, she offered her the teat, squeezing a little milk out so she knew it wasn't formula, but Kizzy wasn't fooled and she spat the teat out.

Great.

Emily didn't know what she was doing. If only she hadn't started this. Well, it was time it stopped. Harry could feed her. Maybe that would work better.

She took Kizzy down, handed her and the bottle over and gave him a crooked smile. 'Yours, I think,' she said, and, scooping Freddie up, she hugged him and kissed his sticky, chocolaty little face. 'Hello, gorgeous,' she said, and he snuggled into her and wiped chocolate all over her front.

She didn't care. It didn't matter. All that mattered was that Harry and Kizzy would manage to get the milk down her neck and she could take a back seat.

'Is that my tea?' she asked, and Beth nodded.

'It's not very hot.'

'It'll be fine,' she said firmly, and, turning her back on Harry and the baby, she sipped her tea, nibbled a biscuit— not home made, she noticed—and tuned out the sound of Kizzy fussing.

And then, miraculously, there was peace.

The screaming stopped, there was a suckling noise from behind her, and she felt her shoulders drop about a foot.

Finally.

'Thank you.'

She looked up and smiled at Harry. He was hesitating in the doorway, his eyes studying the gadget, and he shifted awkwardly, jerking his head towards the pump.

'So how does it work?'

Strangely shy suddenly, she showed him the instructions, showed him the bra which held the breast shields in place while the pump was working, and how the milk was collected, and his brows clumped together in a frown.

'I had no idea it was so complicated,' he said. 'Hell, Em, I'm sorry. It's a real drag having to do all that.'

'It's fine,' she said, all too conscious of the fact that he'd never asked her to start this.

'But it's going to take so much time—all the sterilising and stuff, never mind the time linked up to the pump.'

'Well, that's OK. You'll have plenty of opportunity in between milking times to hose down the parlour,' she said with a grin, and his face dropped.

'Me? You want me to wash it out and sterilise it and stuff?'

'Well, why not? She's your baby. I'm just the dairy cow—and, no, you can't call me Daisy,' she added, and his mouth quirked in a smile.

'Sorry. I didn't think. Of course I'll do it. Just one thing?'

'Mmm?'

'Can I call you Buttercup?'

He ducked out of reach, laughing, and she stood up and grabbed a cushion and lobbed it at him just as he turned the corner into the hall.

It bounced off the wall, and she heard the sound of his retreating chuckle, then the noise of the kettle boiling. Two minutes later he was back with a cup of tea for her.

'Kids are all settled. Anything I can do for you?'

A massage, to take the kinks out of her neck from falling asleep in the chair this morning after she'd fed Kizzy?

She shook her head. 'No. I'm fine.'

'You don't look fine, you look tense,' he said, and, turning her round in her swivel chair, he put his big, gentle hands on her shoulders and squeezed. 'Tight as a bow-string,' he said, tutting, and worked the muscles carefully.

Bliss. It was absolute bliss. The only thing that could be better would be if they were lying down, and then when he'd massaged her shoulders, he'd run his hands down her back, over her bottom, her legs, then back up, really slowly, teasing, slipping his finger under the elastic of her knickers and running it round, just enough to torment her. Then he'd roll her on her back and start again, kneading—

'Are you OK?'

Oh, lord, had she really groaned aloud?

'I'm fine. Sorry, bit tight there,' she flannelled, wondering if she'd get away with it. He paused a moment longer, then his fingers started working again and she let her breath go in a long, silent sigh.

'Better?'

Was she imagining it, or was his voice a little husky? No. Don't be silly, she told herself. You're imagining it.

'Yes, thanks,' she said, and wondered if her voice was a little off kilter or if she was just imagining that, too. But then she turned to smile her thanks, and met his unguarded eyes.

Need.

That was what she saw. Need, and hunger, and reluctance. Well, she knew all about that. All of them, in fact. Just at the moment reluctance was way down her list, but it was still there, smothered by the need and hunger and the unrequited ache that had been there for what seemed like half her lifetime.

Was half her lifetime.

Oh, hell.

She turned back to the desk. 'I'd better drink my tea,' she said, a touch unsteadily. 'It'll be cold. Thanks for the massage—I'll be able to put in another couple of hours at the drawing board now.'

She felt him hesitate, then with a murmured, 'See you later, then,' he went out and closed the door softly behind him.

She sagged against the desk and closed her eyes. Why? Why on earth had he had to come back and torment her like this? And why was it all so incredibly complicated?

She straightened up, pulled the file towards her and

sorted through the pages, considering the next project she had to do for Nick. She couldn't afford to think about Harry now. She had work to do, to earn her living. And Harry Kavenagh was just a distraction she could do without.

He shouldn't have touched her.

Just the feel of her shoulders, tense under his hands at first, then gradually relaxing, and that little moan—hell, he'd nearly lost it.

Bit tight? Rubbish. She'd been utterly floppy and she'd only tensed up again after she'd made that needy little noise.

And her eyes, when she'd turned—wary, longing—he had no idea how he'd got out of there. If she hadn't turned away when she had, God knows what would have happened.

He snorted. Well, of course she'd realised that. That was why she'd turned back to her desk, because she'd realised that if she kept looking at him like that, he would have lost it.

Might still.

He growled with frustration and checked his watch. Eight-thirty. He'd fed Kizzy at seven-thirty. With any luck he'd got another hour, at least. He tapped on the study door and opened it a crack.

'Are you OK if I go for a walk? Kizzy should be all right for a bit.'

'Sure,' she said, her voice a little strained. 'Take your mobile.'

'Done,' he said, and went out into the blissful evening. It was gorgeous—a light breeze to take away the heat of the day, the sun low in the sky, creeping down to the horizon. He walked to the clifftop and sat watching the sun brush the sky with colour. It was the wrong way round for a sunset, of course, facing east as it did, but sunrise would be glorious.

If he was up one night, woken by Kizzy, he might bring her here and let her see the dawn.

He glanced at his watch, surprised at how dark it had become, and realised he'd been longer than he'd meant to be. Still, his phone hadn't rung, so Kizzy hadn't woken.

Unless Em just hadn't phoned him.

He jogged back and arrived just as she began to whimper.

'Milk's in the microwave,' Em told him, meeting him in the hall.

'Thanks.' He ran up and lifted the baby into his arms, and she snuggled into him, her little mouth working, feeling the material of his T-shirt and growing impatient.

'Sorry, baby. Do I smell wrong? Never mind. Come on, let's go and find some milk for you.'

Em was waiting for him, handing him the bottle and going back into the study and shutting the door. Just as well. A little space would do them both good at the moment.

He fed the baby, persevering through her fussing until she took the bottle in the end and settled down to suck, then he bathed and changed her and put her to bed.

Ten. Just in time for the news, he thought, and watched it in silence on the edge of his seat, saw friends of his reporting from places he knew well, read between the lines, guessed the things they weren't telling or had been ordered not to report.

Did they miss him? Were they all having to work extra shifts, or were there things not being given coverage because he wasn't there? Maybe some youngster was getting his first chance. Or hers. There were plenty of women now out there working in the field, covering stories every bit as dangerous as the ones he covered.

He laughed softly to himself and shook his head. The most dangerous thing he had to do at the moment was dodge one of Kizzy's special nappies.

Or Emily. Keeping out of her way, keeping the simmering need between them under control because frankly things were complicated enough without that. And then she stuck her head round the door.

'I'm off to bed now. The breast pump's in the sink—it needs washing up and putting in the sterilising solution. There are four bottles in the fridge—should see her through. 'Night.'

'Good night,' he said automatically, and switched off the television. They'd got onto the local news, and he didn't need to know about the local protests about a meat-rendering plant and the woman who'd had her dog stolen.

So he went into the kitchen and picked up the breast pump. Warm. It was still warm, the bits that went over her nipples still holding her body heat, the reservoir warm from the milk.

And he had to wash it, knowing where it had been, aching to have touched her as closely as these bits of plastic.

Dear God, he was losing it. It was just an ordinary, everyday thing, and he was turning it into something huge.

Because it was.

He didn't know anybody else who would have done it for Kizzy, and it brought a lump to his throat. He didn't want to be there in the kitchen. He wanted to be upstairs with Em, cradling her in his arms, holding her close to his heart, listening as her breathing slowed into sleep, but he didn't have the right.

He didn't have any rights.

He washed it up, put it in the solution, checked the bottles and went upstairs to bed.

Kizzy slept right through to four, and when she woke she snuggled down into his arms and fell asleep again, so he went down to the kitchen, warmed the bottle and went back up, laid her carefully down on the bed and pulled on his jeans and T-shirt, wrapped her in her fleecy blanket and went down, took the bottle and headed for the cliff.

'We should just make the sunrise,' he told her, and as they turned the corner, he saw the first tiny rim of gold creep over the horizon.

'Look, Kizzy,' he said, holding her up, and she opened her eyes and stared up at him and smiled.

She smiled at him! Her first smile!

He sat down on the damp grass, cradled her close and lifted the bottle to her mouth, and she took it without a murmur, while he sat there and watched the new day dawn and marvelled at her smile.

'Harry?'

He turned in the bedroom doorway, his face perturbed. 'Em—I'm sorry, did I disturb you?'

'Not really. I heard the door go. I was worried. Is everything OK?'

He nodded, his face somehow lit from within. 'She smiled at me,' he said in wonder. 'I took her out to watch the dawn and she smiled at me.'

Oh, she remembered that so well—the first time Beth and Freddie had smiled at her. Such a wonderful gift. Of course, Kizzy was very young, so it might have been wind, but she wasn't going to spoil his moment. And she'd been staring more and more intently, so it could easily have been a proper smile.

'That's lovely,' she said softly, and reached out her finger to stroke it down the baby's downy cheek. 'Did she take the feed?'

He nodded, and she felt a strange mixture of emotions. Relief, of course, but also—regret? Really?

'I'm just going to change her and put her down. Do you want me to make you a cup of tea, as you're up?'

She nodded. 'That would be nice. In fact, why don't I make it while you do the baby?' she offered, and he smiled gratefully and went into the bedroom to change her.

Emily went downstairs, put the kettle on and made the tea, and she was just at the foot of the stairs when he came out of the baby's room and pulled the door to.

'Ah, cheers,' he murmured, and ran lightly down, smiling at her.

'So where did you go?' she asked, curious about his sudden urge for the dawn.

'The cliff top. I took the bottle and fed her while I watched the sun come up. It was gorgeous. Beautiful. You would have loved it.'

She would have. Sitting on the cliff top with him, leaning against him and watching for that first sliver of gold—they'd done that on the morning of his grandmother's funeral, and then that night, in the summerhouse, he'd kissed her as he'd never kissed her before, with a wildness and desperation that had nearly pushed them over the edge.

Did he remember? Yes, of course he did. He'd mentioned it already, when he'd talked about the creaking garden gate; she'd said they'd been kids, and he'd said not the last time. So clearly he remembered it.

She handed him his tea and curled up on the chair—safest, really, considering how vulnerable she was to him—and he sat in the corner of the sofa opposite and drank his tea and watched her as the sun slowly pushed back the night and the shadows receded.

'I ought to go back to bed and catch a few more minutes—Freddie'll be up soon,' she said, putting down her mug and standing up, and with a fleeting smile she turned on her heel and left him while she still had the determination to do it.

She was out for the count. Not surprising, really, considering how much sleep she'd lost over the last couple of nights, but as he was up anyway with Kizzy, it was no hardship to give Freddie a hug and change his nappy—quite a different proposition to Kizzy's!—and take him downstairs for his juice.

Two babies, he thought, and had to stifle a slightly hysterical laugh. Him, the greatest bachelor of all time, changing nappies at six-thirty in the morning?

His mother would be stunned.

He realised with something akin to astonishment that he hadn't told them yet—not about Carmen, not about his marriage, and certainly not about Kizzy.

Perhaps he should. Give them an opportunity to gloat.

They'd probably earned it, he'd given them a hard enough time when he'd been growing up.

And whose fault was that? an inner voice asked. Yours, for being bored and understimulated by parents that didn't bother, or theirs, for neglecting your basic need for human interaction?

Well, he was getting plenty of human interaction now, both at work and at home—and there was that word again.

'San'castle,' Freddie demanded.

'How about breakfast first?' he suggested evenly. 'Want some eggy bread? Or toast and honey?'

'Eggy b'ed.'

'OK. I tell you what, you drink your juice and watch the telly with me, and I'll give Kizzy her milk, and then we'll have eggy bread. OK?'

''K,' Freddie said round the spout of the feeder cup, and snuggled up under his arm and watched him feed the baby.

He looked exhausted.

He was dozing on the sofa, Kizzy sleeping in the crook of his arm, Freddie next to him watching baby-telly in the crook of his other arm, and Emily felt a wave of emotion that she didn't want to examine too closely for fear of what she'd find.

'Hi, baby,' she said softly, and Freddie lifted his head and gave her his gorgeous beaming smile and held out his arms. She scooped him up, hugged him close and sat down on the chair with him without a word, so as to not disturb Harry. She didn't like leaving Kizzy there like that, in case he rolled over or moved and dropped her, but the first sign of movement and she'd be there.

Plus, of course, it gave her the perfect excuse to study him as he slept.

He was rumpled and tousled and gorgeous, she thought, his jaw dark with stubble, his lashes dark crescents against his cheeks. His nose had been broken at some time, leaving a little bump in the middle, and there was a faint scar slicing through the stubble—from a knife blade? Could be. It wouldn't surprise her, the places he ended up and the trouble he seemed to find.

What was that saying? Don't borrow trouble, it'll find you soon enough—or something like that? It certainly found Harry—or he found it. As a child he'd been a daredevil, and as an adult—well, she couldn't bear to think about the things he'd done in the course of his career as a TV world affairs correspondent.

Still, it was over now. She was sure he'd still travel the world, but once he'd worked his notice, hopefully his life should be a whole lot safer.

And maybe, just maybe, he'd find that life in Yoxburgh wasn't so bad after all…

CHAPTER SIX

'It's looking really good.'

'Mmm.' Harry swivelled round, studying the newly painted sitting room, then glanced down the hall. 'The kitchen's still awful.'

'Well, give them time. I tell you what, if you had the cabinet doors painted while they're in there, it would give it a new lease of life. Just until you decide what you're doing,' she added.

She was fishing, but he didn't rise. 'I'll talk to them,' he said, and disappeared upstairs to where the boss was working, leaving her there with Freddie in her arms and Beth at her side, wrinkling her little button nose at the smell of paint.

Emily was standing by the French doors, keeping an eye on Kizzy outside in the baby-carrier, and she glanced up at the garden, looking at it properly for the first time in ages. As she studied it Harry appeared at her shoulder and made a thoughtful noise.

'Awful, isn't it? It's gone to rack and ruin over the last ten years. My grandparents would be gutted. It just needs tidying when I've got time,' he said, but she laughed.

'I don't think so. Most of the shrubs are too leggy to recover, and it's a high-maintenance garden, anyway. Tenants won't want that, and I don't suppose you do, either.'

'So what do you suggest?'

She shrugged. 'I don't know. Something simple? Some gravel, some paving, some serious pruning and thinning of the shrubbery and some more inventive planting—I'd have to look at it.'

'Would you? I'll pay you to design it for me.'

She turned and frowned at him. 'I wouldn't dream of charging you!' she said, insulted, but he just arched a brow.

'Do you charge Nick?'

'Well—yes, but it's business.'

'Yes. And so's this. Put it like this, if you won't let me pay you, I'll get someone else in—one of the garden centre chains. Most of them have a design department. And you'll have to look at it over the fence and it will annoy the hell out of you.'

'But I'll need someone to look after the children.'

'I'll do that.'

'Only if you let me pay you.' Hah. She had him.

Or not. 'But I still owe you babysitting time,' he pointed out archly, 'and, come to think of it, a massage.'

'You gave me that the other night.'

'Not a proper one. I only did your shoulders.'

And that had been bad enough. The thought of taking her clothes off and lying down on a towel while he massaged her whole body with those incredible hands was enough to make her hyperventilate. She turned back to the garden.

'Fair cop,' she said, her voice a little uneven. 'OK.

Instead of the massage, you can look after the kids and I'll do you a design. If you like it, you can pay me. If you don't, then there's no charge.'

'Is that how you normally work?'

'Yes,' she lied.

He grunted, and she guessed he didn't believe her, but it was tough. She wasn't taking money off him if he didn't agree with her design, and she wouldn't take much off him anyway. And she'd oversee it for nothing and pretend it was part of the service. Maybe even do some of the work. And maybe he could do some, too. They could do it together, working side by side while the children played in the soil and ran around getting grubby.

Just like a family.

The sudden ache in her chest took her by surprise, and she sucked in her breath and turned back to him with an overbright smile. 'Deal?'

'Deal,' he said, but before he could say any more or lay down any conditions of his own, her mobile phone rang.

'Hey, Georgie!' she said with relief. 'How are you?'

'Fine—fancy the beach? We're going down with the kids and taking a picnic. Want me to do enough for you, too?'

'You don't want to do that! I can make something for me and the kids.'

'Aren't you forgetting Harry?' Georgie said, and she shot him a look, wondering if he'd heard. Probably.

'Fancy going to the beach with the kids?' she asked him, hoping he'd say no, but he grinned and nodded.

'Love to. I haven't been to an English beach for years. Bucket–and-spade time, eh, Freddie?'

Freddie was jiggling on her hip and squealing, Beth was

bouncing on the spot and nearly tugging her arm out of its socket, and Harry looked almost as enthusiastic.

'I think that's a yes,' she said to Georgie, giving up the unequal struggle, because, in fact, she couldn't think of anything she'd like more than going to the beach with Harry and the children.

And if it was just another example of them playing happy families, well, maybe he'd find it was so much fun he wanted to do it again and again and again...

'Freddie, no!'

He was being crushed to death! He was lying flat on his back, buried up to his neck in sand, and Freddie was bouncing on his chest and laughing. Beside him Nick was similarly buried, with Dickon sitting on him and giggling helplessly, and he turned his head and caught Nick's eye.

'Enough?' Nick mouthed, and he nodded.

'OK. One, two, three!' Nick yelled, and they both erupted out of the sand, grabbing the giggling children and dumping them in the dents they'd made.

'Look! I can still see you!' Beth said, pointing at his impression in the sand, Freddie sitting in the middle of it— giggling hysterically.

''Gain!' he yelled.

'You've got to catch me first,' Harry said, and headed for the sea, Nick at his side and the children in hot pursuit. As his feet hit the water he stopped dead and gasped. 'Hell, it's freezing!'

'Not quite Sharm-el-Sheikh, I'm afraid!' Nick replied with a grin. 'We can always go back to the house for a proper swim if you want.'

'You've got a pool?'

He nodded. 'And a hot tub. I love my hot tub. I've got one in London at the apartment, and I couldn't bear the thought of not having it, so we built one here.'

They strolled along the fringe of surf, the children giggling and chasing each other round and round in the shallow water and splashing each other, while Georgie sat under a big hat and fanned herself and Em sat with her, the baby at her side under a little parasol she'd found in the loft.

They could have been just two normal families, he thought, but of the four of them only Em was really a parent, although of course time would soon change that for Nick and Georgie, with the birth of their own baby in just a very few weeks.

He glanced up the beach at Em. How would he feel if she was pregnant with his child?

Terrifed, if he had any sense.

But apparently not, because the thought didn't seem terrifying at all, it seemed ridiculously appealing—although that was probably because it was never going to happen. One, because he didn't just go round getting women pregnant and, two, because there was no way he was getting that close to Emily.

And if that left him feeling just a little hollow inside, it was tough. Coming back had caused enough havoc. And he needed to be able to leave again, needed to be free—and he knew, just knew, that if he and Em ended up having an affair, free was the last thing he'd be.

'Stay for the evening. We were going to have a barbeque and a real swim, and the children could lie down in front of a film with Nick's mother while we sit outside in the hot tub and chill. What do you say?'

Emily hesitated for a moment, then thought of all the good reasons why not. Starting with the fact that Kizzy was out of milk.

'That isn't really fair on Liz, dumping three extras on her, and anyway, we can't—we didn't bring enough bottles for the baby,' she said truthfully.

'Well—Harry, why don't you go and pick some up from home and come back? We'll look after Kizzy for you, won't we, Em?'

She met his eyes in desperation, hoping he'd catch on, and he did, bless him, but not in the way she'd thought. Instead he grinned and said, 'Sounds like a plan. Except I've had a beer, so I can't drive. Still, you could go, Em. I'm sure there are things you want to do at home—you said something about putting the washing on before you came out, and I don't think you remembered.'

'No—no, I didn't,' she said, grabbing the lifeline. 'Um—so, I'll go, then, and stick a load in and get everything. Back soon. Kids, be good for Harry, won't you?'

And with a quick kiss for them both, she shot out of the door before Georgie could scupper her by offering to keep her company. The last thing she needed while she plugged herself into Buttercup was an audience!

But she escaped without intervention, and half an hour later she was on her way back, the bottles full and the washing on—just to make it less of a lie, because she hated that. She ought to just tell Georgie and have done with it, but she was afraid her friend would find it somehow repellent.

Still, she'd done her bit for the subterfuge now, and she

arrived back armed with the milk and more nappies and clothes for Freddie and Kizzy, to find them all in the swimming pool, with much shrieking and giggling going on, and Nick and Harry with Dickon and Harry junior on their shoulders, battering each other with brightly coloured foam poles.

Dickon fell off with a great shriek, and the two Harrys punched the air and whooped.

'We-e wo-on,' Harry junior chanted, brandishing his hideous green pole overhead and grinning for England.

'Me, me!' Freddie yelled, reaching out to Harry, his little fists opening and closing in appeal, and so Harry took him on his shoulders, Nick took Beth and, as she'd known she would, Beth let her little brother win, falling into the water with a mock cry. Nick scooped her up instantly, hugging her and whispering something to her that made her giggle deliciously, and then she caught sight of Emily and waved.

'Hello, Mummy! Come in the water, it's lovely!'

Why was it, she thought, that the sea was somehow so much less personal, so much easier to be almost naked in? Because here, in the close confines of the Barrons' pool, she felt suddenly hideously conscious of the scantiness of the perfectly normal one-piece swimsuit that only an hour ago had seemed quite adequate.

Not now, though. Now, it could have been made of gauze, and she could feel Harry's eyes burning holes in it

She slid under the water, mmmed appreciatively and swam away from him to Freddie, bobbing happily in his waterwings and splashing Georgie with his pudgy baby hands. He snuggled up to her, giving her a wet, slightly chlorinated kiss, and she was glad to focus her attention on him. It gave her a chance to ignore Harry, although she could hear another loud and boisterous game behind her with him evidently in the thick of it.

'Get the washing sorted?' Georgie asked, and Emily was so, so glad she'd made the effort.

'Yes, thanks. Baby clothes,' she flannelled. 'Kizzy and Freddie. They get through them so fast.'

'So can't Harry use the washing machine?' she murmured, and Emily felt the colour creeping into her cheeks.

'Of course he can—but he didn't know where Freddie's stuff was. I just popped a few of the baby's things in to make up the load.'

Oh, she was going to be struck by lightning in a minute, and Georgie, who'd known her for years, was giving her a very odd look. She didn't say anything, though, and Nick was getting out of the water and attending to the barbeque, the children were heading for the shower—one mess she was glad she wouldn't have to clear up!—and Freddie was pulling the sort of face that meant she had just a few seconds to get him to a potty.

'Oops. Got to fly,' she said, and hoisted Freddie out of the pool, hauled herself up onto the side, grabbed him and ran.

'That was a great evening.'

She smiled warily. 'Yes, it was.'

'They're lovely people.'

'Yes.'

'You're lucky to have such good friends close by. Mine are scattered all over the world.'

And whose choice was that? she could have said, but she

didn't, she bit her tongue and headed for the kitchen. 'Tea or wine?' she asked, and he shrugged.

'Whatever. I've had wine and beer already today. If you're drinking I'll join you, but I'm quite happy with tea.'

'Tea it is, then,' she said, glad she'd had the excuse of driving to refuse the wine, because while she was still expressing milk for Kizzy she didn't want to drink.

And it would be lovely to reach a point where she didn't have to take that into account at every moment of her life!

With a little sigh she put the kettle on, reached for the mugs and bumped into Harry.

'Sorry,' he said, throwing her an apologetic smile. 'I was getting the mugs for you.'

But the damage was done. After a day of watching him running around on the beach and at the Barrons' three parts naked, water sluicing off his powerful body and beading like tiny gems in the dark hair that covered his legs and arrowed down his abdomen, just the brush of his body against her was enough to start a wildfire that no amount of common sense was going to be able to put out. She'd nearly blown a fuse when his leg had brushed against hers in the hot tub, but she'd been safe there, with Georgie and Nick to chaperone and keep order. Here, there was no one to hold them back, nothing to stop them. Except her fleeting common sense.

Emily turned back to the tea, her fingers trembling, and dropped a teaspoon on the floor.

They bent together, bumped again and he laughed and apologised and moved away, giving her room to breathe at last and her heart time to slow.

'So—fancy having a look at the garden tomorrow?' he said after a long moment that sizzled with tension.

'Sure. If you have the kids.'

'I thought we could do it together—talk it through. It's not as if it's far away. The kids can come, too. After all, it's the weekend. The painters won't be there.'

'No. OK. What did they say about the kitchen, by the way?' she asked, desperately trying not to think about that arrowing hair on his washboard abdomen.

'Oh, he'd been going to suggest it,' he said, taking his mug from her. 'Thought it was a good idea for a short-term fix. He's going to do it.'

'Colour?'

Harry shrugged and grinned. 'I have no idea. Maybe sort of duck-egg, I think he was suggesting, but I can't say I've taken an interest in kitchens, really. My flat's got a stainless-steel and lacquer-red high-gloss laminate kitchen that's a mass of fingermarks and a living nightmare to work in—not my choice, I have to add. It was the developer who put it in. The only bit of it I like is the walnut worktop, because it goes with the floor. Anyway, it doesn't matter. This kitchen can't look worse than it does at the moment, so duck-egg or cream or whatever, it has to be an improvement.'

They went through to the sitting room and she picked up the TV remote. 'Want to watch something, or shall I put music on?'

'Music would be nice,' he said, and she went into her study and came back with a couple of CDs that she used for background while she was working—compilation albums of soft, easy-listening tracks, female singers mostly, but she'd never noticed just how intrinsically romantic all the songs were until that moment.

Damn. She should have chosen something different—something classical. She buried her nose in her mug and tried not to look at him. For a few minutes they sat in silence, then the third track came on, less romantic, and with an inward sigh of relief she shifted slightly so she could see him better and said, 'Tell me about yourself. What have you been doing since I last saw you? Apart from the obvious, of course.'

He gave a quiet huff of laughter. 'Nothing much. Flying about all over the world. It doesn't leave time for much, really.'

'You'd just left uni when your grandmother died, hadn't you? You must have been twenty-one, I suppose.'

He nodded. 'Nearly twenty-two. And you were nineteen, and home from uni for the summer.'

And they'd watched the sun rise, and then that night…

The memory was written on his face, and she looked away. 'So what did you do then? After you left?'

He shrugged. 'Bummed around. Took the gap year I'd never had, saw some of the world, worked in a radio station in Brisbane, got a job on a newspaper in Rio, linked up with a television crew in Nepal, and that was it, really. I started doing odd bits for them, earning a living but nothing great, working as a news researcher when I came home. Did a bit of local television news, then got the break into overseas reporting when I was about twenty-five. I've been doing it for six years now.'

'And you've never married?'

He shook his head. 'Well, except for Carmen, and she didn't really count, because I'd realised by then that I'd never marry. It just doesn't fit with the job.'

'You're not telling me all those reporters are single?'

He laughed. 'No, of course not, but they find it hard to have a normal family life. I didn't want anything in the way. And anyway, I'd never met anyone who made me feel like settling down.' He tipped his head on one side. 'So tell me about you. I know about Pete but what did you do before you met him? How old were you then?'

'Twenty-four. I'd finished my degree, decided biology didn't really qualify me for anything and, anyway, I'd discovered I loved gardens, and so I did a garden design course and started work.'

'Here.'

She laughed. 'Well, yes, my father let me do their garden, and I did some others, and then I worked for one of the garden centre chains—the sort of thing you were threatening me with yesterday.'

He grinned. 'Hardly threatening.'

'Blackmailing, then. Anyway, that's what I was doing when I met Pete.'

'And you stopped when you had Beth?'

'Only for a while,' she told him, remembering her reluctance to go back to work full time. 'I wanted to freelance, to break out on my own and work from home, but he said we couldn't afford the risk. What he really meant was that he wasn't prepared to fund me while it got off the ground, but Pete never really said what he meant—not until he walked out, and even then he didn't discuss it.'

Harry shook his head. 'I can't believe he just legged it while you were at the supermarket.'

'Pausing only to stop the credit card,' she reminded him. 'Still, water under the bridge and all that. And I'm much happier now than I was then.' Except for the fact that she couldn't afford to house her children without her parents' generosity. That was a bit of a killer, always nagging at the back of her mind.

As if he'd read that mind, he said quietly, 'And the house? I don't imagine if you weren't living here your parents would want to keep something this big on into their retirement.'

She shook her head. 'No. Ideally they want to downsize and buy somewhere in Portugal, as well, to be near my grandparents. Well, my mother does. My father would be quite happy here, pottering in his garden, but he loves her, and whither thou goest and all that.'

He frowned. 'I can't imagine a woman in the world who'd want to follow me wherever I go.'

Or a woman, presumably, who he'd follow?

'To the ends of the earth,' she murmured, realising that, were things different, if she hadn't had the children and if he'd asked her, she would follow him anywhere he asked her.

'It sometimes feels like it,' he replied. 'And, like I say, no sane woman would want that.'

No sane woman, possibly, but where Harry was concerned she could never be accused of being sane. If she was sane, she wouldn't have ended up sharing her roof with him, making him welcome, feeding his child for heaven's sake!

'So how's Dan?'

Dan? 'He's fine,' she said, reining in her rambling mind and concentrating on her brother. 'He's working in New York. He breezes in from time to time, sometimes without warning—he's got a partner, Kate, but there's no sign of them getting married, to my mother's disappointment. She wants to see her firstborn settled, she says, before she turns up her toes.'

His eyes narrowed. 'Is she sick?' he asked, and she laughed.

'No, not at all. She's just despairing of Daniel. No, she and Dad are fine. Enjoying life.' And she was holding them back, interfering with their plans for retirement. Oh, damn.

'Em, are you OK?'

She met his eyes, gentle and concerned, and could have crumpled, but she didn't. 'Yes, I'm fine,' she said. 'Just a bit tired.'

'Why don't you turn in?' he suggested.

She gave a wry smile. 'Another appointment with Buttercup before I can go to bed, but I've got half an hour or so to kill, at the least. I might go and sort out the washing and tidy the kitchen.'

But the kitchen was tidy, and the washing could wait for the morning so she could put it on the line, so she just pulled it out of the machine into the plastic basket ready for the morning. She'd stick it by the door and then she wouldn't forget, she thought, but he was in there with her, right behind her again, so that when she straightened up and stepped back with the washing basket in her hands, she cannoned into him and felt her head connect with his chin.

'Ouch!'

'Oh, Harry, I'm sorry!' she said, turning to see if she'd hurt him, and found him ruefully rubbing his jaw, the fingertips rasping over the stubble and sending shivers skittering over her nerve endings.

He took the laundry basket out of her hands and put it down again. 'I think it needs a magic kiss,' he murmured.

'Like the ones you give Beth and Freddie when they hurt themselves.'

'Big baby,' she teased. She must be mad. She shouldn't rise to it, he was just being silly. She hadn't really hurt him. Still, she lifted his fingers away, went up on tiptoe and pressed her lips to the spot, just because it was so irresistible.

'There. Magic kiss, all better now,' she said softly. And just as softly he replied, 'You missed. It was here,' and, turning his head, he touched his lips to hers.

For a moment her heart lodged in her throat, but then it broke free, beating wildly against her ribs, deafening her with the clamour of its rhythm. Deafening her to reason, certainly, because instead of moving away, taking herself out of reach, she went back up on tiptoe, slid her arms around his neck and kissed him right back.

He groaned softly, easing her closer, and she felt his fingers thread through her hair and cup her head, anchoring it against the onslaught of his mouth. Then the kiss gentled, and he lifted his head a fraction, dropping a daisy chain of hot, open-mouthed kisses over her cheek, her eye, down the side of her jaw. He traced a line around her ear, his breath teasing her hair and making it stand on end, then he moved on, down the side of her neck, across her throat, pausing over the wild fluttering pulse before continuing down, down, across her collar-bone, her shoulder, the slope of her breast.

He lifted his head and stared down at her. 'You've caught the sun,' he murmured, one finger trailing over the sensitive skin of her cleavage. 'Do you have any idea,' he went on gruffly, 'just what you've been doing to me all day, running about in that little scrap of black Lycra?'

He traced the line the costume had followed, down, up—back down again...

She sucked in a breath and her ribs lifted, bringing his knuckles into contact with her breast, and he groaned again, his hands sliding down to bracket her waist, easing her closer as he trailed his tongue over the sun-warmed skin, leaving fire and ice in its wake. With a muttered oath he lifted her vest top out of the way, unclipped her bra and tenderly, reverently, cradled the burgeoning fullness of her breasts in his hard, hot hands.

He sucked in a breath, his head lifting so he could stare down at her, and his pupils were huge, his eyes dark as midnight with desire. His thumbs dragged over her nipples, sending sensation arrowing through her and bringing a cry to her lips, and slowly he lifted his hand and stared at it.

There was a bead of moisture on his thumb, pearly white, and as she watched he lowered his head and touched his tongue to it.

His eyes were still locked on hers, smouldering with unspoken need, but the touch of his hands had triggered her natural response, and she felt the milk beading on her nipples.

'Harry, no,' she moaned, anguished, and lifting her hands to his shoulders, she pushed him away, her heart clamouring, her body aching for him but common sense, finally, making itself heard.

And he dropped his hands and stepped back, swallowing convulsively, and turning on his heel he strode away, up the stairs and into his room, closing the door softly but emphatically behind him.

With a whimper Emily crumpled against the worktop, her hands trembling too much to deal with the breast pump for a moment. And so she stood there, her legs like jelly, until her breathing had slowed and the world had righted itself and her hands were hers again.

Then she gathered all the bits and pieces from the steriliser, went into her study and shut the door every bit as firmly. Two doors between them was the minimum they needed at the moment.

She sat down, set up the equipment and reached for her CD player to relax her—and then remembered that her favourite, most relaxing CDs were in the sitting room.

And she'd never be able to listen to them again without thinking of him.

Five more nights, she told herself. That was all it was. Five more nights until he was back in his own home and she had her house back to herself.

It couldn't come a moment too soon.

CHAPTER SEVEN

'THAT'S a bit more like it!'

Em stood back and studied Harry's work, and nodded. 'You'll get there. Take the cut down another notch and run over it again. You never know, you might even find a lawn in there!'

And she turned back to her surveying, measuring, checking sight lines and jotting notes on a pad. Busy. Busy, busy, busy since the sun had crept over the horizon and he'd been dragged out of bed by Kizzy's first whimpering cry. She'd been up minutes later, going downstairs while he'd fed Kizzy and tried so hard not to think about last night.

The feel of her. The taste.

The look of longing in her eyes before she'd pushed him away and stepped back, bringing their unscheduled and very unwise kiss to an end in the nick of time.

More or less. His dreams had been colourful, to say the least, and he'd been glad to get up just to get away from them.

Then while he had been changing Kizzy's nappy and looking out of the window, she'd taken the washing down the garden and hung it out in her nightshirt and bare feet, standing in the dewy grass and stretching up to the washing line so that her nightshirt rose up and gave him the occasional glimpse of her smooth, firm bottom encased in its sensible white knickers.

Since when had sensible white knickers been such a turn-on?

Not that he'd been looking, of course. Just glancing down the garden while he'd changed the baby's nappy and put the kettle on to make them tea and loaded the washing machine with his clothes and emptied the dishwasher—anything that just happened to give him a view out of one of the back windows!

Then she'd come back in, stood with one foot rested on the other like a child, staring at the floor for a moment until she'd lifted her head, sucked in a breath and said, 'About last night.'

And without giving her a chance to get in first, he'd said, 'I know. I'm sorry. It was stupid of me. It won't happen again.'

And she'd stood there, opened her mouth again, shut it, and then finally said, 'Good. Right. So. About your garden.'

And that was that.

No more talk of the kiss. They'd shut the door on it, walked away and now they were laying waste to the jungle that had been his grandparents' pride and joy.

'Right. That looks better. OK, I've done the survey. I just want to walk you through these shrubs and agree which ones should come out and which ones we can prune and rescue.'

'Is August the time to prune?'

She shook her head. 'No, not really. It's too hot. We need to wait a bit, but we can trim them. There are rules, for spring and summer flowering shrubs, for roses, for evergreens. But I think when you're talking this drastic, you just have to do what you have to do and hope they make it through. Most of them do. Right. Let's make some decisions and mark them up.'

And she picked up a can of yellow spray paint and headed down the garden, relentless.

Ten minutes later and the yellow kiss of death was on many of the bushes. 'Your job, I think. I'll put them through the shredder and keep an eye on the children. Beth, put that down, darling, it's sharp. Freddie, no!'

She took the secateurs from Beth, the dirty stick from Freddie before he put it in his mouth again, and handed Harry some very businesslike pruners. 'Get to it, then.'

He lifted a brow, tugged his forelock and set about the mammoth task of flattening the garden.

She really didn't need this.

She was sitting in the shade with the children, Freddie napping on her lap, the baby asleep in the carrier beside her, Beth sitting cross-legged playing a game with stones and talking happily to herself, and in front of her Harry was stripped to the waist and digging.

Rippling muscle, smoothly tanned skin glistening with sweat, streaks of dirt across his forehead where he kept lifting his arm and wiping away the trickles that threatened to run down into his eyes. And the way he threw the spade down into the hole, over and over, slicing through the roots and then grasping the stem and heaving it over, trying again, cutting another root, another tug, another cut, and all the time those muscles bunching and gleaming and driving her crazy.

Finally, victorious, he heaved the rootball of a huge old vibernum out of the ground and straightened, grinning at her. 'At last,' he said, his breath sawing in and out, and he strolled over, dropped down beside them and reached for a glass of fresh lemonade.

'Oh, bliss,' he said, rolling it over his chest and then lifting it to his lips, his throat working as he swallowed it in one.

'I hope you never go to wine-tastings,' she said drily, and he chuckled.

'Oh, I can swill and spit with the best of them, but ice-cold real lemonade on a hot day with a raging thirst? No way. It would be a sin to spit it out.'

'Want another?'

He grinned. 'I thought you'd never ask.'

He held out the glass while she filled it from the Thermos flask, then took a long, reflective swallow and smiled. 'Gorgeous. Nice and sharp. I hate it too sweet.'

'It's got honey in it,' she told him.

'It's lovely. Thank you.'

She dragged her eyes away from him, from those twinkling, smiling eyes, the stubbled jaw—she hadn't given him time to shave she'd been in such a hurry to keep moving—the beads of sweat caught in that fascinating, arrowing hair just above his battered old jeans...

No!

'Want to have a look at the plan? It's only a doodle so far—nothing formal yet—but I'd like your feedback.'

'Sure.'

And he lifted the tray out of the way, set it down on the other side of him and shuffled closer.

Too close. She could smell him, the tang of fresh sweat,

the warmth of his skin, the lemons on his breath—intoxicating. She hauled her pad over and picked up a pencil.

'I thought this might work,' she said, and forced herself to concentrate.

It took two days.

Two days in which Harry thought his muscles were going to die, but it was only because he'd been too busy with the baby to work out. Normally, in his crazy nomadic lifestyle, he stayed in hotels that had gyms—unless they were filming in the back of beyond, in which case very often they'd had a hike to get there—and when he was at home in London he went to the gym round the corner from his flat.

But in the two—or was it nearly three?—weeks since Kizzy had come into his life, he hadn't lifted anything heavier than a basket of wet washing, and he needed this.

Therapy, he told himself, and at least he'd slept last night.

And now, at the end of the second day, the shrubs with the yellow squirt on them had been evicted, a rotten tree was felled and the root hacked down to below ground level, and a huge pile of shredded material was heaped up at the bottom of the garden ready to be composted and put back into the soil. He tipped out the last bag onto the heap with a sigh of relief and surveyed the devastated garden thoughtfully.

'It looks vast,' he told her. 'I'd forgotten the garden was so big.'

'They always look like this when they're cleared. Even cutting the grass can double the apparent size of a garden. And using fine lawn grass does the same thing, because we have a mental scale rule and a blade of grass is x big, therefore the garden must be y long—and so on.'

'Tricks of the trade? Clever. So what's next?'

'Marking out the hard landscaping, deciding on the shape of the lawn, and then getting down to the nitty-gritty of the planting. But to do that, we need a big rope to lay on the ground to give us a line. There's one in the summerhouse. Can you give me a hand? It's quite heavy.'

The summerhouse?

'Sure,' he said, his mouth suddenly dry. He hadn't been in the summerhouse since the night of his grandmother's funeral. He'd been actively avoiding it, because so much of their past was in the place, but it seemed his avoidance tactics were to come to nothing.

Right now.

He followed her, Freddie and Beth running ahead to show him the way, Kizzy sleeping in the carrier in the shade by the back door where they could keep an eye on her from either garden.

And there it was, screened by shrubs, tucked away at the end in a lovely, private little dell, the sort of place that as children had been a magical retreat, and as adolescents in the grip of their hormones had been an ideal trysting place.

'Right, it's in here somewhere,' she said, pulling the door open and picking her way in. 'We don't use it any more, so it's a bit of a dumping ground now. Ah, here it is.'

It smelled the same. Slightly musty, the odd cobweb hanging across the windows, and it had gone downhill a little, but it was basically the same, and the memories slammed through him.

The hedgehog with its fleas. Secret societies with Dan, and Emily and Georgie, on occasions, if the girls insisted. And then later, on her sixteenth birthday, their first kiss.

Tender, tentative, staggering in its impact on the seven-teen-year-old boy with a massive chip on his shoulder and a feeling that he'd never really been wanted.

Until then.

But Emily had wanted him, and, God help him, he'd wanted her. So much.

That innocent, simple kiss had awoken a whole world of sensation that had somehow been much more than straightforward lust. It had been the tenderness that had shaken him. Her tenderness, and his. Particularly his. Until the night of his grandmother's funeral. That hadn't been tender. That had been desperate, and frightening, and wild with a passion that had left them both shaken. They'd stopped, pulled back from the brink, shocked by the force of their emotion—

'Harry?'

He lifted his head and met her eyes, and the memories must have been written all over his face. 'Sorry. Miles away,' he said, and he watched the soft colour sweep her cheeks and she looked away.

'Um—the rope,' she said, but she was between him and it, and the only way to get it was to squeeze past her. She turned away from him, but as she struggled not to fall headlong into the piles of clutter, he took her shoulders in his hands to steady her and her bottom settled briefly but firmly against his groin.

She gasped softly and squirmed past him and away, out of the door, and he sucked in a huge breath, forced himself to concentrate and reached for the rope. If she had any sense, she'd tie him up with it and leave him there to cool down.

'Uncle Dan! Mummy, look, it's Uncle Dan!'

'Hi, Half-Pint. Hello, little sister— —got room for a lodger for a few days?'

Dan's voice came to him through the open door, and Harry took a moment longer to steady himself while Emily ran to greet him.

Then he followed her out of the door and hesitated on the step, the rope in his hands. 'Might be a small problem with that. I seem to have borrowed your bed,' he said, stepping forward out of the doorway, and Dan did a mild double-take.

'Harry?'

He felt the smile start, right in the centre of his chest, along with that strange tightness and the prickling in his eyes. 'Well, hi, stranger.'

'Me, stranger? Coming from you?'

He laughed and—typical Dan—crossed the garden in two strides and engulfed Harry in a hug. 'Ah, hell, you're all sweaty! Since when did you get your hands dirty?' He laughed, and let him go.

'Since your sister started cracking the whip,' Harry replied with a wry smile. 'God, it's good to see you again. You are the world's lousiest communicator. How are you?'

'I'm the world's worst? And you're so darned good at it?' he returned, but Harry noticed he hadn't actually answered the question, and the smile on his face didn't really reach his eyes.

'So what's going on? What brings you back?' he asked, but Dan just shook his head.

'Never mind me, what brings you here?'

And right on cue, Kizzy started to cry.

* * *

It was hours later, and the children were in bed. Dan's luggage was installed in their parents' bedroom, because, as Emily had pointed out, Harry was about to go back to his own house and it would be silly to change the beds just for two or three nights. They'd had supper and were sitting down with a glass of wine and catching up.

Well, she wasn't drinking, and any minute now she'd have to sneak off and deal with Buttercup, but if Daniel was going to be staying there—and he still hadn't said why he was there, or how long for, or where Kate was—he was going to find out sooner or later.

Later, preferably.

'I feel nibbly—jet-lag,' he said, and got up and went out to the kitchen, coming back a few moments later with another bottle of wine and a party-sized packet of hand-fried potato crisps. He ripped them open, tipped them onto the table and sat down, propping his feet up just inches from the crisps.

'So where's Kate?' Emily asked him, fed up with waiting for him to say anything and going for the direct approach. 'Kicked you out because of your disgusting habits?'

He gave a laugh that sounded just a little hollow to her ears, and reached for some crisps. 'Never mind about Kate, what's all the gubbins in the sterilising solution? Looks like bits of a breast pump. Don't tell me Freddie *still* isn't weaned!'

She shot Harry a desperate look, and he just shrugged.

OK. So she was on her own here.

'It's for Kizzy,' she said, being deliberately evasive. 'She doesn't tolerate formula very well.' OK, slight exaggeration, she'd been fine with it until she'd realised there was a choice, but he didn't have to know that.

He stared at her thoughtfully, then turned to Harry and

said, 'So tell me again how this happened? You just found some kid on the street and *married* her? Bet that caused a wave of grief through your little black book.'

Harry's jaw tightened. 'I don't have a little black book,' he replied, and Dan snorted.

'Last time I saw you, you were fighting them off with a stick—and not trying too hard, if I remember correctly.'

'I was young.'

'Oh, and you're so ancient now, poor old man. All of—what are you, six months older than me? That makes you thirty-one, right? Almost thirty-two? And you married a total stranger because you felt *sorry* for her? Man, you are nuts. And now you're living here with Emily and she's feeding your baby? And I thought I'd just pop home for a few quiet days!'

Emily gave him a strained, apologetic smile. 'Sorry. Of course, if you'd rung…'

She left it hanging, and he shrugged and reached for another handful of crisps and another glass of wine. 'Last-minute flight,' he said lightly, and she realised he still hadn't said anything about Kate.

Well, they all had something they didn't want to talk about. And she had no doubt he'd tell her in the end. He always had, but she just had to wait and bide her time. In the meantime, he was still grilling Harry.

'So what did your boss say when you dumped this on him?' he asked.

'Her. And you don't want to know,' Harry muttered. 'Let's just say it wasn't pretty.'

Dan threw back his head and laughed. 'I'll bet. So that's

it? No more crazily dangerous reporting from Harry Kavenagh in Timbuctoo?'

'It's still up in the air,' he said evasively. 'I've got a month.'

'Three weeks,' Emily put in. Not that she was counting. And she didn't dare ask what the outcome of his deliberations would be, because she was hoping against hope that he'd pack it all in and stay there and things would…

Dan was letting his breath out on a long, low whistle. 'That's a tough one. It all backfired a bit on you, didn't it? I mean, if you just married her to give her a better life, you didn't intend presumably to be a father? I mean, not a real one. Not this real, at least. So what the hell are you going to do?'

Harry reached for the crisps and sat back casually. 'We'll see,' he said, but there was nothing casual about the tic in his jaw or the way his free hand was crushing the crisps to dust, one by one in the palm of his other hand.

And for the first time in years, Emily realised she wasn't actually pleased to see her brother, because his arrival would interfere with the dynamics between her and Harry, and the cosy little family unit she was trying to create felt suddenly very threatened…

'So what's the real story, our kid?'

Dan spoke softly, standing beside her and propping up the worktop, long arms folded across his chest, hazel eyes searching.

'Real story?'

'Harry. Why's he back here?'

She shrugged, not sure she knew the answer. 'He just turned up one day with the baby. He'd been sent home from the hospital with her, and didn't know what to do. He came here.'

'The only place he's ever called home,' Dan said quietly.

She met his eyes.

'And you?'

He looked away. 'Just needed space.'

'From Kate?'

'All of it.'

'Business not going well?'

He shrugged. 'Business is fine. I'm just not sure of my direction at the moment. Did Nick Barron tell you I ran into him in New York a few weeks ago?'

'He did mention it. Said you were in good form.'

He chuckled. 'It was the end of a long party. George had the baby yet?'

'No—four more weeks, I think. We spent Friday on the beach with them. She's looking good—coping well.'

'Unlike Harry.'

'Oh, Harry's doing fine. It was a bit of a steep learning curve, but he's great with her now and he's wonderful with Freddie and Beth. Beth adores him.'

'Isn't that dangerous?'

She nodded, biting her lip. 'She knows he's just a friend—that he's going again. I've told her.'

'And you? Have you told yourself, little Em?' he said softly.

'Endlessly.'

'And do you believe it?'

She shrugged away from the worktop. 'I have to, don't I? Because one of these days Harry Kavenagh's going to pack up his bags and go, and I have to be ready for that.'

'And Kizzy?'

She stopped, her heart aching. 'I have no idea what he's planning for Kizzy. It's none of my business, and I'm keeping it that way.'

'If you say so,' he murmured.

'I do,' she said firmly, and headed for the stairs.

'Sis?'

She turned back to him, reluctantly because she knew all she felt would be written on her face, and he gave a quiet sigh and shook his head. 'I thought you would have got over him after all this time.'

'I have,' she said, her voice even firmer than before, and turning on her heel, she walked resolutely away.

Behind her, Daniel shook his head.

'Oh, Harry, what have you done?' he said under his breath, and went to find his old friend.

'So what really brings you back to Suffolk? Em tells me you aren't a frequent visitor.'

'More frequent than you,' Dan replied, but Harry wasn't having that.

'We aren't talking about me, we're talking about you,' he said. 'And I get the distinct feeling that you rocking up here out of the blue is rather more meaningful than you're letting on.'

'I could say the same for you—and since my sister seems to be very much at the heart of this situation, I would very much like to know why.'

'Why what?' he asked wearily. 'Why I came back here? They told me to take my baby home. This came to mind. It seemed like a good idea at the time.'

'And now?'

Harry met his eyes, then looked away, giving his hands an unreasonable amount of attention. 'I'm not here to hurt her, Dan. We're just friends. She's helping me out of a jam—offering me and Kizzy a roof over our heads while the decorators are in and until the new furniture arrives. Nothing else.'

'Except she's feeding your baby.'

Harry felt his neck heat and ran his hand round it, letting out a harsh sigh. 'That wasn't meant to happen. Kizzy wouldn't take the bottle. I was in London for the day, she didn't know what else to do.'

'So she got out the breast pump and fed her?'

He prevaricated for a second, then said, 'Something like that.'

Dan's eyes narrowed. 'Hell! She breastfed her, didn't she? Damn, I might have known. She's as soft as lights, that girl.'

'She's a woman, Dan.'

'Oh, I've noticed—and I might have known you had. Things were never the same after the summer she turned sixteen. I would have thought you'd both moved on from a teenage crush, but perhaps I've been naïve.'

Harry stabbed his hands through his hair and growled softly under his breath.

'Dan, me and Em—there's nothing to it. She's just an old friend.'

'So you haven't touched her, then? I mean, I know you're in my room, but that might just be for the sake of the children. A cover story.'

He jackknifed out of the sofa and strode across to the window, glowering down the garden. 'That's just fantasy.'

'Yours?'

Bastard. He felt the colour rise on the back of his neck, the guilt plucking at him.

'So have you touched her?'

'I really think that whether he's touched me or not is none of your damned business, Daniel,' Em said from the doorway, and Harry swore softly and turned to face her.

'Em, don't chew him out, he's only doing what he's always done.'

'Yeah—interfered! Well, it isn't necessary, Dan, so give it a rest. We aren't kids any longer. I'm going to bed. I suggest you two do the same and maybe by the morning you will have got some common sense.'

And she stalked off, leaving them both suitably reprimanded.

'Bossy little madam.'

Harry turned and gave Dan a thoughtful look. 'Fancy a drop of Irish whiskey?'

'What—for old times' sake?' He grinned wryly and got to his feet, slinging an arm round Harry's shoulder and slapping it affectionately. 'Why not? Got a secret stash?'

'No, but your father always did.'

Dan chuckled. 'I believe he still has. Come on, let's raid it. It won't be the first time.'

And maybe, Harry thought, if he softens up enough, he'll tell me what's really going on.

'So what time did you get to bed last night?'

'God, you sound like my mother,' Harry groaned, and scrubbed a hand over his already rumpled hair.

'I thought your mother had no idea what time you went

to bed because she was there as little as possible? And maybe I have a flicker of sympathy for her,' she said unkindly.

'Ouch.' He winced and sat down on the arm of the sofa. 'And don't waste your sympathy on her. She didn't know, didn't care—didn't want to have anything to do with me. Let me rephrase that. You sound as if you could be my mother.'

She smiled and relented a little. 'So—what time? I feel I have the right to ask, since this is the second feed I've given your daughter since you crashed into your bedroom at three-thirty this morning.'

'So why ask if you know what time?' he groaned, getting up and heading for the kitchen. 'Tea?'

'Thanks, that would be lovely.'

Kizzy—like Harry and Dan—had finished the bottle, so Emily lifted her up against her shoulder and followed him through to the kitchen.

'So did you get anything out of my brother last night?'

He shook his head. 'Nothing that made any sense, but I have to say I think Kate's at the bottom of it.'

'Mmm. I agree. Oh, rats. I did so hope he was settled this time. They seemed to get on well enough.'

Harry looked at her closely. 'Do you like her?'

Oh, blast. Now she was going to be torn between loyalty and truth.

'That's a no, then.'

'I didn't say a word.'

'No. And you don't hang back for nothing. So you don't like her—or you don't think she's right for him.'

'it's not for me to decide that,' she protested, but her heart wasn't in it. She didn't like Kate—never had, never would. She thought she was superficial and self-serving, and she'd never been able to understand what Dan saw in her. But she'd thought he loved her, was happy with her, and so she'd been happy for him.

She sighed and took her tea, then put it down again, took his from him and handed him the baby. 'Yours, I think,' she said. Picking up her tea again, she went back upstairs to bed. Five minutes, she thought. Just five minutes alone, with a cup of tea and a good book—

'Mummy!'

She gave Freddie a tired smile, scooped him up in one arm and carried him back to bed with her. 'Hello, little man. How are you today?'

''K,' he said cheerfully. 'Want tea!' And he slid off the bed and headed for the stairs, turning as he got to the top to look back at her.

She saw it coming. Saw the inevitable, but as if her feet were stuck in treacle, she just couldn't get there in time.

'Freddie, careful!' she said, running towards him, but he laughed and turned and then went, in slow motion, end over end over end until he hit the floor at the bottom and was still. She screamed and flew down the stairs after him, arriving a fraction after Harry.

'Don't touch him!'

His voice checked her, but he held her back, then let her go once he was sure it had registered, but of course it had. She couldn't move him in case of making his injuries worse—oh, dear God, what if he'd broken his neck? What if he'd got a head injury?

'Mummy,' he wailed, and, rolling over, he stumbled into her arms, sobbing pitifully.

She clung to him, tears pouring down her face, rocking

him gently. 'It's all right, baby, it's all right. You're OK, Freddie, I've got you,' she murmured, over and over again, soothing him until his sobs slowed to a steady hiccup.

She became aware of Dan sitting on the bottom step with his arm around her, Harry crouching beyond her, one hand gently, rhythmically stroking her knee. Beth was standing wide-eyed beside him, a look of terror on her face.

She tried to smile. 'He's OK. I think he's probably just bruised. Freddie, let me look at you,' she said, shocked at how shaky her voice was.

'Head,' Freddie said, rubbing his forehead tearfully. She could see a blue bump coming up, and all her fears about head injuries came to the fore again. 'Magic kiss!' he demanded, and she closed her eyes and pressed her lips, oh, so gently to the little bump.

'There,' she said, her voice shaking still. 'Magic kiss—all better now.'

And then she looked up and caught Harry's eyes, and saw the tenderness and concern for her son in them—and the memory of their own magic kiss in his wry, gentle smile.

'Want tea,' Freddie said, but Harry shook his head.

'He ought to be nil by mouth until he's checked over.'

'Shouldn't I just watch him? Keep him awake and check him?' Just the thought of hours in A and E was enough to make her want to weep, but she knew he was right. 'OK,' she sighed, before he could answer. 'I'll get dressed. Freddie, stay with Harry and Uncle Dan and Beth, and I'll get ready, then we'll go in the car to the hospital and you can see the nice doctors again—OK?'

'Again?'

She looked up at Harry. 'Oh, yes. Freddie lives life in

the fast lane. We're regulars. And while I'm gone, could you two find the stairgate and put it up, and give Beth her breakfast, and then, if Kizzy's all right, why don't you both go over to the garden and get started on clearing the patio slabs? But for now a clean nappy on him would be good.'

And handing Freddie over to his uncle, she got to her feet and ran upstairs, her legs like jelly. And shutting her bedroom door, she leant back against it, buried her head in her hands and sobbed.

He couldn't bear it.

'You OK here?' he said to Dan, and he nodded, so Harry went past him and up the stairs three at a time, knocked on Emily's door and pushed it open gently, moving her out of the way and then folding her firmly against his chest.

'Hey, come on, it's all right. He's going to be OK.'

'Not necessarily,' she sniffed, 'and what if he isn't? I took the stairgate down because he was climbing over it, but he just wasn't paying attention. If it had been there, it would have slowed him down. I would have been with him—'

'Shh. It's OK. It's not your fault, it's just life. Stuff happens, Em. Don't beat yourself up. Come on, let's see you smile.' And he tipped up her head and smoothed the tears from her cheeks. Her mouth wobbled, but to give her credit she drew herself up and smiled.

And he couldn't help himself.

He bent his head, brushed her lips with his and drew her back into his arms. 'There. Magic kiss. All better now,' he said gruffly, and then forced himself to let her go.

'You'd better get dressed and get off. Want one of us to come with you?'

She shook her head. 'I'll be fine. Can you cope without me? I might be hours,' she said unevenly.

'Sure. You go ahead. And don't worry. Beth will be fine. You just concentrate on Freddie, and let us know if they want to keep him in or anything.'

She nodded. 'Will do.'

He went back out, closing the door carefully behind him, and found Dan struggling with Freddie's nappy.

'Want a hand?'

Dan grunted and stood back. 'He's all yours,' he said with a grin. 'How is she?'

'OK. Bit shaken up.'

She wasn't alone. Just hearing her scream and seeing Freddie tumbling end over end like that down the stairs was enough to make his blood run cold.

If anything had happened to the little lad…

Damn. He was getting in too deep. So deep.

Right in over his head.

He had to get the hell out of there and back to his own house before it was too late, he thought, and ignored the little voice that told him it already was—far, far too late…

CHAPTER EIGHT

FREDDIE was fine.

After three hours in A and E of being poked and prodded and X-rayed, they sent her home with him, armed with a head injuries card listing all the things she should keep an eye out for.

He was in fine form. He'd had a good time in A and E, he'd got a sticker on his hand and he'd had lots of cuddles and new toys to play with—life, as far as Freddie was concerned, was great.

Not so for his mother.

She was exhausted, she needed the breast pump fast, Harry's garden was in chaos and all she could think about was going to sleep. She turned into the drive, cut the engine and sat there, eyes shut, wondering if she could find the energy to deal with the day.

It was all Harry's fault, she thought unreasonably. Him and Dan, between them, had kept her awake half the night, and Kizzy had kept her awake the other half. She couldn't do it any more.

'Em? How is he?'

'He's fine. Harry, I can't do it any more,' she whispered.

'Feeding her, being up in the night—I just can't do it. I'm so tired. I've got so much work to do for Nick, and I know we spent the weekend in your garden, but I really ought to be getting on with Nick's stuff today, but I can't because your garden is utterly destroyed and the kids need me and Kizzy needs me and I just can't do it all—'

'Shh,' he murmured, drawing her into his arms and rocking her gently. 'You go to bed. Dan and I will look after the kids and sort out the garden. You have a sleep, and we'll worry about the rest later—OK?'

'But you don't know what to do—'

'Rubbish. We're not stupid. I'm sure we can read your plan well enough to do the basic groundwork.'

'And watch the children?'

'And watch the children. Stop worrying. And I'm sorry we kept you awake.'

'I need to see Buttercup,' she told him, and he frowned.

'I've been thinking—we ought to try her back on the formula,' he said. 'This can't be helping.'

'I still need Buttercup.'

He gave her a fleeting smile. 'OK. Come on, let's get you both in and sort you out. Want a cup of tea?'

'Want tea!' Freddie chimed in. 'And biscuit.'

'He needs breakfast, he must be starving.'

'So do you. Come on.'

And he led her inside, sent her into the study with Buttercup and tapped on the door a few minutes later. 'Room service,' he murmured, and she opened the door a crack and stuck her head round it.

'Tea and toast,' he said, and handed them to her one at a time so she could take them from behind the door.

Breastfeeding was one thing. Being connected to the pump was quite another, and she felt ridiculously shy and self-conscious.

She thanked him and shut the door, sat down again at her desk and while Buttercup did her job, Emily looked through Nick's file and studied the brief for her next contract.

It was mercifully simple, but it needed to be stunning and she didn't have it in her to be stunning at the moment. She rested her head on the desk, closed her eyes and sighed. 'Just a few minutes,' she murmured to herself. 'Then I'll do it…'

She'd been ages. He couldn't believe how long she'd been in there, and he could hear the pump still running.

'Em?'

He tapped on the door and opened it a crack, then said her name again, but there was no reply, so he stuck his head round the door and saw her slumped forward on her arms, fast asleep.

'Em?' he murmured, stroking her shoulder gently, and she woke with a start and sat up, her arms flying up to cover her breasts, cheeks burning.

'Sorry,' she said. 'Um…'

'I'll go,' he said, sensing her discomfort at his presence, and he went out and shut the door, resting his head back against it with a sigh.

It was crazy. She was worn out, and helping him with Kizzy wasn't doing her any good at all.

Behind his back he heard the door opening, and he straightened and turned, to find her there with all the pump's paraphernalia in her hands. 'Oh,' she said, and he held out his hands and she put the stuff into them, her cheeks still flushed.

That could have been with sleep, of course, but maybe it was just because she was shy. And he'd pushed her into something she wasn't comfortable with.

She touched his hand. 'Harry, don't look like that, it was my idea to feed her.'

'Well, it's time it stopped. I'll get her back on formula—mix them, perhaps. And the decorators will be done tomorrow, and the carpets come on Wednesday, and the furniture's due then as well. And we'll move out, and you won't have us underfoot or keeping you awake all night any more, and you'll be able to get on with your life. Now, go to bed and get some sleep.'

And he turned on his heel and walked into the kitchen, leaving her there with a lost and mournful expression on her face.

'Fine,' she said softly, and, turning round, she went upstairs to bed.

Kizzy was having none of it.

The best-laid plans and all that, he thought wearily, and went back to the fridge for the real McCoy.

He was exhausted. He'd spent the day in the garden with Dan, lifting the slabs on the patio and breaking up the concrete path that led to it, and in the middle of that he had been keeping an eye on the children, getting them food and drinks, watching Freddie like a hawk for signs of head injury and feeding Kizzy in between.

Only she had other ideas, the little madam, and if he hadn't loved her so much he would have throttled her.

'Problems?' Dan said, dropping down beside him on the grass in the shade and watching him try again.

'She likes Emily milk. Only Emily milk.'

Dan frowned. 'So what's going to happen when you go back to work? Are you leaving her here with Em?'

'I can't.'

'So you'll take her away with you?'

He let his breath out on a sharp sigh and shot Dan a troubled glance. 'I can't do that, either.'

'Rock and a hard place come to mind,' Dan said mildly, lying back on the grass. 'So what, then? You need to do something. I mean, she's not a puppy. You can't just stick her in kennels every time you race off to the other side of the world.'

He felt sick.

For the rest of the day, all he'd been able to hear had been Dan's voice, those words echoing in his head.

She's not a puppy. You can't just stick her in kennels.

So what the hell was he supposed to do?

Especially now she was so inextricably linked to Emily.

He'd begun to realise that every time he got some formula into her, it upset her little tummy. Clearly her system couldn't tolerate cows' milk.

The next day he went to the doctor's surgery and saw the health visitor and explained the situation, leaving Emily's name out of it.

'Oh, this must be Emily's little one,' she said with a smile. 'She's been on the phone, asking for advice.'

He felt silly. 'Oh,' he said. 'So what did you say?'

'Try all the things you've been trying,' she told him. 'Only if she's got a problem with cows' milk, then you've got to try soya milk or carry on as you are. Personally I think breast milk is best, obviously, because it's designed for human babies, and in cases of lactose intolerance like Kizzy's, your choices are strictly limited.'

'Tell me about it,' he muttered, and she smiled and patted his hand.

'It doesn't last for ever. This is only a short phase of her life. Once she's weaned it all gets much easier.'

Really? With him on the other side of the world? He didn't think so.

She's not a puppy. You can't just stick her in kennels.

He thanked her and left, bought some soya milk and tried that. It was better, but she still didn't like it, and when he tried her back on Emily's milk exclusively, she settled straight away.

And his decorators were finished, the carpet fitters were in and the furniture was stacked up on the drive, waiting. He didn't have the time or the energy for any more experiments, and Kizzy was beginning to distrust the bottle.

He found Dan in the swing seat under the old apple tree, reading a book. 'Dan, they've finished in the sitting room. Could you give me a hand to get the suite in?'

He grinned. 'As an alternative to lying here, doing nothing? It'll be a pleasure.'

'Don't be sarcastic. You need the exercise.'

'Exercise?' he grumbled. 'I've been doing nothing but exercise since I got here,' he pointed out.

'I'll bring you a beer under the tree when we've finished,' he promised, and Dan chuckled.

'You must think I'm really cheap.'

'I know you're really cheap,' he replied, and headed for the drive of his house, Dan trailing behind and grumbling.

They found Emily in there with the children, Beth picking up the little bits of carpet that the fitter had missed, Freddie making piles of tufts in the middle, and Emily vacuuming up the rest.

She finished the last bit and turned off the machine. 'You'd better give me Kizzy,' she said, and he took the sling off and handed her over reluctantly.

Strange, how odd it felt without her on his front. He'd got so used to the sling he didn't even think about it now, but obviously he couldn't carry her and move furniture any more than he'd been able to do the gardening with her on his front.

And he missed her.

'Right, let's get this suite in,' he said, and didn't let himself think about how he'd feel when he'd gone back to work and left her behind.

You can't just stick her in kennels.

It looked good.

They'd worked all day, following the fitters round, cleaning up each room in turn and unpacking the furniture, and now it was done. Beth and Freddie had been wonderful, but the novelty was definitely wearing off, and the fridge was low on milk.

And Kizzy was starting to grizzle.

So Emily went to pump, and Harry took the last bottle of milk and went to feed the baby, and she sat in her study linked up to Buttercup and thought, How stupid. What a pointless exercise, when she could just be giving it to Kizzy direct.

It wasn't as fresh, there was an infection risk, there was infinitely more work—crazy.

But necessary, for her peace of mind, for Kizzy's independence from her and for the future.

Whatever that might hold.

Emily realised that she had no idea. Dan had told her that Harry was still undecided about what he was going to do, and she had to have answers. She had to know what the future held, she couldn't go on like this indefinitely.

She'd have to tackle him—but how?

And that night he'd be sleeping in his house again.

It felt so odd, not being at Emily's.

It smelt strange—that new-carpet smell, a brand-new bed, the sheets stiff and creased from the packets, the down duvet not yet quite fluffed up.

Not that he really needed it. It was still hot at night, and he lay with the windows wide open and stared through the uncurtained window at the house next door.

Emily.

She was all he could think about.

The landing light was on, the trees filtering the light, but he could still see it.

Kizzy was asleep in the room next door. She'd been unsettled, but that might be because it smelt different. But finally she'd gone to sleep, her tiny mouth working rhythmically, and he'd been able to get his head down.

But just like his daughter, sleep eluded him for a while. Not that he wasn't tired. He was. He was exhausted. Days in the garden, today spent heaving furniture around—all on top of weeks of broken sleep, starting after a hectic fortnight dodging mortars and sniper fire—it was no wonder he was shattered.

But it wasn't enough to stop his mind working.

He went down to the kitchen—a soft ivory, in the end—and made himself a cup of tea. He didn't have anything else apart from coffee in the empty kitchen, and he really didn't need that. And he sat in his sitting room overlooking the now orderly but barren garden, pale in the moonlight, and wondered what the hell he was supposed to do about Kizzy.

'So have you decided what you're going to do?'

He didn't pretend not to understand. He was sitting in the garden with Emily, more than a week after he'd moved back to his house, less than two weeks of his month's grace left, and he still hadn't made a decision about where he went from there.

He shrugged. 'I don't know. I can't see the way forward. I need a nanny, I suppose, but I can't bear the thought of leaving her with a stranger. I just don't know what else I can do, though. I can hardly drag her with me if I get sent to a war zone or a hurricane or an earthquake.'

'You didn't really think this through, did you?'

He looked at her. 'Think what through?'

'Bringing up a baby.'

He frowned, remembering the rain-lashed night when Carmen had been mugged, the night he'd landed and been greeted by horizontal rain and the news that his wife was on life support.

'Of course I didn't think it through,' he said savagely. 'I didn't have time. I'd adjusted to the idea that I was going to be a father, but that was all. Not the implications. Not this. But she was my wife—for better, for worse and all that crap. What was I supposed to do, Emily? Tell them to throw the switch? Let the baby die, just because she was going to be a bit of an inconvenience?'

Em blanched and shook her head. 'No, of course not.'

'No. And you're right, at the time I just didn't think it through. So now we have to deal with it. Correction. *I* have to deal with it.'

'Except it seems to be involving me.'

'Yes. I'm sorry. Well, I've tried. She'll take soya milk. Perhaps we should just give her that from now on, cut you out of the equation.'

'That doesn't help you.'

'It gives me more choices.'

'Of child care?' She shook her head. 'Maybe you should look at your job,' she offered softly, and he stared at her in astonishment.

'My job? I can't change my job.'

'Why not?'

He was shocked. 'Because it's me. It's what I am.'

'No, Harry, it's what you *do*.'

He thought about it for a second. Barely. 'Isn't that the same thing? Aren't you a garden designer?'

'No. I'm a mother, and I'm me, and I design gardens for people to earn a living. And I'm lucky that I enjoy it. But it isn't me. It's not what I *am*.'

He stared at her for a long, puzzled moment, then reached for his tea, retreating behind it while he thought over her words. Do something else? He couldn't imagine doing anything else. Nothing. The noise, the drama, the terror and pain, the injustice—bringing all that into people's homes and showing them what was going on in the world was how he spent his life.

It was what he *was*.

'I *have* to do it,' he said urgently. 'I have to show people what's happening out there.'

'No. Someone has to, Harry—but it doesn't have to be you.'

'Yes—yes, it does, Em. It does have to be me. It *is* me.'

'In which case perhaps you'd better think about whether you're the right person to be bringing Kizzy up, because if you go back to work and leave her with a succession of unsupervised nannies, then you're no better than your parents, and frankly, you'd all be better off if you gave the baby up for adoption,' she said quietly, and, picking up her tea, she went back inside without another word.

He stared after her, stunned.

Adoption? *Adoption*?

He looked down at the baby on his lap, her head lolling in sleep, and felt a wave of emotion so powerful it nearly unravelled him.

But maybe she was right. Maybe he wasn't the ideal parent for this beautiful little girl. He'd never meant to be her father, not in this way. He'd meant to pay her way, secure her future, make sure Carmen had everything she needed for a good life. A safe life.

And she'd died, as a result of his interference.

Hot tears scalded his eyes, and he scrubbed them away angrily. No. He wouldn't wallow in self-pity. This wasn't about him, it was about Carmen, and her daughter, little Carmen Grace—the tiny Mini-Dot who'd stolen his heart.

And he owed it to her to do this right.

If he could only know what that was—but he was beginning to wonder if Emily hadn't already told him...

'Seen Harry?'

Emily shook her head. 'Not for ages. Um—I might have upset him.'

Dan tipped his head on one side and studied her thoughtfully, and she swivelled her chair round from the drawing board and recapped their conversation.

'You told him to put her up for adoption? Ouch. I thought *I'd* been harsh.'

'What did you do?'

'Oh, it was days ago. I told him she wasn't a puppy and he couldn't just stick her in kennels every time went off after a news story.'

'Ow. What did he say?'

'Not a lot. He was talking about nannies.'

'Mmm. He was talking about them today, as well, but I don't think he's considered things like time off and shift patterns. He'll need a fleet of them. I don't suppose he's even thought about it.'

'No, he's good at that. Fancy a coffee?'

'No. I've just had one. Now, go away and amuse yourself. I've got work to do.'

'Actually, I was looking for Harry for a reason. I was thinking I might go up to London for a few days. I was wondering about his flat—thought if it was empty, I might scab it off him as a base.'

She felt a rush of relief, followed by guilt, because she still didn't know what he was doing over here from New York and yet all she wanted was time alone with Harry—

time in which to change his mind, to convince him that
there was more to life than running away from it. And
she'd got less than two weeks left.

'I don't think there's anyone in the flat at the moment.
You'll have to ask him. Phone his mobile, he's usually got
it with him. Is Beth OK?'

'She's fine. She's colouring in the kitchen while I read
the paper.'

'Send her in to me if you go out.'

'Will do.'

She heard the door close, and looked down at the
drawing in front of her.

Rubbish. It was rubbish, the planting totally wrong. And
she couldn't for the life of her work out what was right.

Seemed to be a lot of that going on at the moment, one
way or another, she thought, and pushed back her chair.
She could hear Freddie stirring from his sleep, the thump
of his cot as he turned over and sat up, followed by a little
wail. She went up to his room and was greeted by outstretched arms and a watery smile, and she lifted him out
and cuddled him close and wondered what on earth she'd
do without him.

'Want to go for a walk?' she asked, and he nodded.

'Beach,' he said.

'Maybe. Let's find Beth and ring Georgie. If they're
busy we can go the other way and feed the ducks—'

'Want beach! Want Harry!' he said, his voice rising,
and she soothed him and changed his nappy and took him
downstairs past the reinstated stair gate.

'Beach!' he told Beth cheerfully. 'San'castle. Mummy,
down!'

She put him down and he ran to the door, beaming up at her. 'Harry,' he demanded, but she wasn't at all sure Harry would want to come.

'We'll see. I think he's gone for a walk.'

'With Kizzy?' Beth asked.

'Probably.'

They went without him, taking the buggy in case Freddie's legs got tired, and met him on the cliff top. He was sitting with Kizzy in his arms, staring out to sea, and as Beth and Freddie ran over to him, he lifted his head and looked across at her, and for a fleeting moment his face was bleak.

Then a shutter seemed to come down, and he smiled at the children. 'Hi, kids,' he said, and his voice sounded rusty and unused. 'Going to the beach?'

'The buckets and spades are a bit of a give-away,' Emily said with a laugh, but it cracked in the middle and he shot her a glance.

'Come with us,' she said softly. 'I've brought your shorts—you left them drying in the bathroom. And I brought bottles and stuff for Kizzy. I had a feeling you might be here.'

'Did you come looking for me, Emily?'

His voice was a little hard, and she looked away. 'I'm sorry. I shouldn't have said what I did. I know it's difficult.'

'You have no idea,' he murmured, and got to his feet, tucking Kizzy back in the sling. 'Come on, then, kids. Let's go and build sandcastles.'

They buried him again.

Buried him and jumped on him, while Em sat with Kizzy and laughed and told them to be gentle, and then Georgie came down with Harry and Dickon and Maya, and they ended up back at the Barrons' house, having juice and biscuits and playing in the swimming pool.

And Kizzy ran out of milk.

'Sorry, guys, time to go, we have to feed the baby,' he said, and helped Em dry the children and walk them reluctantly home.

'I wanted to stay,' Beth said mournfully. 'I like Dickon. He's my friend. Freddie's a baby.'

She wasn't much more than a baby herself, he thought, smiling indulgently and hugging her slim shoulders as they walked along.

'There'll be other days. Maybe you can see them again tomorrow or the next day.'

'Tomorrow,' she said decisively, and ran to her mother. 'Can we see them tomorrow?'

'We'll see,' she said, and Beth pouted.

'That means no,' she explained to Harry. 'But I want to see them.'

'Well, we can't always have what we want,' he said, his heart aching, because this little family outing was getting to him, reaching parts of him that had been dormant all his life, and the process, like letting blood back into a limb that had gone to sleep, was a mass of alien sensations. And not all of them were pleasant.

She was sitting in the study, wrestling with the plans for Nick's contract, when she heard the back door open and shut.

'Em?'

She stood up, stretching out the kinks, and went into the kitchen to see Harry there with Kizzy in his arms, his face troubled.

'What's up?' she asked.

He swallowed, looked down at Kizzy and pressed his lips together. 'I've had a phone call from my boss. There's been an earthquake.' He hesitated, then said, 'She wants me to go.'

'But you've got another twelve days!'

'I know. But she wants me now. It's not for long, just three or four days, but…' He shrugged, and she felt a cold, sinking feeling in the pit of her stomach.

'Are you going?'

'I have to.'

'And Kizzy?'

He frowned. 'I wanted to ask you if you'd look after her. I wouldn't have asked, but she hasn't given me any notice. And I know I haven't sorted out any child care, but I'll do it the minute I get back.'

She ignored that. She was too busy thinking about him going to an earthquake zone. Not that he hadn't done it before, but that somehow had been more remote. Now, after these weeks, it all seemed much closer to home.

'So, will you? Look after her?'

'This time,' she said, trying to inject some muscle into her voice, but it didn't sound convincing. 'When do you go?'

'In the morning. Early.'

Just like that, her dream was turning to dust. She felt her eyes fill, and turned away.

'Is Dan here?'

'Yes, he's watching a movie.'

'Tell him goodbye from me. I'll bring her round in the morning, just before I go.'

She nodded, and he turned and went out, all the spirit drained from him.

Why? Why go, she wanted to ask him, but she couldn't. She knew why he was going—because he'd convinced himself it was who he was. Even though he clearly didn't even want to go this time.

She snorted, shut the door and stuck her head round the sitting-room door. 'I'm off to bed.'

'Was that Harry?'

She nodded, but couldn't say any more. 'I'll see you in the morning,' she said, and went upstairs.

She took a shower, so the sound of running water would drown out her sobs, and then she went to bed. Not that she slept, and at four-thirty, when she heard Harry's front door open and shut, she tiptoed into Beth's room and watched him walking down the road, Kizzy in the sling on his front.

She pulled on her clothes and ran lightly downstairs, slipped out of the door and followed him.

She knew where he was going, and she followed him to the cliff top and sat beside him on the wet grass and tucked her arm in his, her head on his shoulder as he fed Kizzy and watched the sun come up.

Finally he took a deep breath, let it out on a sigh and stood up, helping her to her feet. They walked back in silence, and when they reached her house, he turned and looked down at her without a word.

And still without a word, she took his hand and led him, not down her drive but down his, and in through the door, and up to the bedroom he'd used as a child.

He put Kizzy down, still sleeping, in her cot, and came back to her, his expression guarded, but a muscle jumped in his jaw.

'Are you sure, Em?' he murmured.

She nodded, blinking away the tears.

'Yes.'

And with a ragged sigh, he drew her into his arms.

CHAPTER NINE

'HERE—my house keys. Get Dan to take the cot over later. I meant to do it when I got back from my walk, but I got a little sidetracked.'

His mouth twisted into a sad, fleeting smile, and he drew her back into his arms, his voice muffled by her hair. 'I'm sorry. I hate dumping her on you. I know it isn't fair, but it won't happen again. I've been thinking about what you said, and I've decided you're right. I'll sort all the details out when I get back, but I'm going to put her up for adoption.'

She lifted her head, unable to stifle a little cry, and took in the bleak, empty look in his eyes. 'Oh, Harry,' she said, but there was nothing she could add. There was nothing to say and, anyway, her throat wouldn't work properly, so she just lifted her hands and cradled his face and kissed him.

'Take care,' she pleaded.

He nodded. 'I'll see you soon.'

He kissed her again, urgently, hungrily, and then broke the kiss abruptly, turned on his heel and strode to his car, driving off without a backward glance. She lifted her hand to her lips, her fingers replacing his lips, holding in the anguish.

'Oh, dear God, take care of him,' she whispered, and picking up Kizzy in her little carrier, she went round the side of her house and in through the kitchen door.

Dan was sitting there, Freddie in his high chair having juice and toast, Beth kneeling on a chair arranging her toast soldiers into neat rows and talking to them, and as she walked in with Kizzy Dan took one look at her, stood up and ushered her straight into the hall.

'He's gone,' she said tonelessly. 'His boss rang last night. There's been an earthquake somewhere.'

'Indonesia. I know. It was on the news. I wondered if they'd call him in.'

She nodded. 'He was there earlier this year, and they want him there again. He knows it well, apparently. It makes sense, but...'

Dan searched her face, then dragged her into his arms and hugged her. 'So what about Kizzy? Are you looking after her until he's back?'

'Yes, but...' She felt the sob beginning to rise and swallowed it down. 'He said I was right. He's going to put her up for adoption. Oh, Dan, what on earth have I done?'

She looked up at him, expecting condemnation, but this was Dan. He just shrugged. 'Helped him organise his priorities?'

'And Kizzy? What about Kizzy?' She swallowed again and stared down at the sleeping baby in her carrier, then answered her own question. 'I guess she'll end up somewhere with a couple who are desperate for a baby. And they'll love her to bits—'

She broke off, and Dan sighed and rubbed her arms comfortingly. 'She'll be fine, Em.'

'But she might not be. What if they split up? What if she ends up in the middle of a divorce?'

'She'll be brought up by a single parent. It hasn't done Beth and Freddie any harm.'

She frowned. 'But—what if she doesn't have the infra-structure I've got? The family and friends, giving support?'

He gave a bemused laugh and shook his head. 'You're making a hell of a lot of assumptions here. They might be fantastic parents.'

But she wouldn't see her again. Ever.

She shook her head and turned away. 'I'm going to put her down in the study and get some breakfast. Thank you for looking after the kids.'

'Any time. But next time you might let me know you're going.'

'There won't be a next time,' she said firmly, and went into the study, put the baby down and then caught sight of the television through the sitting-room doorway. They were showing scenes of the earthquake, and she sat down, hands knotted together, and watched it.

It was dreadful. Scene after scene of devastation. She felt gutted for them, but more than ever afraid for Harry. What if there was another one? There often was.

She was aware of Dan coming up behind her, placing a hand on her shoulder, watching it with her. 'I've made you fresh tea,' he said.

'Thanks.'

'Come on, he's not there yet. He won't be there for hours.'

He was right. He'd said it was a twelve-hour flight, and then he had to get in and out of the airports. It would be tomorrow morning before he appeared on TV. She turned off the television, went through to the kitchen and gave the kids a hug. Freddie gave her one of his special sticky kisses, and Beth snuggled up beside her while she ate her breakfast, mechanically spooning in the cereal without even tasting it.

And he hadn't even left the country yet!

Nick phoned at eleven, when she'd just put Freddie down for a nap and she was working on his plan, Beth at her side colouring.

'Hi,' he said, sounding exhausted and yet euphoric. 'Just had to let you know—Georgie's had a little girl—three point seven kilos, or eight-three in old money, and they're both doing really well.' He hesitated. 'We've called her Lucie, after my sister.'

'Oh, Nick, that's lovely!' she said, her eyes filling. 'When's she coming home?'

'This afternoon. She's absolutely fine, and I'm around and so are my mother and her father, so I'm going to pick her up around three.'

She felt herself welling up. 'Give her my love, and tell her I'll come and see her tomorrow some time, the minute I can get away.'

'You running out on me again?' Dan said, lolling in the doorway behind her. 'It's a good job I haven't gone to London yet.'

She smiled at him as she cradled the phone. 'Georgie and Nick have had a little girl. I'm not going far. I thought I'd drop in and see her in the morning. If you don't mind looking after the kids?'

He smiled. 'Of course I don't mind. We could walk

down and they could play with the others for a few minutes, and then maybe we could go on the beach.'

Except she'd be tortured by images of Harry—Harry buried up to the neck in sand, Harry running into the sea, Harry skimming pebbles with the children, showing off, Harry—just Harry, everywhere she looked.

'Sounds lovely,' she said, just for Beth. 'That would be nice, wouldn't it?'

'Can I hold the baby?'

'Not tomorrow, probably. She'll be too tiny.'

'Kizzy's tiny,' she pointed out truthfully. 'And I hold her.'

'We'll see,' she said automatically, and Beth pouted.

'You mean no.'

'No, I mean I'll see what Georgie has to say about it. It's her baby, after all, and Dickon and Harry will want to hold her. That's a lot of holding for a tiny baby. Right, how about a drink and a biscuit to celebrate?'

Harry wasn't on the ten-o'clock news, but he was on the satellite news at midnight.

He must have scarcely landed, and he was flying by helicopter to the epicenter of the earthquake, jammed in amongst aid workers.

'This is the only way to get here,' he was saying, shouting over the noise of the aircraft, 'because the roads are rubble. They've only just cleared them after the last quake, and now the people of this devastated region are facing destruction and ruin yet again. Down below us everything is flattened, as far as the eye can see. Trees are down, rivers have altered course yet again and every village is showing more signs of destruction. I'm going back to the small community I stayed in last time, to see just how much damage has been done, but early reports aren't good. This is Harry Kavenagh, reporting to you from somewhere over Indonesia.'

The report went to cover other areas, showing more pictures of the damage, but Emily had seen enough. She'd seen him, in his element, back where he belonged.

Being him.

Her eyes pricked with tears, and she blinked hard and turned off the television with an angry stab at the remote.

Dan flicked her a glance, opened his mouth and shut it again. 'Tea?' he said eventually, and she nodded.

'Thanks.'

But she couldn't drink it. She just felt sick, because she'd lost him, and they were on opposite sides of the world.

'I'm going to feed Kizzy and get to bed,' she said, and went to the fridge. One last bottle after this. She contemplated Buttercup, but frankly she was too tired. She'd do it later, when she'd fed Kizzy.

But she didn't. She was exhausted, struggling to stay awake long enough to feed and change her, and then when she fell into bed she slept so soundly she didn't wake for hours.

Kizzy was starting to cry, and Dan and her children were still asleep, so she crept downstairs, got the bottle out of the fridge and put it in the microwave to heat. She flicked on the television, and there Harry was again, on the early breakfast news, describing the damage sustained by the little town.

She heard the microwave ping and, still watching the screen through the open doors, she went into the kitchen and took out the bottle, but as she turned back, her watch caught on the door and the bottle spun out of her hand and shattered on the floor.

She stared at it blankly. How could it shatter? They were unbreakable—unless it had already been cracked? She didn't know. All she knew was that the fridge was empty and Kizzy was crying in earnest now.

Forgetting the television, she turned to the steriliser and realised, to her dismay, that she hadn't put Buttercup's bits and pieces in there. They were lying in the sink, rinsed but not nearly sterile enough to use.

And Kizzy was crying, and her nipples were prickling, and the utter futility of it struck her like a brick.

What on earth was she doing? Why on earth express the milk, decant it from the pump into a bottle, then give it to Kizzy?

Especially if she was going to lose her so very, very soon.

With a sigh of gentle resignation, she went back into the sitting room, picked the baby up and sat down with her.

'Look, Kizzy,' she said softly, lifting her nightshirt out of the way. 'Daddy's on the telly.'

And while she watched him, hanging on his every word, his tiny daughter snuggled into her, latched on and fed, contented at last.

'You're crazy.'

'Dan, I had no choice. I broke the last bottle and the things weren't sterilized.'

He smiled and shook his head. 'I didn't mean that. I meant you're crazy trying the pump in the first place when you should have been doing this all along.'

'I was trying to keep some distance,' she explained, and he laughed softly.

'You? I don't think so. I think you're doing what you should have been doing all along—and I think you think so, too.'

She looked down at Kizzy, so dear to her, and swallowed. 'Except when she goes to her new home, it's just going to be even harder for her.'

'Well, I guess there's only one thing for it.'

'What?'

'You'll just have to adopt her yourself.'

She stared at him, aghast, and then turned back to Kizzy, blinking away the sudden tears.

'Don't be silly,' she said, her throat clogged. 'I can't do that. I've already got Beth and Freddie.'

'So what's one more? And you can't tell me you don't love her. I've seen you with her. Look at you—made for each other. How can you let her go?'

She couldn't—and it was going to tear her apart. She looked up at Dan in anguish. 'What part of no don't you understand? I can't do it. I can't afford another child. Especially not this one.'

'Because she isn't really Harry's?'

She shook her head. 'No. Because she is, in every way that matters. And—'

She broke off, and Dan finished the sentence for her. 'And because you love him?'

She looked away. 'I'm so silly. I didn't mean to do it. I didn't mean to let myself get so involved.'

'So why go to him in the night?' he murmured.

'We watched the sun come up,' she said, remembering.

'And because it was in the east, I realised that he'd see it hours before me, and if I go and watch it come up, it'll be over him, getting low in the sky, but he'll still be able to see it.' She looked at Dan and smiled sadly. 'I couldn't let him go again. Not without knowing. I could lose him, Dan. He might be killed. Maybe not this time, but the next, or the next. Maybe when he's reporting on a war. They get shot, taken hostage, murdered, blown up—it happens regularly. And there could be another earthquake where he is now. It's terribly dangerous, everything he does. And I thought, if he dies, and I've never found out what it would be like with him, never held him, never shared that…'

She broke off, not knowing how to say it, but she didn't need to. Dan was beside her, holding her, offering her a tissue and giving her a gentle hug. 'I understand. I would feel the same. And I guess he did, too.'

'It was sort of goodbye,' she said unevenly. 'And maybe—perhaps there was a part of me that hoped it might bring him back to me. Bring him to his senses. Make him realise all the things here waiting for him at home.'

'Maybe this tour will. Maybe it's just what he needs— to go from this to that.'

She shook her head. 'It'll just remind him of what it's like to be free, to have nothing more significant to think of than picking up his passport on the way out of the door.'

She looked down at Kizzy. 'Dan, I can't adopt her. I have to let her go. If I don't, I'll never be able to let go of Harry and move on.'

She was sleeping now, her little rosebud lips still white with milk, and carefully, so as not to wake her, Emily lifted her against her shoulder and walked with her until she brought up her wind, then carried her upstairs and changed her and put her down.

Then she went into Freddie's room and stared down at him, her baby, flat out on his back, arms and legs outstretched, sprawled the full length of his cot. He was outgrowing it, she realised. He'd need a bed soon. Maybe Beth's. She was getting big for her little bed, but it would be perfect for Freddie.

And then who would have the cot?

No! She mustn't let herself think about it. It was madness. Anyway, he probably wouldn't want her to have Kizzy, because it would mean he would never be able to let her go, either. He'd always be thinking about her, and if he ever came back, he'd want to see her, and they'd never be able to move on, any of them.

And she wasn't foolish enough to imagine that one short hour in his arms would make any difference to him, no matter how wonderful it was. For her, at least.

For him, it had probably been simply a matter of propinquity. She'd been there, he'd felt a need to hold someone close.

Freddie stirred, his eyes flickered open and he smiled. 'Mummy,' he said, holding out his arms, and she lifted him from his cot and cradled him tight and inhaled the warm baby smell of him.

She'd been happy before Harry had come back into her life—happy with Beth and Freddie and holding the fort for her parents, happy working for Nick and Georgie and doing other contracts locally.

Worried about money, yes, but happy, for all that. Contented. At peace.

Not so now. Now she was in turmoil, and she couldn't imagine it feeling any better for a long, long while.

If ever.

Georgie's baby was gorgeous.

Georgie was in the family room, ensconced on the sofa with the baby in her arms, and Harry and Dickon were playing with Maya on the floor.

'Oh, she's beautiful,' Emily breathed, her eyes filling as she set Kizzy's carrier down and hugged Georgie gently.

'She's really pretty,' Beth sighed, standing up on tiptoe and leaning over to get a better look.

'You think? I reckon she's got her father's nose.'

'There's nothing wrong with her father's nose,' Nick said, following them into the room with a grin he couldn't hide and an indulgent look about his eyes.

Emily reckoned if he could have crowed, he'd be doing it, and she laughed at him softly. 'I don't need to ask how the proud father's feeling this morning.'

He chuckled and sat down on the end of the sofa, scooping up Freddie and holding him so he could have a look. 'How about I take this lot out into the garden for a few minutes, give you two time to chat?'

Georgie smiled gratefully at him, and Nick ushered the children out through the French doors and into the garden, still within sight but out of earshot. Emily turned to her and took her friend's hand. 'So how are you? Really?'

'Really? Sore, a little bit battered and absolutely ecstatic. It's just wonderful. So different. Last year when we suddenly ended up with Harry and Dickon and Maya as a newborn baby, it was such a sad time. It shouldn't have been,

Lucie dying was all wrong, and it was a time of massive adjustment for all of us. But this—this is just how it ought to be, another baby coming into the family, and oddly it doesn't feel all that different. I love the other three so much I can't imagine I'll love this one any more, but there is a difference. Carrying her, giving birth to her—it just makes it so much easier to love her. You know, I grew to love Maya, just as you've grown to love Kizzy, but I loved baby Lucie before she was born. Does that make sense?'

'Absolutely.' Emily nodded, thinking of Kizzy and how quickly she'd fallen under her spell, despite her best attempts to stay detached.

'I don't suppose there's any progress with you and Harry, is there? I'd so love to see you two settled. You belong together—you always have.'

'I don't think so.' She gave a strangled little laugh. 'Actually, I've got something to tell you. You know Harry's gone? He's in Indonesia, reporting on an earthquake.'

'Really? Oh, Emily, I didn't know! I'm so sorry—I haven't noticed anything but the baby since I went into labour.'

'No, well, I wouldn't expect you to. But anyway, just before he went, he told me…' She broke off, took a breath and went on, 'He said he was thinking of putting Kizzy up for adoption.'

Georgie's expression was horrified. 'Oh, Em, no! Oh, poor little thing! How can he?'

She shrugged. 'Says he can't be a full-time father and carry on with his job. And I don't know what to do. Dan says I should adopt her myself, but—I'll never be free of him if I do that. And it's so much worse this time.'

She closed her eyes, letting her head fall forward so her

hair shielded her face, but Georgie just reached out an arm and drew her down, holding her while she cried.

'I miss him,' she sobbed. 'It's so silly. But I've been really stupid and let myself fall for him all over again, and now he's on the other side of the world and I just have this really bad feeling—'

'Hush. You've had that really bad feeling every time you've seen him reporting from some hellhole or other. You need to get him out of your system—sleep with him. Maybe it'll reveal some truly awful habits.'

Emily straightened up and sniffed, rummaging for a tissue. 'Nice theory. Unfortunately he doesn't seem to have any truly awful habits, so it didn't work.'

Georgie's jaw dropped. 'Oh, my, you've done it. After all this time.'

She nodded. 'Stupid. Stupid, stupid, stupid, but I just couldn't let him go without knowing—just in case. And now…'

'Oh, Em. I'm so sorry.'

She sniffed again and tried for a smile. 'No, I'm sorry. I should be here celebrating the baby with you, and all I can do is pour out my troubles. I'm a dreadful friend.'

'Rubbish. You're wonderful. Want to hold her?'

'I'd love to,' she said, and took the baby into her arms. 'Gosh, she feels heavier than Kizzy!'

'She probably is. She's a real porker, and Kizzy was very tiny.'

She nodded. 'She was. She's catching up now, though. Actually, there's something else I should tell you—something else I've done which is incredibly stupid and just makes letting her go even harder. I've started breastfeeding her.' She swallowed and forced herself to meet Georgie's eyes, waiting for the revulsion, but there was only sympathy and compassion.

'Oh, Em,' she whispered. 'Oh, how can you let her go? Now, after that?'

'Wet nurses always did.'

'They were usually poor women doing it for money or members of the same family. But you've done it for love.'

She looked down at little Lucie, and sighed. 'Yes. Yes, I have, but I shouldn't have done. It was silly, but it turns out that formula upsets her, so I don't know what would have happened if I hadn't been around.' She brushed her finger over Lucie's tiny palm, and it was immediately enclosed in a tight grasp. 'Oh, she's beautiful. Really strong. I'm so happy for you. I think you've been fantastic, both of you, taking on the kids, and I'm so glad you've got your own baby now. It just ties all of you together.'

She sighed and handed her back. 'I have to go. I've got work to do, and—'

'Television news to watch?' Georgie said astutely, and she gave a sad little laugh.

'Maybe. You get some rest. She'll be crawling before you know where you are. Enjoy her while she's tiny, it's over so very fast.'

'I will. And ring me—any time you want to talk. Or come over. You know you're always welcome.'

Emily hadn't lied.

She did have lots to do, not least bringing order to Harry's garden. If she could get it into some sort of shape before he came back, then it would be one less thing for them to have to deal with.

She was convinced they had no future. Sleeping with him had been rash and stupid—and she wouldn't have changed it for the world, but it hadn't been her cleverest move. And she was more than ever certain that when he came back, he'd put the house on the market, give Kizzy up for adoption and that would be the last she'd see of him. If the garden was done, he'd be gone all the sooner and she could get back to normal.

She scrubbed the silly, foolish tears from her eyes and marshalled the children. 'Who fancies a picnic in the garden?' she said brightly. They chorused, 'Yes!' at the tops of their voices.

'Right, in the kitchen, everybody. Let's make it now. Uncle Dan?'

Uncle Dan unfolded himself from his chair, grabbed Beth and tickled her in passing and presented himself in the kitchen. 'Give me a job,' he said, and she handed him a pile of bread and the butter.

'Just a scrape,' she reminded him. 'We're having sand-wiches.' And she busied herself pulling out food from the fridge and the cupboards, and refused to allow herself to think about Harry or what he might be doing...

It was horrendous.

The heat, the flies, the stench of bodies trapped beneath the buildings. Harry scrambled over the rubble in his path and walked down a street he'd known for years—a street now unrecognisable. The buildings had crumbled, the shops and houses falling in on each other, and everywhere there were desperate people digging.

He paused beside a house and spoke to a young man who was digging in the rubble with his bare hands. They were running with blood, but he didn't seem to notice.

'My wife and child,' he told Harry, and the dust on his face was streaked with tears. 'Just a baby. Help me.'

Harry's knowledge of the language was patchy, but the man's simple plea was universal. He questioned him a little more, then turned back to the cameraman.

'This is Ismael. His wife Rom is inside, with their two-week old baby son. He's desperate, because he can hear them crying, but there aren't enough rescue workers to help him find them, and time's running out. They won't have any food or water, and the baby's cries are so weak now he can hardly hear him. He's found a hole, and he's trying to clear it to see if he can get inside. I'm going to help him.'

He turned back to the man, tapped him on the shoulder and took the rock from his hands, lobbing it behind him. Together they shifted a large slab of what had once been wall out of the way, and crouched down, peering in through the hole. Ismael called his wife, and they heard a whimper from deep inside the building.

Fresh tears spilled over the man's cheeks, and he set about the rubble with renewed energy. Finally they shifted the last big lump of concrete out of the way, and the man lay down and squirmed in, calling as he went. He had a torch, and he was shining it around, then there was a shout from inside and Harry lay flat and stared after him.

There, in the mass of rubble and wood and twisted metal that had been their house, he saw a hand, reaching out, and he saw the man take it, clasping it as if his life depended on it.

Or hers.

He turned back to the camera. 'He's reached her. Tim, get help. I'm going in.'

'You can't, Harry!' the cameraman said, but Harry ignored him. He had no choice. There was enough room in there for two of them, and if they shifted that pile of rubble, there was a good chance they could get her out, or get medical aid to her. He shrugged off his jacket, emptied his pockets and crawled inside.

'Ismael,' he said, touching the man's leg, and he turned his head. 'Let me help. We can get her out.'

He could hear the shouts outside, the chorus going up, 'Survivors!'

But at that moment, as they were so close to success, he felt the ground gather itself.

No. Not again. Not another one, he thought, and as the shaking started, he heard the woman scream.

CHAPTER TEN

'Em?'

There was something about Dan's voice that sent a chill right through her. He was watching the news—something she'd steadfastly refused to allow herself to do—and she left her desk and went through to the sitting room.

Dan was standing there in front of the television, and he took her hand. 'Em, it's Harry, they're filming this live. He's pulling some crazy stunt. He's gone inside this house to help the man find his wife and baby, and—

The picture shuddered, and the cameraman exclaimed in shock, but he kept filming, live, on the other side of the world, as a cloud of dust rose up and the building shifted and settled.

She stared at it, her mouth open, and her heart all but stopped.

No.

Please, God, no.

She sat down abruptly and watched the rescue workers desperately trying to clear the rubble. The cameraman who'd been filming at the time was being interviewed now, and he was clearly shocked.

'I told him not to go in, but he just went anyway. He's

never listened to reason, I guess this is just another of those occasions. We all do it and we try not to think about the consequences, but you never think it's going to happen to you.'

He turned back, staring at the rubble. 'I'm sorry, I can't talk to you. I have to help.'

And he went over to the gang working on the house and joined in, while Emily sat in shocked silence, twisting her hands together and forgetting to breathe.

'Dan, he's going to die,' she whispered. 'He may already…'

She broke off, distraught, and grabbed the remote control from his hand, switching to the satellite news and selecting the newsflash. Then Nick rang. Dan answered the phone, and a few minutes later he arrived to collect Beth and Freddie and take them to play. He'd seen the news, and knew what it would have done to her.

'Hang in there,' he said to Emily, hugging her, but she was numb.

All she could think of was Harry, the body she'd held so lovingly, that had brought her such joy, crushed by the weight of the rubble. All the tenderness, the passion, that wicked sense of humour and enormous energy snuffed out like a candle.

Kizzy woke, and she sat there in front of the endless news and fed his daughter while the tears streamed unheeded down her cheeks and her eyes stared unblinkingly at the unfolding drama before her.

God, he hurt.

Everywhere.

There was something pressing on his back and shoulders so he could scarcely breathe, and just beyond him he could hear Ismael's wife weeping. Ismael was silent, and he hadn't heard the baby cry at all.

He could hear rescue workers, though, the shouted instructions, the sound of machinery. And then they called for silence, and he tried to yell, but his breathing was so restricted he couldn't do more than whisper.

He could knock, though. He managed to make his hand into a fist around a rock, and he smacked it as hard as he could against the slab above him.

'I can hear something,' someone shouted, and he recognised the voice of Tim Daly, the cameraman.

He banged again, and again, and then he heard the scrape of a shovel and the urgent voices.

Thank God. He closed his eyes and assessed the situation.

He was lying on his front, his head turned to one side and his left arm twisted up behind his head. He must have lifted it up to protect his head and neck, but it was stuck now, and he didn't want to think about the pain. But he couldn't move at all. He could feel everything—only too well—but apart from his right arm and a very small amount of movement in his left leg, he was trapped. And if they managed to free him, he might end up with crush syndrome, from all the muscle proteins pouring into his bloodstream when the circulation was restored. And then he'd go into multiple organ failure and die.

He felt panic begin to rise, and squeezed his eyes shut, concentrating on slowing his breathing and not wasting energy. He wasn't getting enough oxygen into his body to waste it on futile panic.

So he thought about Em, and the baby, and how he

would have felt if it had been them in here and he'd been in Ismael's place.

What was it Dan had said about being between a rock and a hard place? He nearly laughed, but the laugh turned to a sob, and he forced himself to be calm. He focussed on Emily's face, the tender smile as she reached up and touched his mouth when he'd made love to her, her fingers exploring him.

He should have stayed there with her. He should have told his boss to go to hell, and stayed there with her, with the woman he loved, and with the family that had become his own.

But then he wouldn't have been there to help Ismael.

And Ismael might have been outside still when the aftershock had hit, instead of inside, lying still and silent while his wife wept at his side.

Just like Carmen, dead and cold in the hospital chapel while her tiny motherless daughter had struggled for life in the special care baby unit. All because he'd interfered.

He felt bile in his throat, but he could hardly swallow, and it seared his parched throat. He ignored it. Precious little else he could do, and all he could think about was Kizzy and what would become of her if he died.

If only Emily wasn't so set on not having her. They'd make such a wonderful family, but she'd made it quite clear that she didn't want any more to do with her than was absolutely essential. Take the breast pump, for example. He'd thought it was crazy right from the start, taking the milk out of Emily into the pump and then a bottle to give to her, when the sensible, best and most convenient thing would have been to feed her directly.

But she'd been adamant, and who was he to argue? Just a relic from her past come back to complicate her carefully ordered existence.

It hadn't done a lot for his, either. Well, a lot for his existence, but damn all for the careful order. Or was it careless disorder he meant? Being able to walk out of the door at a moment's notice with nothing more than a phone, his wallet and his keys. A far cry from leaving the house with a baby. You had to be seriously orderly to achieve that. It was like a military operation.

He thought of his flat in London. He'd given Dan the keys the day before he'd left, so he could go and stay there. Was he still there? He hoped not, because when—if—he got out of this mess, he'd have to move back there.

Back there, alone, without Kizzy, without Em, without Beth and Freddie, without Nick and Georgie and their children. He wondered if they'd had the baby yet. Maybe not. It wasn't quite due, he didn't think, but he couldn't remember.

It seemed suddenly very important that he did, but he was losing focus. His right leg had gone to sleep, and his left arm was beginning to break through the mental block he'd put on it and give him hell. If only he could breathe…

It took ten hours to get him out.

Ten hours, during which Emily sat glued to the screen, watching the endless loop of tape until she knew it by heart, waiting for any further news to dribble through.

And then suddenly, without warning, they cut live to the scene where they'd been working all night, and they showed the rescue workers freeing him, lifting him carefully onto a sheet of corrugated iron and carrying him out.

Alive!

He was alive! His hand was moving, his legs shifting, and they cut to his face, battered and dusty, his mouth crusted and bleeding, and the emotion she'd held back for so many hours poured out in a torrent.

'Shh, baby, I've got you,' Dan said, cradling her against his chest, and she sobbed and sobbed, her eyes never leaving the screen as they carried him over the rubble and off down the street, Tim Daly, the cameraman, at his side.

'He'll be all right, won't he?' she asked, and Dan hesitated for a second and then nodded.

'Hopefully. At least he's alive. That's a good start.'

She straightened up and shot him a keen look. 'You think he could die? You do, don't you? Dan, he can't die. I can't live without him.'

She phoned the television centre but she got nowhere. She didn't know the name of his boss, and even if she had, who was she? A neighbour. That was all she could say. Not his lover, the woman looking after his baby. Not to the person on the switchboard. He might not want it to be common knowledge.

But she was desperate to get a message to him.

'Send him a text,' Dan said, reading her mind. 'He might have his phone on him.'

But it was lying in the rubble where he'd left it, together with the rest of the contents of his pockets, and it had been crushed beyond repair.

He was alive.

Sore—he gave a humourless laugh at that—but alive. His left arm was broken in two places and they'd pulled it out straight and put a cast on it without anaesthetic because he had been in danger of losing his hand because of the kinked arteries. That had been a bundle of laughs. And as for the rest of him, he was scraped and filthy and bruised to the point of Technicolor, but he was alive.

And so, to his relief, were Ismael and his wife and child. Ismael had a broken leg and concussion, but Rom and the baby were miraculously unharmed by their ordeal.

He went and saw them before he left the field hospital, and Rom took his bandaged hand and pressed it to her cheek and cried.

He hugged her gently, touched the baby's tiny hand with his bandaged finger and left them to it. They were all alive, and together. That was all that mattered. They were the lucky ones.

And so was he.

He knew what he had to do. Right now, before he did anything else.

But there was no reply, either on her house phone or her mobile, and he didn't feel he could leave a message. He didn't know what to say, in any case. He just knew he had to talk to her.

Face to face.

Yes. That was better. He'd do that.

Tim got him back to their base, helped him pack up his few things and took him to the airport.

'Good luck.'

'Thanks.'

Tim went to shake his hand, took one look at the bandages and hugged him instead. 'It's been good working with you, you crazy bastard,' he said, his voice choked, and then he let him go and gave him a little shove towards the departure lounge.

He needed no further encouragement.

There was no word from him.

She'd thought, in all the time that had elapsed, that either he or one of the team could have given her a call, but no. There had been nothing.

She knew he was all right. She'd seen him landing at Heathrow two hours ago, battered and bruised, his left eye swollen shut, his arm in a sling and both hands bandaged to the fingertips, but she'd had no word.

Well, what had she expected? That was Harry all over, dropping in and out of her life as if nothing had ever happened, breezing through and leaving her a mangled wreck in his wake.

She stared at the ceiling, wondering when he'd turn up. He would, of course. There was no question about that. He'd come back to sort out Kizzy, as he'd put it. And if she was stupid enough to encourage him, he'd probably stay for a while, but he'd go in the end, like he always had.

Well, she wouldn't encourage him. She'd let him make his arrangements for the baby, and she'd wave him goodbye and get on with her life.

Somehow.

She turned over and banged the pillow, but she couldn't sleep. She heard a car stop on the street, then drive on, and then a few moments later there was the sound of stones against her bedroom window.

What on earth…?

She heard it again, and got out of bed and peered round the curtain.

'Harry? What on earth are you doing?' she whispered hoarsly, throwing up the window and telling her heart to stop it, but he just grinned, and her heart flipped again and raced.

So did she, all the way downstairs, out of the back door and round the corner, straight into his arms. Well, arm. The other one was a hard line across her chest, and she realised it was in a cast.

'Ouch,' he said, laughing, and then the laughter died and his face contorted a little. His bandaged right hand came up to touch her face. 'It's nice to see you,' he said, and she gave a little hiccup of laughter that could just as easily have been a sob, and nodded.

'It's nice to see you, too. I wondered—when they showed it...'

She broke off, unable to finish, and he hugged her hard against his side with his right arm and led her into the house.

'Do you want a drink?' she asked, but he shook his head.

'All I want is to talk to you. To hold you. To try and let myself believe that I'm really here with you. But first I need to get my head down.'

'Do you want your keys?'

'Keys?'

'To your house. So you can go to bed.'

His eyes searched her face. 'Where's Dan?'

'Here. Upstairs in bed.'

'Then come with me.'

She shook her head. 'I'll need to feed Kizzy.'

'Can't Dan do it?'

She shook her head. 'No, because...' She looked away.

'I gave up with the pump. It seemed pointless. Wrong. So I need to be here. But you could stay,' she added, and then held her breath.

'Em?'

She shrugged. 'I know I shouldn't. I know you said you were going to give her up for adoption, and it'll tear me apart to let her go, but—it was all I could do for her, and you weren't here for her, and I just…'

'Oh, Em,' he breathed, and wrapped his arm around her. 'Come to bed with me. We need to talk, but I have to lie down. We'll go in your room.'

So they went upstairs, Harry limping slightly, his right leg reluctant to bend, and she led him into her bedroom, closed the door and undressed him, her eyes filling at the sight of the bruises.

'Sorry. It's a bit gaudy,' he said with a strained smile as she helped him ease back onto the mattress.

'You could have stuck to one part of the spectrum, instead of going for the whole rainbow,' she said, but her voice cracked unconvincingly and he sighed and drew her down against his chest.

'Come and lie next to me,' he murmured, and she lay down carefully and cuddled up, her head on his shoulder, worried about the bruises.

'Doesn't that hurt?' she asked, but he shook his head.

'Not so much that I'm going to let you go.' He turned his head and kissed her, just a brush of his poor, bruised lips against her brow, and she lifted her head and touched her mouth to his.

'Oh, Em,' he sighed, and his arm eased her closer. 'I thought I'd never see you again. I lay there, listening to

Rom crying in the darkness, and I wondered if any of us would get out of there alive.'

'Rom?'

'Ismael's wife. She'd got a two-week-old baby in there with her. Em, if you'd seen the look on that man's face—heard his voice…'

'I did,' she told him. 'Tim was filming it. He filmed it all, right up to the aftershock, and then he put the camera down and left it running while he got help and joined in. Someone else picked it up and carried on filming, and they interviewed him, but he wouldn't talk, he wanted to help. They showed it live. I was watching when it all went shaky and the buildings shuddered, and I knew you were in there…'

She couldn't go on, couldn't relive it, and his arm tightened. 'Shh, it's OK, I'm here,' he said, and his mouth found hers again, his kiss urgent in the darkness.

He rolled towards her, his cast bumping against her hip, and she lifted her hand and cradled his jaw. 'Harry, we can't. It'll hurt you.'

'You'll have to be gentle, then, won't you?' he replied, and drew her tighter against his body. 'Because I need you, Em. Don't imagine for a moment that once was ever going to be enough.'

She took a ragged breath and let it out. 'I thought…it was goodbye.'

'No way. There's something you have to know. I've handed in my notice. You were right. It isn't what I am, it's just what I do. What I did. But there are other things, more important now. Other people can do my job. It's time for a change. In all sorts of ways.'

He shifted, his bandaged right hand stroking up and

down her back, the touch strangely soothing. 'About Kizzy,' he said softly. 'How would you feel about adopting her?'

For a moment she thought she hadn't heard him right, because until that moment it had sounded as if there was hope for them, but this…?

'You ought to know, though,' he went on, his hand still stroking her, 'that she comes complete with her father. So if you did feel you wanted to take her on, you'd be taking me on, too. For better, for worse etcetera. And if you agreed, I'd very much like to adopt Beth and Freddie, too. So we all belonged to each other. Because I've realised that home isn't a place, it's the people, and my home is with you. You and Kizzy and Beth and Freddie. And I want to come home for good, Em. To you.'

He was holding his breath, she realised. His chest had frozen under her cheek, his heart thudding wildly.

'Oh, Harry,' she whispered, unable to speak. Instead she lifted her face to his, and kissed him.

'Well?' he demanded, his voice shaking, and she gave a funny little laugh that cracked in the middle.

'Oh, yes,' she said unsteadily. 'Yes, please. I can't think of anything I'd like more.'

His mouth found hers, cutting her off, and she lifted herself up so she could kiss him back better. Then gently, tenderly, so as not to hurt him, she eased out of his arms and settled down beside him.

'Hey!'

'Shh,' she told him. 'Just rest now. There's no hurry. We've got the rest of our lives ahead of us.'

And snuggling against his side, her hand over his, she

listened as his breathing eased into sleep. He gave a soft snore, and her mouth kicked up into a contented smile.

So he did have some habits she'd have to get used to, she thought, but she didn't care. She'd embrace every one with joy.

Harry was finally home.

* * * * *

BAREFOOT BRIDE

JESSICA HART

CHAPTER ONE

'GUESS who I bumped into in town?'

Beth bounced down the steps into the garden and plonked herself onto the lounger next to Alice.

Alice had spent a blissful morning by the pool, feeling the tension slowly unwinding as the tropical heat seeped into her bones, and guiltily enjoying some time on her own. There was a puppyish enthusiasm about Roger's wife that could be quite exhausting at times, and, ever since she had arrived two days ago, Alice had been conscious of how hard Beth was trying to distract her from the fact that Tony was getting married tomorrow.

No one could be kinder or sunnier-natured than Beth, though, and Alice would have been very fond of her even if she wasn't married to Roger. And this was, after all, Beth's pool that she had been lying beside all morning. A good guest would be opening her eyes and sitting up to take an interest in her hostess's morning.

On the other hand, Beth *had* told her to relax before she'd gone out. Alice had done as she was told, and was now so relaxed she honestly couldn't summon the energy to open her eyes, let alone care which of Beth's many acquaintances she had met in town.

'Umm… Elvis?' she suggested lazily, enjoying the faint stir of warm breeze that ruffled the parasol above her.

'No!' Beth tsk-tsked at Alice's failure to take her exciting news more seriously, but she was much too nice to take offence. 'Someone we know… At least, I think you know him,' she added, suddenly dubious. 'I'm pretty sure that you do, anyway.'

That meant it could be anybody. Beth was unfailingly sociable, and gathered lame ducks under her wing wherever she went. When Roger and Beth had lived in London, Alice had often been summoned to parties where Beth fondly imagined her disparate friends would all bond and find each other as interesting as she did.

Sadly, Alice was by nature as critical and prickly as Beth was sweet and kind. She settled herself more comfortably on her lounger, resting an arm over her eyes and resigning herself to one of her friend's breathless accounts of someone Alice had met for five minutes several years ago, and who she had most likely hoped never to see again.

'I give up,' she said.

At least she wouldn't have to pay much attention for the next few minutes. Beth's stories tended to be long, and were often so muddled that she would get lost in the middle of them. All Alice would be required to do was to interject an occasional 'Really?' or the odd 'Oh?' between encouraging murmurs. 'Who did you meet?' she asked dutifully.

It was the cue Beth had been waiting for.

'Will Paxman,' she said.

Alice's eyes snapped open. 'What?' she demanded, jerking upright. *'Who?'*

'Will Paxman,' Beth repeated obligingly. 'He was a friend of Roger's from university… Well, you must have known him, too, Alice,' she went on with an enquiring look.

'Yes,' said Alice in a hollow voice. 'Yes, I did.'

How strange. She had convinced herself that she'd forgotten Will, or at least succeeded in consigning him firmly to the past, but all it had taken was the sound of his name to conjure up his image in heart-twisting detail.

Will. Will with the quiet, serious face and the stern mouth, and the disconcertingly humorous grey eyes. Will, who had made her heart jump every time he'd smiled his unexpected smile. He had asked her to marry him three times, and three times she had said no.

Alice had spent years telling herself that she had done the right thing.

She felt very odd. The last four years had been consumed by Tony, and she'd been braced for memories of him, not Will. Ever since Tony had left, she had done her best to armour herself against the pain of if onlys and what might have beens, to convince herself that she had moved on, only to be ambushed now by the past from quite a different direction.

Alice was totally unprepared to think about Will. She had thought that relationship was long over, and that she was safe from those memories at least, but now all Beth had to do was say his name and Alice was swamped by the old turbulence, uncertainty and bitter-sweetness of that time.

Beth was chatting on, oblivious to Alice's discomposure. 'I didn't recognize him straight away, but there was something really familiar about him. I've only met him a couple of times, and the last time was at our wedding, so that's…how long?'

'Eight years,' said Alice, carefully expressionless.

Eight years since Will had kissed her one last, fierce time. Eight years since he had asked her to marry him. Eight years since he had turned and walked away out of her life.

'It's hard to believe Roger has put up with me for that long!' Beth smiled, but Alice had seen the faint shadow cross her eyes

and knew that her friend was thinking of the years she had spent
trying to conceive. She and Roger had been open about their
plans to start a family as soon as they were married, but it hadn't
worked out that way. And, although they were unfailingly
cheerful in company, Alice knew the sadness they both felt at
their inability to have the children they wanted so much.

'Where did you meet Will?' she asked, wanting to
distract Beth.

'In the supermarket, of all places!' Alice was pleased to see
Beth's expression lighten as she swung her legs up onto the
lounger and settled herself into a more comfortable position
to recount her story. 'Isn't that an *amazing* coincidence? I
mean, bumping into someone in a supermarket isn't that
unusual, I know, but a supermarket in *St Bonaventure*? What
are the odds of us all ending up on a tiny island in the Indian
Ocean at the same time?'

'Will *is* a marine ecologist,' Alice felt obliged to point out.
'I guess the Indian Ocean isn't that odd a place to find him.
It's more of a coincidence that Roger's been posted here. Not
many bankers get to work on tropical islands.'

'No, we're so lucky,' Beth agreed happily. 'It's like being
sent to Paradise for two years! And, now you're here, and
Will's here, it's not even as if we've had to leave all our
friends behind.'

She beamed at Alice, who immediately wondered if Beth
was hatching a plan for a cosy foursome. It was the kind of
thing Beth would do. It was Beth who had suggested that Alice
come out for an extended visit while Tony was getting married.

'There are lots of single men out here,' she had told Alice.
'They won't be able to believe their luck when you turn up!
A few weeks of uncritical adoration, and you won't care about
Tony any more!'

Alice had no fault to find with this programme in principle, but not with Will. He knew her too well to adore her, and the last thing she wanted was Beth taking him aside and telling him how 'poor Alice's' world had fallen apart. He might be persuaded to take pity on her, and pretend he didn't remember how she had boasted of the great life she was going to have without him.

She would have to squash any matchmaking ideas Beth might have right now.

'I'm only here for six weeks,' she reminded Beth. 'And Will's probably just on holiday too. I don't suppose either of us will want to waste our precious holiday on politely catching-up on old times,' she added rather crushingly.

'Oh, Will's not on holiday,' said Beth. 'He's working here on some long-term environmental project. Something to do with the reef, I think.'

'But you'd have met him already if he'd been working here,' Alice objected. 'St Bonaventure is such a tiny place, you must know everybody!'

'We do, but Will's only been here a week, he said. I got the impression that he knows the island quite well, and that he's been here on various short trips, probably before Roger and I came out. But this is the first time he's brought his family with him, so I imagine they're going to settle here for a while.'

Alice's stomach performed an elaborate somersault and landed with a resounding splat, leaving her with a sick feeling that horrified her. 'Will's got a *family*?' she asked in involuntary dismay. She sat up and swung her feet to the warm tiles so that she could stare at Beth. 'Are you sure?'

Beth nodded, obviously surprised at Alice's reaction. 'He had his little girl with him. She was very cute.'

Will had a daughter. Alice struggled to assimilate the idea of him as a father, as a husband.

Why was she so surprised? Surely—*surely*, Alice—you

didn't expect him to stay loyal to your memory, did you? she asked herself.

Why on earth would he? She had refused him. End of story. Of *course* he would have moved on and made a life of his own, just as she had done. It wasn't as if she had been missing *him* all these years. She hadn't given him a thought when she'd been with Tony. Well, not very often, anyway. Only now and then, when she was feeling a bit low. If things had worked out, she would have been married by now herself.

Would that have made the news less of a shock? Alice wondered with characteristic honesty.

She could see that Beth was watching her curiously, and she struggled to assume an expression of unconcern. So much for her fears about Beth's matchmaking plans!

'I didn't know that he had married,' Alice said, hoping that she sounded mildly surprised rather than devastated, which was what she inexplicably felt. 'What was his wife like?'

'I didn't meet her,' Beth admitted. 'But I asked them to your welcome party tomorrow, and he said they'd like to come, so I guess we'll see her then.'

'Oh.' The sick feeling got abruptly worse. Somehow it seemed hard enough to adjust to the mere idea of Will being married, without having to actually face him and smile at the sight of him playing happy families, Alice thought bitterly, and then chided herself for being so mean-spirited.

She ought to be glad that Will had found happiness. She *was*, Alice told herself.

She was just a bit sorry for herself, too. None of the great plans she had made for herself had worked out. How confidently she had told Will that her life would be a success, that she wanted more than he could offer her. Alice cringed now at the memory. She wouldn't have much success to show off tomorrow. No marriage, no child, not even a job, let alone a good one.

Will, on the other hand, apparently had it all. He probably hadn't even been thinking about her all those years when the thought of how much he had loved her had been somehow comforting. It was all very…dispiriting.

'It's not a problem, is it?' asked Beth, who had been watching Alice's face rather more closely than Alice would have liked. Beth might be sweet and kind, but that didn't mean that she was stupid.

'No, no…of course not,' said Alice quickly. 'Of *course* not,' she added, although she wasn't entirely sure whether she was trying to convince herself or Beth.

How could it be a problem, after all? She and Will had split up by mutual agreement ten years ago, and she hadn't seen him for eight. There was no bitterness, no betrayal to mar their memories of the time they had spent together. There was absolutely no reason why they shouldn't meet now as friends.

Except—*be honest, Alice*—that he was married and she wasn't.

'Honestly,' she told Beth. 'I'm fine about it. In fact, it will be good to catch up with him again. It was just funny hearing about him suddenly after so long.'

She even managed a little laugh, but Beth was still looking sceptical, and Alice decided that she had better come clean. Roger was bound to tell his wife the truth anyway, and, if she didn't mention how close she and Will had been, Beth would wonder why she hadn't told her herself, and that would give the impression that she *did* have a problem with seeing Will again.

Which she didn't. Not really.

Slipping her feet into the gaudily decorated flip-flops she had bought at the airport at great expense, Alice bent to adjust one of the straps and let her straight brown hair swing forward to cover her face.

'You know, Will and I went out for a while,' she said as casually as she could.

'No!' Beth's jaw dropped. 'You and Will?' she said, suitably astounded. 'Roger never told me that!' she added accusingly.

'We'd split up long before he met you.' Alice gave a would-be careless shrug. 'It was old news by then. Roger probably never gave it a thought.'

'But you were both at our wedding,' Beth remembered. 'I do think Roger might have mentioned it in case I put you on the same table or something. I had no idea!' She leant forward. 'Wasn't it awkward?'

Unable to spend any more time fiddling with her shoe, Alice groped around beneath her lounger for the hair clip she had put there earlier.

'It was fine,' she said, making a big thing of shaking back her hair and twisting it carelessly up to secure it with the clip, all of which gave her the perfect excuse to avoid Beth's eye.

Because it hadn't been fine at all. There would have been no way she'd have missed Roger's wedding, and she had known that Will would be there. It had been two years since they had split up, and Alice had hoped that the two of them would be able to meet as friends.

It had been a short-lived hope. Alice had been aware of him from the moment she'd walked into the church and saw the back of his head. Her heart had jerked uncomfortably at the sight of him, and she had felt ridiculously glad that he was wedged into a pew between friends so that she wouldn't have to sit next to him straight away.

She had been going out with someone from work then. Clive, his name had been. And, yes, maybe he *had* been a bit of a stuffed shirt, but there had been no call for Will to talk about him that way. They had met, inevitably, at the reception after the service, and Alice had done her best to keep up a flow of increasingly desperate chit-chat as Will had eyed Clive and made absolutely no attempt to hide his contempt.

'You've sold out, Alice,' he told her later. 'Clive is boring, pretentious and self-obsessed, and that's putting it kindly! He's not the man for you.'

They argued, Alice remembered, in the hotel grounds, away from the lights and the music, as the reception wore on into the night. Clive had too much to drink, and to Alice's embarrassment was holding forth about his car and his clients and his bonuses. Depressed at her lack of judgement when it came to men, she slipped away, but, if she had known that she would encounter Will out in the dark gardens, she would have stuck with Clive showing off.

Will was the last person she wanted to witness Clive at his worst. She had been hoping to convince him that her life had been one long, upward curve since they had agreed to go their separate ways and that she was happily settled with a satisfying career, a stable home and a fulfilling relationship. No chance of him thinking that, when he had endured Clive's boasting all evening.

Mortified by Clive's behaviour, and tense from a day trying not to let Will realise just how aware she was of him still, Alice was in no mood for him to put her own thoughts into such brutal words.

'What do you know about it?' she fired back, glad of the dim light that hid her flush.

'I know you, and I know there's no way on earth a man like Clive could ever make you happy,' said Will, so infuriatingly calm that Alice's temper flared.

'You didn't make me happy, either!' she snapped, but Will just shook his head, unfazed by her lie.

'I did once,' he said. 'We made each other happy.'

Alice didn't want to remember those times. She turned her head away. 'That was then and this is now,' she said.

'We haven't changed.'

'*I* have,' Alice insisted. 'It's been nearly two years, Will. I'm not the same person I was before. I've got a new life, the life I always wanted.' She lifted her chin. 'Maybe Clive gives me what I need now.'

'Does he?' Will took a step towards her, and instinctively Alice backed away until she found herself up against a tree.

'Does he?' Will asked again softly, taking her by the wrists and lifting her arms until she was pinned against the tree trunk. 'Does he make you laugh, Alice? Do you lie in bed with him and talk and talk?' he went on, in the same low voice that reverberated up and down Alice's spine. 'The way you did with me?'

Her heart was thumping and she could feel the rough bark digging into her back through the flimsy material of her dress. She tried to pull her wrists away, but Will held her in place with insulting ease. He wasn't a particularly big man, but his spareness was deceptive, and his hands were much stronger than they looked.

And Alice, too, was conscious that she wasn't fighting as hard as she could have done. She could feel her treacherous body responding to Will's nearness. It had always been like that. Alice had used to lie awake sometimes, watching him while he slept, and wondering what it was about him that created such a powerful attraction.

It wasn't as if he were especially good-looking. In many ways, he was quite ordinary, but there was something about him, something uniquely Will in the line of his jaw, in the set of his mouth and the feel of his hands, in all the lean, lovely planes and angles of him that made her senses tingle still.

Will's voice dropped even further as he pressed her back against the tree. 'Do you shiver when he kisses you here?' he asked, dropping a light kiss on Alice's bare shoulder where it curved into her throat, and in spite of herself Alice felt that familiar shudder of excitement spiral slowly down to the very centre of her, where it throbbed and ached with memories of all the times they had made love.

Closing her eyes, she sucked in her breath as Will pressed warm, slow kisses up the side of her throat. 'That's none of your business,' she managed unsteadily.

'Does he love you?' Will whispered against her skin, and the brush of his lips made her shiver again.

She swallowed hard, her eyes still squeezed shut. 'Yes,' she said, but she knew it was a feeble effort. 'Yes, he does,' she tried again, although it sounded as if she was trying to convince herself.

Alice wanted to believe that Clive loved her, otherwise what was she doing with him?

'No, he doesn't,' said Will, and, although she couldn't see him, she knew that he was shaking his head. 'Clive doesn't love anybody but himself.'

There was a long pause, then Alice opened her eyes and found herself staring up into Will's face, the face that had once made her heart clench with the knowledge that she could touch it and kiss it and feel it whenever she wanted.

'Do you love Clive, Alice?' Will asked quietly.

Alice couldn't answer. Her throat was so tight it was hard enough to breathe, and all she could do was stand there, her arms pinioned above her head, and look back at him while the world stopped turning, and there was only Will and the feel of his hands over her wrists.

To her horror, her eyes filled with tears, and Will bent with a muffled curse to kiss her, a fierce, hard kiss that seared Alice to the soul. Nearly two years since they had said goodbye, but her mouth remembered his instantly, and she found herself kissing him back, angrily, hungrily, until Will released her wrists at last and yanked her into him to kiss her again.

Instinctively Alice's arms reached round him and she spread her hands over his back. It had been so long since she had held him, so long since she had felt the solidity and the hardness of the body she had once known as well as her own. She had forgotten how much she missed the feel of him and the wonderfully warm, clean, masculine scent of his skin.

'I've missed you,' Will echoed her thoughts in a ragged voice. 'I don't want to miss you again.'

'Will…' Alice was reeling, shocked by the emotion surging between them and the power of her own response.

'I'm going to Belize next week to work on the reef,' he went on, taking her face between his hands. 'Come with me,' he said with an urgency she had never heard from him before. 'Come with me and marry me, Alice. We need each other, you know we do. Clive has got his big, fat bonuses to keep him warm. He won't even notice you're gone. Say you'll come with me, and we can spend the rest of our lives making each other happy.'

And the truth was, Alice remembered by Beth's pool in St Bonaventure, that for a moment there she hesitated. Every fibre of her body was clamouring to throw herself back into his arms and agree.

And every cell in her brain was clanging a great, big warning.

She had the security she had yearned for at last. She had a good job, and in a year or two she would be in a position to get a mortgage and buy her own flat. Wasn't that what she had always wanted? A place of her own, where she could hang up her clothes in a wardrobe and never have to pack them up again? She was safe and settled. Did she really want to give that up to chase off to the Caribbean with Will, no matter how good it felt to kiss him again?

'Say yes,' Will urged her, encouraged by her hesitation.

Very slowly, Alice shook her head. 'No,' she said.

She would never forget the expression on his face then. Alice felt as if she had struck him.

'Why not?' he asked numbly.

'It wouldn't work, Will.' Alice pulled herself together with an effort. 'We went through all this two years ago. We agreed that we're different and we want different things. Our lives were going in different directions then, and they still are now. What's the point of pretending that they're not?'

'What's the point of pretending that what we have doesn't exist?' he countered, and she swallowed.

'It's just sexual chemistry,' she told him shakily. 'It's not enough.'

'And Clive and his bonuses are, I suppose?' Will made no attempt to hide the bitterness in his voice.

Alice didn't—couldn't—answer. It wasn't Clive, she wanted to tell him. It was the way her life seemed finally under control. She was settled, and had the kind of reassuring routine that she had craved when she was growing up.

And, yes, maybe Clive and the other boyfriends she had had weren't kindred spirits the way Will had been, but at least she knew where she was with them. They didn't make her entrails churn with excitement the way he had done, it was true, but they didn't make her feel superficial and materialistic for wanting to root herself with tangible assets either. Will was like her parents. He wanted things like freedom, adventure and independence, but Alice had learnt that you couldn't count on those. You couldn't put them in the bank and save them for when you needed them. Freedom, adventure and independence might be great things to have, but they didn't make you feel safe.

So all she did was look helplessly back at Will until he

dropped his hands, his expression closed. 'That's three times I've asked you to marry me,' he said bleakly as Alice lowered her trembling arms and rubbed them unsteadily. 'And three times you've said no. I've got the message now, though,' he told her. 'I won't ask you again.'

He had stepped away from her then, only turning back almost against his will for one last, hard kiss. 'Goodbye, Alice,' he said, and then he turned and walked out of her life.

Until now.

Alice sighed. For a while there, the past had seemed more vivid than the present, and her heart was like a cold fist in her chest, just as it had been then.

'Are you sure?' asked Beth, whose blue eyes could be uncomfortably shrewd at times.

'Of course.' Alice summoned a bright smile. 'It was fine,' she repeated, knowing that Beth was afraid that tension between her and Will would mar the party she had planned so carefully. 'And it will be fine this time, too. Don't worry, Beth. I promise you I don't have a problem meeting Will or his wife,' she went on bravely, if inaccurately, as she got to her feet. 'Will probably won't even remember me. Now, why don't I give you a hand unpacking all that shopping?'

Will watched anxiously as Lily took Beth's hand after a moment's hesitation and allowed herself to be led off to the pool, which was already full of children squealing excitedly. His daughter had looked apprehensive at the thought of making new friends, but she hadn't clung to him or even looked to him for reassurance. He was almost as much a stranger to her as Beth was, he reflected bitterly.

'She'll be fine.' Roger misread Will's tension. 'Beth loves kids, and she'll look after Lily. By the time the party's over, she won't want to go home!'

That was precisely what Will was afraid of, but he didn't want to burden Roger with his problems the moment that they met up again after so long. He'd always liked Roger, and Beth's delight at bumping into him the day before had been touching, but the truth was that he wasn't in the mood for a party.

He hadn't been able to think of a tactful way to refuse Beth's invitation at the time, and this morning he had convinced himself that a party would be a good thing for Lily, no matter how little he might feel like it himself. Beth had assured him that it would be a casual barbecue, and that several families would be there, so Lily would have plenty of other children to play with.

Will hadn't seen his daughter play once since they had arrived in St Bonaventure, and he knew he needed to make an effort to get her to interact with other children. But, watching Lily trail reluctantly along in Beth's wake, Will was seized by a fresh sense of inadequacy. Should he have reassured her, or gone with her? He was bitterly aware that he was thrown by the kind of everyday situations any normal father would take in his stride.

'Come and have a beer,' said Roger, before Will could decide whether to follow Lily and Beth or not, so he let Roger hand him a bottle so cold that the condensation steamed. There wasn't much he could do about Lily right now, and in the meantime he had better exert himself to be sociable.

The two men spent a few minutes catching up and, by the time Roger offered to introduce him to the other guests, Will was beginning to relax. He didn't know whether it was the beer, or Roger's friendly ordinariness, but he was definitely feeling better.

'Most people are outside,' said Roger, leading the way through a bright, modern living-area to where sliding-glass doors separated the air-conditioned coolness from the tropical heat outside.

Will was happy to follow him. He had never minded the heat, and, if he was outside, he'd be able to keep an eye on Lily at the pool. Roger glanced out as he pulled open the door for Will, then hesitated at the last moment.

'Beth did tell you who's staying with us, didn't she?' he asked, suddenly doubtful.

'No, who's that?' asked Will without much interest as he stepped out onto the decking, shaded by a pergola covered in scrambling pink bougainvillaea.

He never heard Roger's answer.

He saw her in his first casual glance out at the garden, and his heart slammed to a halt in his chest.

Alice.

She was standing in the middle of the manicured lawn, talking to a portly man in a florid shirt. Eight years, and he recognized her instantly.

Even from a distance, Will could see that her companion was sweating profusely in the heat, but Alice looked cool and elegant in a loose, pale green dress that wafted slightly in the hot breeze. She was wearing high-heeled sandals with delicate straps, and her hair was clipped up in a way that would look messy on most other women, but which she carried off with that flair she had always had.

Alice. There was no one else like her.

He had thought he would never see her again. Will's heart stuttered into life after that first, jarring moment of sheer disbelief, but he was still having trouble breathing. Buffeted by a turbulent mixture of shock, joy, anger and something perilously close to panic, Will wasn't sure what he felt, other than totally unprepared for the sight of her.

Dimly, Will was aware that Roger was saying something,

but he couldn't hear it. He could just stare at Alice across the garden until, as if sensing his stunned gaze, she turned her head, and her smile froze at the sight of him.

There was a long, long pause when it seemed to Will as if the squawking birds and the shrieking children and the buzz of conversation all faded into a silence broken only by the erratic thump of his heart. He couldn't have moved if he had tried.

Then he saw Alice make an excuse to the man in the ghastly shirt and turn to walk across the garden towards him, apparently quite at ease in those ridiculous shoes, the dress floating around her legs.

She had always moved with a straight-backed, unconscious grace that had fascinated Will, and as he watched her he had the vertiginous feeling that time had ground to a halt and was rewinding faster and faster through the blur of the last ten years. So strong was the sensation that he was half-convinced that, by the time she reached him those long years would have vanished and they would both be back as they had been then, when they'd loved each other.

Will's mouth was dry as Alice hesitated for a fraction of a second at the bottom of the steps that led up to the decking, and then she was standing before him.

'Hello, Will,' she said.

CHAPTER TWO

'ALICE.' Will's throat was so constricted that her name was all he could manage.

Roger looked from one to the other, and took the easy way out. 'I'd better make sure everyone has a drink,' he said, although neither of them gave any sign that they had even heard him. 'I'll leave you two to catch up.'

Will stared at Alice, hardly able to believe that she was actually standing in front of him. His first stunned thought was that she hadn't changed at all. There were the same high cheekbones, the same golden eyes and slanting brows, the same wide mouth. The silky brown hair was even pulled carelessly away from her face just the way she had used to wear it as a student. She was the same!

But when he looked more closely, the illusion faded. She must be thirty-two now, ten years older than the way he remembered her, and it showed in the faint lines and the drawn look around her eyes. Her hairstyle might not have changed, but the quirky collection of dangly, ethnic earrings had been replaced by discreet pearl studs, and the comfortable boots by high heels and glamour.

Alice had never been beautiful. Her hair was too straight, her features too irregular, but she had possessed an innate stylishness and charm that had clearly matured into elegance and sophistication. She had become a poised, attractive woman.

But she wasn't the Alice he had loved. That Alice had been a vivid, astringent presence, prickly and insecure at times— but who wasn't, when they were young? When she'd talked, her whole body had become animated, and she would lean forward and gesticulate, her small hands swooping and darting in the air to emphasise her point, making the bangles she wore chink and jingle, or shaking her head so that her earrings swung wildly and caught the light.

Will had loved just to watch the way the expressions had chased themselves across her transparent face. It had always been easy to tell what Alice had been feeling. No one could look crosser than Alice when she was angry; no one else's face lit like hers when she was happy. And when she was amused, she would throw back her head and laugh that uninhibited, un-expectedly dirty laugh, the mere memory of which was enough to make his groin tighten.

Ironically, the very things that Will had treasured about her had been the things Alice was desperate to change. She hadn't wanted to be unconventional. She hadn't wanted to be differ-ent. She'd wanted to be like everyone else.

And now it looked as if she had got her wish. All that fire, all that quirkiness, all that personality…all gone. Firmly suppressed and locked away until she was as bland as the rest of the world.

It made Will very sad to realise that the Alice who had haunted him all these years didn't exist any more. In her place was just a smart, rather tense woman with unusual-coloured eyes and inappropriate shoes.

'How are you, Alice?' he managed after a moment.

Alice's feet were killing her, and her heart was thumping and thudding so painfully in her chest that it was making her feel quite sick, but she produced a brilliant smile.

'I'm fine,' she told him. 'Great, in fact. And you?'

'I'm OK,' said Will, who was, in fact, feeling very strange. He had been pitched from shock to joy to bitter disappointment in the space of little more than a minute, and he was finding it hard to keep up with the rapid change of emotions.

'Quite a surprise bumping into you here,' Alice persevered in the same brittle style, and he eyed her with dismay. When had the fiery, intent Alice learnt to do meaningless chit-chat? She was treating him as if he were some slight acquaintance, not a man she had lived with and laughed with and loved with.

'Yes,' he agreed slowly, thinking that 'surprise' wasn't quite the word for it. 'Beth didn't tell me that you were here.'

'I don't think she made any connection between us,' said Alice carelessly. 'It wouldn't have occurred to Beth to mention me to you. She didn't know that we'd been…'

'Lovers?' suggested Will with a sardonic look when she trailed off.

A slight flush rose in Alice's cheeks. 'I didn't put it quite like that,' she said repressively. 'I just said that we had been close when we were students together.'

'It's not like you to be coy, Alice.'

She looked at him sharply. 'What do you mean?'

'You and Roger were *close*,' said Will. 'You and I were in love.'

Alice's eyes slid away from his. She didn't want to be reminded of how much she had loved him. She certainly didn't want a discussion of how in love they had been. No way could she cope with that right now.

'Whatever,' she said as carelessly as she could. 'Beth got the point, anyway.'

He had changed, she thought, unaccountably disconsolate. Of course, she had known in her head that he wasn't going to be the same. Ten years, marriage and children were bound to have had an effect on him.

But in her heart she had imagined him still the Will she had known. The Will she had loved.

This Will seemed taller than she remembered, taller and tougher. His neck had thickened slightly and his chest had filled out, and the air of calm competence she had always associated with him had solidified. He still had those big, capable hands, but there was none of the amusement she remembered in his face, no familiar ironic gleam in the grey eyes. Instead, there were lines around his eyes and deeper grooves carved on either side of his mouth, which was set in a new, hard line.

It was strange, talking to someone at once so familiar and so much a stranger. Meeting Will like that was even worse than Alice had expected. She had planned to be friendly to him, charming to his wife and engaging to his child, so that they would all go away convinced that she had no regrets and without the slightest idea that her life wasn't quite the glittering success she had so confidently expected it to be.

She might as well have spared herself the effort, Alice thought ruefully. In spite of all her careful preparations, her confidence had evaporated the moment she'd laid eyes on him, and she was as shaken and jittery as if Will had turned up without a moment's warning. She knew that she was coming over as brittle, but she couldn't seem to do anything about it.

'Beth said that you were working out here,' she said, opting to stick with her social manner, no matter how uncomfortable it felt. It was easier than looking into his eyes and asking him if he had missed her at all, if he had wondered, as she had done, whether life would have been different if she had said yes instead of no that day.

Will nodded, apparently willing to follow her lead and stick to polite superficialities. 'I'm coordinating a major project on sustainable tourism,' he said, and Alice raised her brows.

'You're not a marine ecologist any more?' she asked, surprised. Will had always been so passionate about the ocean, she couldn't imagine him giving up diving in favour of paperwork.

'I am, of course,' he corrected her. 'But I don't do straight research anymore. A lot of our work is assessing the environmental impact of major development projects on the sea.'

Alice frowned. 'What's that got to do with tourism?'

'Tourism has a huge effect on the environment,' said Will. 'The economy here desperately needs the income tourists can bring, but tourists won't come unless there's an international airport, roads, hotels, restaurants and leisure facilities…all of which use up precious natural resources and add to the weight of pollution, which in turn affects the delicate balance of the environment.'

Will gestured around him. 'St Bonaventure is a paradise in lots of ways. It's everyone's idea of a tropical island, and it's still unspoilt. Its reef is one of the great undiscovered diving spots in the world. That makes it the kind of place tourists want to visit, but they won't come all this way if the development ends up destroying the very things that makes this place so special.

'The government here needs to balance their need to get the money to improve the living standards of the people here with the risk to the reef,' he went on. 'If the reef is damaged, it will not only destroy the potential revenue from tourism, it'll also leave the island itself at risk. The reef is the most effective protection St Bonaventure has against the power of the ocean.'

Will stopped, hearing himself in lecture mode. The old Alice might have been interested, but this one certainly wasn't. Instead of leaning forward intently and asking awkward questions, the way she would have done before, she wore an expression of interest that was little more than polite.

'Anyway, the project I'm coordinating is about balancing the needs of the reef with the needs of the economy before tourism is developed to any great extent,' he finished lamely.

'Sounds important,' Alice commented.

He glanced at her, as if suspecting mockery. 'It is,' he said.

Alice had deliberately kept her voice light to disguise the pang inside. For a moment there he had been the Will she remembered, his face alight with enthusiasm, his eyes warm with commitment.

What would it be like to work on something you believed in, something that really mattered, not just to you but to other people as well? Alice wondered. When it boiled down to it, her own career in market research was just about making money. It hadn't changed any lives other than her own.

That had never bothered her before, but she had had to question a lot of things about her life in the last year. What did her much-vaunted career amount to now, after all? Nothing, thought Alice bleakly.

Will had built his career on his expertise and his passion. He had done what he wanted the way he'd wanted to do it. He had found someone to share his life and had fathered a child. His life since Roger's wedding had been successful by any measure, while hers... Well, better not go there, Alice decided with an inward sigh.

'What about you?' Will asked, breaking into her thoughts and making her start.

'Me?'

'What are you doing on St Bonaventure?'

Alice wished she could say that she was here for some interesting or meaningful reason. 'I'm on holiday,' she confessed, immediately feeling guilty about it.

'So you'll just be here a couple of weeks?'

She was sure she detected relief in his voice. He was

probably delighted at the idea that she wouldn't be around for long so that he could get on with his happy, successful, *married* life without her.

The thought stiffened Alice's resolve not to let Will so much as guess that all her careful plans had come to nothing. It wasn't that she begrudged him his happiness, but a girl had her pride. She needed to convince him that she had never had a moment's regret. She wouldn't lie—that would be pathetic, obviously—but there was no reason why she shouldn't put a positive slant on things, was there?

'Actually,' she said, 'I'm here for six weeks.'

He lifted one brow in a way that Alice had often longed to be able to do. 'Long holiday,' he commented.

'I'm lucky, aren't I?' she agreed with a cool smile. 'Roger and Beth have been telling me I should come and visit ever since they were posted here last year, but I just haven't had the opportunity until now.'

Redundancy could be seen as an opportunity, couldn't it?

'You must have done well for yourself,' said Will. 'Not many people get the opportunity for a six-week holiday.'

'It's not strictly a holiday,' Alice conceded. 'As it happens, I'm between jobs at the moment,' she explained, tilting her chin slightly.

That wasn't a lie, either. She might not have another job lined up just yet, but when she went home she was determined that she was not only going to get her career back on track, but that she would be moving onto to bigger and better things. With her experience, there was no reason why she shouldn't aim for a more prestigious company, a promotion *and* a pay raise.

'I see,' said Will, his expression so non-committal that Alice was afraid that he saw only too well. He had no doubt interpreted being 'between jobs' as unemployed, which of course was another way of looking at it, but not one Alice was prepared to dwell on.

'I was in a very pressurised work environment,' she told him loftily. 'And I thought it was time to take a break and reassess where my career was going.'

Strictly speaking, of course, it had been the company who had taken over PLMR who had decided that Alice could have all the time she wanted to think about things, but Will didn't need to know that. It wasn't as if it had been her fault. Almost all her colleagues had been made redundant at the same time, she reminded herself. It could happen to anyone these days.

'Market research—it *is* market research, isn't it?—obviously pays well if you can afford six weeks somewhere like this when you're between jobs,' said Will, with just a hint of snideness. 'But then, you always wanted to make money, didn't you?'

'I wanted to be secure,' said Alice, hating the faintly defensive note in her voice. 'And I am.' What was wrong with wanting security? 'I wanted to be successful, and I am,' she added for good measure.

Well, she had been until last year, but, when your company was the subject of a hostile takeover, there wasn't much you could do about it, no matter how good you were at your job.

It hadn't been a good year. Her only lucky break had been winning nearly two thousand pounds in the lottery, and that had been a fluke. Normally, Alice wouldn't even have thought about buying a ticket, but she had been in a mood when she was prepared to try anything to change the dreary trend of her life.

It wasn't as if she had won millions. Two thousand pounds wasn't enough to change her life, but it was just enough for a ticket to an out-of-the-way place like St Bonaventure, and Alice had taken it as a sign. At any other time, she would have been sensible. She would have bought herself a pair of shoes and put the rest of the money towards some much-needed repairs on her flat—the unexpected windfall would have covered the cost of a new boiler, for instance—but that hadn't been any other time. That had been the day she heard that Tony and Sandi were getting married.

Alice had gone straight out and bought a plane ticket. *And* some shoes.

Still, there was no harm in letting Will think that she had earned so much money that she didn't know what to do with it all. Not that it would impress him. He was more likely to disapprove of what he thought of as her materialistic lifestyle, but Alice was desperate for him to believe that she had made it.

'We all make choices,' she reminded him. 'I made mine, and I don't have any regrets,'

'I'm glad you got what you wanted, then,' said Will flatly.

'You too,' said Alice, and for a jarring moment their eyes met. It was as if the polite mask they both wore dropped for an instant, and they saw each other properly for the first time. The sense of recognition was like a blow to Alice's stomach, pushing the air from her lungs and leaving her breathless and giddy and almost nauseous.

But then Will jerked his head away, the guarded expression clanging back into place with such finality that Alice wondered if she had imagined that look.

'You didn't marry Clive, then?' he asked abruptly.

'Clive?' Alice was thrown by the sudden change of subject.

'The Clive you were so in love with at Roger and Beth's wedding,' Will reminded her with an edge of savagery. 'Don't tell me you've forgotten him!'

'I didn't—' Alice opened her mouth to strenuously deny ever loving Clive and then shut it again. If she hadn't loved Clive, why had she let Will believe that she did? Why hadn't she been able to tell him the truth that day?

'No, I didn't marry Clive,' she said quietly. 'We split up soon after…after Roger's wedding,' she finished after a tiny moment of hesitation.

She had so nearly said 'after you kissed me', and she might as well have done. The memory of that dark night in the hotel gardens jangled in the air between them. Those desperate kisses, the spiralling excitement, the sense of utter rightness at being back in each other's arms.

The tightness around her heart as she'd watched him walk away.

Alice could feel them all as vividly as if they had kissed the night before.

Will had to be remembering those kisses too. She wanted to be able to talk about it, laugh about it even, pretend that it didn't matter and it was all in the past, but she couldn't. Not yet.

So she drew a steadying breath and summoned another of her bright smiles. 'Then I met Tony, and we were together for four years. We talked about getting married, but…well, we decided it wouldn't have worked.'

Tony had decided that, anyway.

'We stopped ourselves making a terrible mistake just in time,' Alice finished.

OK, it might not be the whole story, but why should she tell Will all her sad secrets? Anyway, it might not be the *whole* truth, but it *was* the truth. It *would* have been a mistake if she and Tony had gone ahead with the wedding. Nothing but unhappiness would have come from their marriage when Tony was in love with someone else. Alice's world might have fallen apart the day Tony had sat her down to tell her about Sandi, but she'd accepted even then that he had done the right thing.

Today was Tony and Sandi's wedding day, Alice was startled to remember. She had spent so long dreading this day, imagining how hard it would be for her to think about another woman taking what should have been her place, and, now that it was here, she hadn't even thought about it.

Perhaps she ought to be grateful to Will for distracting her?

Will drained the last of his beer and turned aside to put the empty bottle on the decking rail. 'Still avoiding commitment, I see,' he commented with a sardonic glance over his shoulder at Alice, who flushed at the injustice of it.

She wasn't the one who had called off the wedding. If it had been down to her, she would be happily married to Tony right now, but she bit back the words. She had just convinced him that ending her engagement to Tony had been a mutual decision, so she could hardly tell him the truth now.

Which was worse? That he thought she was afraid of commitment, or that he felt sorry for her?

No question.

'Still determined not to get married until I'm absolutely sure it's perfect,' she corrected Will. 'So…I'm fancy free, and on the lookout for Mr Right. I'm not going to get married until I've found him, and, until then I'm just having fun!'

Will was unimpressed by her bravado. 'You seem very tense for someone who's having fun,' he said.

Alice gritted her teeth. 'I am *not* tense,' she snapped. Tensely, in fact. 'I'm a bit jet-lagged, that's all. I only got here a couple of days ago.'

'Ah,' said Will, not bothering to hide the fact that he was totally unconvinced by her explanation. Which just made Alice even crosser, but she sucked in her breath and resisted the temptation to retort in kind. She didn't want Will to think that he was getting to her, or that she cared in the slightest what he thought of her.

Friendly but unobtainable, wasn't that how she wanted him to think of her? Pleasant but cool. His long-lost love who had turned into a mysterious stranger. Anything but sad and tense and a failure.

She fixed a smile to her face. 'I gather you weren't as hesitant about taking the plunge,' she said.

'The plunge?'

'Marriage,' she reminded him sweetly, and a strange expression flitted over his face.

'Ah. Yes. I did get married,' he agreed. 'Why? Did you think I would never get over you?'

'Of course not,' said Alice with dignity. 'If I thought about you at all—which I can't say was that often—' she added crushingly, 'it was only to hope that you were happy.'

Will raised his brows in disbelief. 'Really?'

'Yes, really.' Alice had been nursing a glass of Roger's lethal tropical punch, but it didn't seem to be having a very good effect on her. She set it on the rail next to Will's empty bottle.

'*Have* you been happy?' she asked him, the words out of her mouth before she had thought about them properly.

Will didn't answer immediately. He thought about Lily, about how it had felt when he had held his daughter in his arms for the first time. About drifting along the reef, fish flitting past him in flashes of iridescent colour and looking up to see the sunlight filtering down through the water to the deep blue silence. About sitting on a boat and watching dolphins curving and cresting in the foamy wake, while the water glittered and the sea breeze lifted his hair.

He had been happy then. It hadn't been the same feeling as the happiness he had felt lying next to Alice after they had made love, holding her into the curve of his body, smoothing his hand over her soft skin, breathing in her fragrance, marvelling that this quirky, contrary, vibrant woman was really his, but, still, he *had* been happy since.

In a different way, but, yes, he'd been happy.

'I've had times of great happiness,' he said eventually, very conscious of Alice's great golden eyes on his face. 'But not in my marriage,' he found himself admitting. 'We weren't as sensible as you. We didn't realise what a mistake we were making until it was too late.'

It had been his fault, really. He had vowed to move on after Roger's wedding, had been determined to put Alice from his mind once and for all. The trouble was that every woman he'd met had seemed dull and somehow colourless after Alice. They might have been prettier and nicer, and certainly sweeter, but, when he'd closed his eyes, it had always been Alice's blazing golden eyes that he saw, always Alice's voice that he heard, always Alice's skin that he tasted.

Nikki had been the first woman with the strength of personality to match Alice's, and Will had persuaded himself that she was capable of banishing Alice's ghost once and for all. They had married after a whirlwind holiday romance in the Red Sea where he had been researching at the time.

It had been madness to take such a step when they'd barely known each other. Will should have known that it would end in disaster. Because Nikki hadn't been Alice. She had been forceful rather than colourful, efficient rather than intense. The only thing the two women had shared, as far as Will could see, was a determination to make a success of themselves.

Nikki, it had turned out too late, had had no intention of wasting her life in the kind of countries where Will felt most at home. 'My career's at home,' she had told him. 'There's nothing for me to do here, nothing works, and, if you think I'm having the baby in that hospital, you've got another think coming!'

Lily was the result of a failed attempt to make the marriage work. She'd been born in London, just as Nikki had planned, but by then Nikki had already sued for divorce. 'It's never going to work, Will,' she'd told him when he came to see his new daughter. 'Let's just accept it now rather than waste any more time.'

'We were married less than two years,' he told Alice.

'So you're divorced?' she said, horrified at the instinctive lightening of her heart, and ashamed of herself for feeling even a smidgeon of relief that his life hadn't turned out quite as perfectly as it had seemed at first.

And that she wouldn't have to face his wife after all. Although she wished now that she hadn't said that about 'looking for Mr Right'. She didn't want Will thinking that she would try and pick up where they had left off the moment she realised that he was single.

'I'm sorry,' she said, when he nodded curtly. 'I didn't realise. Beth said that you had your family with you, so we just assumed that you were married.'

'No, it's just me and Lily,' he said. 'My daughter,' he added in explanation. 'She's six.'

'Is she spending the holiday with you?' Alice didn't have much to do with children, and was a bit vague about school terms, but she supposed mid-March might conceivably mean the Easter holidays. It seemed a bit early, though. Perhaps it didn't matter so much for six-year-olds?

'No, she lives with me,' said Will, almost reluctantly.

'Oh? That's unusual, isn't it?' Alice looked surprised. 'Doesn't the mother usually have custody?'

'Nikki did,' he said. 'She died recently, so now Lily only has me.'

'God, how awful!' Alice was shocked out of her cool pose, and Will was absurdly pleased to see the genuine compassion in her eyes. He had been wondering if there was anything left of the old Alice at all. 'What happened? Or maybe you don't want to talk about it?' she added contritely.

'No, it's OK. People are going to have to know, and obviously it's difficult to explain in front of Lily.' Will sighed. 'That's why I couldn't tell Beth when we met her in the super-market. Lily is finding it hard enough to adjust without hearing the whole story talked over with perfect strangers.'

'I can imagine.'

'Lily used to go to the after-school club, and Nikki would pick her up after work. But that day there had apparently been some meeting that had run on, so she was going to be very late at the school. They'd warned her before about being late, so she was rushing to get there, and I suppose she wasn't driving as carefully as she should …'

'A car accident?' said Alice when he trailed off with a sigh.

'She was killed instantly, they said.' Will nodded, and Alice wondered just how much his ex-wife still meant to him. You could say that the marriage had been a mistake, but they had had a child together. He must have had some feelings still for Lily's mother.

'Meanwhile, Lily is still waiting for her mother to come and pick her up?' she said gently.

Will shot her a curious look, as if surprised by her under-standing. 'I think she must be. She hasn't talked about it, and she's such a quiet little girl anyway, it's hard to know how much she understands.'

He looked so tired suddenly that Alice felt guilty for being so brittle and defensive earlier. 'It must have been a shock for you, too,' she said after a moment.

Will shrugged his own feelings aside. 'I was in Honduras when I heard. It took them some time to track me down, so I missed the immediate aftermath. I wasn't there for Lily,' he added, and, from the undercurrent of bitterness in his voice, Alice guessed he flayed himself with that knowledge.

'You weren't to know,' she said in a deliberately practical voice. 'What happened to Lily?'

'Nikki's parents live nearby so the school called them when she didn't turn up, and they looked after Lily until I got there. My work's kept me overseas for the last few years, though, and I haven't had the chance to see her very often, so I'm virtually a stranger to her.' Will ran his fingers through his hair in a gesture of defeat. 'To be honest, it's all been a bit…difficult.'

Difficult? Alice thought about his small daughter. Lily was six, he had said. What would it be like to have the centre of your world disappear without warning, and to be handed over instead to a father you hardly knew? Alice's heart was wrung. Her own parents had been dippy and unreliable in lots of ways, but at least they had always been there.

'When did all this happen?' she asked.

'Seven weeks ago.'

'Seven *weeks*? Is that all?' Alice looked at Will incredulously, her sympathy evaporating. 'What are you doing out here?'

Will narrowed his eyes at her tone. 'My job,' he said in a hard voice. 'I've already delayed the project by over a month.'

'You shouldn't be thinking about your *job*,' said Alice with a withering look. 'You should be thinking about your daughter!'

'I am thinking about her.' Will set his teeth and told himself he wasn't going to let Alice rile him. 'I'm hoping that the change of scene will help her.'

He couldn't have said anything more calculated to catch Alice on the raw. His casual assumption that a change of scene could only be good for a child reminded her all too painfully of the way her own parents had blithely uprooted her just when she had settled down in a new country and started to feel at home.

'We're off to Guyana,' they had announced gaily. 'You'll love it!'

After Guyana, they had spent a year on a croft in the Hebrides. 'It'll be good for you,' her father had decided. Then it had been Sri Lanka— 'Won't it be exciting?'—followed by Morocco, Indonesia, Exmoor (a disaster) and Goa, although Alice had lost track of the order they had come in.

'You're so lucky,' everyone had told her when she had been growing up. 'You've seen so much of the world and had such wonderful experiences.'

But Alice hadn't felt lucky. She hadn't wanted any more new experiences. She had longed to settle down and feel at home, instead of being continually overwhelmed by strange new sights and sounds, smells and people.

And she hadn't had the loss of a mother to deal with at the same time. Alice's heart went out to Will's daughter.

Poor Lily. Poor little girl.

CHAPTER THREE

'YOU don't think it would have helped her more to stay in familiar surroundings?' Alice asked Will sharply, too irritated by his apparent disregard for his daughter to think about the fact that it was probably none of her business.

A muscle was twitching in Will's jaw. 'Her grandparents offered to look after her,' he admitted. 'But they're getting on. Besides, we all thought that it would be easier for Lily to start a new life without continual painful reminders of her mother. She's going to have to get used to living with me some time, so it's better that she does that sooner rather than later.'

His careful arguments were just making Alice crosser. 'Why couldn't *you* get used to doing a job that meant you could stay where Lily would feel at home?' she demanded.

'There's not a lot of work for marine ecologists in London!'

'You could change your job.'

'And do what?' asked Will, stung by her tone, and annoyed with letting himself be drawn into an argument with Alice, who was typically holding forth on a subject she knew little about.

Her brittleness had vanished, and she was vivid once more, her cheeks flushed and her tawny eyes flashing as she waved her arms around to prove her point. Suddenly, she was the

Alice he remembered, and Will was simultaneously delighted and exasperated.

It was an uncannily familiar feeling, he thought, not knowing whether he wanted to shake her or catch her into his arms. The rush of joy he felt at realising that the real Alice was still there was tempered by resentment of her unerring ability to home in on the very issue he felt most guilty about. He wouldn't have minded if they'd been arguing about something unimportant, but this was his daughter they were discussing. Will was desperate to be a good father, and he didn't need Alice pointing out exactly where he was going wrong five minutes after meeting him again.

'Marine ecology is all I know,' he tried to explain. 'I have to support my child financially as well as emotionally, and the best way I can do that is by sticking with the career that I know rather than launching wildly into some new one where I'd have to start at the beginning. Besides,' he went on as Alice looked profoundly unconvinced. 'Lily isn't my only responsibility. This project has taken five years to set up, and a lot of futures depend on it being successful. Of course Lily is important, but I've got responsibilities to other people as well. That's just the way things are, and Lily's going to have to get used to it.'

'That's an incredibly selfish attitude,' said Alice, twirling her hand dramatically so that she could poke her finger towards Will's chest. 'It's all about what suits *you*, isn't it? All about what *you* need. What about what *Lily* needs?'

'I'm her father,' said Will tersely. 'Lily needs to be with me.'

'I'd agree with you, if being with you meant staying in a home she knew, with her grandparents and her friends and her routines.'

Alice knew that it wasn't really her business, but Will's complacency infuriated her. 'Losing a mother would be hard enough for her to deal with even if she had those things to hang on to, but you've dragged her across the world to a strange country, a place where she doesn't know anyone or anything, and by your own admission she doesn't even know you very well!'

She drew an impatient breath. 'Did you ever think of asking Lily what *she* wanted to do?'

'Lily's six.' Will bit out the words, too angry by now to care whether Alice knew how effectively she was winding him up. 'She's not old enough to make an informed decision about anything, let alone where she wants to live. She's just a little girl. How can she possibly judge what's best for her?'

'She's old enough to know where she feels comfortable and who she feels safe with,' Alice retorted.

Will gritted his teeth. Her comments were like a dentist drilling on a raw nerve. Did she really think he didn't feel guilty enough already about Lily? He hated the fact that he was practically a stranger to his own daughter. He *hated* the fact that Lily was lost and unhappy and he seemed powerless to help her. He was doing the best that he could, and, yes, maybe it wasn't good enough, but he didn't need Alice to point that out.

That brief surge of joy he had felt at her transformation from a brittle nonentity into the vibrant, fiery creature he remembered was submerged beneath a wave of resentment, and he eyed her with dislike.

'I thought you'd changed, Alice,' he said. 'But you haven't, have you?'

She tilted her chin at him in a characteristically combative gesture. 'What do you mean?'

'You still hold forth about subjects you know absolutely nothing about,' he said cuttingly. 'You know nothing about my daughter, nothing about the situation and nothing about me, now, but that doesn't stop you, does it?'

He gave a harsh laugh. 'You know, I used to think it was quite amusing the way you used to base your opinions on nothing more than instinct and emotion. For someone so obsessed with fitting things into neat categories, it always seemed odd that you refused to look at the evidence before you made up your mind. But I don't think it's very funny anymore,' he went on. 'It's pointless and narrow-minded. Perhaps, just once, you should try finding out the facts before you open your mouth and start spouting your personal prejudice!'

There was a stricken look in Alice's golden eyes but Will swept on, too angry to let himself notice and feel bad about it.

He was fed up. It had been a hellish seven weeks. He was worried sick about his daughter, and he had a daunting task ahead to get a complex but incredibly important project off the ground. The last thing he needed was the inevitable turmoil of dealing with Alice.

This was typical of her. Time and again over the last eight years, Will had told himself that he was over her. That he was getting on with his life. That he wouldn't want her even if he *did* meet her again. And then he would catch a glimpse of a straight back through a crowd, or hear a dirty laugh at a party, and his heart would jerk, and he would feel sick with disappointment to realise that it wasn't Alice after all.

And now—*now* when he had so much else to deal with— here she was, with characteristically perverse timing, threatening to turn his world upside down just when he least needed it!

Well, this time it wasn't going to turn upside down, Will determined. He had wasted the last ten years of his life getting over Alice, and he wasn't going to waste another ten minutes. It was just as well that they had come face to face, he decided. It had reminded him of all the things about her that had used to irritate him, and that made it so much easier to walk away this time.

'You know, I could stand here and pontificate to you if I could be bothered,' he told Alice, his words like a lash. 'I could tell you that you've thrown away everything that was warm and special about you, and turned yourself into someone brittle and superficial with dull earrings and silly shoes, but I won't because, unlike you, I don't believe in passing judgement on people I've only met for five minutes!'

Alice only just prevented herself from flinching at his tone. She had no intention of showing Will how hard his words had struck home. She managed an artificial laugh instead, knowing that she sounded just as brittle as he had accused her of being.

'You've got a short memory, if you think we've only known each other for five minutes!'

'You're not the Alice I knew,' said Will in the same, hard voice. 'I liked her. I don't like you. But that doesn't give me the right to tell you how to live your life, so don't tell me how to live mine. Now, if you'll excuse me, I'll go and find the daughter you seem to think I care so little about before you accuse me of neglect.'

And, with that, he turned and headed down the steps towards the pool, leaving Alice alone on the decking, white with fury mixed with a sickening sense of guilt. She shouldn't have said all that about his daughter. Will was right, she *didn't* know the situation, and she had probably been unfair. She had let the bottled-up resentment about her own childhood get the better of her. She should apologise.

But not yet.

I don't like you. Will's bitter words jangled in the air as if he had shouted them out loud. Alice felt ridiculously conspicuous, sure that everyone had heard and everyone was looking at her. They were probably all thinking that they didn't like her either, she thought miserably

Her throat was tight with tears that she refused to shed. She hadn't let anyone see her cry about Tony, so she certainly wasn't about to start blubbing over Will. She didn't care if he didn't like her. She didn't care what he thought. She didn't care about anything.

'You haven't got a drink, Alice.' Roger materialised beside her. 'Is everything OK?'

Roger. Alice nearly did cry then. Dear Roger, her dearest friend. The only one she could rely on through thick and thin.

She blinked fiercely. 'You like me, don't you, Roger?'

'Oh, you're all right, I suppose,' said Roger with mock nonchalance, but he put his arms round her and hugged her close. 'What's the matter?' he asked in a different tone.

'Nothing,' said Alice, muffled against his chest.

'Come on, it's just me. Was it seeing Will again?'

Alice drew a shuddering breath. 'He's changed,' she muttered.

'We've all changed,' said Roger gently.

'You haven't.' She lifted her head and looked up into his dear, familiar face. She had met Roger on her first day at university, and they had been best friends ever since. For Alice, he was the brother she had never had, and not Beth, not even Will, had come between them. 'That's why I love you,' she said with a wobbly smile.

Roger pretended to look alarmed. 'An open declaration of affection! This isn't like you, Alice. You *are* upset!'

'Only because Will was rude about my shoes,' said Alice, tilting her chin. 'They're not silly, are they, Roger?'

Straight-faced, Roger studied the delicate sandals, decorated with sequins and blue butterflies. 'They're fabulous,' he told her. 'Just like you. Now, come and have another drink before we both get maudlin and I tell you I love you too!'

'All right.' Alice took a deep breath and steadied her smile. 'But only if you introduce me to all these single men Beth promised me,' she said, determined to put Will Paxman right out of her mind. 'And not that guy in the awful shirt with the perspiration problem,' she added, following Roger into the kitchen.

'Colin,' said Roger, nodding knowledgeably as he handed her another glass of punch. 'No, we'll see if we can do better for you than that!'

He was as good as his word, and Alice soon found herself the centre of a circle of admiring men, all much more attractive and entertaining than the hapless Colin. Alice was under no illusions about her own looks, but she appreciated that, living in a small expatriate community with a limited social life, these men would be interested in any single, available female, and she did her best to sparkle and live up to the reputation Beth had evidently created for her. But it was hard when all the time she was aware of Will's dark, glowering presence over by the pool.

Alice turned her back pointedly, but it didn't make much difference. She could practically feel his cold grey eyes boring into her spine, and the thought made her shiver slightly and take a gulp of her punch.

Why was he bothering to watch her, anyway? There were no shortage of women simpering up at him by the pool, all of them wearing shoes and lipstick and apparently indulging in small talk. Alice was prepared to concede that she might be wrong, but none of them gave the impression of being intellectual giants. How come Will didn't find *them* prickly and false?

Defiantly, Alice emptied her glass and let someone whose name she had already forgotten rush off to get her a refill. If Will thought her brittle and superficial, superficial and brittle she would be!

Flirting was not something that came naturally to her but it was amazing what she could do when glacial grey eyes were watching her with open disapproval. What right had Will Paxman to disapprove of her, anyway? She was just being sociable, which was more than he was doing, and she was damned if she was going to skulk away to the kitchen just because he didn't like her.

So she smiled and laughed and made great play with her eyelashes while she shifted her weight surreptitiously from foot to foot to try and relieve the pressure from her shoes, which might look fabulous but which were, in truth, becoming increasingly uncomfortable. Not that Alice would ever have admitted as much to Will.

The tropical sun combined with Roger's punch was giving her a thumping headache, and Alice's bright smile grew more and more fixed as she concentrated on being fun and ignoring Will. Still, she was doing all right until someone mentioned honeymoons and suddenly she remembered that today was Tony's wedding day.

All at once Alice's bottled-up misery burst through its dam and hit her with such force that she only just managed to stop herself doubling over as if from a blow. The pain and anger and humiliation she had felt when Tony had left her for Sandi was mixed up now with a nauseating concoction of shock, regret, guilt and hurt at Will's reaction to meeting her again after all this time.

Not to mention an excess of Roger's punch.

Unable to keep up the façade any longer, Alice murmured an excuse about finding a hat and headed blindly for the house. At least there it would be cool.

And full of people. She hesitated at the bottom of the steps leading up to the decking. The large, airy living area would be packed with people enjoying the air conditioning and someone would be bound to see her sneak off to her room. The next thing Beth would be there, knocking on the door, wanting to know what was wrong.

Changing her mind, Alice glanced over her shoulder to

make sure that Will wasn't watching her, and realised that she couldn't see him. All that time she had spent simultaneously ignoring him and trying to convince him that she was having the best time of her life, and he hadn't even been there!

Humiliation closed around her throat like a fist. She had been so sure that he was watching her—he *had* been at first!—and now the idea that he had got bored and gone off while she'd been still desperately performing for his benefit made her feel an idiot. No, worse than an idiot. *Pathetic*.

Close to tears, Alice slipped unnoticed along the side of the house and ducked beneath an arch laden with a magnificent display of bougainvillaea that divided the perfectly mani-cured front garden from a shady and scrubby patch of ground at the back behind the kitchen and servants' quarters.

Beth had a maid to help with the housework, a smiling woman called Chantelle, and this was her domain. There were wooden steps leading down from the kitchen verandah where she would sit sometimes, her fingers busy with some mindless task while she sang quietly to herself. Alice wouldn't normally have intruded, but Chantelle, she knew, was busy clearing up after the barbecue lunch, and Alice didn't think she would mind if she sat there for a little while on her own.

The garden here was blissfully shady and overgrown, so dark that Alice was almost at the steps before she realised that she was not the only person needing some time alone. A little girl was sitting on the bottom step, half-hidden in the shadow of a banana tree. Her knees were drawn up to her chin, and she hugged them to her, keeping very still as she watched a butterfly with improbably large iridescent blue wings come to rest on her shoe.

Alice stopped as soon as she saw them, but the butterfly had already taken off and was flapping languidly in and out of the patches of sunlight. The child spotted her at the same time, and she seemed to freeze. Alice was reminded of a small, wary animal trying to make up its mind whether to bolt for cover or not.

She was sorry that she had interrupted, but it seemed rude to turn on her heel and walk off without saying anything. Besides, there was something very familiar about the scene. Alice couldn't work out what it was at first, but then she realised that the little girl reminded her of herself as a lonely, uncertain child.

'I'm sorry, I didn't mean to disturb you, or the butterfly. I was just looking for somewhere quiet to sit for a while.' She paused, but the little girl just looked guardedly at her, still poised for flight.

She wasn't a particularly pretty child. She had straight, shapeless hair and a pinched little face dominated by a pair of huge, solemn dark eyes. Her expression was distrustful, but Alice was conscious of a pang of fellow feeling.

How many times had she slipped off to find a place to hide while she'd waited for her parents to take her back to wherever they were calling home at the time? This child's parents were probably having a great time by the pool, totally oblivious to the fact that their daughter had slipped away, intimidated by the other children who were noisy and boisterous and seemed to be able to make friends without even trying.

'I wanted to escape from the party for a bit,' Alice explained. 'It's too noisy and I didn't know anyone to talk to properly. Is that what you did?' she asked as the girl glanced sharply at her.

The child nodded.

'The thing is, I don't want to go back yet,' said Alice. 'And I can't think of anywhere else to hide. Do you mind if I sit next to you, just for a little while? I won't talk if you don't want to. I hate it when people talk to me when I'm trying to be quiet.'

There was a flash of recognition in the girl's watchful eyes, and, while she didn't exactly agree, she didn't say no either, and as Alice went over she shifted along the step to make room for her. Encouraged, Alice settled next to her, drawing her knees up to mirror the child's posture.

A strangely companionable silence settled round them. In the distance, Alice could hear the buzz of party conversation, punctuated by the occasional burst of laughter, and the squeals and shrieks and splashes from the pool, but they seemed to be coming from a long way away, far from the dark, drowsy green world of the kitchen garden where there was only the squawk of a passing raucous bird and the low-level hum of insects to break the hot quiet.

She was glad of the chance to settle her nerves. Meeting Will again had left her jangled and distressed, and it was hard to disentangle her feelings about him from all the hurt and confusion she had felt since Tony had left. Between them, they had left her feeling utterly wretched.

If only she could rewind time and do things differently, this afternoon at least, Alice thought miserably. Seeing Will hadn't been at all the way she had imagined. *He* wasn't the man she had imagined him to be. If she had become brittle and superficial, he had grown hard and bitter. The young man with the humorous eyes and the reassuring steadiness had gone for good. Now that she knew what he had become, she couldn't even dream of him the way he had been.

The realisation that the Will she had loved was lost for ever felt like a bereavement. Alice's throat worked, and she pressed her lips hard together to stop herself crying.

There was no point in this, she told herself. She was upset because it was Tony's wedding day, but that was no excuse. She had behaved badly. She had been defensive and unsympathetic and rude. No wonder Will hadn't liked her. Now he had obviously left the party without saying goodbye, and she might not have another chance to say that she was sorry.

It was no use trying to tell herself that she didn't care. Here in the quiet garden with her restful companion she could acknowledge that she did.

'There's the butterfly again.' The little girl broke the silence in hushed tones, and they both sat very still as the butterfly alighted on an upturned bucket. It was so big that it seemed almost clumsy, its wings so heavy that it blundered from perch to perch, flapping slowly through the hot air as if barely able to keep itself aloft.

The child's eyes were huge as she watched it. 'I've never seen such a big butterfly before!'

She obviously hadn't been on the island that long, Alice reflected, although she could probably have told that anyway from her pale skin.

'When I was a little girl I lived in Guyana,' Alice said. 'That's in South America, and it was hot and humid, like this. Our house was on the edge of the jungle, and the garden was full of butterflies—blue ones and green ones and yellow ones, and butterflies with stripes and spots and weird patterns. Some of them were enormous.'

'Bigger than that one?'

'Much bigger.' Alice spread out her fingers to demonstrate the wing span. 'Like this.'

The girl's eyes widened further as she looked from the butterfly to Alice's hand and back again, clearly trying to imagine a garden full of such creatures.

'It must have been pretty,' she commented.

'They were beautiful,' Alice remembered almost in surprise. Funny, she hadn't thought about the garden in Guyana for years. 'I used to sit on the verandah steps, just like we're doing now, and watch them for hours.'

The little girl looked solemn. 'Didn't you have any friends?'

'Not then,' said Alice. 'It was very isolated where we lived, and I didn't know many other children. I used to pretend that the butterflies were my friends.'

How odd to remember that now, after all these years! She smiled, not unkindly, at her younger self.

'I imagined that they were fairies in disguise,' she confided to her small companion. It was strange how she felt more comfortable sitting here with the child than she had in the thick of a party thrown especially for her. Alice had never been a particularly maternal type, but she felt a strong sense of affinity with this quiet, plain little girl with her dark, wary eyes.

'Fairies?' the child breathed, riveted.

'At night I thought their beautiful wings would turn into silk robes and gorgeously coloured dresses.' Somehow it didn't sound silly in this dark, tropical garden. 'You know the sound the insects make when it's dark here?'

The girl nodded but her mouth turned down slightly. 'I don't like it. It's loud.'

'It was loud in Guyana, too,' said Alice. 'I used to think it was frightening, and then my father told me one night that it was just the sound of all the insects having a great party!'

Her father had been good at nonsense like that. He'd told the young Alice extravagant stories, embellishing them until they were more and more absurd, and she had struggled to know how much to believe. She ought to remember the good times more often, Alice thought with a sudden pang. It wasn't often that she thought of her childhood with affection, but it hadn't been all bad.

'So after that, whenever I couldn't sleep because it was too hot, I'd lie there listening to the noise and imagine the butterflies talking and laughing and dancing all night.'

She laughed softly, but the little girl looked struck. 'I was a bit frightened by the noise too,' she confessed. 'But now I'll think about them having a party like you said, and it won't seem so strange.'

'You'll soon get used to it,' Alice reassured her, and then nudged her, pointing silently as the butterfly came lumbering through the air towards them again. They both held their breath as it came closer and closer, fluttering indecisively for what seemed like ages before it settled at last on Alice's foot.

The child's eyes widened in delight as she noticed for the first time that Alice's shoes were decorated with tiny fabric butterflies, their beads and sequins catching the light, and she put a hand to her mouth to smother a giggle.

'He likes your shoes,' she whispered. 'Do you think he knows those butterflies aren't real?'

Alice considered. 'I'm not sure. Probably not. He doesn't look like a very clever butterfly, does he?'

A laugh escaped through the rather grubby little fingers, rousing the butterfly to flight once more, but Alice didn't mind. It was such a pleasure to see the small, serious face lighten with a real smile. She guessed it didn't happen very often and her heart constricted with a kind of pity. A little girl like this should be laughing and smiling all the time.

'I like your shoes,' she said to Alice, who stretched out her legs so that they could both admire them.

'*I* like them too,' she agreed. 'But somebody told me today that they were silly.' Her face darkened as she remembered Will's comment.

'I don't think they're stupid. I think they're really nice.'

'Well, thank you.' Alice was ridiculously heartened by her approval. She peered down at the small feet next to her. 'What are yours like?'

'They're just shoes,' the child said without enthusiasm.

Alice could see what she meant. She was wearing sturdy

leather sandals which were perfectly practical but lacked any sense of fun or fashion.

'When I was little I wanted a pair of pink shoes,' she said sympathetically. 'I asked my parents for years, but I never got them.'

'I'd like pink shoes too, but my dad says these are more sensible.' The little girl sighed.

'Dads don't understand about shoes,' Alice told her. 'Very few men do. But, when you grow up, you'll be able to buy any shoes you want. I bought a pair of lovely pink shoes as soon as I was earning my own money. Now I've got lots of shoes in different colours. Some of them are lots of fun. I've got shoes with polka dots and zebra stripes,' she said, illustrating the patterns by drawing in the air. 'Some of them have got sequins, or bows, or fancy jewels or—'

'*Jewels?*' she interrupted, starry-eyed. 'Real ones?'

'Well, no, not *exactly*,' Alice had to admit. 'But they look fabulous!'

The child heaved an envious sigh. 'I wish I could see them.'

Alice opened her mouth to offer a view of the collection she had brought with her, but before she could ask the little girl her name a voice behind them made them both jump.

'Lily?'

Will stepped out of the kitchen onto the wooden verandah, letting the screen door bang into place behind him. He had been looking for his daughter everywhere.

Unable to bear the sight of Alice flirting any longer, he had been avoiding the front lawn, and had endured instead a tedious half-hour making small talk in the air-conditioned coolness of the living room. Only when he'd thought that he could reasonably make an excuse and leave had he realised that Lily was not among the children around the pool where he had left her.

Since then he had been searching with rising panic, flaying

himself for ever taking his eyes off her in the first place, and now acute relief at finding her safe sharpened his voice.

'What do you think you're—'

He stopped abruptly as he reached the edge of the verandah and saw who was sitting at the bottom of the steps next to his daughter, both of them staring up at him with identically startled expressions.

'Alice!'

Will glared accusingly at her. If Alice hadn't annoyed him so much, he wouldn't have left the poolside, and he would have kept a closer eye on Lily. This was all her fault.

'What are *you* doing here?' he asked rudely. It was bad enough when he had imagined her out front, making a spectacle of herself with all those fawning men, but it was somehow worse to find her here with Lily, a witness to his inadequacies as a father.

Why did it have to be *her*? He wouldn't have minded finding anyone else with Lily, would even have been glad that his daughter had found a friend, but not Alice. She had been free enough with her opinion of him as a father earlier. There would be no stopping her now that she had met Lily. Alice would have taken one look at his quiet, withdrawn daughter and decided just how he was failing her, Will thought bleakly.

CHAPTER FOUR

ALICE took her time getting to her feet. Slowly brushing down the back of her dress, she wondered how best to deal with him. She didn't want to argue in front of Lily—how stupid of her not to have guessed who she was, but she didn't look anything like Will—but it was obvious that Will was still angry with her.

Obvious too that he hadn't liked finding her with his daughter. She just hoped he wouldn't think that she had done it deliberately.

'We were just talking about shoes,' she said carefully at last. 'We hadn't got round to introducing ourselves, had we?' she said to Lily, who had turned away from her father and was sitting hunched up, her fine hair swinging down to hide her face.

Lily shook her head mutely. With the appearance of her father, she had lost all her animation.

'I'm Alice,' said Alice, persevering. 'And you're…Lily? Is that right?'

Lily managed a nod, but she peeped a glance under her hair at Alice, who smiled encouragingly.

'Nice to meet you, Lily. Shall we shake hands? That's what people do when they meet each other for the first time.'

It felt like a huge victory when Lily held out her hand, and Alice shook it with determined cheerfulness. She wished she could tell Will to stop looming over his daughter. He looked so forbidding, no wonder Lily was subdued.

'What are you doing out here, Lily?' Will asked stiffly. 'Don't you want to play with the other children in the pool?'

Lily's face was closed. 'I like talking to Alice,' she said, without turning to look at him.

There was an uncomfortable silence. Alice looked from Will to his daughter and back again. He had told her that he was practically a stranger to his own child, but she hadn't appreciated until now just what that meant for the two of them. Will was awkward and uncertain, and Lily a solitary child still trying to come to terms with the loss of her mother. Neither knew how to make the connection they both needed so badly.

It wasn't her business. Will wanted her to leave him alone with his daughter, that much was clear. She should just walk away and let them sort it out themselves.

But when Alice looked at Lily's hunched shoulders, and remembered how she had laughed at the butterfly, she couldn't do it. Will didn't have to accept her help, but his little girl needed a friend.

'I liked talking to you, too,' she said to Lily. 'Maybe we can meet again?' She glanced at Will, trusting that he wouldn't jump on the offer before Lily had a chance to say what she wanted. 'Do you think your dad would let you come round to tea one day?'

'Can I see your shoes?' asked Lily, glancing up from under her hair.

'You can see some of them,' said Alice. 'I'm only here on holiday, so I didn't bring them all with me, but I've got some fun ones. The others are at home in London.'

Lily thought for a moment and then looked over her shoulder at her father. 'Can I?'

Most other little girls would have been jumping up and

down, swinging on their daddy's hand and cajoling him with smiles and dimples, supremely confident of their power to wrap their fathers round their perfect little fingers, but not Lily. She would ask his permission, but she wouldn't give him smiles and affection. Not yet, anyway.

A muscle worked in Will's jaw. He wished that he knew how to reach her. He knew how sad she was, how lost and lonely she must feel. If only he could find some way to break down the barrier she had erected around herself.

Torn, he watched her stiff back helplessly. He wanted to give Lily whatever she wanted, but Alice and her shoes and her talk about London would only remind her of her mother and her life in England, and she would be unsettled all over again. Surely that was the last thing she needed right now?

He was still hesitating when Beth burst through the screen door with her customary exuberance. 'Will?' she called. 'Are you out here? Did you—' She stopped as she caught sight of the three of them. 'Oh, good, you've found her—and Alice too!'

Belatedly sensing a certain tension in the air, she looked from one to the other. 'I'm not interrupting anything, am I?'

'Of course not.' Alice forced a smile. 'I was just inviting Lily round for tea one day.'

'What a lovely idea!' Beth clapped her hands together and beamed at Will. 'Come tomorrow!'

Will could feel himself being swept along by the force of her enthusiasm and tried to dig in his heels before it all got out of hand. 'I'm sure you'll have had enough visitors by then,' he temporised while he thought up a better excuse.

'Nonsense,' said Beth briskly. 'I've hardly had a chance to talk to anyone today. You know what it's like at a party. You're always saying hello or goodbye or making sure everyone's got a drink. It would be lovely to see you and Lily tomorrow. Otherwise it'll all feel like an awful anticlimax, and we'll get scratchy with each other. At least, if you come, Roger and Alice will have to behave.' She laughed merrily. 'It's not as if you'll be working on a Sunday, is it?'

'No,' Will had to admit.

'And Lily needs to make friends for when you're not there,' Beth reminded him.

'I've brought a nanny out from England,' said Will, irritated by the implication that he hadn't given any thought to child-care arrangements. What did they think? That he was planning to go off to work and leave Lily alone in the house every day?

'Oh, you should have brought her along today.' Beth was blithely unaware of his exasperation, but Alice was keeping a carefully neutral expression, Will noticed. She would know exactly how he was feeling.

'It's her day off,' he said, forcing a more pleasant note into his voice. It wasn't Beth's fault that Alice was able to unsettle him just by standing there and saying nothing. 'She wanted to go snorkelling.'

'Well, bring her tomorrow,' Beth instructed. 'Then she'll know where we are, and she and Lily can come again when you're at work.'

Will glanced back at Lily. She had lifted her head and was watching the adults talking. Her face was brighter than he had seen it, he thought, and his heart twisted.

I like talking to Alice, she had said. He couldn't refuse her just because he remembered talking to Alice himself. And what would be the harm, after all? He didn't have to have anything to do with Alice. He could just have tea and then let Dee take over the social side of things.

'All right,' he succumbed, and was rewarded by a flash of something close to gratitude in Lily's eyes. 'Thank you, we'd like to come.'

* * *

Alice disliked Dee, Lily's nanny, on sight. What had Will been thinking of, hiring someone quite so young and silly to look after his daughter? Or had he been thinking more about what a pretty girl she was? How long her legs were, how sparkling her blue eyes, how soft the blonde hair she tossed back from her face as she giggled?

Lily was subdued, and Will positively morose, but Dee made up for both of them with her inane chatter—and he had called *her* superficial! Alice listened in disbelief as Dee rambled on about her family and her friends, and what a good time she had had learning how to snorkel the day before.

As far as Alice could tell, she had absolutely nothing in common with Will or Lily. It was hard to imagine anyone less suited to dealing with a quiet, withdrawn child, she thought disapprovingly. Still, if Dee's particular brand of silliness was what Will wanted to come home to in the evening, that was his business. She was only thinking about Lily.

Unable to bear Dee's inanities any longer, Alice leant over to Lily. 'Would you like to come and see my shoes?' she whispered as Dee talked on, and Lily nodded. She took the hand Alice held out quite willingly and trotted beside her to the bedroom, where a selection of Alice's favourite shoes had been spread out on the bed.

'Which ones do you like best?' Alice asked, after Lily had examined them all seriously.

After much thought, Lily selected pair of black high heels with peep toes and floppy bows covered in polka dots.

'Good choice,' said Alice approvingly. 'They're my favourites too. Why don't you try them on?' she added, and watched as Lily slipped her small feet into the shoes and turned to look at herself in the mirror.

'Wait!' Alice rummaged in a drawer and pulled out a diaphanous sarong. Tying it round the little girl, she draped some pearls over her and added her favourite straw hat with its wide brim. 'There!'

She stood back to admire the effect, delighted by the look on Lily's face as she studied her reflection. The sullen expression was gone and, animated, the piquant face looked positively pretty beneath the hat.

Will would like to see her like this, Alice thought. 'Let's show the others,' she suggested casually.

Biting her lip as she concentrated on her balance, Lily teetered down the corridor. 'May I introduce Miss Lily Paxman?' Alice announced grandly as she flung open the door.

There was a chorus of oohs and aahs, and a broad smile spread across Lily's face. Alice happened to glance at Will just then, and the expression in his eyes as he watched his daughter smile brought a lump to her throat. She would never be able to accuse Will of not caring about Lily now.

Feeling as if she had intruded on a very private moment, she looked away and caught Roger's eye.

'OK?' he mouthed.

Alice nodded and went over to stand next to him, leaving Beth and Dee exclaiming over Lily. Dee, in particular, was going completely over the top with her compliments. Probably trying to impress Will, Alice thought sourly. Too bad Dee didn't know that Will didn't go in for gushing sentimentality.

At least, he never used to. He had changed so much that for all Alice knew sweet, fluffy women were just his type nowadays. He certainly didn't have much time for sharp, astringent ones, that was for sure.

Without quite being aware of it, Alice sighed.

'What's the matter?' asked Roger.

'Oh…nothing.'

Not wanting to look at Will, Alice watched Beth instead.

'She's fantastic with kids, isn't she?' she said, and Roger's smile twisted as his eyes rested on his wife.

'She loves children.'

Roger and Beth had never talked much about their inability to conceive, but Alice knew how much having a baby would mean to both of them. She tucked her hand through Roger's arm and leant against him, offering wordless comfort. 'It must be hard for her at times like this,' she said quietly. 'For you, too.'

'It's just that you can't help imagining what it would be like if it was your own child dressing up ...' Roger trailed off, and Alice hugged his arm closer in silent sympathy. He and Beth were both so easy-going and good-humoured that it was easy to forget that they had their own problems to deal with.

On the other side of the room, Will watched Alice standing close to Roger and frowned. Only a moment ago he had been feeling grateful to her. Lily's smile might not have been meant just for him, but still it had warmed his heart, and it was down to Alice, he knew. She had been able to connect with his daughter in a way that eluded him.

But, when he looked at her to try and indicate his gratitude somehow, he saw that she wasn't even aware of Lily any more. Instead she was leaning against Roger, her arm tucked through his and her head on his shoulder. It was a very intimate pose.

Too intimate for a man whose wife was only a few feet away.

Will glanced at Beth, who was smiling at Lily as she adjusted her hat. She seemed unaware of Roger and Alice over by the window, but Will had noticed a fleeting expression of sadness in her face more than once now, and he wondered how much Beth knew, or guessed, about her husband's feelings for Alice.

It was a long time since he and Roger had shared that drunken evening, but Will had never forgotten the look in Roger's eyes as he confessed the truth. He couldn't remember where Alice had been, but Roger had just split up with yet another girlfriend, and Will had been deputed to help him drown his sorrows and provide a shoulder to cry on.

'I don't want him to be alone,' Alice had said. She'd always been very protective of Roger, which was ironic in its own way, Will reflected.

It had been very late and very dark when Will had helped a reeling Roger home at last. He had never known if Roger had meant to tell him that all the other girls were just an attempt to disguise how he felt about Alice, or if the next day he had even remembered the truth he had blurted out. Neither of them had ever mentioned it again, but Will couldn't shake the memory of the bleakness in Roger's face.

'I'm just her friend,' he had said, slurring his words. 'I'll only ever be her friend.'

Had Roger decided to settle for second best with Beth? Will hoped not. He liked Roger's wife. She deserved better than that.

What was Alice doing, snuggled up to Roger like that? Will scowled. Did she know how Roger felt about her? Had she guessed?

'I'm looking for Mr Right,' she had told him with that bright, brittle smile he hated. Easy to see how Roger might fill that role for her. He was kind, loyal, funny, the rock Alice had fallen back on more than once. It wouldn't be hard to imagine the scales falling from her eyes as friendship turned to love...

But Alice wouldn't do that to Beth, would she? Will's frown deepened. The old Alice would never do anything to hurt her friends, but what did he know of her now? The old Alice wouldn't have stood that close to Roger, either.

She would have been standing close to *him*, leaning against him, touching him.

Will pushed the thought aside and got abruptly to his feet. 'It think it's time we went,' he said.

'What did you think of Dee?' Beth asked Alice when Will had chivvied a disappointed Lily and Dee out to the car.

'Not much,' said Alice, unimpressed. She felt oddly disgruntled. It wasn't that she had wanted to see Will, but he could have stayed a bit longer instead of rushing them off like that. It wasn't very fair on Lily. 'She tries too hard. You can tell she's desperate to impress Will.'

Beth looked at her strangely. 'You can?'

'Well, it's a classic, isn't it?' Alice sniffed. 'Child, nanny, single father...alone together on a tropical island... Of *course* she's going to fall for him!'

'It's interesting you should say that,' said Beth. 'I wouldn't have said that she was the slightest bit interested in Will. He's too old for her.'

'Old?' repeated Alice, outraged. 'He's not *old*! He's only thirty-five!'

'I expect that seems old to Dee,' said Beth, choosing not to comment on how well Alice remembered Will's age. 'She can't be much more than twenty. I'd say she was much more impressed by that hunk who taught her how to snorkel yesterday. Didn't you hear her going on about him?'

'No.' Alice frowned. She wasn't as openly friendly as Beth, and had frankly tuned out most of Dee's prattling. She wasn't quite ready to believe that Dee had no interest in Will, either. He might be a bit older, but Dee could hardly have failed to notice that he was an attractive man—any more than Will would have missed the fact that she was young and very pretty. One could accuse Will of being lots of things, but unobservant wasn't one of them.

'I don't know how Will could possibly have thought she would make a suitable nanny,' she said crossly.

Beth laughed. 'Nannies aren't buxom old ladies in mob caps any more, you know! Dee is young and friendly and enthusiastic. I expect Will thought she would be fun for Lily to have around.'

'Or fun for *him* to have around?' suggested Alice, her voice laced with vinegar. 'You're not going to tell me he didn't clock those long legs and that body when he interviewed her?'

'She's certainly a very pretty girl,' Beth agreed equably. 'But it wasn't Dee he was watching today, and it wasn't Dee he couldn't take his eyes off yesterday.'

Alice, who had prowling restlessly around the room, stopped and stared at Beth, who smiled blandly back.

'I don't think you need to worry about Dee,' she said.

'I'm not worried about Dee,' snapped Alice, severely ruffled. 'Will can do what he likes. *I* don't care. We don't even like each other any more.'

'Ah.' Beth nodded understandingly. 'Right. That'll be why you both spent the entire time watching each other when you thought the other one wasn't looking.' She paused. 'I think there's still a real connection between you.'

Alice flushed. 'There's no connection,' she insisted. 'Not any more.'

And there wasn't, she reminded herself repeatedly over the next few days. Will had hardly spoken to her at the tea, and she certainly hadn't been aware of him watching her. Whenever she'd happened to glance at him—and it wasn't that often, no matter what Beth had said—he'd seemed intent on talking to Roger or Beth, or watching Lily and Dee. If he'd even noticed that *she* was in the room, he'd hidden it extremely well, she thought grouchily.

There certainly hadn't been any opportunity for her to tell him that she was sorry for her tactless comments at the party.

Not that Will would care whether she apologised or not. He had made it very clear how he felt about her now. Beth's idea of a connection between them was ludicrous, Alice thought more than once over the next week, refusing each time to consider why the realisation should make her feel so bleak. Any sense of connectedness that had once existed between her and Will had been broken long ago, and there was no hope of repairing it now.

And she wouldn't want to, even if it had been possible, Alice reminded herself firmly. She hadn't been lying when she had told Will that this time in St Bonaventure was her chance to think about what she really wanted out of life. Redundancy and Tony's rejection had brought her to a crossroads, and, if the last miserable few months had taught her anything, it was that she needed to look forward, not back.

There was no point in hankering after the past or what had been. Of all the options that lay open to her now, the one route she wouldn't take was the one she had already travelled. She had to make her own future, and that certainly didn't include resurrecting old relationships that had been doomed in the first place.

No, she was going to have a good time while she was here, Alice decided, and then she was going to go home and rebuild her life so that it was bigger and better than before. She would get herself a really good job. She might even sell her flat, and make a fresh start somewhere new where memories weren't lurking behind every door, waiting to ambush her when her resistance was low.

And she would do it all by herself. She wasn't going to rely on anyone else to make her happy this time. The only way to be sure was to do it alone.

In spite of all her resolutions, Alice found her mind wandering to Will uncomfortably often over the next few days. Having been catapulted back into her life without warning, Will had disappeared again so completely, it left Alice feeling mildly disorientated.

Had that really been Will standing there, after all these

years? Sometimes she wondered if she had dreamt the entire episode, but she knew that she hadn't made up Lily. That guarded little face with the clouded dark eyes were all too vivid in her memory. Alice hoped that she was adjusting to her new life and learning to trust Will. She kept thinking about the look in his eyes when he had seen his daughter smiling, and every time it brought a lump to her throat.

She would have liked to be able to help them understand each other, but then she would remind herself that they didn't need her help. They had Dee, and no doubt they were already well on the way to being a happy little family.

Alice imagined Will going home every night to Dee, who would already know how he liked his tea—strong and black. By now she would know that he hated eggs, and his gestures would be becoming familiar to her. She would recognize how he rubbed his hand over his face when he was tired, how amusement would light the grey eyes and lift the corner of his mouth.

Oh, yes, Lily and Will would be fine without Alice. They didn't need her when they had Dee.

Which left her free to enjoy her holiday.

She should have been delighted at the prospect, but instead Alice felt scratchy and increasingly restless as the days passed. She had longed and longed for a few weeks doing absolutely nothing in the sunshine, but the truth was that she was getting a bit bored of sitting by the pool all day.

Beth had a full social agenda, and Alice was included in all the invitations, but there were only so many coffee mornings and lunches at the club that she could take. All that gossip and moaning about maids, school fees, how hard it was to get bacon or a decent gin and tonic! Beth was so open and friendly that she was welcome anywhere, but Alice knew that her own brand of acerbity went down rather less well.

In spite of having grown up overseas, she had never come

across the expat lifestyle like this before. Her parents would never have dreamed of joining a club with other expatriates. They didn't care about air-conditioning or supermarkets, and chose to live in remote tribal villages where they could be 'close to the people', a phrase that still made Alice nearly as uncomfortable as a lunch with some of Beth's fellow wives.

Why was it she never seemed to fit in anywhere? Alice wondered glumly. All she had ever wanted was to belong somewhere, but the only place she felt really at home was work. At least this break had taught her one thing, and that was how important her career was to her. Will might think her superficial, but at least she was prepared to go out and do a proper job, not sit around smiling all day like Dee.

'Are you sure you don't want to come?' Roger asked her the following Sunday. He and Beth were off to yet another barbecue, where they would meet all the people who had come to their barbecue the previous weekend, and Alice had opted out. 'Will might be there. They're bound to have invited everybody.'

If Will had wanted to see her, he knew where she lived. Alice had spent far too much of the week wondering if he would think about dropping round some time, and she was thoroughly disgusted with herself for being disappointed when he hadn't. She certainly wasn't about to go chasing after him at some party now!

'I don't think so, thanks,' she said, ultra-casual. She could hardly change her mind just because Roger had mentioned Will. What a giveaway *that* would be! 'I'll just stay here and finish my book.'

But, when Roger and Beth had gone, Alice sat with her book unopened on her lap and wished perversely that she had let herself be persuaded. After all, Will could hardly suspect her of chasing him if she just happened to bump into

him at party, could he? She would have been able to see
how he—how *Lily*, Alice corrected herself quickly—was
getting on.

Then, of course, Dee might be at the party too. What could
be more natural for Will to take her along since they were all
living together? Did she *really* want to see that they were all
getting along absolutely fine?

No, Alice acknowledged to herself, she couldn't honestly say
that she did. Much better not to know. She was better off here.

Determinedly, she opened her book, but it was impossible
to concentrate when all the time she was wondering if Roger
and Beth had bumped into Will at the party, and, if they had,
whether he would notice that she wasn't there. Would he ask
where she was? Would he miss her?

'Oh, for heaven's sake!' Alice slammed her book shut,
furious with herself. Will didn't even like her now. *Remember
that little fact, Alice?* Why on earth would he miss her?

And why was she wasting her time even *thinking* about him?

When the doorbell went, she was so glad of the interruption that she leapt to her feet. It was Chantelle's day off, and
she hurried to the door, not caring who it was as long as they
distracted her from her muddled thoughts for a while.

Flinging open the door, she smiled a welcome, only to
find the smile wiped from her face in shock as she saw who
was standing there.

It was Will, with Lily a small silent figure beside him. The
last people she had expected to see. The sight of them
punched the breath from Alice's lungs, and, winded, she hung
onto the door.

'Oh,' she said weakly. 'It's you.' She struggled to get some
oxygen into her lungs but her voice still sounded thin and
reedy. 'Hi…hello, Lily.'

''Lo,' Lily muttered in response.

Will cleared his throat. He looked as startled to see Alice as she was to see him, which was a bit odd given that he knew perfectly well that she was living there. 'Is Beth around?'

'No, she and Roger have gone to a party.' Alice had herself under better control now. It had just been the surprise. 'At the Normans, I think.'

'Damn, I'd forgotten about that …'

Will raked a hand through his hair and tried to concentrate on the matter in hand and not on how Alice had looked, opening the door, her face alight with a smile. Her hair swept back into its usual messy but stylish clip, and she was wearing loose trousers and a cool, sleeveless top. Her feet were thrust into spangled flip flops, and she looked much more relaxed than she had done at the party.

Much more herself.

'Is there a problem?' she asked.

He hesitated only for a moment. 'Yes,' he said baldly. Alice might be the last person he wanted to ask for help, especially under these circumstances, but he didn't have a lot of choice here. Too bad if she gave him a hard time about neglecting Lily. He had survived worse.

'There's been an accident on the project,' he said, his voice swift and decisive now that his mind was made up. 'I don't have many details yet, and I don't know how bad it is, but I need to go and see what's happened and if anyone's hurt. I can't take Lily with me until I know it's safe.'

'Where's Dee?' asked Alice, going straight to the heart of the problem as was her wont.

'She left yesterday.'

'Left?'

'She met some guy at the diving school last weekend.' Will wondered if he looked as frazzled as he felt. Probably, judging by Alice's expression. 'She's known him less than a week, but when he told her he was going back to Australia she decided to go with him.' He tried to keep his voice neutral, because he was afraid that if he let his anger and frustration show he wouldn't be able to control it.

Alice opened her mouth to ask how on earth that had happened, and then closed it again abruptly. Will was worried about Lily, worried about the accident. He didn't need her exclaiming and asking questions.

'Perhaps Lily could stay with me,' she said instead. 'You wouldn't mind keeping me company this afternoon, would you, Lily?'

Lily shook her head and, when Alice held out her hand, she took it after only a momentary hesitation.

'You go on,' Alice said to Will. 'I'll look after her until you get back.'

Astonished and relieved at her lack of fuss, Will could only thank her. He turned to go, but as he did he saw Alice nod imperceptibly down at his daughter. God, he'd almost forgotten to say goodbye! What kind of father did that make him?

'Goodbye, Lily,' he said awkwardly. If only he could be sure that if he crouched down and hugged her she would hug him back. 'Be good.' She was always good, though. That was the problem. 'I'll be back as soon as I can.'

Alice had to be one of the few people who knew less about parenting than he did, he thought bitterly as he reversed the car out of the drive and headed towards the project headquarters as fast as he could, but she was still able to make him realise how badly he was getting it wrong.

Alice, still able to wrong-foot him after all these years. Will shook his head. He had been waiting for her to take him to task for putting the project before his own child. He couldn't have blamed her if she'd pointed out that it was his fault for employing a silly girl like Dee who would run off and leave him in the lurch after barely more than a week as a nanny. She could have criticised him for not even thinking to say goodbye to Lily.

But she had done none of those things. She had recognized the problem and done exactly what he needed her to do. He would have to try and tell her later how much he appreciated it.

CHAPTER FIVE

'LILY'S asleep,' said Alice, opening the door to him nearly four hours later and motioning Will inside.

'Asleep?' He was instantly anxious. 'Is she OK?'

'Of course. She's just tired, and she dropped off a few minutes ago. It seems a shame to wake her just yet. Why don't you sit down and have a drink?' Her polite façade vanished as she watched Will drop into a chair. 'You look tired,' she added impulsively.

Will rubbed a hand over his face in a gesture so familiar that Alice felt a sharp pang of remembrance. 'I'm OK,' he said gruffly, but he was glad to sit down, he had to admit. The room was cool and quiet after the chaos at the hospital. 'Thanks,' he said as Alice came back with one of Roger's beers, and he drank thirstily.

'Was it a bad accident?' Alice asked. She sat on the end of the sofa, far enough away to be in no danger of touching him by accident, but not so far that it looked as if she was nervous about being alone with him.

'Bad enough.' Will lowered the bottle with a sigh. 'A couple of our younger members of staff had taken one of the project jeeps to the beach. It's their day off, and they had a few beers...you know what it's like. They're not supposed to take any of the vehicles unless they're on project business, but they're just lads.'

He grimaced, remembering the calls he had had to make to the boys' parents after he'd contacted the insurance company. 'Perhaps it's just as well they took one of our jeeps. It had our logo on the side, so when someone saw it had gone off the road they raised the alarm with the office, and the phone there gets switched through to me at weekends.'

'Are the boys OK?'

'They'll survive. They've both recovered consciousness, and the doctors say they're stable. The insurance company is making arrangements to fly them back to the UK, and the sooner that happens the better. The hospital here isn't equipped to deal with serious accidents.' He shook his head. Hospitals were grim enough places at the best of times.

'I'm glad I didn't have to take Lily there,' he said abruptly. 'I don't know how to thank you for looking after her, Alice.'

Alice avoided his eyes. 'It was no trouble,' she said with a careless shrug. 'Lily's good company.'

'Is she?' Will took another pull of his beer, unable to keep the bitterness from his voice. 'I can't get her to talk to me.'

'You need to give her time, Will. Everything's very new to her at the moment, and she's just lost her mother. You can't expect her to bounce back immediately.'

'I know, it's just…I don't know how to help her,' he admitted, the words wrenched out of him.

'You can help her best by being yourself. You're her father, and she knows that. Don't try too hard,' Alice told him. 'Let her get to know you.'

'Who made you such an expert on child care?' Will demanded roughly.

There was a tiny pause, and then, hearing the harshness of

his voice still echoing, he put down the beer and leant forward, resting his elbows on his knees and raking both hands through his hair. 'I'm sorry,' he said after a moment. 'That was uncalled for. Sorry.'

'You've got a lot on your mind at the moment,' said Alice after a moment.

'Still.' He straightened, and the grey eyes fixed on hers seemed to reach deep inside her and elicit a disturbing thrum. 'It's no excuse for rudeness.'

With an effort, Alice pulled her gaze away and reached for her lime juice with a hand that was not nearly as steady as she would have liked it to be.

'You're right, I don't know much about children,' she said. 'But Lily reminds me a lot of myself when I was younger. I was shy, the way she is, and I know what it's like—oh, not to lose my mother—but that feeling of not really knowing where you are or what you're doing there …' The golden eyes clouded briefly. 'Yes, I remember all that.'

'Is that why you were so angry with me at the party?'

Alice flushed. 'Partly. I shouldn't have said what I did, Will. I'm sorry, I was out of order. It wasn't any of my business.'

'No, you were right. I overreacted, mainly because you'd put your finger on all the things I felt most guilty and unsure about.' He smiled briefly. 'So it looks as if neither of us behaved quite as well as we might have done.'

He paused, his eyes on Alice, who had tucked her feet up beneath her and was curled into the corner of the sofa.

'What was the other reason?' he asked.

'Reason?' she said blankly.

'You said that was "partly" the reason you were angry,' he reminded her.

'Oh…' The colour deepened in Alice's cheeks, and she fiddled with the piping on the arm of the sofa. 'It's stupid, but

I suppose it was meeting you again after all this time. I was nervous,' she confessed.

'Me too,' said Will, and her eyes flew to his in disbelief.

'Really?'

He lifted his shoulders in acknowledgement. 'You were the last person I expected to see,' he told her with a rueful smile. 'I was completely thrown.'

'Oh,' said Alice with an embarrassed little laugh. 'Well… I'm glad it wasn't just me.'

'No.'

An awkward silence fell, and stretched at last into something that threatened to become even more difficult. Will drank his beer. Alice traced an invisible pattern on the arm of the sofa and kept her eyes lowered, but beneath her lashes her eyes kept sliding towards the fingers curled casually around that brown bottle.

Those fingers had once curved around her breast. They had drifted over her skin, stroking and smoothing and seeking. They had explored every inch of her, and late at night, when they had been intertwined with her own, she had felt safe in a way she never had before or since.

Alice's throat was dry, and that little thrum inside her was growing stronger and warmer, spreading treacherously along her veins and trembling at the base of her spine.

She reached forward for her glass with something like desperation. She shouldn't be remembering Will touching her, kissing her, loving her. They weren't the same people they had been then. Will was a father, and had more on his mind right now than remembering how the mere touch of his hands had been enough to melt her bones and reduce her to gasping, arching delight.

Sipping her lime juice, she sought frantically for something to say, but in the end it was Will who broke the silence.

'Roger and Beth still out?'

The question sounded too hearty to be natural, but Alice fell on it like a lifeline.

'Yes,' she said breathlessly. 'You know what party animals they are.'

'Why didn't you go?' Will asked her.

'I didn't feel like it.'

She didn't quite meet his eyes as she adjusted her hair clip. Telling him how she had dithered over the possibility of meeting him again wouldn't help. The atmosphere was taut enough as it was, even though they were both labouring to keep the conversation innocuous.

'I've spent all week going to coffee mornings and lunches, and we've been out to supper twice, and every time you meet the same people,' she said. 'To be honest, I had a much better time with Lily this afternoon.'

Will had finished his beer, and he looked around for a mat to put the bottle down on. 'What did you do with her?'

'Oh, you know...we just pottered around.'

'No, I really want to know,' he said. 'I'm going to have to spend more time with Lily, and it would help if I knew what she liked doing.'

'Well, she's very observant,' said Alice, glad to have moved the conversation into less fraught channels. 'And she's interested in things. We spent some time wandering around the garden, and she was full of questions, most of which I couldn't answer, like why the butterflies here are so colourful and why don't bananas grow in England... I think you'll make a scientist of her yet!'

Will's expression relaxed slightly. 'It's reassuring to know that she'll ask questions like that. She's always so quiet when she's with me.'

'She's not a chatterbox,' Alice agreed. 'But she'll talk if

she's got something to say. She got quite animated going through my wardrobe. She loves dressing up.'

'She gets that from her mother.' Will sounded faintly disapproving. 'Nikki was a great one for clothes. Her appearance was always very important to her.'

'Appearance is important to a lot of us,' said Alice, sensing the unspoken criticism in his comment. 'It doesn't always mean that you're superficial,' she added with a slight barb, remembering how his jibe at the party had stung.

'No, I suppose not,' said Will, although he didn't sound convinced, and Alice noticed darkly that he didn't take the opportunity of apologising for calling her superficial.

'It's perfectly normal for Lily to like dressing up,' she said with some tartness. 'Most little girls do. It doesn't mean she's condemned to life as an empty-headed bimbo! Some of us manage to dress well *and* hold down a demanding job.'

'You sound like Nikki,' he said, and from the bleak expression that washed across his face Alice gathered that it wasn't a compliment.

She longed to ask what Nikki had been like and what had gone wrong with their marriage, but it seemed inappropriate just then. Besides, she wasn't sure she wanted to know just how much she resembled Lily's mother.

'At least I stick at my jobs,' she pointed out with a slight edge. 'Unlike Dee.'

'Quite.' Will acknowledged the hit with a sigh. 'I should never have employed her, but she seemed so bright and lively that I thought she would be more fun for Lily to have around than some of the more experienced nannies. We obviously weren't fun enough for her, though,' he said, his mouth turning down at the memory of that dire week with Dee. 'She couldn't wait to go out as soon as I got home in the evening. I should have guessed she'd take the first chance to leave. I just didn't realise it would come quite so soon.'

'You couldn't have anticipated she'd throw up a good job to follow a guy she'd only known for a week,' said Alice, even as she wondered why she was trying to make him feel better.

Perhaps that was what superficial people did.

'If I'd been more experienced, I might have read the signs,' said Will. 'She was the only nanny the agency had on their books who could leave at such short notice, and now I know why!'

'What are you going to do now?'

Will put his arms above his head and tried to stretch out the tension in his shoulders. 'Get another nanny, I guess.' He leant back in his chair with a tired sigh. 'I'll have to get onto the agency tomorrow. I just haven't had a chance today.'

'It might take them some time to find someone suitable,' Alice pointed out. 'What happens in the meantime?'

'I'll just have to manage,' said Will, rubbing his face again. 'Lily's due to start school in a few weeks' time. I might be able to find someone locally who could help out until then, or maybe she could come to the project headquarters some days. It's not a very suitable place for a child, but I can hardly leave her on her own.'

'I'll look after her.'

The words were out of Alice's mouth before she had thought about them, and she was almost as startled by them as Will was. He sat bolt upright and stared at her.

'*You?*'

'Why not?' Some other person seemed to be controlling her speech. Was she really doing this? Arguing to look after Will's daughter for him? She must be mad! 'I managed this afternoon.'

'But …' Will looked totally thrown by her offer. Almost as thrown as Alice felt herself. 'You're on holiday,' he pointed out.

'I'm not suggesting I take on the job permanently. I'm just offering to help out until you can find a qualified nanny.'

'It's extraordinarily kind of you, Alice,' said Will slowly. 'But I couldn't possibly ask you to give up your holiday to look after Lily. You told me yourself that you were here for a complete break.'

'A break from routine is all I need.' Alice got to her feet and walked over to the sliding doors, trying to work out why it felt so important to persuade him.

'I thought I wanted to spend six weeks doing absolutely nothing,' she told him. 'When Beth told me about her life here, about the mornings by the pool, about the parties and the warmth and the sunshine, I was envious, jealous even.'

She remembered sitting at her desk, staring out at the rain and remembering Beth's bubbling enthusiasm. Tony hadn't been long gone, then, and she had still been at the stage of dreading going home to an empty flat.

'It was a bad time for me,' she told Will. She wasn't ready to tell him about Tony yet. 'The idea of just turning my face up to the sun and not thinking about anything for a while seemed wonderful, and when I got the chance to come I took it...'

'But?' Will prompted when she paused.

Alice turned back from the window to face him. 'But I'm bored,' she said honestly. 'It's different for Beth. She makes friends wherever she goes. She likes everybody, even if they're really dull, and she always sees the good side of people, but I'm ...'

'... not like that?' he suggested, a hint of amusement in his eyes, and he looked suddenly so much like the Will she remembered that Alice's heart bumped into her ribs and she forgot to breathe for a moment.

'No,' she agreed, hugging her arms together and drawing

a distinctly unsteady breath. 'You know what I'm like. I'm intolerant, and I get impatient and restless if I'm bored.'

'They don't sound like ideal characteristics for a nanny,' Will pointed out in a dry voice, and she made herself meet his eyes squarely and not notice that disconcertingly familiar glint.

'Lily doesn't bore me,' she said. 'I like her. She reminds me of me, and I'm never bored when I'm on my own. Besides, I'm not planning on being a nanny. If this week has taught me anything, it's how important my career is. I need to work, and if I can't work, I need to do *something*.

'I enjoyed spending this afternoon with Lily,' she told Will. 'I'd much rather spend the next few weeks with her than twitter away at endless coffee mornings.'

'If that's how you feel, why don't you just cut short your trip?'

'Because I can't change my ticket. It was one of those special deals which means you can't get any refund if you change your flight. And Roger and Beth would be hurt if I said I was bored and wanted to go home. They've gone to so much trouble to make me welcome,' Alice added guiltily.

'They might be hurt if you choose to spend the rest of your time with Lily,' Will commented.

'I don't think so. Not if we present it as me helping you out.' Alice hoped she wasn't sounding *too* desperate, but, the more she thought about it, the more she liked the idea.

'I love Roger and Beth,' she said carefully. 'Of course I do. No one could be kinder or more hospitable, but I'm used to being independent and having my own space, making my own decisions.

'When you're a guest, you just fit in with everyone else,' she tried to explain. 'And I'm finding that harder than I thought. It's as if I'm completely passive. I don't decide what we're going to do, or what we're going to eat, or where we're going to go. I just tag along. At least if I was looking after Lily I'd have some say in how we spent the day.'

'I certainly wouldn't try and dictate what you did,' said Will. 'You know what would keep Lily happy better than I do. I do have a cook but I expect she'd be happy to make whatever you felt like.'

By the window, Alice brightened. 'You mean you're going to accept my offer?'

Will studied her eager face, puzzled by her enthusiasm and disconcerted by the way her mask of careful composure kept slipping to reveal the old, vivid Alice beneath.

'I don't know …' he said slowly. 'It doesn't seem right somehow.'

'Is it because it's me?' she demanded. 'You wouldn't be hesitating if the agency had sent me out on a temporary assignment, would you?'

'Of course not. That would be a professional arrangement and I'd be paying you for your time.'

Alice shrugged. 'You can pay me if it makes you feel better, but it's not necessary. It's not as if I'm doing it for you, you know. I'd be doing it for me—and for Lily,' she added after a moment's thought.

Still, Will hesitated. Getting to his feet, he took a turn around the room, hands thrust into his pockets and shoulders hunched in thought. Finally he stopped in front of Alice.

'You don't think it would be a bit…difficult?' he asked. 'Living together again after all these years?'

'I'm not suggesting we sleep together,' said Alice, a distinct edge to her voice. 'Presumably Dee had her own room?'

'Of course.'

'Well, then.' She glanced at him and then away. 'It's different now, Will. What we had before is in the past. We agreed at the time that we would go our separate ways, and we have. There's no going back now.'

She was presenting it as something they had both decided together, but it hadn't been quite like that, not the way Will remembered it, anyway. It had been Alice who had wanted to end their relationship. 'Our lives are going in different directions,' she had said. 'Let's call it a day while we're still friends.'

'I think we both know that there's no point in trying to recreate what we had,' she was saying. 'I don't want that and neither do you, do you?'

'No,' said Will, after a moment. Well, what was he supposed to say—yes, I do? I do want that? I've never stopped wanting that?

That would have been a very foolish thing to say. He had tried to say it at Roger's wedding, and he wasn't putting himself through that again. He had enough problems at the moment without getting involved with Alice again. She was right; it was over.

'So what's the problem?' she asked him. 'It makes much more sense for you to have me living with you than some other woman who might fall in love with you and make things *really* awkward.'

It was her turn to pause while she tried to find the right words. 'We've both changed,' she said eventually. 'We're different people and we don't feel the same way about each other as we did then. We're never going to be lovers any more, but there's no reason why we couldn't learn to be friends, is there?'

Except that it was hard to be friends with someone whose taste you could remember exactly, thought Will. Someone whose body you had once known as well as your own, someone who'd been the very beat of your heart for so long.

With someone who'd made you happier than you had ever

been before. Someone who'd left your life empty and desolate when she had gone.

'It would only be for a few weeks,' Alice went on. 'And then I'd be gone. That wouldn't be too difficult, would it?'

'No,' said Will. 'We could do that for Lily.'

He had a feeling that it was going to be a lot harder than Alice made out, but it would be worth it for Lily. She liked Alice, that was clear, and Alice's presence would help her to settle down much more effectively than introducing yet another stranger into her life. He would just have to find his own way of dealing with living with Alice again.

And living without her once more when she had gone.

'All right,' he said, abruptly making up his mind. 'If you're sure, I expect Lily would love you to look after her until I can find a new nanny.'

He was glad that he had agreed when he saw Lily's face as the news was broken to her that Alice was going to stay with them for a while. She was never a demonstrative child, but there was no mistaking the way her dark eyes lit up with surprise and delight.

'You're going to live with us?'

'Just for a little while,' cautioned Alice. 'Until your dad can find you a new nanny.'

'Why can't you stay always?'

Will waited to see how Alice would handle that. It was a question he had wanted to ask her himself in the past. He had never understood why she had been so determined to end their relationship when they had been so good together. It was as if she had been convinced that everything would go wrong, but she hadn't been prepared to give it a chance to go right.

'Because I have to go home, Lily,' Alice told her. 'My life

is in London, not here. But until I do go back we'll have a lovely time together, shall we?'

Lily seemed to accept that. 'OK,' she said.

Alice was more nervous than she wanted to admit about how Beth would react to the news that she was moving out that night to live with Will and Lily. The last thing she wanted to do was to hurt Beth's feelings. But, once the situation about the missing nanny had been explained, Beth was very understanding, and even surprisingly enthusiastic about the idea.

'It sounds like the perfect solution,' she said, smiling, her gaze flickering with interest between Will and Alice. 'I'm sure you're doing the right thing.'

'I'm doing it for *Lily*,' said Alice pointedly. She didn't want Beth getting the wrong idea.

Beth opened her eyes wide. 'Of course,' she said. 'Why else?'

Roger was less convinced that it was a good idea. 'Are you sure about this, Alice?' he asked under his breath as they came to say goodbye.

'I'm sure,' she said. 'Don't worry about me.'

Roger glanced at Will. 'Maybe it's not you I'm worrying about.'

'We've talked about it,' said Alice firmly. 'It's going to be fine.'

'Well, you're a big girl now, so I guess you know what you're doing.' Roger swept her up into a hug. 'Look after yourself, though.'

'I'm only going up the road!'

'I'll still miss you. I've got used to coming home to find you drinking my gin.'

'I'll miss you, too. I always do.' Alice hugged her dearest friend, holding tightly onto his big bear strength, and her eyes were watery when he finally let her go.

'Oh, good God, she's going to cry!' exclaimed Roger in mock horror. 'Take her away, man!'

Will, who had observed that tight hug, thought it would not be a bad idea to get Alice away from Roger for a while. He was worried about Beth. At first glance, she seemed as bright and cheerful as ever, but on closer inspection Will thought there was a rather drawn look about her. It might be best all round if Alice came with him.

'Come on, then,' he said to Alice and Lily. 'Let's go home.'

They had decided that Alice might as well start her new role straight away, so she had already packed a bag by the time Beth and Roger got home. Now Will slung it in the back of his four-wheel drive and hoped to God he was doing the right thing.

Will's house had no pool, no air-conditioning, and was some way away from the exclusive part of St Bonaventure up on the hill where Roger and Beth lived in manicured splendour, but Alice felt instantly much more at home there. An unassuming wooden house set up on stilts, it had a wide verandah shaded by a corrugated-iron roof, and ceiling fans that slapped at the air in a desultory fashion.

It was set on a dusty, pot-holed road and an area of coarse tropical grass at the rear led down to a line of leaning coconut palms. 'The sea's just there,' said Will, pointing into the darkness. 'Go through the coconuts, cross a track and you're on the beach.'

He carried Alice's cases inside and put them in what had been Dee's bedroom. 'I need to make some calls, I'm afraid,' he said. 'I want to ring the hospital and see how the boys are, and then I'll have to talk to our head office in London. Lily, perhaps you could show Alice the house?' he suggested.

'That was a good idea, getting Lily to show me round,' Alice said to him later when they had eaten the light supper left by his cook and Lily had gone to bed. They were sitting out on the back verandah, listening to the raucous whirr of the insects in the dark and, in the distance, the faint, ceaseless suck of the sea upon the sand. Alice could just make out the gleam of water through the trunks of the palms. 'Knowing more about the house and where everything was made her realise that she was more at home than she thought. It was good for her to be able to explain everything to me,' Alice told Will. 'She might not have been talking much, but she's certainly been taking it all in.'

'I'm glad about that.' Will handed her a mug of coffee that he had made, unthinkingly adding exactly the right amount of milk. He hadn't forgotten how she took hers any more than she had forgotten how he liked his tea, Alice thought with an odd pang. She took the mug gingerly, taking care that her fingers didn't brush against his.

'This is going to be her home for a couple of years at least,' he went on, picking up his own mug and sipping at it reflectively. 'So she needs to feel that it's where she belongs.'

He paused to look sideways at Alice, who was curled up in a wicker chair, cradling her coffee between her hands. The light on the verandah was deliberately dim so as not to attract too many insects, but he could make out the high cheekbones that gave her face that faintly exotic look and the achingly familiar curve of her mouth. It was too hard to read her expression, though, and he wondered what she was thinking.

'I want to thank you, Alice,' he said abruptly. 'I know I didn't seem keen when you first suggested it, but I think it will be a very good thing for Lily to have you here.'

'I hope so,' she said.

'What about you? Do you think you'll be comfortable at least?' He glanced around him as if registering his conditions for the first time. 'I know it's not as luxurious as Roger's house.'

'No, but I like it better,' she said. Tipping back her head, she breathed in the heady fragrance of the frangipani that blossomed by the verandah steps. The wooden boards were littered with its creamy yellow flowers. 'This reminds me of the kind of places I lived in as a child.'

Will grimaced into his coffee. 'I'm not sure that's a good thing. You hated your childhood.'

'I hated the way my parents kept moving,' she corrected him. 'It wasn't the places or the houses—although we never lived anywhere as nice as this. It was the fact that I never had a chance to feel at home anywhere. My parents never stuck at anything. They had wild enthusiasms, but then they'd get bored, or things would go wrong, and they'd be off with another idea.'

She sighed. She loved her parents, but sometimes they exasperated her.

'I was shy to begin with. It was hard enough for me to make friends without knowing that in a year or so I'd be dragged somewhere new, where I'd have to learn a new language and make completely new friends. After a while, it didn't seem worth the effort of making them in the first place. It was easier if I was just on my own.'

It was her unconventional upbringing that had made Alice stand out from the other students. Will had noticed her straight away. It wasn't that she'd been eccentric or trying to be different. She'd dressed the same as everyone else, and she'd done what everyone else did, but there had been just something about the way she'd carried herself that drew the eye, something about those extraordinary golden eyes that had seen places that most of the other students barely knew existed.

Alice might complain about being endlessly uprooted by her parents, but continually having to adapt to new conditions had given her a self-sufficiency that could at times be quite intimidating.

It was a kind of glamour, Will had always thought, although Alice had hooted with laughter when he'd suggested it. 'There's nothing glamorous about living in a hut in the middle of the Amazon, I can tell you!' she had said.

'That's why I identify with Lily, I think,' she said now, sipping reflectively at her coffee. 'She's a solitary child too.'

'I know,' said Will, anxious as always when he thought about his daughter. 'But I hope she'll have a chance to settle down now. I should be here for two or three years.'

'And then?'

'Who knows?' he asked, a faint undercurrent of irritation in his voice. He wasn't her parents, moving his child around the world on a whim. 'It depends on my job. I'm not like you. I don't plan my life down to the last minute.'

'I've learnt not to do that either, now,' said Alice, thinking about Tony and the plans they had made together. 'There are some things you just can't plan for.'

Will arched a sceptical brow. 'I can't imagine you not planning,' he said. 'You were always so certain about what you wanted.'

'Oh, I still know what I want,' she said, an undercurrent of bitterness in her voice. 'The only thing that's changed is that now I'm not sure that I'll get it.'

CHAPTER SIX

'I GUESS that's something we all learn as we get older,' said Will. 'You can't always have what you want.'

His voice was quite neutral, but Alice found her head turning to look at him, and as their eyes met in the dim light she was suddenly very sure that he was thinking about Roger's wedding when he had told her what he wanted and she had said no.

She kept her own voice as light as possible. 'That's true, but perhaps we get what we need instead.'

'Do you think you've got what *you* need?'

Alice looked out into the darkness to where the Indian Ocean boomed beyond the reef.

'I've got a career,' she said, ignoring the little voice that said it wasn't much of one at the moment. 'I've got a flat and the means to pay my mortgage and earn my own living. I've got security. Yes, I'd say I've got everything I need.'

'Everything?' She didn't need to be looking at Will to know that his brows had lifted sardonically.

'What else would I need?'

'Let's say love, just for the sake of argument,' he said dryly. 'Someone you love and who loves you. Someone to hold you and help you and make you laugh when you're down.

Someone who can light up your world, and close it out when you're too tired to cope.'

Someone like he had been, Alice thought involuntarily, and swallowed the sudden lump in her throat.

'Why, Will, you've turned into a poet!' she said, deliberately flippant. 'Have they started doing an agony column in *Nature* and *Science Now*?'

'I read books too,' he said, unmoved by her facetiousness. 'So, do you?'

'Need love?' Alice leant down to put her coffee mug on the table between them. 'No, I don't. I used to think I did, but I've discovered I can manage quite well without it.'

'That's sad,' said Will quietly.

'Love would be great if you could rely on it, but you can't,' she said, wrapping her arms around herself as if she were cold. 'You can't control it. You think it's going to be wonderful and you trust it, and then you end up hurt and humiliated.' Her jaw set, remembering. 'If you want to be safe, you need to look after yourself, not put your whole happiness in someone else's hands.'

She glanced at Will. 'You asked me what I need. Well, I need to feel safe, and that's why I'm not looking for love any more.'

'You've been hurt,' he said, and she gave a short, bitter laugh.

'You can tell you've got a Ph.D., the speed you worked that one out!'

Will ignored her sarcasm. 'What happened?'

He thought at first that she wasn't going to answer, but suddenly Alice needed to tell him. It was too late to pretend that her life was perfect now. Will's clearly wasn't, so he might as well know the truth.

'I met Tony four years ago,' she began slowly. 'I'd had a few boyfriends, but there hadn't been anyone serious.'

There hadn't been anyone like Will. Alice pushed that thought aside and carried on. 'I hadn't exactly given up on meeting someone special, but I'd decided it probably wasn't going to happen. And then Tony came to work in my office.'

She paused, remembering that day. 'He was everything I'd ever wanted,' she said, oblivious to the wry look that passed over Will's face. 'We clicked immediately. We had so much in common. We liked doing the same things, and we wanted the same things out of life. I really thought he was The One,' she said, with an effort at self-mockery.

'Tony's careful,' she went on, even though she knew Will wouldn't understand. 'I felt safe with him. He's committed to his career, and he makes sure he invests his money sensibly. He thinks before he acts. He doesn't take stupid risks. That's why…'

She stopped, hearing her voice beginning to crack like a baby. Swallowing hard, she forced herself to continue. 'That's why I found it hard to believe that he would do something so out of character.'

'What did he do?' asked Will, part of him still grappling with disbelief at the idea that his lovely, vibrant Alice had decided after all to settle for safe, sensible and boring. He wouldn't have minded so much if she had fallen in love with someone wild, passionate and unsuitable, but how could she choose a man whose main attribute seemed to be a sensible approach to financial investments?

Alice drew a breath. 'He went out one day and fell in love at first sight.'

For a moment, Will was nonplussed. 'It happens,' he said, remembering that dizzy, dropping feeling he'd had the first time he'd laid eyes on Alice.

'Not to someone like Tony,' she said almost fiercely. 'We were together three and a half years, and I thought I knew him through and through. He was never impetuous. He never did anything without thinking it through.'

God, Tony sounded dull, thought Will. He wasn't a particularly reckless man himself, but he got the feeling that he would seem a positive daredevil next to Tony. What on earth had been his appeal for Alice?

'I couldn't believe it when he told me,' she was saying. 'He was very honest with me. He said that he'd thought that he did love me, but he realised when he met Sandi that he hadn't known what love was. It had taken us three years to decide that we would get married,' she added bitterly. 'It took him three minutes to know that he wanted to marry Sandi.'

'I'm sorry,' said Will, not knowing what else to say.

'Sandi's sweet and good and kind and pretty,' Alice went on. 'She really is,' she insisted, seeing Will's sceptical look. 'It's really hard to dislike her, and, believe me, I've tried. No one who meets her is at all surprised that Tony fell for her. The only surprising thing is that he thought he loved *me* for so long. Sandi's about as different from me as she could be.'

'She doesn't sound very interesting,' Will said, but Alice wasn't to be consoled.

'Tony doesn't want interesting. Interesting is too much like hard work,' she said. 'I thought I was making an effort for him, but it turned out I was "challenging" him,' she remembered, bitterness creeping back into her voice. 'I don't know how. I didn't think I had particularly high expectations, but there you go. Apparently I'm very demanding.'

'You're not easy,' Will agreed. 'But you're worth the effort. If Tony couldn't be bothered to make that effort, you're better off without him.'

'It didn't feel that way,' said Alice bleakly. 'We have lots of friends in common, so I see Tony with Sandi quite often. I don't think he's regretted his decision for a minute. In fact, I think he wakes up in a cold sweat sometimes, realising what a narrow escape he had!'

She tried to sound as if she didn't mind, but Will could hear the thread of hurt in her voice.

'They're still together, then?'

'They got married last week,' said Alice, her eyes on the dull gleam of the sea through the darkness. 'The day I met you at Roger and Beth's party.'

Will remembered how tense she had been that day. Alice had always been too proud to show how much she hurt inside. He should have guessed that something more than the passage of time was wrong, but he had been too shaken by his own reaction to give any thought to hers.

'I'm sorry,' he said again. 'It must have been difficult for you.'

Alice lifted her chin. She had always hated any suspicion of pity. 'I survived,' she said curtly. 'But that's why I'm doing without love at the moment.'

'You know, we all get hurt sometimes,' said Will mildly. 'Some of us more than once.'

'Once is enough for me,' said Alice.

Silence fell. They sat together in the hot, still night, each wrapped in their own thoughts, while the insects shrilled frantically in the darkness and the lagoon whispered onto the sand.

Alice was very aware of Will beside her. It was strange, being with him again, feeling that she knew him intimately, and yet hardly at all. He wasn't the same man he had been, she reminded herself for the umpteenth time. He was harder, more contained than he had been, and he had grown out of his lankiness to a lean, solid strength.

Her eyes slid sideways under her lashes to rest on the austere profile. She couldn't see them in the darkness but she knew there were new lines creasing his eyes, a tougher set to his jaw, a sterner line to his mouth.

That capacity for stillness was the same, though. She had often watched him sitting like that, his body relaxed but alert, and envied his ability to withdraw from the chaos and just be calm. She had loved his competence, his intelligence, the ironic gleam in the humorous grey eyes. Even as a young man, he had had an assurance that was understated, like everything else about Will, but quite unmistakeable.

There was something insensibly reassuring about his quiet presence. Whatever happened, you felt that Will could deal with it and everything would be all right. Even now, after everything that had happened, he made her feel safe.

If only that was all he had made her feel! The initial attraction she had felt for the ordinary-looking student had deepened into a dangerous passion that made Alice uneasy. She didn't like feeling out of control, and the strength of her emotions scared her.

Will had started out a good friend, a good companion, and he had become a good lover, but soon it went beyond even that. Alice was out of her depth. She didn't like the feeling of needing him, of not feeling quite complete without him. All her experience had taught her to rely on herself, and she had forced herself to resist the lure of binding herself to him for ever.

Because she had been so in love she hadn't seen that they wanted very different things out of life. The future Will enthused about hadn't been the one Alice had dreamed of. She had yearned all her life for security, and that had been the one thing Will couldn't offer. He'd wanted to continue his research, to work wherever he could find a coral reef, to do what he could to protect them. She'd wanted a wardrobe, somewhere she could hang up her clothes and never have to unpack them. She'd wanted a place she could call her own. She'd been sick of scrimping and saving to put herself through university. She'd been sick of window shopping. If she saw a pair of wonderful shoes in a window, she wanted to be able to go in and buy them.

There were no shoe shops on coral reefs. If she'd married Will, as he had asked her to, she'd have had to give up all her dreams to live his. Alice had decided that she couldn't, wouldn't, do that.

She had made the right decision, she told herself, but there was no denying that the physical attraction was still there. It was very hard to explain. There was nothing special about the way Will looked. He had a lean, intelligent face that could under no circumstances be called handsome, but the contrast between the severe mouth and the humorous grey eyes made him seem more attractive than he actually was.

The first time Alice had seen Will, she hadn't been conscious of any instant physical attraction. Later, that seemed strange. She'd thought he was nice, but it was only as she'd got to know him that she'd begun to notice those things that made him uniquely Will: the firmness of his chin, the texture of his skin, the angle of his jaw. The way the edges of his eyes creased when he smiled.

Once she had start noticing, of course, it had been impossible to stop. It hadn't been long before Alice had found her body utterly in thrall to his, and she'd only had to look at his mouth for her breath to shorten and for her entrails to be flooded with a warmth that spread through her until it lodged, tingling and quivering with excitement, just beneath her skin.

The way it was doing now.

Alice tucked her feet beneath her once more and drew herself in, willing the jangling awareness to fade. 'It's not enough,' she had told Will at Roger's wedding, and she knew that she had been right. If she let herself be sucked back into those dark, swirling depths of sexual attraction, she would lose control of her life and her self completely, and the last ten years would have been for nothing.

She swallowed, hard. 'So, what about you?' she asked to break the lengthening silence. 'Do you know what you want?'

For years Will would have been able to say instantly that he wanted her. And then he would have said that he wanted to forget her. Now …

'Not really,' he said slowly. 'I've learnt not to want anything too specific. I don't want a Porsche or a knighthood or to win a million pounds. But I want other things, I suppose,' he went on, thinking about it.

'I want to keep Lily safe. I want her to grow up with a sense of joy and wonder at the world around her. I don't want her to be afraid of it.' He turned his head to look at Alice. 'I don't want her to end up frightened of love or too proud to admit that she needs other people.'

'Oh, so you don't want her to end up like me?' Alice asked flippantly, but there was no answering smile on Will's face as he met her gaze steadily.

'No,' he agreed. 'I want her to be happy.'

Was that really how he saw her—unhappy and afraid? Alice lay in bed that night, scowling into the darkness, hating the memory of the pity she had seen in Will's face. She didn't need him to be sorry for her. She was fine. She could look after herself. She didn't need anybody.

She had thought that she needed Tony, and look where that had got her. She had placed him at the centre of her life and told herself that she was safe at last. Tony hadn't made her head whirl with excitement, it was true, but it wasn't passion that Alice was looking for. She had had that with Will, and the power of those unmanageable emotions had left her uneasy and out of control. With Tony, she had felt settled and as if her future was safe at last. It had been a wonderful feeling.

Until Sandi had come along, and her carefully constructed world had fallen apart.

All those years she had dreamed of feeling secure, and with one meeting it had been shattered. Was it the loss of that dream that hurt more than losing Tony himself? Alice wondered for the first time. And did that mean that she had never really loved Tony at all?

For some reason, it was that thought that made Alice cry in a way she hadn't been able to cry since Tony had left. Trapped in a straitjacket of hurt and humiliation, she had taken refuge in a stony pride, but all at once she could feel the careful barriers she had erected around herself crumbling, and she lay under the mosquito net and wept and wept until at last she fell asleep.

Her eyes were still puffy when she woke the next morning, but she felt curiously released at the same time. Having spent her childhood trying not to let her parents guess how unhappy she was, Alice felt uncomfortable with crying. Until now, it had just seemed another way of admitting that everything was out of control, and she'd been afraid that, once she started, she might never be able to stop.

But this morning it felt as if a heavy hand had been lifted from her heart.

Perhaps she should try tears more often, Alice thought wryly.

Will had gone by the time she got up. She found Lily in the kitchen with the cook, a severe-looking woman called Sara. Alice was quite intimidated by her, but Lily seemed to accept her and was already picking up some words of the local language, a form of French Creole.

Alice was relieved not to have to face Will just yet. She might feel better for a good cry, but she had told him more than she wanted about herself last night, and now she felt exposed. At least she hadn't cried in front of him—that was something—but he had still been sorry for her, and that wasn't a feeling Alice liked at all.

She spent the morning exploring the garden with Lily, and together they crossed the track to the beach. In the daylight, the lagoon was a translucent, minty green, its surface ruffled occasionally by a cat's paw of breeze from the deep blue ocean that swelled and broke against the protecting reef. The leaning coconut palms splashed the white sand with shade, but it was still very hot and Alice was glad to keep on the shoes she had put on to pick her way through the coarse husks and roots that littered the ground beneath the trees.

She had bought the sandals on impulse at a market the previous summer, and Lily was frankly envious. They were cheap but fun, their garish plastic flowers achingly bright in the dazzling sunshine.

'I wish I could have some shoes like that,' said Lily wistfully.

'Let's see if we can find you some in town,' Alice said without thinking, and Lily's face lit up.

'*Could* we?' She sounded dazzled by the prospect.

'We'll go this afternoon,' said Alice.

'Look what I've got,' Lily said to Will when he got home that evening, and she lifted one foot so that he could admire her new shoes.

There hadn't been a great deal of choice in town—St Bonaventure would have to give some thought to modernising its shops if it wanted to attract large numbers of tourists and relieve them of their money, Alice thought—but they had found a pair of transparent pink sandals in Lily's size, and she could hardly have been more delighted if they were Manolo Blahniks.

Will shot a glance at Alice before studying the shoe Lily was showing him so proudly. 'They're very...pink,' he said after a moment.

'I know,' said Lily, deeply pleased.

'Lily and I thought we'd do a spot of shopping,' said Alice, who could tell that Will was considerably less delighted with the shoes but was trying hard not to show it.

'So I see.'

Lily looked earnestly up at her father. 'Alice is good at shopping,' she said, and Will's jaw tightened.

'There are more important things to be good at in life than shopping,' he said.

'Did you have to be quite so crushing?' Alice demanded crossly much later, when Lily was in bed. 'She was so thrilled with her shoes. It wouldn't have killed you to have shown some interest.'

'How can you be *interested* in a pair of shoes?' snarled Will, who was in a thoroughly bad mood, exacerbated by guilt at so comprehensively pricking his daughter's balloon earlier.

It had been the first time Lily had volunteered any information when he'd come home. Part of him had been ridiculously moved that she had come to show him her new shoes without prompting. She had been chattier than usual, too, but he had had to go and spoil things by his thoughtless comment.

Will sighed. He was very tired. It had been a long day, dealing with the fall-out from yesterday's accident, and it hadn't helped that he had slept badly the night before. His mind had been churning with what Alice had told him about her broken engagement. In the small hours, Will had had to acknowledge that he didn't like the fact that Tony had obviously been so important to her.

It was Tony who had given her what she wanted, Tony she was missing now. Alice could say all she wanted about not needing anybody; it was clear that she had loved Tony, and that he was the one she was always going to regret. Will knew exactly what that felt like.

He was sorry, of course, that she had been hurt so badly. But his pity was mixed with resentment at the years *he* had spent believing that he would never find anyone who could make him feel the way she did, the years spent hoping that somehow, somewhere, she was missing him too, and was sorry that she had ended things when she had.

And all the time she had been in love with Tony, dull, safe, sensible Tony who had broken her heart! Will was furious with her for making it so clear how ridiculous his fantasy had been all along, and more furious with himself for caring.

As if that wasn't enough of a slap in the face, now she was the one who was getting through to Lily. It was Alice who was making the bond with his daughter that should really be his, and he resented that too. Will knew that he was being unreasonable and unfair, and he was ashamed of himself, but there it was, something else to add to the mix of his already confused feelings about her.

The next few weeks were going to be even harder than he had feared. Lily went to bed early, which meant that there would just be the two of them alone together every evening like this. Alice still stirred him like no other woman he had ever met. She made him feel angry, and resentful and regretful and grateful and irritated and amused and sympathetic and muddled and disappointed and exhilarated and aroused, often all at the same time. And all it took was for her to turn her head and he was pierced by such joy at her presence that it drove the breath from his lungs.

'Look,' he said, 'I'm sorry I wasn't more enthusiastic about the shoes. I know she likes them. I just don't think it's a good idea for you to encourage her to think that happiness lies in shopping.'

Alice was exasperated. 'I bought her a pair of cheap shoes,' she said tightly, and was aware, deeply buried, of relief that

Will was being so objectionable. It was much easier to be cross than to be aware of him and his mouth, his hands and the way he made her *feel* again. 'It wasn't a philosophical statement, and it won't turn her into a raging materialist. It was just a present, and not a particularly expensive one at that.'

'It's not about the money,' said Will irritably. 'It's about giving her false expectations of the kind of life she's going to have now. Nikki used to buy her things the whole time—toys, clothes, the latest brands, whatever made her feel better for being away at work so much—but that's not going to happen now. I'm not going to try and buy Lily's love, even if I had the time to do it. Little shopping trips like today's will just remind Lily of a life that's gone, and I'm afraid it will just make it harder for her to settle down here.'

'There's a difference between buying affection and giving your child some security,' snapped Alice. 'Lily's been wrenched out of the only life she's ever known. Where *are* all these toys and clothes that her mother bought for her? Did it not occur to you that she might like a few familiar things around her? Or would that have been making things too easy for her? I suppose you thought what she really needed was a clean break and the equivalent of an emotional boot camp to help her settle!'

'Of course not,' said Will stiffly. 'It's true I only brought what I could carry this time, but all her other things are being shipped out. They should arrive in a couple of weeks.'

'Oh,' said Alice, wrong-footed. She had been ready to whip herself into a fury at his stupidity and intransigence. 'Well… good,' she finished lamely.

'Is there anything else she needs—apart from pink shoes, that is—until the shipment arrives?'

'She could do with more to keep her occupied during the day.' Alice was glad that Will had given her the opening. She had intended to raise it, but was afraid she might have pushed him a bit too far to suggest it herself. 'If I didn't think you'd throw a fit at the idea of going to the shops again, I'd suggest getting her some books and maybe some paper and crayons.'

'If I give you some money, will you take her and let her choose whatever she wants?'

'What?' She clapped a hand to her chest and opened her eyes wide. 'You mean we're going to be allowed to go *shopping*?'

Will clamped down on his temper, not without some difficulty. 'For things Lily really needs,' he said repressively. 'I don't want it spent on rubbish.'

'Heavens, no! We don't want to risk Lily having something silly that would give her pleasure, do we?' Alice got up in a swish of skirt. 'That would be spoiling her, and we can't have *that*!'

He had handled that all wrong, thought Will glumly as she swept off saying that she was going to read in her room. He had to stop letting her get to him like this. He needed to forget that she was Alice and treat her the way he would any other nanny. Dee hadn't wound him up this way, and she hadn't done nearly as good a job as Alice. Somehow he would have to find a way to start again.

Alice was decidedly frosty the next morning, and Will's nerve failed at the thought of a tricky discussion before breakfast, but he was determined to make amends when he came home. He left work as early as he could, and found Alice and Lily on the back verandah playing cards.

Hesitating behind the screen door, he looked at the two heads bent close together over the little table, and his chest tightened so sharply that he had to take a deep breath before he pushed open the door.

At the sound of the door banging to behind him, Lily looked up with a shy smile. She didn't cry 'Daddy!' or throw herself into his arms, but it was such a big step for her that

Will felt enormously heartened. Alice was looking aloof, but that didn't bother him. He knew he would have to work harder to win her round, but in the meantime he was content to go over and ruffle Lily's dark hair.

'Hello,' he said with a smile. 'What are you playing?'

'Memory.'

'Who's winning?'

'Alice is,' Lily admitted reluctantly.

That was typical of Alice. She would never patronise a six-year-old by letting her win. When Lily *did* win, her victory would be the sweeter.

'It won't be easy to beat her,' Will warned Lily. 'She's got a good memory.'

Too good a memory, Alice thought, trying not to notice how the smile softened his face. She didn't want to be able to remember too well at the moment. It would be much easier if she could forget the times she and Will had played cards together. Neither of them had had any money as students, and they hadn't been able to go out very often, but Alice had been perfectly happy to stay at home with him, to sit on the floor and play cards, while outside the rain beat against the windows.

Once, when she'd got a distinction for an essay, Will had taken her out to dinner to celebrate. He had only been able to afford an old-fashioned brasserie on the outskirts of town with plastic tablecloths and a dubious taste in décor, but it had still been one of the best meals Alice had ever had. She wanted to forget that, the way she wanted to forget the long walks along winter beaches, the lazy Sunday mornings in bed, all those times when they had laughed until it hurt. She wanted to forget the feel of those hands curving over her body, to forget the taste of his mouth, of his skin. The last thing she wanted was to be able to remember the sweet, shivery, swirling and oh-so-seductive pleasure they had found in each other night after night.

She wanted to remember why it had been such a good idea to end it all.

Will was still talking to Lily. 'That was a good idea to buy cards.'

'We went shopping again.' Lily eyed her father with a certain wariness after his unenthusiastic response to her shoes the day before, but he kept his smile firmly in place.

'Did you buy anything else?'

'Some books.'

'Show me what you bought.'

Lily ran off quite willingly to find the books, and Will glanced at Alice, who immediately turned away, mortified to have been caught watching him.

'Don't lift your chin at me like that,' he said. 'I know I deserve it, but I really am sorry. I was in a bad mood yesterday, and I shouldn't have taken it out on you and Lily, but I did.'

Alice's chin lowered a fraction.

'I'm truly grateful to you, Alice, for what you've done. You've made a huge difference to Lily already, and I know I'm going to have to try harder to make things work if we're going to spend the next month together. Say you'll forgive me,' he coaxed. 'It'll make it much easier for us all if you do!'

The chin went down a bit further.

'Would you like me to go down on my knees and apologise?'

'That won't be necessary,' said Alice with as much dignity as she could muster. She wished he would go back to being grumpy and disagreeable, but she could hardly sulk for a month. 'Apology accepted.'

'I really am sorry, Alice,' Will said quietly, and, in spite of herself, Alice's head turned until she met his steady gaze.

That was something else she remembered—how those grey eyes could tip her off balance so that she felt as if she was toppling forward and tumbling down into their depths, falling out of time and into a place where there was nothing but Will and the slow, steady beat of her heart and the boom of her pulse in her ears.

And when she had managed to wrench her eyes away it had almost been a shock to find, like now, that the world had kept turning without her. Alice had once been sitting on a train, waiting for it to depart and watching the train beside them turn into a blur of carriages as they pulled out of the station. She had never forgotten the jarring shock of realising that it was another train that had left, and hers hadn't moved at all. As the last carriage had disappeared and she'd seen the platform once more, it had felt as if her train had jerked to a sudden, sickening halt. It was the same feeling she had now.

'Let's both try harder,' she muttered.

'All right,' said Will. 'Let's do that.'

CHAPTER SEVEN

'Do you want to see my books?'

It was a tiny comfort that Will seemed as startled as Alice was by Lily's reappearance. She was clutching a pile of books to her chest and watching them with a doubtful expression, as if sensing something strange in the atmosphere.

'Of course I do.' Will forced a smile. 'Let's have a look.'

Lily's face was very serious as she stood by his chair and handed him the books one by one. Will examined them all carefully. 'This looks like a good one,' he said, pulling out a book of fairy stories. He glanced at his daughter. 'Would you like me to read you a story?'

Lily hesitated and then nodded, and, feeling as if she were somehow intruding on a private moment, Alice got to her feet. She suspected that this was the closest Will had ever been to Lily, and the first time he read her a story should be something special for both of them.

'That sounds like a good idea,' she said, firmly quashing the childish part of her that felt just a tiny bit excluded. 'You two read a story together, and I'll go and heat up the supper Sara left for us. She left very strict instructions, and I'm frightened of what she'll say if I get it wrong!'

Alice lingered in the kitchen, giving them time alone

together. It wasn't a bad thing for her to have some time to herself too, she reflected. She had spent all day feeling furious with Will, and there had been something almost comforting in that, but all he had had to do was say sorry and look into her eyes and her anger had crumbled. Like a town without a wall, she was left without defences, and it made her feel oddly vulnerable and uneasy. Will shouldn't still be able to do that to her.

Oh, this was silly! Alice laid the table with unnecessary vehemence, banging down the knives and forks, cross with herself for making such a fuss about nothing. She should be glad that Will had apologised and was obviously prepared to be reasonable. She *was* glad for Lily's sake, if not her own. They couldn't have spent the next month arguing with each other. That would have been no example to set a six-year-old.

It would be so much easier if she could just think of Will as Lily's father, if she could wipe out the memories of another time and another place. It was all very well to tell him that she wanted to be friends, but that was harder than she'd thought it would be.

Alice sighed. Her feelings about Will weren't simple. They never had been and they never would be, and she might as well accept that. Nothing had changed, after all. She had meant what she had said. When her holiday was over, she was going home and she was starting life afresh on her own. No more looking back, no more wanting something from love that it just couldn't give.

When Alice went back out onto the verandah, Will and Lily were sitting close together on the wicker two-seater. Will's arm rested loosely around his daughter and she was leaning into him, listening intently to the story.

Reluctant to disturb them, Alice sat down quietly and listened too. The sun was setting over the ocean, blazing through the trunks of the palm trees, and suffusing the sky with an unearthly orange glow in the eerie hush of the brief tropical dusk. Lily's face was rapt. Will's deep voice resonated in the still air and, watching them, Alice felt a curious sense of peace settle over her. Time itself was suspended between day and night, and suddenly there was no future, no past, just now on the dusty wooden verandah.

'… and they lived happily ever after.' Will closed the book, and his smile as he looked down at his daughter was rather twisted. It was sad that Lily already knew that things didn't always end as happily as they did in stories.

'Did you like that?' he asked, and Lily nodded. 'We could read another one tomorrow, if you like,' he said casually, not wanting her to know how much it had meant to him to have her small, warm body leaning against him. It was like trying to coax a wild animal out of its hiding place, he thought. He wanted desperately for her to trust him, but he sensed that, if he was too demonstrative, she would retreat once more.

'OK,' she said. It wasn't much, but Will felt as if he had conquered Everest.

It was all getting too emotional. Alice had an absurd lump in her throat. Definitely time to bring things down to earth. 'Let's have supper,' she said.

'You're starting to make a real bond with her,' she said to Will.

Lily was in bed, the supper had been cleared away, and by tacit agreement she and Will had found themselves back on the verandah. She had thought about excusing herself and spending the evening reading in her room, but it was too hot, and anyway that would look as if she was trying to avoid him, which would be nonsense. They had cleared the air, and there was no reason for them to be awkward together.

Besides, she liked it out here. It reminded her of being a child, when she would lie in bed and listen to the whirr and click and scrape of the insect orchestra overlaid by the comforting sound of her parents' voices as they sat and talked in the dark outside her room.

She had been thinking of her father a lot this evening. He used to read to her the way Will had read to Lily earlier. He would put on extraordinary voices and embellish the stories wildly as he went along, changing the ending every time, so that Alice had never been quite sure how it was going to turn out. No wonder she had grown up craving security, Alice thought with a rueful smile. She hadn't even been able to count on books to stay the same until she could read them for herself!

Funny how she kept thinking of her childhood here. Normally, she kept those memories firmly buried, but she was conscious that she was remembering it not with her usual bitterness and frustration, and not with nostalgia either, but, yes, with a certain affection. Perhaps she should have remembered more of the good times as well as the bad.

'Lily's learning to trust you,' she went on, and Will leant back in his chair and stretched with a sigh that was part relief, part weariness.

'I hope so,' he said. 'Just doing something simple like reading a story makes me realise how much time I've missed with her. I've got a lot of catching up to do.'

Alice hesitated. 'How come you're such a stranger to her?' she asked curiously, hoping that she wasn't opening too raw a wound. 'Didn't you want a child?'

Will glanced at her and then away. 'Do you want the truth?' he said. 'When Nikki first told me that she was pregnant, I was appalled. Lily was the result of a doomed attempt to save a failing marriage. That's not a good reason to bring a child into the world. Nikki had already made arrangements to leave when she found out she was pregnant. So, no, I didn't want a child then.'

'But Nikki decided to keep the baby?'

'Yes. I don't know why, to be honest,' said Will. 'She couldn't wait to get back to her career, and as far as I could make out Lily spent more time with her grandparents than she did with her mother. Nikki made it very clear that it was her decision whether or not to keep the baby, and I had to respect that. I accepted my responsibility to support the child, but I couldn't really imagine what it would be like to be a father,' he admitted. 'I hadn't been involved in the pregnancy the way most fathers are. I didn't get to see the first scan, or go to antenatal classes. I was just someone who would be handing over a certain sum of money every month.'

'Would you rather Nikki had chosen not to have the baby?' Alice asked curiously.

'There was a time when I thought that would have been the best solution,' said Will. 'But then a funny thing happened. Nikki didn't want me there at the birth, but she did let me see Lily a couple of days later.'

'You cared enough to see her, anyway.'

He looked out at the night. 'I can't honestly say I cared, not then,' he said slowly. 'I felt responsible, that's all. Nikki was in London by then, and I was working in the Red Sea, but my child was being born. I couldn't just pretend it wasn't happening, could I?'

Some men might have done, reflected Alice, but not Will.

'So I went to visit,' he went on, unaware of her mental interruption. 'I guess Nikki thought that if she wanted me to pay maintenance she would have to let me see my own child, but she wasn't exactly welcoming. Fortunately, there was a nice nurse there. I'm not sure whether she knew the situation, or just thought I was a typically nervous first-time father, but before I could say anything she picked Lily up and put her in my arms and—'

He stopped, and in the dim light Alice could just see that his mouth was pressed into a straight line that was somehow more expressive of the feelings he was suppressing than a dramatic show of tears and emotion would have been.

'…And I felt…' he began again when he had himself under control, only to falter to a halt again. 'I can't really describe how I felt,' he admitted after a moment. 'I looked down at this tiny, perfect little thing and just stared and stared. She was so new and so strange, and yet I knew instantly—deep in my gut—that she was part of me.

'I've never felt anything like it before,' he said. 'It was such a strong feeling, it was like a tight band around my chest, and I could hardly breathe with it. It was too painful to be happiness, and there was terror in there too, but it was a wonderful feeling too… I don't know what it was.'

Surprised at how moved she was, Alice managed a smile. 'It sounds like love,' she said, lightly enough, and Will turned his head to look at her for a long, intense moment.

'Yes,' he said after a moment. 'I suppose that's what it was. But not love the way—'

He had so nearly said *the way I loved you*. Will caught himself up just in time.

'It's not the same as the love between a man and a woman,' he finished smoothly.

'Of course not,' said Alice. 'But it's still love. I've never had a child, but I recognized the feeling you described straight away.'

She remembered lying in bed next to Will and feeling just that mixture of terror and wonder, a feeling so intense that it was almost pain. Its power had seemed dangerous, overwhelming, uncontrollable, and in the end she had run away from it. She had been a coward, Alice knew, but at the time it had seemed the sensible thing to do.

And now… Well, there was no point in looking back. No

point in wondering what it would have been like if she had given in to that feeling instead of fighting it, if she had chosen love rather than security. She and Will might have had a child together. She would have discovered for herself how it felt to hold a child in her arms.

She wouldn't have been able to run away from *that* feeling.

Aware that she was drifting perilously close to regret, Alice gave herself a mental shake. She had made her own choices, and she would have to live with the consequences.

'I don't think Lily knows that you love her that much,' she said, breaking the silence.

'How could she?' said Will. 'I've hardly seen her since she was a baby. Nikki had already started the divorce process before Lily was born.'

'You'd think the baby would have brought you together,' Alice commented.

'I would have been prepared to give it another go for Lily's sake, but I suspect Nikki was right when she said that we both knew it wasn't going to work, so we'd better accept reality sooner rather than later.'

Will shifted shoulders restlessly, as if trying to dislodge the memory pressing onto them. Of course, that was what Alice had said too. *It'll never work. Let's call it a day while we're still friends. It's not worth even trying.* At least Nikki had taken the risk of marrying him. Alice hadn't even had the guts to give it a go.

'So you didn't contest the divorce?'

'No.' He shook his head. 'Our marriage was a mistake. Nikki was right about that. We should never have got married in the first place.'

'Why did you, then?' asked Alice, who had no patience with people who didn't think through the consequences of their actions. Of course, sometimes you could think about things too much, and you ended up missing opportunities, but Will was an intelligent man, and marriage was a serious business. It wasn't the kind of thing you fell into *by mistake*.

The sharpness in her voice made Will glance at her, but he didn't answer immediately. How could he tell Alice how hard he had tried to find someone else after she had given him that final 'no' at Roger's wedding? How every woman he'd met had seemed either twee or colourless in comparison to her? Nikki had been the first woman he'd met with a strength of personality to match hers. Seduced by the notion of wiping Alice from his memory once and for all, Will had convinced himself that he was falling in love with Nikki's forcefulness and vivacity, and he had been too eager to find out what she was really like until it was too late.

'I think I fell in love with the idea of Nikki, rather than with the person she really was,' he said at last. 'And I think she did the same.'

Alice opened her mouth to tell him it had been madness to even think about marrying an idea, but then closed it abruptly. Hadn't she done the same with Tony, after all? Tony had represented something that she had always yearned for, but she hadn't really known him. If she had, she might not have been so unprepared when he'd met Sandi.

'It was a holiday romance that got out of hand,' Will went on. 'She came out to the Red Sea to learn how to dive, and when we met she was incredibly enthusiastic about diving and the reef. I saw that she was fun, pretty, vivacious…and I think she saw me as someone very different from her friends and business associates in London.'

Alice could imagine it all very clearly. To Nikki, bored with men in suits and ties, escaping from a cold, grey London, Will must have seemed hard to resist with his wind-tanned skin and the glitter of sunlit sea in his eyes. He would have been a step up, too, from the surfers and beach bums. Will's shorts and T-shirts might have been as faded from the sun as theirs, but he had an air of competence and assurance that gave him the kind of authority other men had to put on suits to acquire.

'So you were both carried away by the sea and the stars?' she suggested, with just a squeeze of acid in her voice.

'You could say that,' Will agreed dryly. 'And of course, once reality set in, the sea and the stars weren't enough. Nikki was full of how she wanted to start a new life with me, but it didn't take long before she was bored, and then she started to resent me for "making" her give up her career in London.'

His mouth twisted. 'It wasn't a good time. We tried to patch things up—hence Lily—but in the end it was obvious it wasn't going to work. Nikki wanted to pick up her career where she'd left off, and the truth was that by then I wanted out of the marriage too. I just didn't count on how Lily's birth would change things.'

'It must have made everything more complicated,' said Alice, and he gave a mirthless laugh.

'You could say that. Nikki insisted on having full custody of Lily, and I was prepared to accept that. What I wasn't prepared to accept was not having any access to my daughter at all.'

'No access? But that's completely unreasonable!' Alice protested, shocked. '*And* unfair!'

Will shrugged. 'Unreasonable…unfair… You can shout all you like, but, when you're up against the kind of hot-shot lawyers Nikki hired, saying that it's unfair doesn't get you very far. For two years she refused to communicate with me except through the intimidating letters her lawyers would send me.'

'But why would she be like that? You'd have thought she'd have wanted her child to grow up knowing its father!'

'I don't know.' Will rubbed a weary hand over his face. 'The only thing I can think was that she was afraid I'd somehow take Lily away, but I wouldn't have done that, and she had no grounds for suspecting that I would.'

'I'm sorry,' said Alice, appalled at what Will had been through. 'It must have been very hard for you.'

'I didn't react quickly enough.' Will's face was set in grim lines as he remembered that bleak period. 'I'm a scientist. I understand about ocean currents, and protogyny among coral-reef fish, and sampling by random quadrats, but I wasn't well equipped to deal with divorce lawyers. It took me too long to get my own hot-shot lawyers and take the fight back…and by the time I did Nikki had changed tactics.'

Alice frowned. She didn't like the image of Will, bruised from the wreckage of his marriage, frustrated by lawyers and manipulated by Nikki. No wonder there were harsh lines on his face now. 'In what way?'

'She opted for emotional blackmail next,' he said, and, although he was clearly trying to keep his voice neutral, it was impossible to miss the underlying thread of bitterness. 'And very effective it was, too. Lily was already a toddler by then, and Nikki claimed it would be too unsettling for her to see me regularly. I wouldn't understand her needs the way Nikki did. It would distress Lily to go and stay somewhere strange. She didn't know who I was. I wouldn't know how to look after her properly. She needed to be in a familiar environment. It would be too disruptive for her to spend longer than a couple of hours with me. And so on and so on.'

'With the result that you became even more of a stranger to Lily?'

'Exactly. The few times I did manage to see Lily I was only able to take her out for a few hours, and frankly they weren't successful visits. I think Nikki was so paranoid about the possibility of me taking her away altogether that she'd transferred all her tension and suspicion to Lily. It's not surprising that she was nervous of me. As far as she was concerned, I was a stranger her mother didn't trust.'

He rubbed his face again, pushing his fingers back through his hair with a tired sigh. 'It wasn't just Nikki's fault. I didn't know how to reach Lily either. I wanted to tell Lily how much she meant to me, but I didn't know how, and I still don't. I've got no experience of being a father, and, now that I've got Lily all the time, I just feel inadequate. I either try too hard, or I get it completely wrong.'

He sounded so dispirited that Alice found herself reaching out to lay a comforting hand on his arm.

'You got it right tonight,' she told him.

She was burningly aware of his hard muscles beneath her fingers, and wished that she hadn't touched him. She had reached out instinctively, but now that her hand was on his arm it seemed suddenly a big deal, and she felt jolted, as if she had done something incredibly daring.

Which was ridiculous. It was only a matter of a hand on his forearm, after all. No reason to feel as if she had done the equivalent of clambering onto his lap, unbuttoning his shirt, pressing hot kisses up his throat …

Alice swallowed. She wasn't even touching his skin, for God's sake! Will was wearing a long-sleeved shirt rolled back at the wrist, but there was only a thin barrier of cotton between his skin and hers, and she was sure that she could feel his warmth and strength through the fine material anyway.

Horribly conscious of the way her body was thrumming in response, she made herself pull her hand away. She couldn't have been touching him for more than a few seconds, but her heart was beating so hard she was afraid Will would be able to hear it above the crescendo of the night insects.

In this light it was impossible to tell whether he had even reg-

istered her touch, and his voice sounded perfectly normal as he
credited her with the small progress he had made with Lily.

'Thanks to you,' he said. 'The books were your idea.'

'But you were the one who read to her.' Sure that her
cheeks were still burning with awareness, Alice was very
grateful for the darkness that she hoped hid her expression as
effectively as it did Will's.

'You're good with children,' he said abruptly. 'Somehow
I never imagined that you would be.'

'I'm not really,' she confessed, glad that her voice seemed
steadier now. 'I'm not usually that interested in them. But I
like Lily.'

'You've never wanted children of your own?'

Alice thought about the years she had spent trying to find
a man she could settle down and be happy with, a man she
could build a family with, a man who would make her forget
Will and all that she had walked away from. She had thought
she had found him at last in Tony. They had talked about
having children, when they were married, when the time was
right. But sometimes the time was never right, and, even if it
was, it wasn't always that easy. Look at Roger and Beth.

'You can't always have what you want,' she said in a low
voice, and Will turned to her, wondering if she was thinking
about Tony who she had loved so much, and thinking about
how much he had wanted her for so long.

'No,' he agreed. 'Sometimes you can't.'

'It'll rain soon.' Will handed Alice a glass of fresh lime juice
chinking with ice, and sat down next to her with a cold beer.

'I hope so.' Alice took the glass with a murmur of thanks
and held it against her cheek, letting the condensation cool her
skin. 'Mmm…that feels nice,' she told Will, who had to make
himself look away from the sight of her, her eyes closed in

pleasure as the condensation on the glass trickled down her throat and into her cleavage. It was dark on the verandah, but sometimes not dark enough.

'It's been so hot today,' she went on, languid with heat. 'I took Lily over to see Beth today so we could sit in the air-conditioning for a while.'

With her free hand, Alice lifted a few damp strands of hair that had fallen from their clip onto the back of her neck. 'The heat doesn't usually bother me, but for the last couple of days it's been suffocating. It's like trying to breathe through a scarf.'

'It's the pressure.' Will was dismayed at how hoarse his voice sounded. 'A good storm will clear the air.'

'I can't wait,' she sighed. 'There's no sign of any rain clouds, though. I've been looking at the horizon all day.'

'They'll be boiling up now,' said Will. 'Didn't you notice them at sunset? That's always a sign. It has to break soon.'

He wished that he was just talking meteorologically. A different kind of pressure had been building inexorably over the ten days since Alice had arrived, and Will was finding it harder and harder to ignore.

He had done his best to try and think of her simply as Lily's nanny, but it wasn't any good. She was resolutely Alice, impossible to ignore. It didn't matter if she was just sitting quietly next to him in the dark, or playing cards with Lily or laying the table. It was there in every turn of her head, every gesture of her hands, every sweep of her lashes.

Will struggled to remember how he had disliked her at Roger and Beth's party, but that tense, brittle, superficial Alice had somehow been whittled away by the heat, the sunlight and the warm breeze that riffled the lagoon and rustled through the coconut palms. He had to remind himself constantly that she hadn't really changed that much. She still wore that absurd collection of shoes. She flicked through magazines and talked about clothes, make-up and God knew what else, encouraging Lily to remember her life in London more than Will wanted. She still talked about the great career she was going to resume.

She was still going home.

He needed to keep that in mind, Will told himself at least once a day. She would only be there for another few weeks, and then she would be gone. He would have to start thinking about life without her all over again.

It alarmed him how easily they had slipped into a routine, and he was afraid that he was getting used to it. He left early for work, but for the first time in years found himself looking forward to going home at the end of the day. Alice and Lily were usually on the verandah, playing games or reading together, and he would often stand behind the screen door and watch them, unobserved for a while, disturbed by the intensity of pleasure the peaceful scene gave him. Sometimes he tried to tell himself he would have felt the same no matter who was with Lily, but he knew that he was fooling himself.

It wasn't just the fact that Lily was gradually settling down. It was Alice.

Every night when Lily was asleep, they would sit on the verandah, like now, and they would talk easily until one of them made an unthinking comment that reminded them of the past and all they had meant to each other. And when that happened, the tension a routine kept successfully at bay most of the time would trickle back into the atmosphere, stretching the silence uncomfortably until one or other of them made an excuse and went to bed.

Will had hoped that the weekend would break that pattern, and things had certainly been different since then. He just wasn't convinced that it was for the better.

On the Saturday he had taken the two of them out to the reef in the project's tin boat. Half-submerged in a life jacket that was really too big for her, Lily had clutched onto the wooden seat. Her face had been shaded by a floppy cotton hat, but, sitting opposite her at the helm, Will could peer under the brim and see that her expression was an odd mixture of excitement and trepidation. She'd looked as if she wanted to be thrilled, but didn't quite dare to let herself go.

'Would you like to drive the boat?' he asked her, and her eyes widened.

'I don't know how.'

'I'll show you.'

Will held out his hand, and after a moment, with some encouragement from Alice, she took it and let herself be handed carefully across to stand between his knees. He showed her how to hold the tiller, and kept her steady, guiding the boat unobtrusively from behind. Lily's small body was tense with concentration, and it was hard to know whether she was terrified or loving it.

Over her head, he could see Alice, straight-backed as ever on the narrow seat, holding her hat onto her head. Her eyes were hidden by sunglasses, but when she met his gaze she smiled and nodded at Lily. 'She's smiling,' she mouthed, as if she knew what he most wanted to hear, and Will felt his heart swell with happiness.

The sun glittered on the water, bouncing off every surface and throwing dazzling patterns over Alice's face as the little boat bounced over the waves. Everything seemed extraordinarily clear, suddenly: the breeze in his hair, the tang of the sea in his lungs, his daughter smiling as she leant into him… And Alice, contrary, prickly, unforgettable Alice. At that moment, Will felt something close to vertigo, a spinning sensation as if he were teetering on the edge of a cliff, and he had to jerk his gaze away before he did something stupid like telling her that he loved her still.

Bad idea.

It had been a happy day, though. They pulled the boat onto a tiny coral island, where they could wade into the warm water and watch the fish dart around their ankles, flashing silver in the sunlight. Will taught Lily how to snorkel while Alice sat under a solitary leaning palm and unpacked the picnic they had brought.

Afterwards, Lily dozed off in the shade, and Will watched Alice wandering along the shore. The set of her head on that straight spine was so familiar it made Will ache. Her loose white-linen trousers were rolled up to her knees, her face shadowed by the brim of her hat, a pair of delicate sandals dangling from her hand.

'You won't need shoes,' Will had said when they'd got into the boat that morning, but Alice had refused to leave them behind in the car.

'I feel more comfortable with shoes on,' she had said. 'You never know when you're going to need them to run away.'

'You won't be able to run very far on the reef,' Will had pointed out, but she'd only lifted her chin at him.

'I'm keeping them on.'

Alice would always want an escape-route planned, he realised as he watched her pause and look out across the translucent green of the lagoon to where the deep blue of the Indian Ocean frothed in bright white against the far reef. She would always want to be able to run away, just as she had run away from him before.

She wouldn't be here now if she didn't have that ticket home, Will remembered. It would be foolish to let himself hope that she might stay. She wasn't going to, and he had to accept that now. Consciously steadying his heart, he made himself think coolly and practically. He mustn't be seduced by the sea and the sunlight and Alice's smile. Sure, he could enjoy today, but he wouldn't expect it to last. There were no for evers where Alice was concerned.

When Lily woke up, she ran instantly down to join Alice at the water's edge. Will watched them both, and tried not to mind that his daughter so obviously preferred Alice's company to his. Tried not to worry, too, how she would manage when Alice was gone.

He could see them bending down to examine things they found on the beach. Alice was crouching down, turning something in her hand and showing it to Lily, who took it and studied it carefully.

And then it happened.

'Daddy!' she cried, running up the beach towards him. 'Daddy, look!'

It was a cowrie shell, small but perfect, with an unusual leopard pattern on its back, but Will hardly noticed it. He was overwhelmed by the fact that Lily had run to him, had called him Daddy, had wanted him to share in her pleasure, and his throat closed so tightly with emotion that it was hard to speak.

'This is a great shell,' he managed. 'It's an unusual one, too. You were very clever to find it.'

'Alice found it,' Lily admitted with reluctant honesty, and Will looked up to see Alice, who had followed more slowly up the beach. Their eyes met over Lily's dark head, and she smiled at him, knowing exactly what Lily's excited dash up the beach had meant to him.

Will smiled back, pushing the future firmly out of his mind. He knew the day wouldn't last for ever, but right then, with Lily's intent face, the feel of the shell in his palm, and Alice smiling at him, it was enough.

CHAPTER EIGHT

WILL was thinking about that day out on the reef as he sat on the verandah with Alice and the hot air creaked with the pressure of the oncoming storm. He had done his best to keep his distance from her since then.

Again and again, he had reminded himself that she would be leaving soon and that there was no point in noticing the curve of her mouth, or the line of her throat, or the sheen of her skin in the crushing heat. No point in remembering how she felt, how she tasted. No point in thinking about how sweet and exciting and *right* it had felt to make love to her.

Not doing any of that was definitely the sensible thing to do. But it was hard.

'Listen!' Alice held up a hand suddenly, startling Will out of his thoughts.

'What is it? Is it Lily?' he asked, instantly anxious in case he had missed a cry.

'It's the insects.'

Will looked at her puzzled. 'What insects?'

'Exactly. They've stopped.'

And, sure enough, the deafening rasp, scratch and shrill of the insects, that was such a familiar backdrop to the evenings here that Will barely heard it any more, had paused and in its place was an uncanny silence.

The next instant there was a rip of lightning in the distance, an almighty crack of thunder overhead, and a deluge of rain came crashing down onto the roof. One second there had been the hot, heavy, *waiting* silence, the next there was nothing but sound and fury and the pounding, thundering, hammering rain. It fell not in drops but as a solid mass, bouncing back in the air as it hit solid ground, and overwhelming the gutters so that it simply cascaded in a sheet over the edge of the verandah.

Alice laughed with sheer delight. 'I *love* it when it rains like this!' she shouted to Will, but it was doubtful that he could hear her over the deafening roar of the rain.

Caught up in the elemental excitement of the downpour, she jumped to her feet. The sheer power of it was awe-inspiring, almost frightening, but exhilarating at the same time. Alice could feel the raw energy of it surging around the verandah, pushing and pulling at her, making her blood pound.

Normally she hated feeling so out of control, but a tropical downpour was different. She knew it wouldn't last very long, but while it did she could feel wild and reckless, the way she would never allow herself to be the rest of the time.

She looked at Will, who had got to his feet too, moved by the same restless excitement generated by the breaking of the pressure that had been pressing down on them for the last few days. He was watching the rain, his intelligent face alive with interest, the stern mouth curling upwards into an almost-smile, and, as her eyes rested on him, Alice was gripped by a hunger to touch him once more, to feel his hard hands against her skin, to abandon herself to the electricity in the air.

Instinctively, she took a step towards him, just at the moment when the force of the rain finally succeeded in dis-

lodging part of the roof and poured through a hole directly
onto her head. If Alice had stayed where she was, the water
would have splashed harmlessly onto the verandah, but as it
was she was drenched instantly.

It felt as if someone had tipped a bucket over her, and she
gasped with the shock of it before she started to laugh again.
It was like standing under a waterfall, the water cool and in-
describably refreshing after the suffocating heat, and as it
was too late to get dry Alice closed her eyes and tipped her
face up to the cascading water.

In seconds her dress was clinging to her, and her shoes—
her favourite jewelled kitten-heels—were probably ruined,
but right then Alice didn't care. Pulling the clip from her
hair, she shook it free and let the rain plaster it to her head as
it ran in rivulets over her face and down her throat.

Will had been unable not to laugh at the sight of her
ambushed by the leak in the roof, but as he watched her close
her eyes and turn her face up to the water, as he watched the
fine fabric of her dress stick to her breasts and hips, as he
watched the rain sliding over skin, his smile faded at the extraordinary sensuality of the scene, and his body tightened.

As if sensing his reaction, Alice opened her eyes. Her
lashes were wet and spiky, and she had to blink against the
water running over her face, but her gaze was dark and steady.

There was no need for either of them to say anything. They
both knew that the careful defences they had built over the last
couple of weeks were no match for the downpour. For tonight,
the rules, their hopes and their fears, meant nothing. There
was only the two of them, the crackle of electricity, and the
drumming rain. When Will reached for her, Alice reached out
at the same time and tugged him under the rain still pouring
through the hole in the roof.

They kissed with the water spilling around them, trickling

from his skin onto hers, and from hers to his, their bodies pressing so close that it couldn't find a way between them. They kissed and kissed and kissed again, hard, hungry kisses that fed on the power of the downpour and on the spiralling excitement that spun and surged as they touched each other with increasing urgency. Their hands moved instinctively over each other, clutching, clasping, sliding, shifting, finding long-remembered secret places, rediscovering the feel and the taste and the touch of each other.

'Will…' Alice pressed her lips to his throat in fevered kisses, revelling in the feel of his body, in the wonderful, familiar smell of his skin, arching and shuddering with pleasure at the touch of his hands, the taste of his mouth, How could she have told herself that she had forgotten how it felt? 'Will…' she gasped, inarticulate with need.

'What?' he murmured raggedly against her throat. They might as well have been naked already. Their clothes were plastered to their wet bodies, and should have felt cold and clammy, but the heat of their beating blood was keeping them warm. Will wouldn't have been surprised to see steam rising.

Alice didn't know what she wanted to say, didn't know how to tell him how she felt. Her mind was reeling with pleasure, and all she could think about was the clamour of her body, the desire that was running rampant, unstoppable, out of control…

'Tell me what you want, Alice,' Will whispered, and then lifted his head so that he could look down into her face, his own streaked with water now too.

'I don't know,' said Alice helplessly.

But she did know. She wanted him. She wanted more of him, all of him. She wanted him closer, harder, inside her. She wanted him completely—but the very strength of her need was beginning to alarm her, while a small voice of reason inside her was insinuating itself into the wild recklessness that had gripped her, telling her to be careful, reminding her about the past and the future, about the risk of abandoning herself utterly to the moment.

Oh, how she wanted to, though!

'I want …' she began unsteadily, and then swallowed. 'I want to pretend that this is all there is,' she told him at last.

'This *is* all there is,' said Will. 'This is all that matters.' And, taking her hand, he led her inside and out of the rain.

Alice lay next to Will and let her pounding blood slow, her breathing steady. Her entire body was still thrumming with satisfaction, and she felt heady and boneless. It was impossible to regret what had happened, even now the wildness and the excitement of the night had dissipated. Their bodies had remembered each other with a heart-stopping clarity, their senses snarling and tangling and tantalizing, surrendering together to the soaring rhythm of love until they'd shattered with release.

It had been wonderful. She could hardly pretend otherwise when the glory was still beating through her veins and shimmering out to the very tips of her toes. And it hadn't been wrong. They were both single, both free, both responsible adults. No one was going to be hurt by what they had done.

But…

Why did it feel as if that huge 'but' was hovering, just waiting to be acknowledged?

Alice turned her head on the pillow to look at Will. He was lying on his back, and she could see his chest rising and falling unevenly as his breathing returned to normal. Outside it was still raining, although not with the ferocity of earlier, and the sound was comforting rather than exhilarating. If it had rained like this earlier, would they have still ended up in bed?

Perhaps. Probably, even. If Alice was going to be honest, she would have to admit that she had been finding it harder and harder to resist the tug of attraction as the days had passed. She'd only had to look at him reading a story to Lily, or at the helm of the boat, his hair lifting in the breeze and his eyes full of sunlight, or lifting a glass to his lips, and her mouth would dry and her stomach would clench. She could say what she liked about being friends, but the old chemistry was still there, and they both knew it.

So, yes, perhaps tonight had been inevitable, but what now? They couldn't just go back to the careful way they had been before, but what other choice did they have? A tiny sigh escaped Alice as she stared up at the ceiling. She should have made it clear to Will that it had just been the storm, and that she wasn't expecting anything to change just because they had made love tonight.

'You know, you don't need to fret.' Will's voice came unexpectedly out of the darkness, making Alice jump.

'I'm not fretting!'

'Yes, you are.' Will rolled so that he could prop himself up on one elbow and look down at where she lay, her bare skin luminous in the faint light and her hair still wet and tangled on the pillow. 'I know you, Alice. You're planning your escape route right now.'

'What do you mean?' she asked uneasily.

'You always look for a way out before there's any chance that you might end up committing yourself.'

'That's rubbish!' she scoffed, but not quite as convincingly as she would have liked. Will certainly wasn't fooled.

'Is it? Don't try and tell me you weren't lying there trying to work out how soon you could tell me that you only wanted this for tonight, that it didn't mean anything to you and that it wasn't meant to be for ever.'

'What did you think it was?' retorted Alice, glad that he had found the words for her.

'I wasn't thinking at all.' Will's wry smile gleamed in the darkness. 'I can't say I regret it, though. It wasn't something either of us planned, but I think it was something we both wanted—or are you going to deny that?'

'No, I'm not going to deny it,' she said in a low voice. 'There's always been a special chemistry between us.'

'I know that. You don't need to worry, Alice.' Will reached out and lifted a lock of her wet hair, rubbing it gently between his fingers. 'You don't need to explain or make excuses. I know you're leaving, so you don't have to think of a way out. Let's just leave tonight as an itch that we both scratched.'

It ought to have made Alice feel better, but somehow it didn't. She knew that Will was right, and that he was giving her exactly what she needed, but she didn't want to be an *itch*.

Sitting up, she pushed her damp hair away from her face and reached down for the sheet that had slipped unheeded to the floor much earlier. 'Is that it?' she asked almost sharply as she wrapped it around her.

'What more can it be?'

'Well…there's still three weeks or so until I go,' she found herself saying.

There was a pause. 'What are you suggesting, Alice?' he asked, and it was impossible to tell from his voice what he was thinking. 'That we keep scratching that itch?'

'If that's how you want to think of it.' Alice bit her lip and pulled more of the sheet onto the bed. 'You were right about the way out. There's no point in pretending that I'm not leaving in three weeks' time, so I'm not making any promises. I wouldn't want you to think that I'm talking about for ever.'

'Don't worry,' said Will, at his most dry. 'I learnt a long time ago never to think of you and for ever in the same sentence.'

'Then, if we both know that, why not make the most of it?'

Part of Alice was rearing up in alarm at her insistence, and warning her that nothing good could come of getting involved with Will again. It was all very well to talk about scratching an itch, but, once you had given in to the need, it was almost impossible to stop. It was madness to think that she could sleep with him for three weeks and then calmly walk away. Better to leave things as they were, as Will himself had suggested, and treat tonight as a one-off. She had a nice house and a life to go back to in London. That was enough, wasn't it?

But another, more reckless, part had her in its grip tonight. Why not? it was asking. How long was it since she had felt that gorgeously, fabulously good, that relaxed, that *sexy*? What was the point of not doing it again, when they had another three weeks or more to get through? They both knew where they were. They had no expectations of each other. And it had been great. Did she *really* want that to be the last time?

No, she didn't.

'It would be fun,' she coaxed, realising at that moment that it was a very long time since she had let herself simply have fun. Ten years, in fact.

Will was silent for a moment. 'I don't want to fall in love with you again, Alice,' he said.

'We won't fall in love,' she said. 'We've been there, and we know it doesn't work. That doesn't mean we can't have a good time together.'

'So you just want me for my body?' said Will, but Alice was sure she could hear a smile in his voice.

'We-el…' She let the sheet fall and slid back down beside him, letting her hand drift tantalisingly over his flat stomach, and scratching him very, very lightly with her nails. 'If the itch is there, we might as well scratch it, don't you think?'

The downward drift of her fingers was making it hard for

Will to think clearly. 'So we'll have the next few weeks and then say goodbye?' he managed.

Alice's hand paused for just a second. 'Then we'll say goodbye,' she agreed.

Will knew that he was probably making a mistake but right then, with her fingers teasing him and her lips against his throat, and her body warm and soft and close, he didn't care. Moving swiftly, he pinned her beneath him and put his hands on either side of her face. 'All right,' he said as he bent to kiss her. 'Three weeks. Let's make them good ones.'

It didn't work, of course. They had about a week when they both resolutely closed their minds to the future, and thought only about the days with Lily and the long, hot nights together. It was easy to fall into their old ways, talking, laughing, arguing, making love... And inevitable, Will thought, that he should start wishing that it could go on for ever.

Knowing that, it made him increasingly tense and irritable. He was angry with Alice for her dogged refusal to consider taking a risk on the unknown, angrier with himself for agreeing to the one situation that he had most wanted to avoid.

Because of *course* he had fallen in love with Alice again. The truth was that he had probably never fallen out of love with her, and it wasn't helping matters to have her there whenever he went home, as combative, challenging and stimulating as ever, as warm and responsive every night. Every time Will looked at her, his heart seemed to stop, and the knowledge that he would have to let her go gnawed relentlessly at him.

Three weeks, that was all they had. After the heady delight of that first week, Will did his best to distance himself from her. But how could he when she was there in his bed, when she lay warm against him all night, and her very nearness made his head reel?

Alice sensed his withdrawal, even understood it. It had been a wonderful week, but slowly the sensible side of her was regaining its natural ascendancy. Ah-ha! it cried. Told you you'd regret it! Look what a mess you've got yourself into *now*!

The three-week deadline changed her whole sense of time. Sometimes it seemed to rush forward with dizzying speed, making her panic, and at others it slowed to a lethargic trickle that made it impossible to imagine the future. Alice tried to focus on going home, but her life in England seemed increasingly unreal.

She had expected to start feeling bored by now, to start yearning for shops, cinemas, bars and the gossip and pressure of a proper job, but it hadn't happened yet. She tried to make herself miss them, but how could she think about London when Lily chattered as she swung on her hand, and the lagoon glittered behind the coconut palms, and Will closed the bedroom door every night with a smile?

The arrival of Lily's trunk only underlined how far she was from home. Having made such a fuss about Will not bringing his daughter's things with him, Alice had to admit that none of the clothes were suitable for a tropical island. There were surprisingly few books, and a lot of very expensive and hardly-used toys, none of which seemed to interest Lily very much.

She had to find *some* way of detaching herself from life here, Alice thought with increasing desperation. It was too comfortable, too intimate, with just the three of them. She needed to get out and meet more people, make her life bigger again so that when she left there wouldn't be an aching gap where Will and Lily had been. Deep down, Alice was afraid that she might have left it too late for that, but at least it was a plan.

When Will told her that he and his team were preparing for an open day at the project headquarters that Friday, Alice leapt at the opportunity.

'Can we come?'

'To the open day?' Will looked taken aback at the idea.

'Why not? It would be a chance for Lily to see what you do all day.'

'I'm not sure it'll be of any interest to a child. We've got a government minister coming, but it's really about trying to involve the local community in the project, especially the fishermen, and getting them to understand what we're trying to do.'

'Why don't you lay something on for all the children?' said Alice. 'They're part of the community too, and if you get them on board now it'll make things much easier in the future. You could lay on little trips for them,' she went on, warming to her theme. 'Or have a competition with little prizes…you know, they have to find out information as they go round and answer questions, or find something, like a treasure hunt.'

'I suppose we *could* do something for the children,' said Will slowly.

'It'll be good for Lily to start meeting other children before she goes to school, too,' Alice pointed out.

Impressed by her enthusiasm, Will considered. 'Could you run some activities for the children?'

'Me?'

'It was your idea.'

'But I don't know anything about marine ecology!'

'We can give you the information you need. It's putting it into an appealing format we'd find more difficult, even if we had the time to think about it, which we don't. We've got enough to do setting up displays for the open day as it is, and we're running short of time.'

So Alice and Lily found themselves at the project headquarters. The building was simply, even spartanly, furnished, but everything was very well organised. It was clear that all the money was spent on expertise and research equipment—

no surprise with Will in charge. The whole project had his stamp on it; high quality, integrity, and absolutely no frills.

Will showed them round and introduced them to various members of the team, all of whom welcomed Lily kindly and eyed Alice with unmistakable curiosity. He had introduced her simply as 'a friend', and it was obvious that they were all wondering just how close a friend she was. Alice found herself unaccountably miffed that he wouldn't acknowledge a closer relationship, because clearly they *were* more than friends. They were lovers.

Desire shivered through her at the thought of the nights they spent together. She would never guess it to look at Will now. He was dressed casually but with characteristic neatness in shorts and a short-sleeved shirt, and his face was absorbed as he discussed some obscure issue to do with phytoplankton, whatever that was, with a bearded marine biologist. Looking at the back of those long, straight legs, Alice felt quite weak with the knowledge of how they felt against hers, of what it was like to kiss the nape of his neck and slide her arms around that lean, hard body.

'Shall we go and look at the lab?' Will turned to find Alice staring at him, and she gulped and jerked her gaze away.

'Fine,' she said brightly. 'Lead on!'

In spite of herself, Alice was impressed by what she saw. She hadn't realised quite what a major project it was, and she remembered how glibly she had suggested to Will that he give up his career and find another job in London. It seemed an absurd idea now. For it was clear that he was key to the project's success. The staff made no secret of how much they admired him, and Alice could see why. He didn't raise his voice, or show off or patronise anyone, but somehow he was at the centre of everything. She saw a young diver glow at Will's quiet word of congratulation, and a secretary nod with enthusiasm at one of his suggestions. This was Will in his element, intelligent, focused, completely assured about who he was, what he was doing and why he was doing it.

It was very different from her own world of work where status symbols were so important, and how you looked and talked sometimes mattered more than what you actually did. Alice couldn't help comparing Will with Tony, who was always so careful of his appearance and so competitive. Tony would talk himself up in meetings, never missing an opportunity to tell everyone how dynamic and successful he was, and even at home he hadn't been able to wait to tell Alice how well he had performed in a meeting or how much better his results had been than any of his colleagues.

Alice's own drive was less for success in itself than for the security it brought, but she sensed that the team had some reservations about her, and she supposed she did look a bit out of place in her narrow skirt, sleeveless top and high peep-toe shoes with their pretty candy stripes. Alice told herself that she didn't care what they thought of her, and threw herself into the challenge of taking what she had learnt and making it fun and accessible for children.

Will found her a desk, and she and Lily spent the rest of the day happily playing around with ideas and thinking up simple questions that a child like Lily could answer by looking at the various display boards that were being prepared. Will disappeared out to the reef, and Alice found it easier to settle once he had gone. She chatted to the two locally employed secretaries, who adored Will, and were obviously longing to know more about his relationship with Alice but were too polite to ask outright.

'I'm just helping out with Lily until the new nanny arrives,' she told them, since there didn't seem any reason to keep it a big secret. 'I'm going home soon.'

Perhaps, if she said it enough, it would start to seem real.

She liked the atmosphere in the office. It made her realise how much she missed having to think and be part of a team, a train of thought Alice was keen to encourage in herself. Because missing that meant that she was missing work, which meant, obviously, that she was looking forward to going back to London and applying for what she was determined would be the job of her dreams.

Together with Lily, she came up with a competition and a treasure hunt, and begged the use of a computer to draft fun forms for the children to fill in. Then she rang Roger and cajoled him into sponsoring prizes for everyone who took part, as she was pretty sure Will wouldn't approve of using his precious budget to finance frivolities.

'It'll be good PR for your company,' she told him.

'A bunch of children in fishing villages aren't exactly our target market,' said Roger, but he was happy to humour her, and the cost was negligible for a company like his in any case.

It wasn't long before Alice was coming up with other ideas. She told Will about Roger's offer as they drove home at the end of the day. 'Why don't you make this an opportunity to get more sponsorship?'

'I haven't got time for schmoozing,' said Will, changing gear irritably. He was tense after a day spent trying to ignore Alice's warm, vibrant presence in the office. It had been bad enough trying to concentrate on work before, when his senses had still been reeling with memories of the night before, but today had been virtually impossible. Wherever he looked, there she was, sitting on the edge of the desk, swinging those ridiculous shoes, chatting to the secretaries, bending over pieces of paper with Lily, their faces intent, studying the display boards …

Her questions had been intelligent, and she had made some

acute observations, which shouldn't have surprised him.
Nobody could ever have accused Alice of being stupid, and
he could see that, although the team had been wary of her initially, they had all been impressed by her ideas in the end. She
had flair, Will had to admit. It was hard to put his finger on
it, but there was a certain stylishness about everything she did,
and there was no doubt that she had already made a huge contribution to the plans for the open day.

So he ought to be feeling pleased with her, not edgy and
cross. Grateful as he was for her ideas, he wished that she had
stayed at home. Now, when she had gone, he wouldn't even
be able to go to the office without memories of her waiting
to ambush him.

'You wouldn't need to spend any extra time,' said Alice,
taking out her clip and wedging it between her teeth as she shook
out her hair. 'You're having the open day anyway,' she pointed
out, rather muffled through the clip. 'Why not invite businesses
along at the same time and show them what you're doing?'

Twisting her hair back up with one hand, she took the clip
from her teeth and deftly secured it into place. 'You're the one
who said how important the protection of the reef is to the
economy. That makes it of interest to companies who operate
here, local and international, and I'm sure lots of them would
be interested in sponsoring you. Jumping on the environmental awareness bandwagon makes good PR for them.'

'The point of the open day is to keep government support
and to involve the local communities,' Will grumbled. 'You're
wanting to turn it into a jamboree.'

'Nonsense,' said Alice briskly. 'All you need to do is lay
on a few more drinks, and it'll be worth it if you get some extra
money for the project, won't it? Besides,' she said, turning to
wink at Lily in the back seat, 'if we make it a party, it'll be a
chance for Lily and I to dress up.'

Lily brightened. 'Can I wear my pink shoes?'

'You can,' said Alice. 'And I'll wear my shoes with the bows. What do you think?' she asked, ignoring Will's snort.

'I like them.'

'I'm so glad we've got the footwear sorted out,' said Will sarcastically as they turned into their road. 'Now there's nothing else to worry about!'

Although, as it turned out, there was.

An email from the agency in London was waiting for him when he went into the office the next day. Will sat at his desk and stared at the screen. They had found an excellent candidate, the email informed him. An experienced nanny, mature and sensible, Helen would be able to fly out to St Bonaventure as soon as required. Would he please read the attached CV and their comments on Helen's interview and let them know as soon as possible if he wished to offer her the post.

Will lifted his eyes from the screen. Through the glass wall of his office he could see Alice on the phone. She had taken responsibility for the refreshments, and her face was animated as she talked, one hand holding the phone to her ear, the other gesticulating as if the person on the other end could see her.

When she had gone, he wouldn't be able to look at that phone without imagining her as she was now. He wouldn't be able to sit on the verandah in the evening without feeling her beside him, talking, stretching, waving her arms around, laughing, arguing, her face vivid in the darkness. He wouldn't be able to lie in bed without remembering her kisses, her softness and her warmth, the silken fire of her.

When she had gone, there would be an aching, empty void wherever she had been.

'I need to talk to you,' he said to her that night after they had put Lily to bed.

'That sounds serious,' said Alice lightly. 'Had we better sit down?'

So they sat in their accustomed places on the verandah, and Will tried to marshal the churning thoughts that had been occupying him all day. He hadn't been able to talk to her at the office, and he didn't want to say anything in front of Lily. He'd thought he'd decided what he was going to say, but now that he was here his careful arguments seemed to have vanished.

'What is it?' asked Alice after a while.

'I had an email today from the agency in London. They've found a nanny who sounds very suitable and she can come out next week if I want.'

Alice sat very still. Funny, she had known this was going to happen—it was what she had insisted should happen—but, now that the moment was here, she was completely unprepared. Everything had worked out perfectly. A nanny was available. Lily was going to school soon, and there would be someone to look after her when Will wasn't there. She could go home.

It was just what she wanted.

So why did her heart feel as if it had turned to a stone in her chest?

'I see,' she said, and from somewhere produced a smile. 'Well, that's good news. What's her name?'

'Helen.'

Helen would soon be sitting here with him. Helen would meet Lily from school and kiss her knees when she fell down. Helen would be waiting for him when he got home in the evening.

Is she pretty? Alice wanted to ask. Is she young? Will you fall in love with her?

'When's she coming?' she asked instead.

'I haven't replied yet,' said Will. 'I wanted to talk to you first.' He hesitated. 'I wanted to ask if you would stay.'

CHAPTER NINE

'STAY?' Alice echoed blankly.

'Yes, stay. Lily loves you, she'll miss you. And I'll miss you too,' Will admitted honestly. 'I'm not asking you to stay for ever, Alice. I know how you feel about commitment, but the last couple of weeks have been good, haven't they?'

'Yes,' she said, unable to deny it.

'Then why not carry on as we are?' he said, uncomfortably aware of the undercurrent of urgency, even desperation, in his voice. He cleared his throat and tried to sound more normal. 'You told me yourself that your engagement had fallen through and that you didn't have a job at the moment. What have you got to go home to?'

'My home,' said Alice a little defensively. 'My life.'

'You could have a home and a life here.'

'For how long?' she asked. 'I can't pretend I haven't enjoyed the last few weeks, Will. It's been a special time, but special times don't last.'

'They don't if you don't give them a chance,' said Will.

She bit her lip. The thought of saying goodbye to him and Lily tore at her, but he was asking her to give up her whole life, and for what?

'How can they last?' she said. 'Lily will be going to school soon, and what would I do then? You've got an absorbing job, Sara looks after the house. There's no place for me here, Will. How long would it be before I get bored, and everything that's made this such a wonderful time disappears?'

'You could find something to do,' said Will. 'Look at how you've taken over with the open day. Someone with your organisational skills will always find a job.'

'I might find some temporary or voluntary work, but that's not what I want. I've got a career, and the longer I stay away from it the more difficult it will be to go back to it. I've worked hard to get to this stage,' she told him. 'I can't just chuck it all in now on the basis of a few happy weeks.'

'At least you admit you have been happy,' said Will with an unmistakable thread of bitterness. 'Are you going to be happy in London? No, don't answer that,' he said as Alice hesitated. 'You've always put your career before your happiness, haven't you?'

'At least I can rely on my career to give me satisfaction and security,' she retorted. 'You can't rely on being happy.'

'But if you don't take the risk you'll never know how happy you could be.'

Alice sighed and pushed a stray strand of hair behind her ear. 'We've been through all this before, Will,' she reminded him. 'You've got your career, I've got mine, and they don't fit together. We still want different things from life.'

'So you won't stay?' he asked heavily. 'Not even for a while?'

She swallowed. 'No.' And then, when he said nothing, 'Surely you can see that the longer I stay, the harder it's going to be to say goodbye? It's going to come to goodbye sometime, and I think it would be easier for both of us to do it sooner rather than later.'

'All right,' said Will after a moment, his voice empty of expression now. 'I'll email the agency tomorrow and get them to send Helen out as soon as possible.'

Alice didn't reply. She sat unmoving in her chair, paralysed by the weight of the decision she had made. It was the right one, she knew, but that didn't stop her feeling leaden inside, and her throat was so tight she couldn't have spoken if she'd tried.

Beside her, Will looked out at the darkness, his jaw clenched with disappointment and a kind of rage for allowing himself to even hope that she would say yes when he must have known that she would say no.

The insects shrilled into the silence, and for a while there was nothing else but the sound of the ocean beyond the reef and the sadness of knowing that the love and the joy they had shared wasn't going to be enough.

At last, Will drew a long breath and got to his feet. 'Come on,' he said, holding a hand down to her. 'Let's go to bed.'

He stopped as he saw her expression rinsed with surprise, and the hand which he had reached out so instinctively fell to his side. 'Would you rather not?'

'No, it's not that,' said Alice, faltering. 'It's just…I didn't think *you* would want to.'

'We've still got a week left,' he said. 'You were the one who said that we should make the most of the time we had.'

'Yes.' Alice got up almost stiffly, overwhelmed by the relief that had rushed through her when she'd realised that Will wasn't going to reject her. She wouldn't have blamed him if he had, but the thought that she would never again lie in his arms had been a bitter one. Reaching out, she took his hand deliberately. 'Yes, I did.'

They didn't say a word to each other, but there was a desperation and a poignancy to their love-making that wrenched Alice's heart. There was no need to speak when every kiss, every touch, said more than words ever could how much they were going to miss each other.

By tacit agreement, they both threw themselves into the preparations for the open day. Anything was better than thinking about how they were going to say goodbye.

On Friday morning, Will sat impatiently in the car, waiting for Alice and Lily to appear. He had done his best to talk himself into believing that Alice's departure was for the best. She had worked really hard on the open day, but she didn't really fit in here, he reminded himself constantly. She had been right. There would be nothing for her to do on St Bonaventure, and she would soon get bored and restless. Look how little time it had taken for her to get fed up with staying with Beth. Far better for her to go now than to hang around until her frustration soured everything.

He should never have asked her to stay, Will told himself, drumming his fingers on the steering wheel and glancing at his watch for the umpteenth time. Alice had a pattern of running away at the first suggestion of commitment. She had always done it, and she always would. For someone with such forceful opinions, she was pathetic when it came to taking risks.

Will was conscious of the growing resentment inside him, which he fed deliberately because it was easier to be angry with Alice than to contemplate life when she was gone. Why had she had to come and upset everything? She could have stayed with Roger and Beth. They could have met a couple of times for some polite conversation and everything would have been fine. But no! She'd had to come and live with them. She had turned his world upside down all over again. She had made him fall in love with her all over again, and, now that she had made sure that she was right at the centre of his life and Lily's, she was going to leave them both feeling desolate.

Now the tension between them was worse than ever. They

hardly talked about anything except the open day. The only way they could communicate was in bed, where they made love with a fierceness and an intensity that left them both shattered. Will didn't know whether it making things better or worse. He just knew that his stomach felt as if a heavy stone were lodged inside it.

If nothing else, the delay allowed an outlet for his feelings. He leant on the horn. 'If you're not ready in two minutes, you can get a taxi,' he shouted. 'I've got to go.'

'We're coming!'

Alice and Lily came hurrying down the steps from the front door. Alice was holding Lily's hand and had a straw hat in the other. Will didn't know whether it was deliberate or not, but she was wearing the green dress she had worn at the party when he had first seen her again. She even had the same silly shoes on. It was almost as if she was making an effort to revert to the brittle, superficial person she had seemed then.

His daughter looked charming in a floppy hat, pink shoes, and a straight pink shift that Will didn't recall seeing before.

'New dress?' he asked, cocking an eye over his shoulder as she clambered into the back seat and Alice helped her fix her seat belt.

'Alice bought it for me.'

'A goodbye present,' Alice explained, getting in beside Will and settling herself with much smoothing and twitching of her skirt. 'I thought it was time to get her used to the idea of me going,' she added in an undertone as Will let out the clutch.

Big of her, thought Will sourly, resenting the way she seemed to treat the matter so practically.

'I don't want her to go,' said Lily, whose hearing was better than Alice had imagined.

Now look at the mess Alice had left him in. It was all very well for Alice, swanning back to her oh-so-important career in London, but he was going to be left trying to find a way to comfort a desolate daughter, and he had know idea how he was going to do it.

'Alice has to go home,' he said. 'I'm sure you'll like Helen. She sounds nice.'

Lily's bottom lip stuck out. 'I don't want Helen. I want Alice.'

'I'm not going yet,' Alice interrupted, determinedly bright. 'So let's all enjoy today.'

She might be able to enjoy it, Will thought darkly, but he couldn't. The only advantage was that he was too busy to think much. The open day proved to be a surprisingly popular event and, once the government minister's tour was out of the way, a steady stream of curious visitors came in to look around and find out what the project was all about and how it would affect them. Fishermen mixed with the expatriate crowd Alice had persuaded to come with a view to drumming up some financial support, and between them all ran what seemed like hordes of children who had got a whiff of the prizes. Alice's competition was a huge success, and even some of the adults tried it for fun.

It was a hot day, but Alice was cool and elegant at the centre of it all. It was hard to believe that this was the same woman who had rolled laughing with him in bed, her hair tickling his chest and her mouth curving against his skin, and his heart twisted as he watched her.

She seemed to be everywhere, organizing children, making sure people had drinks, smiling and talking, working unobtrusively to make the day a success. He couldn't help thinking that it would be easier for him if she were being selfish and false. As it was, her every move seemed designed to underline how much he would miss her when she was gone.

And how little she herself cared.

Alice was not, in fact, enjoying the day as much as Will

thought. It was a huge effort to keep the smile fixed to her face, especially when she kept catching glimpses of Will between the crowds. He was dressed rather more smartly today in honour of the minister, but she noticed that he talked to the fishermen in exactly the same way as he talked to the politician.

He'd told her that he only had the rudiments of the local language which he had picked up on previous trips, but he seemed to Alice to be able to communicate perfectly well, laughing and joking with the locals or explaining the project's objectives. She only had to look at how people reacted to him to know that he was able to do that clearly and without being condescending or patronising.

Studying him through the milling crowds, Alice was struck anew by the cool self-containment that set him apart from the others, and she was engulfed suddenly in a giddying thrill of pride and possession that she was the only one there who knew how the muscles flexed when she ran her palms over his back, who knew the taste of his skin, how warm and sure his hands felt.

Her breath shortened as she watched him, and her mouth was dry, and for the umpteenth time since that awful night on the verandah she dithered. Stay, he had asked her, and she had said no. Was she making a terrible mistake? Sometimes, like now, it felt as if saying goodbye would be the hardest thing she had ever done. And why do it if she didn't need to?

But, if today proved anything, it was that Will's career was as important to him as hers was to her. His marine research was an integral part of him, and she clung to her work as the one thing she had ever been able to feel sure of. She loved Will, Alice realised sadly. She just couldn't be sure whether she loved him enough to give up everything else that mattered to her, and, unless she *was* sure, it would be better for her to go home.

'Alice!'

Startled out of her gloomy thoughts, Alice turned to see Roger and Beth advancing on her, both smiling broadly, and quickly she fixed her own smile back into place.

'It's lovely to see you,' she said, hugging first one then the other. 'Thank you for coming—and for all those prizes, Roger! They've been a huge success with the children.'

'Where's Will?'

Alice didn't even have to look. She was always aware of where he was and what he was doing. 'Over there,' she said, indicating to where Will stood talking to a group of fishermen.

Rather overwhelmed by all the strangers, Lily was leaning against his leg, nibbling her thumb, and he had a reassuring hand on her head. Every time she saw them close together, a choked feeling clogged Alice's throat and she had to bite her lip.

Roger whistled soundlessly. 'What a change in them both! Is that thanks to you, Alice?'

'They just needed time to get used to each other,' said Alice, but deep down she hoped that she *had* made a difference. At least Will and Lily would have each other from now on.

She would have nobody.

Roger wandered off to have a word with someone he recognized, and Beth turned to Alice with mock reproach. 'We've hardly seen you recently!'

'I know, I'm sorry,' said Alice, guiltily aware that she had been so involved with Will and Lily that she hadn't given her old friends the attention they deserved. 'It's been…busy.'

'Well, as long as you've been having a good time.'

Alice thought about the day out on the reef. About reading with Lily on the verandah. About lying under the ceiling fan with Will breathing quietly beside her, and the thrill of anticipation when he rolled towards her with a smile. To her horror, she felt tears sting her eyes, and she was very glad of her sunglasses.

'Oh, yes,' she said with a careless shrug. 'It's been fun.'

'We wondered if you'd think about staying,' said Beth, ultra-casual. 'You and Will must have got quite close.'

'Yes, it's been nice seeing him again.' Alice was shocked by how unconcerned she could sound when she tried. 'But, you know, when it's time to go…A new nanny is coming out next week, so there's not much point in me staying any longer. Besides, I've still got my ticket home.'

'Oh, you're going?' Beth looked disappointed. 'You will come and see us before you— Oh!' She broke off abruptly and put a hand to her stomach.

'Beth?' said Alice in quick concern. 'Are you all right?'

'Just a bit sick,' muttered Beth, and when Alice looked closely she saw that, beneath her hat, Beth was looking grey and drawn.

'Come inside,' she said, taking Beth's arm. 'It's cooler in there, and you can sit down.'

She made Beth sit in a cool quiet room while she went to find some cold water. 'Shall I get Roger?' she asked worriedly when she came back. It wasn't like Beth to be ill. 'You don't look at all well.'

'I'll be fine in a minute,' said Beth, sipping the water. She smiled at Alice. 'Don't look so worried. It's good news. Oh, Alice, I'm pregnant at last!'

Alice gasped. '*Beth!* That's *fantastic* news!'

'It's early days yet,' Beth warned, 'so we're not telling anyone yet, but I wanted you to know.'

'Oh, Beth …' Tears shone in Alice's eyes as she hugged her friend. 'I won't tell anyone, I promise, but I'm so, so happy for you! And Roger…he must be thrilled!'

'He is. Neither of us can quite believe it yet,' Beth confessed. 'We've wanted this for so long, and we were just beginning to think it wasn't going to happen. Of course, I didn't count on quite how sick I'd feel!'

Alice was so elated by Beth's news that she forgot her own misery about saying goodbye to Will for a while. Leaving Beth to recover in the cool, she sailed out with a wide smile to find Roger.

Roger being Roger, she found him in the middle of a laughing group. Mindful of the need for secrecy, it took all her ingenuity to extricate him but she finally managed to drag him to a quiet place behind the laboratory where she threw her arms around him and promptly burst into tears.

'Hey, what's the matter?' asked Roger in alarm, enveloping her in a comforting hug.

'I'm just so happy for you,' Alice snuffled against his broad chest.

'Ah.' Roger began to smile. 'You've been talking to Beth?'

'Yes, and I'm sworn to secrecy, but it's such fantastic news,' she said, lifting her head to smile at him through her tears. 'I know how much it means to you both.'

'Well, we're expecting you to be godmother, so you'd better come back when the baby is born.'

For a fleeting moment Alice wondered how on earth she would cope with coming back when she would be bound to meet Will again, but she pushed that thought resolutely out of her mind. It was Roger and Beth who mattered now.

'Of course I will,' she told him. 'Try keeping me away from my first godchild!'

She was still smiling when she and Roger rejoined the party. Beth had recovered by then, but Alice was glad to see that Roger took her away soon afterwards. She couldn't help noticing the tender way he put his arm around his wife, and she watched wistfully as he ushered Beth out to the car.

Their devotion to each other brought a lump to Alice's throat. Roger and Beth were lucky. They loved each other completely and they faced everything together. They had had

their sadnesses, but their life seemed so much less complicated than her own. Everything was simple for Roger and
Beth. Why had she had to fall in love with someone whose
life was incompatible with hers?

Sighing, she turned to find Will watching her. His jaw was
set and his mouth was pressed together in a decidedly grim
line, but Alice's heart still skipped a beat at the sight of him.

'Oh... Hi,' she said.

'You look very sad, Alice,' he said, an edge to his voice that
Alice was too full of emotion to analyse.

'I'm not sad,' she said. 'Envious, perhaps.'

'Of Beth?'

'Yes.' She was a little surprised that he had guessed so
quickly. 'I think she knows how lucky she is.'

'Does she?'

This time there was no mistaking the hardness in his voice,
and Alice looked at him, puzzled. But, before she could ask
what he meant, Will's attention was claimed by someone who
came up to say goodbye.

The event seemed to be winding down, anyway, and,
feeling deflated after the earlier high, she began to help with
the clearing up. In spite of her hat, she was beginning to feel
the effects of standing in the sun too long, and her head was
thumping, so when Will told her that one of the divers had
offered her and Lily a lift home she was glad to accept.

'I'll need to wait and lock up when everyone else has
gone,' he said brusquely.

Alice had put an exhausted Lily to bed by the time he
came back, and she was sitting on the verandah and trying not
to think that this time next week she would be home. She tried
to imagine herself in her flat. She would pick up the accumulated post from the doormat. She would unpack her case, and
put some washing on.

And then what? Desolation washed over her at the realisation that there would be no one to sit down with, no one to have missed her, no one to pour her a drink or put an arm around her and tell her that they were glad she was home. She would be alone again.

'There you are.' Will let the screen door crash behind him. He was carrying a bottle of beer, and although he sat down in his usual chair nothing else was normal. His expression was stony, and he was taut with suppressed feeling, wound up so tight that Alice looked at him in concern. *Something* had obviously happened, but she had the nerve-racking feeling that if she put a foot wrong he would explode.

'Long day,' she ventured cautiously.

'Yes.'

'Still, I think it was a success.'

'Yes.'

There was a pause while Alice eyed him warily. 'Do you want anything to eat?'

'No,' he said, adding grudgingly as Alice raised her brows, 'Thank you.'

'I wasn't hungry either,' she said, and gave up. If Will wanted to tell her what the problem was, he could, but she was in no mood to sit here and coax it out of him if he didn't feel like cooperating. Let him keep it all bottled up inside him, if that was what he wanted.

The silence lengthened uncomfortably. Will drank his beer grimly, until at last he put the bottle down on the table between them with a sharp click.

'I think you should be more careful of Beth's feelings,' he said abruptly.

Alice wasn't sure what she was expecting, but it certainly wasn't that!

'What on earth do you mean?' she asked in astonishment.

'I saw you with Roger this afternoon.'

She stared at him. Surely he wasn't jealous of *Roger*? 'Yes, we're friends. Of course I talked to Roger!'

'What were you talking to him about?'

Opening her mouth to tell him, Alice remembered her promise to Beth just in time and closed it again. 'That's none of your business,' she said after a moment.

'Because *friends* don't usually sneak away behind the lab to have a conversation, or kiss and cuddle each other when they're doing it!'

Will had been gripped by a white-hot fury ever since he had watched Alice drag Roger out of sight. He didn't know what had prompted him to follow them—all right, he did know, he was jealous—but he was completely unprepared for the fist that had closed around his heart as he had seen Alice bury her face in Roger's broad chest and cling to him.

Unable to watch any more, he had turned on his heel and left them to it, and he might have left it at that if he hadn't caught sight of Beth emerging from the office a few minutes later, looking pale and wan. She'd asked him if he had seen Roger, so of course he had said no. He couldn't have her interrupting that scene behind the lab, but, from her drawn look, he couldn't help thinking that she already suspected that something was wrong.

And now Alice wasn't even bothering to deny it.

'Roger and I have always hugged and kissed each other,' she said, her eyes blazing at his tone. 'He's a *friend* and that's what we do. We're not all repressed scientists,' she was unable to resist adding snidely.

'Is Beth a friend too?'

'You know she is.'

'You don't treat her like one,' said Will harshly. 'I saw her today too. She looked wretched, and I'm not surprised, if she has any idea of what you and her husband are up to!'

For a moment, Alice was so outraged that she couldn't speak, could only gulp in disbelief and fury. 'Are you implying that Roger and I are having an affair?' she asked dangerously when she could get the words out.

'I'm saying that you don't behave to him the way you should if you were a good friend to Beth.'

'How dare you!' Alice surged to her feet, shaking with fury. 'I've known Roger for years and there's *never* been anything between us. You should know that better than anyone! I love Roger dearly, but we've never felt like that about each other.'

'Are you sure about that?' Will asked unpleasantly, remembering that disastrous evening when Roger had confessed how he really felt about Alice.

'Yes, I'm sure! And, even if I wasn't, do you really think that I'm the kind of person who would break up a friend's marriage?' She shook her head, unable to believe that Will could be saying such things. 'What do you think I *am*? We've been sleeping together, for God's sake! What did you think, that I was just making do with you because I couldn't have Roger?'

Turning away with an exclamation of disbelief and disgust, she wrapped her arms around her in an attempt to stop herself shaking. 'I suppose you think that after Tony left, I came out here deliberately to ensnare Roger because I didn't have a man of my own!'

'I'm a scientist,' said Will, who didn't believe anything of the kind but who was too angry to think about what he was saying. Seeing Alice with Roger had provided an outlet for all the pent-up anger, confusion and bitterness he had been feeling ever since she had refused to stay, and he wasn't capable of thinking clearly right now. 'I believe the evidence, and I've seen you cuddling up to Roger at every opportunity. You can't tell me that you've never thought what that does to him!'

Alice turned slowly to stare at him. 'I don't believe this,' she said. 'How can you possibly think that about me? You know me!'

'I used to,' he said bleakly. 'I'm not sure I do know you any more.'

There was an appalled silence.

'I think I'd better go,' said Alice in a shaking voice at last, and she turned blindly for the door.

The expression on her face brought Will to his senses too late, and he scrambled to his feet. 'Alice, wait!'

But she only shook her head without looking at him. 'I'll leave tomorrow,' she said, and let the screen door click back into place behind her.

Alice sat carefully down on the back steps next to Lily. She had broken the news at breakfast that she was leaving that day and it had gone even worse than she had feared. Not that Lily had cried or had a tantrum. She had simply stared disbelievingly at Alice out of dark eyes, then had got up without a word and run out into the garden. Heavy hearted, Alice had finished her packing. Now Roger was waiting with a bleak-faced Will by the car, and she had come to try and say goodbye to Lily.

Lily wouldn't acknowledge her presence at first. Her body was rigid, her face averted, and Alice was dismayed to see the closed, blank expression that she remembered from their first meeting.

'Lily,' she began helplessly. 'I'm sorry I have to go like this. I was going anyway in a few days, but I didn't want it to be this way.'

'I don't care,' said Lily, but a spasm crossed her face, and Alice's heart cracked. It wasn't long since this child had lost her mother, and now the next person she had allowed close seemed to be abandoning her too. She tried to put a comforting arm around her, but Lily shook it off.

'Oh, Lily, it's not that I want to leave you,' she sighed.

'Then why are you going? Is it because I've been naughty?'

'Of course not,' said Alice, appalled. 'Of *course* not, Lily. It's nothing to do with you. I wish I could explain but it's…complicated…adult stuff,' she said lamely. She wasn't going to leave Lily thinking that it had anything to do with Will. Her father was the only constant in her life now, and, hurt as Alice was, she wouldn't do anything to jeopardise his relationship with his daughter.

'Helen will be coming soon,' she went on. 'And it'll be difficult for her if I'm still here. I'm going to miss you more than I can say, but you'll like Helen, I promise you.'

'I won't!' Lily jumped furiously to her feet. 'I'll hate her like I hate you!' she shouted, and ran off before Alice could reach out to her.

Unable to keep back the tears any longer, Alice buried her face in her hands and wept.

The screen door creaked, and she could hear steps on the wooden verandah before someone sat down beside her. 'She doesn't hate you,' Will's voice said gently. 'She loves you. She's only angry because you're leaving her, and she doesn't understand why.'

There was a pause, punctuated by Alice's hiccupping sobs.

'I don't have Lily's excuse,' Will went on after a moment. 'I *do* understand why you're going, but I was still angry because I love you, too, and I don't want you to go, even though I know that you must.'

Alice's hands were still covering her face, but her sobs had subsided slightly, and he could tell that she was listening.

'I'm so sorry about last night, Alice,' he said quietly. 'I said some unforgivable things, and I said them because I'm a jealous fool, but really because I was looking for an excuse to hate you, like Lily, because making myself hate you seemed like the only way I could bear the thought of you leaving me.'

Drawing a shuddering breath, Alice lifted her head at last and wiped her eyes with a wobbly thumb. She didn't say anything, but Will was encouraged enough to go on. 'It was a childish reaction, I know, but I haven't been thinking straight recently. I've been flailing round, so wretched and miserable because you were going that I would say anything.

'I lied when I said I didn't know you, Alice,' he said. 'I *do* know you. You're the truest person I know. You would never do anything to hurt Roger or Beth, and I knew it when I was saying it. I just wanted to hurt you so that you felt what I was feeling.'

Alice opened her mouth, but he put a gentle finger on her lips. 'Let me finish. I've made such a bloody mess of everything, Alice. I've hurt you, and because I've hurt you I've hurt Lily, and I don't know how I'm going to forgive myself for either.'

He looked into Alice's golden eyes, puffy now and swimming with tears, but still beautiful. 'I won't ask you again if you'll stay. I know you've got your life to go back to, and goodbyes like these are too hard to go through again. Go with Roger now, and fly home as you planned. I'll look after Lily. She'll be all right.

'I hope you find what you're looking for, Alice,' he went on, although his throat was so tight he had to force the words out. 'I hope you'll be happy, as happy as we were here, and all those years ago. I've always loved you, and I know now that I always will. It's only ever going to be you, Alice,' he said with an unsteady smile. 'I want you to know that if you ever change your mind, and think you can take a chance on being loved utterly and completely, Lily and I will be here for you, and we'll take as much or as little as you can give.'

'Will…I…I don't know what to say,' said Alice hopelessly.

'You don't need to say anything.' Will put a hand under her

elbow and helped her to her feet. 'You need to go home and decide for yourself what you really want, without me shouting at you and Lily piling on the emotional blackmail!'

'Tell Lily ...' Alice's voice cracked and she couldn't go on, but Will seemed to understand what she needed to say.

'I'll explain why you're going,' he said. 'I'll tell her that you know that she doesn't really hate you, and that you love her too.'

'Thank you,' she whispered. She didn't seem to be able to stop crying as she walked through the screen door for the last time and out to the front where Roger was waiting by the car.

'Come on then, waterworks,' he said gruffly. 'I've got your cases.'

'Alice,' said Will as she was about to get into the passenger seat, and she paused, a hand on the door and one foot in the well. 'Thank you,' he said simply. 'Thank you for everything you've done for Lily, and for me.'

Unable to speak, she nodded.

'And remember what I said about being here if you ever change your mind,' he added, his voice strained, and Alice bit her lip to stop the tears spilling over once more.

'I will,' she said. Then she ducked her head as she got into the car and closed the door, and Will could only watch in desolation as Roger drove her away.

CHAPTER TEN

THERE was so much post piled up behind the front door that Alice had to push her way into her cramped hallway. The flat smelt musty and unused, and even when she had switched on the lights the rooms seemed cheerless. Perhaps it was something to do with the dreary drizzle and the muted grey light of a wet Spring afternoon, she thought, and tried not to think of the aching blue ocean, the mint-green lagoon and the vivid colours of hibiscus and bougainvillaea.

Her feet had swollen on the long flight, and she kicked off her shoes with a weary sigh as she sat down on the cream sofa. This was the home she had worked hard for, the home she had been insistent she wanted to come back to. It represented everything she had ever wanted: security, stability, being settled at last. She had decorated it with care in the cool, minimalist style that appealed to her, and it had been her refuge whenever things had gone wrong.

Until now, she had always thought of her home as calm and restful. There was no reason suddenly to find the ivory walls cold, or to notice the roar of the traffic along the busy road outside, the dismaying wail of a siren in the distance, and the intrusive blare of a television next door.

No reason to find herself overwhelmed with homesickness

for a verandah thousands of miles away, where the insects whirred and rasped and shrilled, and the scent of frangipani drifted on the hot air. Alice looked at her watch and calculated the time in St Bonaventure. Will would be sitting there now, still and self-contained, listening to the sound of the sea he loved so much.

The memory of him was so sharp that Alice closed her eyes as if at a pain. Was he thinking of her? Was he missing her?

She had thought about him constantly since Roger had driven her away. The worst thing was realising that she hadn't said goodbye, to him or to Lily.

His words went round and round in her head. It's only ever going to be you, Alice. Lily and I will be here for you if you ever change your mind and think you can take a chance on being loved...

'I don't understand what the problem is,' Beth had said. 'Why are you putting yourself through all this misery? Will loves you, Lily loves you, and you wouldn't be this upset about leaving if you didn't love them back.'

'Love's not the problem,' Alice had tried to explain.

'Then what is?'

'It's everything else. It's not being sure if love would be enough.' She'd twisted her fingers in an agony of indecision. 'Yes, I could go back to Will now, but it would mean giving up my whole life for something that might not work out. It didn't work out last time, so why should it now?'

'You know yourselves better now,' Beth had pointed out, but Alice hadn't been convinced.

'I'm not sure that I do. I feel differently here,' she'd said, waving her arms at the tropical garden. 'But who's to say that what I feel is real? It might just be about being on holiday in a beautiful place. Maybe I'm just getting carried away by the romance of it all.'

Beth had looked thoughtful. 'Then perhaps Will is right. You need to go home and see how you feel when you're there. He's told you that he loves you, and he's not going anywhere, so it's up to you to decide what you want.'

It was deciding that was the problem, Alice thought in despair. She who had always been so clear about what she wanted before was now being tossed about in a maelstrom of indecision that was making her feel quite sick. One minute the thought of never seeing or touching Will again seemed so awful that she was ready to jump into a taxi and rush back to the house by the lagoon, the next she would think about selling her flat and committing herself to an expatriate life where they would move from house to house and none of them would be a home. And she would be swamped by memories of her childhood and all the times she had sworn that as soon as she was old enough she would settle down and make a home for herself.

She wasn't ready to give that up, Alice told herself. At least, she didn't think she was …

She was having to readjust so many of her ideas at the moment, that it was difficult to know *what* she thought. She had been astounded when Beth had told her just why Will had been so convinced that her relationship with Roger was inappropriate.

'It's not so far-fetched an idea,' Beth had said. 'Roger was in love with you for years.'

'*What?*' Alice had goggled at her, and Beth had nodded calmly.

'He confessed to Will once when he'd had too much to drink, and he was always grateful that Will never told you. He thought it would have embarrassed you if you'd known.'

'But I… But I …' Alice had floundered in disbelief. 'I had no *idea*!'

'Roger knew that. He'd probably have been better to have

told you and got you out of his system, but you know what fools men can be about these things,' said Roger's fond wife.

Alice regarded her curiously. 'Didn't you mind when he told you?' she asked a little awkwardly, not at all sure it wasn't a bit tacky to ask a man's wife how she felt when she'd found out he was in love with you.

'No,' said Beth, smiling. 'He told me that when he met me he realised that what he'd felt for you wasn't the real thing, and I believe him. I know Roger loves me, Alice. He loves you too, but in a very different way. I've always been sure of that.'

'It must be nice to be so sure,' said Alice wistfully, and then her face darkened as she remembered Will's bitter accusations. 'I can see why Will might be suspicious, I suppose, but it doesn't change the fact that he actually thought me capable of coming out here and making a play for Roger.'

Beth sighed. 'He apologised for that, didn't he? The man's desperate, Alice! If you won't go and see him, will you at least ring him?'

But Alice shook her head. 'It wouldn't be fair to do that until I was sure, the way you're sure about Roger, and I'm not. Helen's arriving today. It would just upset everyone if I went back now. My flight's tomorrow, and we'd just end up having to say goodbye all over again. No, I'm going to go home, and when I can think clearly again maybe I'll know how I feel.'

It was all very well deciding to think about her situation clearly, but it wasn't that easy in practice. Alice was convinced that all she needed was a good night's sleep and to wake up in her flat and suddenly she would know what to do, but it didn't work like that.

She did her best to get back into a routine as quickly as possible. She unpacked, shook the sand out of her shoes, washed and put away her holiday clothes and set about finding a new job. She filled in application forms, bought herself a smart new suit for interviews, and contacted friends she hadn't seen before the break-up with Tony.

Grimly determined to enjoy herself if it killed her, she went out as much as she could. Once she bumped into Tony and Sandi, and was appalled to discover how indifferent she felt as the three of them made polite chit-chat. She had been sure that Tony was the man she wanted to spend the rest of her life with, but how could she have wanted him when he didn't have Will's mouth or Will's smile or Will's ironic grey eyes? But, if her feelings towards him could change so completely in a matter of months, who was to say that her feelings for Will wouldn't change too?

So Alice continued, miserably unsure, torn between her determination to get back into her old life and her inability to put her time in St Bonaventure out of her mind. She would be sitting having coffee with a friend, and her eyes would slip out of focus momentarily at the memory of Will's hands around a mug. She let herself into the flat, and found herself listening for the click of the screen door, and if she caught a glimpse of a dark-haired little girl her heart would lurch with the bizarre hope that it was Lily.

She ached for Will, for his cool, quiet presence, his wry smile and his hard body. She missed the constant sigh of the sea and the soughing of the warm wind in the palm trees. She missed the hot nights. She missed Lily desperately, but most of all she missed Will.

Alice longed to hear from him. Every time she went home, she would check for an email, a message on the answering machine, a postcard, anything to show that he was still thinking about her. There was never anything. *You need to go home and decide for yourself.* She could still hear Will saying it, and she wanted to shout at him that she *couldn't* decide.

If only he would make some move, it would take nothing to convince her. Why didn't he just contact her?

She began to set herself little tests. If she could get through the morning without thinking about him, that must mean that she was getting over him, and then she'd know she'd made the right decision. If she hadn't heard from him by next week, she'd know he didn't really care and that it wasn't meant to be. If she could walk to the end of the street without stepping on the cracks in the pavement, she'd be able to make up her mind.

None of them worked.

When her dream job was advertised in the trade journal, Alice could hardly believe it. This, surely, was the sign that she had been waiting for. The job was everything she'd ever wanted. A prestigious company, a promotion, a challenging position that would launch her into a new stage of her career. If she got this job, she was meant to stay in London and get on with her life. What could be clearer?

Carefully, Alice filled in the application form, and when she passed the first hurdle and was asked for interview she had her suit cleaned, and bought a spectacular pair of new shoes to go with it. She prepared for the interview as thoroughly as she could, but she was very nervous as she waited to go in. It felt as if her whole future would be decided by that hour's interview.

Her shoes pinched horribly, but otherwise it seemed to go quite well, and then all Alice had to do was wait.

When her phone rang a few hours later, she practically jumped out of her skin. She had spent the afternoon prowling restlessly about the flat, unable to settle to anything. Too jittery to take off her suit, she was barefoot on the carpet, her poor toes enjoying a respite from being pushed into the shoes that might look fabulous but were in fact extremely uncomfortable.

This was it. Alice stared at the ringing phone for a moment and then picked it up. 'Hello?'

'Ms Gunning?' said a voice she recognized from the interview that morning. 'Thank you so much for coming to see us this morning. We're absolutely delighted to offer you the post.'

The rest of the conversation was a blur of congratulations, but it finished with a suggestion that she go in and see them the next day to sort out the practicalities of salary and starting date. In the meantime, they would courier over her contract so that she could read it at her leisure.

'Thank you so much.' Alice put the phone down slowly.

So the job was hers. Finally her decision had been made for her. She was to stay here, with a great job, a nice flat, and friends. She had a good life, and she was safe and settled again, just as she had always wanted.

She was ecstatically happy and relieved, naturally.

She burst into tears.

Aghast at herself, Alice sank on to the sofa, brushing the tears angrily from her face. What on earth was the matter with her? She had wanted a sign, and this was it. She should be delighted, not sick to her stomach with disappointment.

But, the more she tried to convince herself that she had got what she wanted, the more she cried, until her face was blotched and piggy, and her throat was clogged with sobs.

As if that wasn't enough, the doorbell pealed imperatively. 'Oh, God, now what?' mumbled Alice. She didn't want to explain her wretched state to a neighbour, and she was in no mood for a survey, but it might be the contract. She would have to check.

Cautiously, she put her eye to the peephole and peered through the door. If it was a courier, she would open the door, take the contract and close it again. If it was a friend or a neighbour, she would just have to pretend that she wasn't there.

But it wasn't a friend or a neighbour, or a market researcher, or even a courier. Standing on the other side of the door were the very last people she had expected to see.

Her parents.

Alice was humming as she jumped off the bus and walked back to the flat past the little parade of shops. She waved at the owner of the Turkish greengrocer, and the young boy who helped at the Indian corner shop that sold everything she could ever want in the middle of the night. Stopping at the street market, she bought a bunch of hyacinths, and sniffed appreciatively as she passed an Italian restaurant where something very garlicky was cooking. Two elderly ladies swathed in black were coming towards her, deep in conversation, and Alice smiled as she stood aside for them.

She loved this multi-cultural side to London. The city was looking at its best in the spring sunshine. In the centre of town, the great parks were green and bright with flowers nodding gaily in the breeze, and the very air seemed sharper and clearer, as if the world was conspiring to reassure her that she had made the right decision. Even the bus had come just when she wanted it, and she had enjoyed the ride on the top deck back to her suburb. It might not be as attractive as the centre of town, but it had its own vibrancy and charm. Yes, this was a great city to live in.

Alice couldn't believe how much better she felt for making up her mind. Filled with a sense of well-being, she was smiling as she turned into her street, and it wasn't until she was halfway along that she saw that someone was standing on her doorstep. Someone whose shape and stance was achingly familiar.

Her steps slowed in disbelief, until she stopped altogether with her hand on the gate, her smile fading. He turned at her approach, and as they looked at each other the beat of the great metropolis, the jabber of languages, the constant throb of traffic, the rattle of trains, the blare of music, and the car alarm that everyone was ignoring, faded into a blur. And then silence, until there was just the two of them, looking at each other.

Will.

Alice drank in the sight of him. He looked tired, she thought, but it was unmistakably him. It was as if a high-definition lens had been slotted over her eyes so that she could see him in extraordinary detail: every line around his eyes, every crease in his cheek, the way his hair grew, the set of his mouth…

Oh, that mouth… Her knees went suddenly weak, and she had to hang on to the gate.

'Hello,' she said.

'Hello, Alice.'

He didn't smile, he didn't rush to sweep her into his arms, he just stood there and looked directly back at her. But that was the moment nonetheless when the last piece clicked into place for Alice, and she realised that she wasn't even surprised to see him. All that misery, all that indecision, all that dithering…all had led inevitably to this time and this place, to this certainty that everything would be all right.

Discovering that she was able to move after all, Alice pushed open the gate and pulled out her keys as she walked towards him.

'Have you been waiting long?'

'About forty minutes.'

About ten years, Will amended to himself.

Alice looked wonderful. The mere sight of her was enough to lift his heart, but he was conscious of a sinking sense of consternation too. Part of him, *admit it,* had hoped that she would have been wretched and miserable without him, and that it would have showed, but there was no evidence of that. Instead, she looked glowing and confident in a short jacket with a long flowing skirt and boots, and flowers in her arms. Her hair fell to her shoulders, and when she stood at the gate it shone gold and copper and bronze in the spring light, and her eyes were full of sunshine.

She looked happy, Will realised dully, and he was terribly afraid that he had left it too late.

Alice went into the kitchen and put the hyacinths into some water, bending to breathe in their heady perfume. 'Coffee?' she asked.

'Thanks.' Will wasn't sure how to begin. He stood to one side and watched her moving around the kitchen. She hadn't asked what he was doing there, but presumably she could guess, and surely they had known each other long enough for him not to need to dance around with polite conversation before coming to the point?

'I've been wondering if you'd thought at all about what I said before you left,' he said abruptly. 'Have you decided what you want yet?'

Alice had sat on a chair and was pulling off her boots, but she stopped in the middle of unzipping the second one and smiled at him. 'Yes,' she said. 'Yes, I have.'

'I see,' said Will bleakly. She had decided to stay in London, that was obvious. You didn't buy flowers for a home you were about to leave.

'Shall we go into the sitting room?' Alice suggested before he could say any more, and she carried the tray into a bright room. It was cool and uncluttered, and Will sat gingerly on the edge of a cream sofa. She looked perfectly at home here. If this was her life, he wasn't surprised that she hadn't wanted to give it up for a rickety verandah and creaking ceiling fans.

Alice pushed the plunger into the cafetière and poured out the coffee, wriggling her toes on the carpet. Will was so used to seeing her in shoes that the sight of her bare feet was strangely arousing, and he looked away.

'What are you doing here, Will?' she asked as she handed him a mug of coffee. 'I thought you were going to wait for me to decide what I wanted to do?'

'I was going to—I *meant* to wait—but there came a point when I couldn't wait any longer.' Will put down his coffee without drinking it. 'It's terrible since you left, Alice,' he told her honestly. 'Lily has closed in on herself again.'

Alice bit her lip. 'Doesn't she get on with Helen?'

'Helen's all right. She's done her best. It's not her fault that she's not you,' said Will. 'The truth is that Lily and I are in a bad way. I can't sleep, I can't eat, I can't work properly... We don't seem to be able to do anything but miss you.'

A wry smile touched his mouth. 'I know this sounds like emotional blackmail, Alice, but it's not meant to be that. It's just that it suddenly seemed stupid to just sit out there and hope for the best. I couldn't just watch my daughter getting quieter and quieter. I realised that if we wanted you back in our lives— and we do—I would have to do something to make it happen.

'So I've applied for a job here in the UK,' he told Alice. 'It's as a consultant with an engineering company, doing environmental impact assessments for their marine projects. I'd be based in the North, not London, but it's a permanent job, and a good one. I'd still have to do research overseas, but it would be in short stints, so we could buy a house and settle down somewhere. Lily could go to school, and you could carry on with your career ...'

Will stopped, realising that he was in danger of babbling. He looked at Alice, who was clasping her mug with a very strange expression on her face, as if she couldn't quite believe what she was hearing.

'I suppose what I really came to ask you, Alice, was

whether it would make any difference to your decision if I did get that job.'

Very slowly, Alice shook her head. 'No,' she said. 'No, it wouldn't make any difference.'

'I see.' The belief that deep down Alice still loved him had been keeping Will going through the last ghastly weeks. He knew that she was scarred by her restless childhood and he knew how important the idea of home was to her. Once he had made the decision to change his own career, he had thought that would solve the problem, but he could see now that it had been arrogant of him. Alice had never promised anything beyond the short term.

Somehow he managed a smile. 'I understand,' he said. 'Now that I've seen you here, I can appreciate what this place means to you.' He looked around the room, approving its simple, tasteful décor. 'It's nice here. You've obviously got a good life, and I know how important your career is to you. I hope you'll find just the job you want,' he added heroically.

'It's funny you should say that,' said Alice, a smile hovering around her mouth. 'I was offered the job of my dreams just a couple of days ago.'

'Well…great,' said Will heartily. Abandoning his coffee, he got to his feet. He wasn't sure how he was going to tell Lily, but he would have to find a way. She had been happy to see her grandparents again. Perhaps he should think about moving to the UK anyway, just as Alice had once suggested. 'Good luck then, Alice.'

'Where are you going?'

'I should go and pick Lily up. It was good to see you again,' he said, looking into Alice's golden eyes for the last time. 'And… Well, there doesn't seem much more to say.'

He was turning for the door when her soft voice stopped him in his tracks. 'Even if I tell you that I didn't take the job?'

Very, very slowly, Will turned back. 'You didn't take it?'

Alice shook her head, her smile a little wavery. 'You haven't asked me what decision I made yet,' she reminded him.

'I thought…I assumed …' he stammered as a tiny spark of hope lit in his heart. 'You look so happy, so at home here.'

She tutted. 'That's not very scientific of you, Will. I'd have expected you to look at the evidence, not make assumptions on how you think I look.'

'Evidence?'

Getting to her feet, Alice went over to the table and rummaged among some papers, pulling out a rectangular card. 'Evidence like this,' she said, putting it into a flabbergasted Will's hand. 'It's a plane ticket,' she told him unnecessarily. 'Open it.'

'It's to St Bonaventure.' Will lifted his head from the ticket to stare at her, a smile starting at the back of his eyes.

'And it's in my name.' She took the ticket from him and tossed it back onto the table before turning back to him and taking his hand, smiling as his fingers closed convulsively around hers. 'What does that evidence tell you, Will?'

'Alice …' Unable to find the words for how he felt, Will pulled her into his arms. He didn't kiss her, he just held her very tightly, his eyes squeezed shut, his face pressed into her hair as he breathed in the scent of her, and felt the iron bands that had been gripped around his heart ever since she had driven off with Roger start to loosen.

'I made my decision, Will.' Alice turned her face into his throat and clung to him. 'I chose happiness. I chose you.'

Will's arms tightened around her even further, but she didn't mind. 'You were right about me looking happy,' she went on, rather muffled. 'I was happy because I'd just finished making all the arrangements to let this flat and could go back to you and Lily.'

'But Alice, this is your home,' Will protested.

'It was, but when I came back from St Bonaventure it wasn't home any more,' she said. 'It was just a flat. For a while it seemed as if I didn't have a home at all, and then I realised that I do. It's just not bricks and mortar. Home is wherever you are.'

'Alice… Oh, Alice …' Will pulled back slightly so that she could turn her face up to his, and their lips met at last in a long, sweet kiss. He felt almost drunk with relief and happiness. He wasn't sure quite how it happened, but his dream had just come true, and the proof of it was Alice's lips beneath his, her arms around him, the softness and scent of her hair. 'Tell me that again,' he said raggedly when they broke for air.

'I love you, Will. I think I've always loved you, but I was too stupid and afraid to realise how lucky I was to have found you.' Lovingly, she traced the line of his cheek with her fingers. 'I've walked away from your love three times now, and I don't deserve to be given another chance, but, if you will, I promise I'll never walk away again. I just want to be with you, and I don't care where we are, or what we do, as long as we're together.'

'And you're sure?' asked Will as he bent to kiss her again, and she smiled against his lips.

'Yes, this time I'm sure.'

'What made you change your mind?' Will asked much later when they were lying, lazily entangled, in Alice's bed. He smoothed the hair tenderly from her face. 'You were so insistent that you had everything you needed here.'

'Everything except you and Lily,' said Alice, rolling onto her side to face him. 'It didn't take me long to realise that I might have the security of material things, but none of them were worth anything without you. I knew I loved you, and that you loved me, but I still couldn't bring myself to trust that feeling.

'I was afraid to let go of what I had,' she confessed. 'It was just what you said. I was afraid to give it all up for the chance of happiness.' She linked her fingers with his. 'Once you know what you want, it all seems obvious, and I can't believe now that I hesitated for so long. But then I was going round and round in circles, not knowing what I wanted or what I really thought.

'Strangely, it was being offered that job that convinced me,' she remembered. 'I'd told myself that I would take it as a sign that I should stay here if I got it, but of course, when it happened, I realised it wasn't the sign I wanted. I felt a fool,' she told him with a twisted smile. 'I'd just been offered the job of my dreams, and all I could think was that I didn't want it if it meant I couldn't be with you and Lily. Then my parents turned up.'

'Your parents?' Will sat up in surprise. 'I thought they were in India?'

'They were. Now they're on their way to keep bees in Normandy.' Out of habit, Alice rolled her eyes, but her smile held a kind of wry affection as well. 'They thought they would call in and see me on their way through London, and, being them, they didn't think to give me any warning. They simply turned up on my doorstep, at the very moment I'd just realised that I wanted to be with you, and I was in a terrible muddle about everything.'

Will twisted a strand of her hair around his finger. 'Did they help?'

'Well, that's the funny thing. They did.' Alice pulled herself up to sit next to him, and adjusted a pillow behind her back. 'They've never been what you'd call conventional parents. They're two old hippies,' she said with an affectionate smile, thinking of her mother with her anklets and long braid, her father with his tie-dyed T-shirt and his grey hair pulled back into a pony-tail. 'But when they saw what a state I was in, they swung into their traditional roles straight away! They sat me down and made me tea, and got the whole story out of me.'

She ran her hand over Will's shoulder, loving the sleekness of his skin. 'I told them about you and Lily, and how much I loved you, and that I'd let you down three times now. I told them I was afraid of doing it again, that I was scared that it wouldn't work unless I was sure that I could get it right this time and that it would be perfect.'

Her mother had simply shaken her head. 'Alice, you can never be sure,' she had said. 'All you can do is trust each other and be true to each other and believe in each other. Love isn't something that comes and goes. It's something you have to make together, and if you both work at it, if you're kind and patient and prepared to compromise, if you can stay friends through thick and thin, then you can make it last, but you can't *ever* be sure of it.'

Alice would never forget the way her mother had smiled at her father then, and suddenly they hadn't seemed like faintly ridiculous hangovers from another era, but two people who had found their own way and loved each other a long time.

'Loving someone completely isn't easy,' her father had added. 'It's hard work, and you can decide it's easier never to try, but, if you never do, you'll never be completely happy either.' He'd reached out and took her mother's hand. 'Yes, it's a risk committing yourself to loving someone for the rest of your life. It's a leap in the dark, but it's a leap out of the dark too, and if you don't take it you'll never know the joy and the wonder and the real security which is loving and being loved.'

Alice felt quite teary with emotion as she told Will what her parents had said. 'As I listened to them talk, I realised that I'd spent my whole life running away from the unsettling effects of my childhood—the moving from place to place, never having any real friends, never feeling at home—when I could have been thinking about all the wonderful things my parents did for me.'

She shook her head at herself. 'They gave me the best example I could have of a loving relationship. My father didn't wear a suit, and my mother didn't put on an apron and stay in the kitchen, but they were always friends and always lovers. They laughed and they talked and were true to each other. They took me to places most children never get to see, and showed me how wonderful the world is.

'I had the most incredible experiences growing up,' Alice remembered. 'But, instead of realising how lucky I was, I turned it all into something negative. I became afraid of change, and I confused the security of place with the security of love.' She curved her hand around his cheek and leaned over to kiss Will's mouth softly. 'I won't do that again.'

'Your parents sound like great people,' said Will when he had kissed her back. Alice had never talked much about her parents when they'd been students. He had the feeling they had been in South America then, so he had never been introduced. 'I'd like to meet them.'

'That's good, because they're coming out to St Bonaventure.'

'They are? When?'

'For our wedding,' said Alice calmly, and a smile twitched the corner of Will's mouth.

'Oh, we're getting married, are we?'

'Yes, we are.' She leant over to Will until he slid beneath her, and her face was suddenly serious. 'You've asked me to marry you four times now, and each time I've been the fool that said no, so this time it's up to me. Will you marry me, Will?'

'Alice.' He cupped her face with infinite tenderness. 'My heart, I've wanted to marry you since I first laid eyes on you fourteen years ago, but we don't have to get married if you don't want to.'

'I do want to,' she said, dropping soft kisses over his face. 'You know what a thing I've got about security, and, now I've decided that you're my security, I want to tie you up as close as I can!'

'The tying up bit sounds fun,' mumbled Will between kisses. 'You can tie me up as tight as you like!'

'Good, I hoped you'd agree,' said Alice with satisfaction, and then her blizzard of kisses had reached his mouth and neither of them said anything more for a long time.

'We don't have to get married in St Bonaventure,' Will pointed out some time later, when they had both discovered that they were starving and were in the kitchen making cheese on toast, which was the best Alice could do. 'If I get this job, we'll be moving back to the UK and we could have the wedding here if you like.'

Alice picked a piece of cheese from the grater and studied him. 'When's the interview?'

'The day after tomorrow.'

'I think you should ring up and cancel,' she said. 'Let's go back to St Bonaventure and finish the project. If I'm married to you, I'll be able to find a job doing something, and as long as I've got something to do I'll be fine. I could sort out your fund-raising for a start! Then, when the project's finished, we can think again. Maybe that'll be the time to come back to the UK, and Lily can settle in a school here.'

Will slid his arms about her from behind and kissed the side of her neck, making her arch with pleasure. 'You're a dream come true,' he said, and she smiled.

'That's the plan.'

The sun was just starting to sink towards the horizon as Alice took Lily's hand and walked down the garden and across the track. Ducking under the trunk of a coconut palm that leant down at an extraordinary angle, they kicked off their shoes and walked barefoot across the beach to where Will was waiting for them.

Lily was in a pale pink dress, which she had been allowed to choose herself, and her dark curls were held in place by a satin headband decorated with rosebuds. Her tongue was sticking out slightly as she concentrated on remembering her bridesmaid's duties. Next to her, Alice was wearing a very simple cream-coloured dress with fine straps that left her arms and shoulders bare, and the chiffon stirred against her legs as cat's paw of wind ruffled across the lagoon. There were frangipani flowers in her hair, and she carried a spray of vivid bougainvillaea.

The sky was flushed with a pink that was deepening rapidly to a brief blaze of red and orange as Will turned to watch them walk across the sand towards him, and he smiled. Their plans for a small ceremony had been overtaken by the insistence of the entire project staff on being invited, together with Roger and Beth, Alice's parents, his mother, Sara and a whole lot of other people who'd seemed so genuinely happy for them that it had seemed churlish not to include them in the wedding party too. They all gathered round as Will stood with Alice and Lily before the celebrant.

Alice bent and handed her flowers to Lily, who took them as if they were made of glass and stepped carefully back to join her grandmother. Will took Alice's hand and, as they turned to face each other, his grey gaze travelled lovingly over her, from the tawny hair to those golden eyes and the warm, generous mouth, and then down over the enticing curves of her body to stop at her bare feet.

'What, no shoes?' he murmured as the celebrant cleared his throat. 'How are you going to run away?'

She smiled back at him. 'I'm not running anywhere,' she said. 'From now on I'm staying right by your side.'

* * * * *

THE COWBOY'S
SECOND-CHANCE
FAMILY

JULES BENNETT

To all the readers who requested more books set
in Stonerock...here you go!
I also threw in a cowboy. You're welcome :)

Chapter One

The mysterious man sitting in the back of the room didn't want to be seen. Too bad, because Lucy Brooks had spotted him the second he'd tried to slip in unnoticed twenty minutes ago.

A sexy man with broad shoulders, perfectly tanned skin, denim worn out in all the proper places, and clutching a black cowboy hat could not simply blend in. That square, stubbled jaw alone would grab any woman's attention. Not that Lucy wanted to be grabbed.

She tried to focus as one of the regular attendees discussed her one positive experience from the past week. The Helping Hands support group Lucy had started with her best friends Tara and Kate was a way to encourage others struggling with grief. Everyone brought something different to the meetings because everyone handled the loss of a loved one differently. And nobody had the same story to tell.

Which brought her gaze back to the cowboy in the back. Stonerock, Tennessee, had its fair share of ranchers, but she'd never seen this man before. The fact he was new explained the jumbled nerves in her belly. She refused to believe they were caused by the dark stare he was returning in her direction.

"Does anyone else have anything they'd like to share?" Tara asked, pulling Lucy back to the moment. When nobody stepped forward, Tara went on. "Remember, we will be changing the starting time next week. We'll be switching to seven instead of six. Have a great week, everybody."

All in attendance tonight were regulars, save for the cowboy. They'd all had a positive week and tonight's meeting had mostly been smiles and laughter—the whole reason for forming this group nearly two years ago.

Lucy excused herself from her friends and headed toward the back of the church where the new guy was trying to sneak out as quickly and quietly as he'd snuck in.

Lucy wasn't having any part of that. She made her way through the aisles, smiling and nodding to familiar faces. But when she reached the back, the stranger was gone. Jogging out the open doors, she spotted him striding toward a big black truck. What else would a mysterious cowboy drive?

A fine mist covered her face as she picked up the pace to catch up with him. Those long legs of his ate up some serious ground.

He must've heard or sensed her because he glanced over his shoulder and stopped. Swiping the dampness from her face, Lucy finished closing the gap between them.

"Hi. I'm Lucy." Okay, that sounded lame, but she didn't know what else to lead with. She was usually fine with greeting new guests, but this man was different. "I wanted to welcome you to the group, but you slipped out before I could say hello."

The stranger shoved his black hat back on and fished the keys from his pocket. "I'm not joining. Just wanted to come by and see what it was about."

She recognized that emptiness she saw in his dark eyes, knew that denial, that unspoken insistence he'd be all right without help. Even with the light rain and only the glow from the church lights, she had become all too familiar with that look. Two years ago she'd seen it every day staring back at her in the mirror.

"You've lost someone recently?" When his jaw clenched, she knew she'd hit the mark. He was the angry griever. There were all types and she'd come to know them all. "Would you like to come back in and talk?"

The stranger snorted and shook his head as he

turned toward his truck and held out his key fob. Lights flashed as the locks were released.

"No, I wouldn't. I'm not baring my soul to a group of strangers."

Lucy wrapped her arms around her waist. Occasionally rude people came through, but she'd had to remind herself the words weren't necessarily directed at her. They were targeted toward the person's inner anger.

The stranger cursed on a sigh and turned back to her. "Noah. My name is Noah."

Lucy smiled. Apparently his guilt trumped his anger where she was concerned. A cowboy *and* a gentleman.

"I didn't plan on making you bare your soul, just so you know. I didn't know if you'd like to come in and just talk, not necessarily about loss or grieving. We actually get together once a week and discuss a variety of things."

One thick, dark brow quirked. "Like what?"

Lucy shrugged. "One rule is if you're going to speak, you have to start with something good that happened since you were here last. It can be anything. We are really just here to lift each other up, not focus on why we're hurting."

His eyes darted away for a brief second before returning to her. "That's great, what you're doing. It's just…not for me."

Nodding, Lucy knew when not to push. "Well,

we're here every Monday. If you change your mind, you're welcome to come back."

When she turned to go, she dropped her head as the rain started to pick up intensity.

"I lost my wife six months ago."

His low tone was nearly drowned out by the rain, but Lucy froze, knowing full well she'd heard correctly. Shoving her damp hair off her forehead, she turned back around.

"My husband has been gone for two years," she replied, wanting him to know they already had something in common and he wasn't alone. Still, saying the words never got any easier. It was just an ugly fact she'd learned to live with. "I'm available to talk one-on-one, too, if you prefer."

He stared at her a bit longer, as if he was trying to process what move to make next. That internal struggle was real, but something he had to battle himself. She waited for his reply, not caring how wet she was getting, how her hair was clinging to her cheeks or how her shirt had plastered itself to her skin.

With a tip of his hat, he nodded toward the church. "You'd best get inside. Storm's comin'."

Gripping the steering wheel until his knuckles turned white, Noah Spencer headed home. Well, to the house he was renting. Calling the place he'd lived in only a few days a home was quite a stretch.

He'd lost his ranch, a portion of his life that he'd never get back. Noah swallowed as guilt and grief threatened to overtake him. The loss of his wife was far greater than that of the land and livestock. But losing nearly everything all at once was damn near soul-crushing.

Settling into this small town, ready to start his new job with the Stonerock Police Department tomorrow night, was the fresh start he needed. Being a rancher was his first love, but the failing ranch he'd had in Texas was gone and the money to rebuild simply wasn't there.

If he were all alone he would've tried to come up with a way to fight for that dream…or close himself off from the world and curse fate for taking so much from him.

But he hadn't quite lost everything and he wasn't alone. He had a little girl depending on him to provide security, a stable home, and the vision of a brighter future.

Noah smiled despite the pain. Just the thought of Emma, his girly-girl with her pink bows and her curly blond hair, always brightened his mood. She'd dealt with this move far better than he had. To her, everything in life was an adventure and he'd do well to learn from her positive outlook.

And it was that positive attitude of Emma's that drove him to check out this support group he'd heard of. When his real estate agent had lined up this rental until he could find a house worth buying in his budget, she'd mentioned various things around town: a few trustworthy babysitters, good restaurants, pediatricians…and this group. Helping Hands was free to the community, to help lift up people who had lost someone.

Noah truly didn't care about being lifted up or any other mind tricks meant to make him feel better about his life. Right now it sucked. Plain and simple. There was no way to sugarcoat things and he was too mentally exhausted to try.

Forcing the bitterness away, he pulled into his drive. For the sake of his daughter, he always put up a strong front. That was his job as her sole parent now. She mourned the loss of her mother, of her pets back at the leveled ranch, so he needed to always keep her surroundings positive.

Killing the engine, Noah sat there and thought back to the blonde beauty who'd followed him out to his truck. She'd been determined to get him to open up and he'd been just as determined not to. Yet something about her sweet smile, those piercing green eyes, and her soft tone had made him reveal more than he'd wanted to.

Her opening up about her late husband had surprised him. Even through the sadness in her tone, she'd smiled. For him. A total stranger reaching out to him. She'd invited him back, but…

Noah sighed and jerked his door handle. He wasn't

going back. Attending meetings like that would only make him relive the nightmare of six months ago. He'd moved to Stonerock for a fresh start and that's exactly what he planned on getting. How could he move forward if he was constantly reminded about how drastically his life had changed?

Heading up the walkway, Noah glanced toward the bay window where his whole reason for living was waving wildly. Curls bouncing, plastic tiara askew, Emma made a silly face. Noah couldn't help but laugh as he reflected one back to her. He knew the second he walked through that door and relieved the baby-sitter that he'd be trading his cowboy hat for a tiara and Emma would pull out her makeup so they could play dress-up.

There was nowhere else in the world he'd rather be. He didn't need a support group to help him move on; he only needed his four-year-old princess.

Yet the blonde and her open invitation stayed in the forefront of his mind and he refused to even ac-knowledge the knot in his gut when he thought of how striking she was, how patient and how compassionate. And he sure as hell needed to forget how her wet shirt had plastered itself to her curves, punching him full-on with the first taste of attraction he'd had since—

No. He refused to even go there right now. All he needed was his daughter, his job and this new beginning. No way in hell was he adding a woman to that list.

* * *

Taking a deep breath, Noah stepped inside the Stonerock Police Department and was hit with the scent of burned coffee. Good thing he'd already had two cups before he left his house. He wasn't used to working the midnight shift back in Texas, but he was the low man on the totem pole at this station, and he needed the job.

He'd always loved the mountains of Tennessee; he and his wife had honeymooned there. When he'd wanted to get away from Texas, he'd immediately thought of Tennessee. It didn't take long to narrow his search down to other departments that were seeking another officer.

A bulletin board hung immediately to his left, full of images of missing persons and various announcements from other authorities, local and national. A couple of old scarred desks filled with folders and papers, but no one manning them, were to his right. He'd been here only twice before for interviews and to turn in paperwork, but he knew the town was low on crime and the office usually only had a handful of staff at a time.

Noah moved through the department and headed toward the captain's office. Cameron St. John was one hell of a captain, and rumor had it he'd put a stop to drug runners threatening this humble town only a year ago. While Noah may long to be back on the ranch, no matter how rough finances had been, he was also anxious and excited to be working for such a well-respected department.

"That's because you always burn the coffee. If you'd let me make it, at least we could drink it without choking on it."

Noah froze. That feminine voice washed over him, instantly taking him back to the parking lot the night before, to the silky tone from the blonde with rain dampening her face. She'd talked to him as if she weren't getting soaked, as if she didn't look like she'd stepped from a wet T-shirt contest. Her only concern had been for him...which said quite a bit about her character.

Noah gritted his teeth and forced those wet T-shirt images aside. Before he could take a step forward, Lucy stepped from the captain's office and smacked right into him. Instinct had him reaching up to grip her arms—toned yet delicate arms. She was a petite little thing, the top of her head hitting below his chin.

Noah dropped his hands, but her palms were flat against his chest. The second she tipped her head back and her eyes focused on his face, she raised her brows in surprise.

Lucy took a step back. "You're the new officer?" she gasped, then shook her head. "Clearly you are. I mean, you're in uniform. I just..."

She trailed off as pink tinged her cheeks, and something about having her flustered when she'd been in such control last night had him fighting back a grin. Other than Emma, nobody had made him grin in a long, long time.

He took in her buttoned-up white sweater and dark jeans. She had some sparkly earrings that his daughter would covet on sight and deem princess material.

"I didn't see you when I came in before." Damn it, why had he said that?

"I'm a part-time night dispatcher," she explained, tucking her hair behind her ear. "I'm finishing up my online master's classes and it eats up most of my time."

And she also ran a free outreach program for the community. Clearly she stayed busy, which was exactly what he needed to do. Ogling his new coworker was not the hobby he needed to look into.

Noah gestured behind her toward the open door. "If you'll excuse me, I need to check in."

Lucy blinked, then stepped aside. "Sorry, I didn't mean to hold you up. I'm just surprised to see you again. I mean…"

"Yeah," he agreed, not wanting to discuss last night.

He'd had a moment of weakness, but his head was on straight now and he was moving forward, starting with this new position. No way in hell would he be seen as vulnerable. What type of cop would that make him? His duties included being strong, fierce, in control—none of which he felt one hundred percent about. But he had to start somewhere and re-hashing last night wasn't the place.

"I'm sure I'll see you later. I better go fix that coffee."

With a smile, Lucy headed down the hallway and Noah cursed himself for watching her go. This beautiful woman who'd caught him at a fragile moment could not interfere with his goal of building a new life for his daughter.

Chapter Two

Lucy cursed her shaky hands. She knew the rookie officer was coming on board tonight, but she'd had no idea the mysterious man she'd met last night would be one and the same.

She wasn't sure if he looked better in a Stetson and jeans or the navy blue uniform, but she wouldn't turn away a chance at looking at both. Looking was harmless, right? Mercy, but he did get her heart rate up and there wasn't a doubt in her mind that once the single ladies of Stonerock realized there was a new officer, they'd be all over him. Parking tickets could quite possibly multiply in the foreseeable future.

The glorious aroma of freshly brewed coffee filled

the tiny break room, masking the burned odor that had pervaded previously. She didn't know how this crew got along without her on her nights off. Soon she'd have her degree in psychology and she could find a job counseling military wives and families.

"Lucy."

She jerked around, startled at the gruff tone of Officer McCoy. He was a giant teddy bear, older and a little pudgy in the midsection, but an amazing cop.

"Hey." She greeted him with a smile. "I didn't hear you come in."

"I need you to spend a few hours with Officer Spencer. Carla was going to, but she had to leave suddenly to get to the nursing home for her mom and there's a last-minute meeting so he's getting paired with you for just a bit."

Perfect. Spending some up close and personal time with the town's newest officer would be fine... if she weren't a bundle of nerves just looking at the man.

All she knew was that he was a widower; she'd learned that last night after the meeting. Word around the station was that he was from a small town outside of Houston, Texas. That was pretty much the extent of what she knew of Noah Spencer.

Well, that wasn't entirely true. She knew he had a swagger that could make a woman's knees go weak and he had that Southern drawl that had her belly curling with arousal.

Still, she shouldn't be eyeing the new guy with such affection, or any coworker for that matter. The town was small and everyone in this department was like one big, happy family.

"No problem," she stated, lying through her teeth. "I'm happy to help out." That part was true; she'd pinch hit for her fellow dispatchers whenever she was needed. "I just had to get this coffee going since Officer James burned the last pot."

"James tries hard, but she's never made a decent pot in her life," McCoy grumbled. "Thanks for saving us. James just went out on a domestic dispute, by the way. She's better on the streets than in this break room."

Lucy laughed as she turned to reach for a mug from the counter. "At least she tries. Let me get a cup and I'll be right out to talk to Officer Spencer."

First she needed some caffeine because this was going to be a long night. A dose of coffee to add to her jitters. Perfect.

But she was a professional and so was Noah. Besides, he hadn't shown the slightest interest, so this little infatuation was quite possibly one-sided. The man was still mourning his wife for pity's sake. She could appreciate his looks and perhaps this learning period would get him to open up. He didn't have to come to meetings to heal.

She poured her cup of coffee and just as she turned, she ran into a solid chest. The hot liquid spilled onto her hand, burning her skin and causing her to drop the mug, which then hit the floor and shattered.

Firm hands gripped her shoulders. "You all right?"

Noah's worried look had her nodding, though her hand burned. "Did I spill coffee all over you?"

Great first impression, Lucy. Way to get him to notice you.

"How's your hand?" he asked, ignoring her question as he took her wet hand in his. "Did you burn yourself?"

"It's fine." Could she be more of a fool? "Let me get something to clean off your shoes. Are you sure it's not on your uniform?"

Thankfully the uniform was navy blue, but still, she didn't want to have him soaking wet and smelling like he was a barista on patrol.

Still holding on to her hand, Noah led her to the sink and turned on the cold water. "This is looking a little red."

Was it? Because the way he was holding on to her and the way his body aligned with hers, she really had no clue anything else existed except him.

"You okay?"

Lucy glanced over her shoulder at Officer McCoy, who stood in the doorway. "Just dropped my coffee," she replied.

"I'll clean it up."

He disappeared for a moment and came back with

the mop. As he started cleaning, Lucy realized Noah was still holding her hand under the water. She focused her attention on him and smiled.

"I'm fine. Really."

Noah's dark eyes seemed so dull, so…sad. She wanted to reach out to him, somehow. Nobody should live in misery. Wasn't that the whole reason she and her friends had started the group? They were each recovering and wanted to get others to live again.

Noah turned the water off and reached for a paper towel. When he started to wrap her hand, she took the towel from him and did it herself. Too much touching was dangerous…at least to her mental state. She was to work with him, and hopefully get him to open up and recover from his loss, so anything beyond that wasn't an option.

Besides, she'd vowed never to fall for a man who risked his life on a daily basis ever again. Living through hell once was more than enough for her.

"I can get that," she said as she turned her attention to McCoy.

"You made the coffee, that's enough." He picked up the large jagged mug pieces and tossed them in the trash before soaking up the liquid. "Get to work and make sure you don't pull any pranks on Spencer here."

She glanced to Noah, who was still standing far closer and smelling far better than should be legal.

"I'll have you know that last stunt with the sugar and salt with the coffee was not me. It was Carla."

When he grunted, Lucy merely glanced to Noah and shrugged. She headed from the break room, well aware the new officer was directly behind her. If only Carla were here tonight to help take some of this pressure from Lucy. She'd never had this instant attraction before so she seriously needed to get ahold of herself.

Why did the first interest since her husband's death have to be a man dealing with such grief? He was in no place to even look her way, let alone flirt.

Flirt? Mercy sakes, what was she saying? They had a job to do and she'd do well to remember they were technically coworkers.

"Are you sure your hand is okay?" he asked as they came to the dispatch desks with all of the monitors and phones.

"It's fine." How many times could she say fine? "Did you get cleaned up?"

He glanced to his shiny, patent leather shoes. "They just got splashed. I think your hand and the floor took everything."

When he looked back up, his eyes went straight to her chest. Well, maybe this attraction wasn't one-sided.

"You have coffee on your sweater."

And perhaps it was, because he wasn't looking at her boobs at all, but the coffee she'd spilled. She

knew her sweater was damp, but she didn't exactly
have another shirt to put on. And of course it was a
white sweater. Classy. So classy.

"It will dry," she stated, waving a hand through
the air as if she wasn't bothered, though she was
cringing each time his eyes dropped to the stain.

She took a seat at her desk and gestured to the
empty chair beside her. "How long have you been
in Stonerock?"

"Almost a week."

Lucy pointed to one of the monitors with the lay-
out of the town. "I assume you've been out driving
around and familiarizing yourself with the area."

He nodded. "The streets are a grid. Pretty easy
to get around."

"This won't be much different from where you
were before," she explained. "Stonerock is small,
low crime. I'm sure you know all of that, but you
will get to know the people in no time."

As she explained how things would work from
her end, he nodded and listened without interruption. When the line lit up, Lucy held up her hand
and took the call.

The frantic voice of a child came over the headset
and Lucy went into that calm mode she had to settle
into when trying to offer comfort to the stranger on
the other end. And when that stranger happened to
be a child, Lucy tried to compartmentalize her feelings and remain in control.

"My mommy is having a baby," the little boy screamed. "Right now!" The child's voice was drowned out by a woman's cries.

Lucy went to the flip cards on the desk and found the one she needed to issue the proper orders. This wasn't her first baby call and it wouldn't be her last. She managed to get a neighbor's name and called her while keeping the child on the line. While paramedics were on their way, Lucy wanted another adult there for the child.

All in all, the call took about four minutes before the medical squad arrived on the scene and the neighbor came to take the little boy. Lucy disconnected the call once everyone was safe and taken care of.

As she eased back in her seat, she caught a side glance of Noah. The adrenaline during the call had her completely forgetting about him—and that was saying something.

"You did good," he commented.

Lucy laughed. "Well, that's my job, so…"

"It takes a special person to be able to do that, though." He eased forward and met her eyes. "Not everyone could remain calm in a time of distress. You're literally the lifeline to those people in need."

Lucy shrugged. She'd never thought of it that way, but he was correct. Still, she didn't take to praise very well. She was doing her job, helping others who couldn't help themselves, and she only hoped in some small way that she made a difference.

As more calls came through, she took them and talked to Noah in between. After about an hour, Officer McCoy came through to take Noah out on a call.

Part of Lucy hated to see him go, but the other part was relieved. She was having a difficult time sitting here ignoring his domineering presence.

As Noah stood up, he started to say something but a call came in and she tuned out everything else. This was going to be one of those nights where the phones were nonstop. Some days were like that and she was grateful she had something to occupy her time other than the mysterious new officer.

She wanted to know more about him, and living in this tiny town, she'd definitely find out. It wouldn't take long for the busybodies to be all abuzz with the backstory of their newest resident.

After they'd finished the call, which amounted to a couple of guys getting too rowdy outside of Gallagher's, the local bar, Noah climbed back into the patrol car. He wasn't used to riding on the passenger side, but he also wasn't used to this town, nor life without his ranch, not to mention life without his wife.

Each day was better than the last, but there was still that void he figured he'd always carry around.

Just as Officer McCoy started the car, Lucy's calm voice came over the radio.

"We've got a missing child at 186 Walnut Street.

The mother reported he was in his room and was supposed to be changing for bed, but now he's missing."

Just because he was a police officer didn't mean he didn't feel. Each case he encountered was different, and each one deserved his full attention and compassion. Noah's heart clenched at the fear that mother must be facing. He knew that fear of loss and the unknown.

"There's a creek that runs behind their house so the mother and some neighbors are there now," Lucy added.

McCoy turned on the siren and raced through the streets. Lucy's voice continued to keep them updated as she stayed on the line with a family friend. Lucy's sweet voice was exactly what he'd told her earlier—a lifeline. She was the link between the caller and the officers and she truly didn't see what an important job she had.

He should feel guilty thinking of her in any way except as a coworker, but there was something so innocent, yet so… He couldn't find the right word. Recognizable? Yes, definitely. He recognized the pain in her eyes, too. She did well to mask it, but it was there all the same. Perhaps she used that support group more for herself than she realized. And that was all fine and good, but talking among a group of strangers wasn't for him. He could get over his grief just fine on his own time.

Within minutes they were pulling up in front of

a small white cottage. Already people had congregated on the lawn. Adrenaline pumping, Noah raced toward the back of the house where he was told the mother was. McCoy went to talk to neighbors to get a description of the boy.

With the rains lately, the creek was up and Noah prayed this would only be a search and not a recovery.

Flashlights shifted all over the backyard, Noah's included. He tried to focus on the water, because if the boy was in there, he was in the most danger. Hopefully he was just in a neighbor's tree house or something that innocent and safe.

"He's there!" someone shouted. "He's caught under that shrub on the other side of the creek."

Noah followed the light stream from someone's flashlight. Immediately he took off running in the direction, his light bouncing as he ran faster.

He heard a woman scream and take off down the edge of the creek just in front of him. "Hold on, baby!"

Noah didn't think twice and he didn't stop to say anything. He raced past the frantic mother and the other people who were trying to figure out how to get the boy out.

As he ran into the cold water, Noah called out to the boy, "Hang on. I'm coming for you." The poor little guy was crying and the hood of his jacket had gotten caught on a dead limb sticking out from a bush along the creek side. His jacket was dark, but the bright yellow shirt made it a little easier for Noah to focus in on him.

The water was nearly to Noah's waist and colder than he'd initially thought. He didn't know how long the boy had been out here, but with the sun down, things had cooled off quite a bit.

The frantic mother continued to encourage her son to hang on as Noah trudged through the water. Blocking out all the chaos behind him, Noah focused solely on this boy.

"I've got you," Noah told him when he finally reached the child. "Wrap your legs around my waist and put your arms around my neck. I'm going to untangle your jacket."

The boy continued to cry and didn't move.

"My name is Officer Spencer, but you can call me Noah. What's your name?"

"C-Conner."

The boy's teeth were chattering. "Okay, Conner. I need you to be a big boy. I need a partner since my partner is in your house helping. Can you be my partner out here?"

Conner nodded. "I just wanted to see the storm and then I saw a c-cat run to the water. I wanted to s-save it."

"You're a brave boy, but right now I need you to wrap yourself around me so I can get you out of here. I don't know about you, but I think this water is cold."

Finally, little arms and legs went around Noah. Realizing the boy was about Emma's age, he felt a tug on his heart. Calls with kids always hit closer to home.

If he didn't get this jacket untangled in the next few seconds, Noah was going to cut it off. This boy had been waist deep in the water long enough. He shivered, not just from the cold, but from fear.

Finally, the material came free with a rip. Noah wasted no time. He waded back through the chilly water as the boy clung to him. On the bank, the crowd had grown and the mother stood sobbing, reaching her arms out, anxious to take her son.

The paramedics were right beside her, also ready to take the boy. Noah reached Conner out to his mom and climbed up the embankment. McCoy grabbed Noah's elbow to help him out.

The paramedics and the boy's mother were racing through the backyard, toward the driveway around front to the ambulance. The boy would be fine, but protocol required he get checked out. Noah would bet Conner wouldn't venture out to explore by himself anytime soon, and probably not near that creek for a long, long time.

"Good job, Spencer." McCoy slapped him on the back. "Already playing hero on your first serious call. You'll fit in just fine."

Noah smiled as they walked through the yard. He didn't want praise for doing his job, but he was glad he could help.

"At least the dip in the creek got the coffee off me," he joked.

McCoy laughed. "I thought you didn't get any coffee on you."

Noah shook his head. "I just told Lucy that so I wouldn't hurt her feelings. She'd already burned her hand and felt bad enough."

They reached the car and just as Noah pulled the handle, Conner's mother came up and wrapped her arms around him.

"Thank you," she cried, pulling back. "I promise I don't let him get near the creek. He's never done that before."

Noah placed a hand on her arm. "And I'm sure he won't do it again. You both had a scare, but you've got a brave boy. He wanted to see the storm and then tried to save a cat. You're doing a good job, mama. Kids are curious creatures by default."

She swiped the tears from her eyes and offered a smile before turning to go back to the waiting ambulance. Conner sat up on the cot inside the open doors and waved at Noah. Waving back, Noah offered his own grin.

Within minutes he and McCoy were headed back to the station where Noah could change and get dry. And see Lucy. On the short trip back, McCoy and Lucy exchanged some information about the boy being transported to the hospital.

Once again, her tone stirred something inside

Noah. Something he didn't want to address because he shouldn't be having these feelings. Should he?

He was human, he was a man, and he had natural desires. There was something about Lucy that made him not want to brush aside these unwanted emotions. No one had been able to reawaken the dead inside him for months. But whether it was her sweet voice, the compassion he already saw in her, or the underlying vulnerability she tried to hide, something about her drew him and made him want to get to know her more.

At this point, he figured they'd be seeing each other on a near daily basis. He might as well just roll with it and see what happened. But at the same time, he had to guard his heart. He was still healing, he was still in new territory...but he was also still fascinated by the gentle blonde with wide, expressive green eyes.

As they pulled into the station, Noah couldn't help but wonder what the next few days, weeks, and months would bring.

He hadn't known what to expect from this new town, but a reawakening in his desire certainly hadn't been on his list.

Chapter Three

Her nerves were near shot. Noah had been on the force for nearly a week and she'd worked five days out of the seven. Her usual part-time schedule had shifted into full-time since Carla had to be out with her mother for the next couple of weeks.

Which meant more face-to-face time with Officer Brooding and Sexy. Why, why, why did this man have to be the one she found so attractive? Why couldn't she get stirrings for a schoolteacher or a garbage man? A man who put his life on the line every day was an absolute no-no.

Her husband had done the same thing. Day after day he'd put himself out there...until one day he was gone.

Noah had only been on the force a short time and already he'd proven he was a man of loyalty, integrity, and compassion. He'd taken the little boy from the creek incident a stuffed animal before his shift. And the only reason anyone knew of that was because the mother called to tell Captain Cameron St. John what an amazing officer he had.

The back door opened and closed. Before she could turn to see which officer was coming on duty, a call came in. She pressed the key on the computer to answer and adjusted her headset.

"Stonerock Police Department."

"I have someone walking through my backyard carrying a baseball bat."

"Do you know who this person is?" Lucy replied.

"No, but they've been out there for a few minutes just staring at the house."

Lucy dispatched an officer and kept the caller on the line as she made sure the lady's doors were locked and she was away from doors and windows. The woman didn't sound frantic, but concerned.

Stonerock wasn't known for having many crimes, but there were crazy people everywhere. She couldn't take any call for granted.

Once the officer arrived and the caller confirmed it, Lucy disconnected the call. When she turned in her seat, she was alone in the room, but she knew who'd come in earlier. That aftershave still permeating the room had become so familiar, making her insides stir and get all schoolgirl giddy.

She was a grown woman getting giddy. How sad was that?

Keeping her feelings in check was the smart thing to do. She needed to keep her emotional distance from Noah, but each day she saw him, she realized she wanted to see more of him, to learn more about him. That need was a recipe for disaster and heartache. Neither of them was at a place in their lives to act on attraction. Of course, she was still assuming it was one-sided, which was all the more reason for her to rein in her school-girl crush.

Only this didn't feel like anything she'd had as a teenager. Her attraction for Noah Spencer was all grown up...as were the dreams she'd been having since that first meeting in the rain.

Lucy came to her feet and stretched her neck from side to side. She was pulling a double shift today, which was fine. She could use the extra money to put back into the support group fund. Tonight was a meeting, but Kate and Tara were fine without her. It's not like Lucy was ever missed.

"Thought you were off today."

She jerked around to see Noah standing in the doorway drinking a cup of coffee. His dark eyes held hers and she had to force herself to not fidget.

"Taking on a few more shifts while Carla is out. I can always use extra money for my group."

His dark brows drew in. "Aren't you missing a meeting tonight?"

Lucy shrugged. "I am, but my girls understand. Sometimes we have to cover for each other."

He took a sip of coffee from one of the disposable cups. When he pushed off the doorway, Lucy thought he was about to turn and leave, but he crossed the room and headed for her desk. Lucy spun around, pretending to stare at the monitors. It was a slow night, but she still wished for a call to come in right then. She couldn't handle all this tension. Well, the tension on her part at least. She never could get a grasp on what he was feeling.

"What do you do in your spare time?" he asked as he took a seat beside her.

The question threw her off as she glanced to the clock. He was early for his shift by about twenty minutes. Why was he choosing to sit in here with her?

"Spare time?" she asked, fidgeting with her watch. "I'm usually looking for speakers for the group or community projects we can do. Giving back and lifting others up is a great way to—"

"No."

Lucy jerked her attention back to him. "What do you mean, no?"

Noah set his cup on the desk and leaned forward. That dark stare of his zeroed in on her and she could easily see him cornering a suspect with those eyes, or seducing a woman. Those eyes held every secret, letting no emotion slip through. That whole guarded, sultry thing he had going might be the sexiest thing she'd ever seen in her life.

The uniform didn't hurt, either. But she'd rather have a man not so committed to danger and more committed to...well, her. As selfish as that sounded, part of her hated knowing that her husband had sacrificed his life defending their country, but that was the type of man he'd been. And she could tell that was the type of man Noah was.

"I know you work and volunteer your time for the group," he stated, still holding her in place with that mesmerizing gaze. "But I'm asking what else you do."

"Oh, I study. I'm almost done with my online classes."

Noah shook his head. "For fun. What do you do for fun?"

Lucy opened her mouth, then shut it. She thought for a second, but nothing came to her. Surely she'd done something for fun lately...hadn't she? Her friends were always texting her or calling for some reason or another. But she couldn't recall the last time they went out and did anything.

"I have horses," she replied. "Two of them. They were my husband's, so they're mine now."

Before she could even think of something she actually did just for herself, a call came in. It took great effort on her part, but she blocked out the presence of the powerful man beside her. The call didn't take long and didn't require anyone to be dispatched. An elderly lady had locked herself out of her home, but ended up finding her key in the bottom of her purse while she was talking.

When Lucy disconnected the call, Officer McCoy came in the back door. "Evening. Gettin' chilly out there."

Noah spun in the chair. "It's downright frigid to me. I guess I'll have to invest in thicker coats."

"Drink more coffee," McCoy suggested as he passed on through to the break room.

"It's not too bad here," Lucy replied once Noah turned back to her. "But I guess coming from Texas, Stonerock does seem cold in the fall."

"Everything is different from Texas," he muttered.

There went that darkness settling over him again. If she could just break through...but that would require her getting closer and spending more time with him. That probably wasn't smart. Maybe she should have Tara or Kate reach out to Noah. Definitely a better option.

A sliver of jealousy speared through her at the idea of her friends getting one-on-one time with Noah.

"Are you upset about missing the meeting?" he asked.

Lucy tipped her head and eased back in her chair. "Why would you say that?"

"Because you've looked upset since I walked in."

Upset? That's what he got out of her appearance and attitude? She was seriously out of practice. Granted, she'd never had to initiate conversation or flirting with a man. Evan had asked her out and he'd taken charge. He was her first love, so...yeah, right now she was seriously out of her element. Maybe she should give up and stop trying. Had she even started, though?

"I'm not upset," she assured him.

Noah grabbed his cup, but never took his eyes off her. "You hide it well, but something is bothering you. None of my business, though."

He rose to his feet and turned to leave the room.

"Wait a minute," she called. "You're the one who seems all brooding and quiet. Over the past week you've barely said a word to me other than hi and bye. You talk to everyone else but me."

Noah glanced over his shoulder. "I speak with you over the radio every day."

Yeah, and that grated on her nerves because his low, gravelly voice always made her tingle and she did not want to tingle. Damn it, she didn't know what she wanted, but she at least wanted him to stop torturing her. Maybe acknowledge her as more than an annoyance or someone not to be bothered with. But the casual greeting as he came and went didn't sit well with her.

Well, maybe she wouldn't mind so much if he

did the same to everyone, but it was only her as far as she could tell. Had she done something to offend him? How was that even possible when she'd barely spoken to him other than to dispatch calls through the radio?

"Face-to-face, you ignore me." That sounded so childish. Lucy came to her feet and sighed. "We're like a family here, so I don't want any tension."

Noah shifted to face her fully. "Are you feeling tension?"

She was feeling sexually frustrated, but she figured announcing that wasn't professional. Was this what it would be like getting back into the dating world? She wasn't so sure she was up for this game.

Instead of answering his question, she asked one of her own. "Are you telling me you aren't?"

Shut up, Lucy. Just shut up.

"Because I don't try to cover my feelings," she went on, ignoring that inner voice. "Attraction is a natural emotion."

When his eyes widened, she seriously wanted to die. He seemed shocked, whether at her blunt statement or the fact he wasn't feeling the same, she had no clue. Regardless, it was out there now and she really, really wished she didn't always take the advice of her therapist and tell people how she felt.

McCoy came back through, whistling and holding his own cup of coffee. At the same time, another call rang through the room, effectively severing the awkward silence that had descended since she'd opened her mouth and opted to pour out her thoughts.

Lucy took the interruption as a sign that it was indeed time to shut up and stop telling Noah...well, anything. She quickly answered the call and sat back down at her desk. By the time she was done, Noah and Sergeant McCoy were gone and Lucy's heart was still beating like mad.

She'd stepped over some professional boundary and she had no clue how to come back from that. Noah was now well aware of how she felt about him, and from the look on his face, he didn't want to accept it.

Fantastic. How on earth did she come back from this embarrassing moment?

Okay, cooking wasn't necessarily her thing. Actually, she was terrible at it. But Lucy knew how to bake and actually loved doing it.

Which was why she found herself standing on the porch of one adorable little gray-and-white cottage on the edge of town. Lucy secured the basket of cranberry scones under one arm and rang the doorbell with her free hand.

Nerves gathered in her belly and she couldn't believe she was actually standing here. Hadn't she made a big enough fool of herself yesterday? At work, no less.

Maybe she should just leave the basket on the swing and—

The door opened, cutting off her thoughts. Once she recovered from the fact she was actually at Noah's home, it took every single ounce of self-restraint she had not to burst out laughing.

"Are you wearing—"

"Yes. What are you doing here?"

Lucy didn't know whether to be extremely confused or thoroughly entertained at the sight of Noah Spencer sporting a plastic tiara, dangling clip-on jeweled earrings, and a purple beaded necklace.

Before Lucy could make a comment of any sort, a little girl popped out from behind Noah's legs. She too wore fancy accessories, but she had on a sparkly dress with a full skirt that went all the way to the floor.

Lucy immediately glanced back to Noah. He offered a simple smile, flashing that dimple at the corner of his mouth.

"This is my daughter, Emma. Emma, this is one of Daddy's coworkers, Lucy."

His daughter. Lucy hadn't heard a word about a little girl. Noah was one private man and now Lucy felt even sillier coming here unannounced.

"You look beautiful," Lucy stated as she bent down to the pre-schooler. "Do you always play dress-up with your dad?"

"I played with my mommy, but she's not here anymore." Emma's little chin wobbled for a second before she continued. "Daddy lets me put anything on him, but not a dress."

Lucy laughed. Apparently Noah had his limits even with his little girl.

Emma smiled up at her dad and Noah nodded to her. When the little girl turned her wide blue eyes back to Lucy, Lucy couldn't help but smile in return.

"We have tea parties," Emma answered. "Daddy puts extra sugar in it."

As she spoke again, Lucy realized the little girl had the cutest dimple on the side of her mouth, just like her father. Could she be any more adorable?

A flash of old dreams coursed through Lucy's mind. At one time she and Evan had wanted children. They'd bought their home with all the acreage and added two horses, with the intention of filling their home with kids. Then he'd been deployed and that had been the end of her dreams for a family.

She'd always assumed those wishes had died with him, but seeing little Emma brought them back again. A lump settled in her throat, blocking her words.

"Come on in." Noah stepped back, placing a hand on Emma's shoulder to pull her with him. "Sorry. It's cold out there."

Lucy stepped over the threshold and attempted a smile to mask the unexpected hurt. "You've just got to get that Southern blood used to this. It's really not cold in the grand scheme of things."

He grunted as he shut the door. Emma ran through the house and disappeared, apparently getting back to her interrupted tea party. Lucy clutched her basket as more doubts crept in.

"I'm sorry," she began as she turned back to Noah. "I shouldn't just show up unannounced. Especially after yesterday, but... You know, it's really difficult to talk to you when you're dressed like an overgrown princess."

Noah pulled the tiara from his head and snapped the earrings off his ears, but remained in the beads. "What brought you here, Lucy?"

Was it completely pathetic that she liked how he said her name? Most likely, but she couldn't help how she felt. She could, however, keep her mouth shut on that subject and try to get back on some level ground with him.

"I made scones for you." She held up the basket and smiled. "I didn't know you had a little girl or I would've made some of my monster cookies."

"Monster cookies?" he asked as he used his fingertip to push aside the checkered towel to see inside the basket.

"It's a chocolate chip cookie, but you add M&M's and other candies. Really, anything you like. They're pretty amazing."

He pulled a scone from the basket and took a bite. When his lids lowered and he groaned, Lucy felt more confident in her decision to bring the peace offering. She typically only baked for the support group or for family and friends. This was the first time she'd done it for a virtual stranger.

"These are amazing," he said around his second bite. "Is that cranberry?"

"It is, and I put a dash of orange in it."

He finished the scone and dusted his hand on his jeans. "You might as well come on in, but I can't guarantee you won't end up with a tiara on your head and a cup of tea."

A little part of Lucy's heart flipped over.

"I'd love to have a tiara."

Noah reached for the basket. "Come on back."

"Wait." She relinquished the basket and shoved her hands inside her jacket. "I want to apologize for yesterday. I didn't mean to make things uncomfortable between us."

The dark eyes she'd come to appreciate held her as he closed the distance between them. In one hand he held the basket, and in the other he had the girly accessories.

"I wasn't uncomfortable," he murmured. "Intrigued and surprised, but not uncomfortable."

The air between them seemed to thicken because she was having a difficult time breathing. And he still appeared just as calm and in control as ever.

"Why don't you take your jacket off and join our tea party?" he asked.

Lucy couldn't help the nervous laugh that escaped

her lips. "How can I turn down an invitation like that from a man wearing purple beads?"

Emma came twirling back through the house holding a stuffed bear as her dance partner. "Is the pretty lady staying?"

Lucy kept her focus on Noah because that precious girl was a reminder of things she'd once dreamed of. Things Lucy hadn't realized she still wanted until just now. A child of her own. A family.

Honestly, Lucy didn't know what was more damaging to her heart, Emma or Noah. But the combination of the two was downright terrifying. Nevertheless, she wasn't going to pass up the chance to stay.

Part of her rationalized that she was staying as a way to break through to Noah and get him to open up about his feelings. He needed new friends in the town, right? And since he refused to join her meetings, she'd just have to try to get him to open up in other ways. She could be his support team...right? That was totally logical and the right thing to do.

Of course the devil on her other shoulder called her a bald-faced liar. She was staying because she was on this roller coaster of newfound emotions and she had no clue how to stop the ride...or even if she wanted to stop it.

As crazy as it sounded, Noah had reawakened something deep inside her. For two years she'd focused on throwing herself into work, the group, school.

But now maybe she just wanted to be selfish and see what happened.

"I'm staying," Lucy replied as she smiled back to Emma.

The little girl bounced up and down, sending her blond curls dancing around her shoulders. "Yay. I'll have Mr. Bear sit on my lap and you can have his chair."

She scurried off just as fast as she'd entered and Noah shook his head. "You should feel honored. I've never had Mr. Bear's seat."

Lucy slid out of her jacket and hung it on the hook by the door. She completely ignored the fact it was nestled between a tiny pink-and-white polka-dot coat and a large black woolen one. Well, she tried to anyway.

She was seeing a whole new side to Noah she hadn't even known existed, but she liked it. The idea that he was a single father really helped Lucy understand why he'd been so reserved. The man had lost his wife and was protecting all the life he had left.

She could spend all day analyzing this situation from his angle, from hers, but right now she was going to enjoy the moment. She'd have time to analyze it later.

What the hell was he thinking? He should never have let Lucy inside his home. Granted he'd only been here a couple weeks, but this was his home now.

Having Lucy here botched up his plans to keep his life simple and his heart guarded.

But damn, that scone was something else. He hadn't had something that delicious and homemade in…well, ever. His wife hadn't been much of a cook, but that never bothered him. They mostly lived off the ranch anyway, between the livestock and the fields. Noah had cooked, too, taking pity on Cara who panicked at the sight of a recipe or the thought of a casserole.

This new lifestyle was taking some serious getting used to. Between the cooler weather, the free time he had from not ranching, and acclimating to the new force, his entire world had been reshaped. But he was grateful he had a job, a home, and his daughter. They'd make it because he was determined to give her the best life possible, considering the circumstances.

"Want to see my room?" Emma asked Lucy.

Without waiting for a reply, Emma hopped up from her little chair and grabbed Lucy's hand.

"Calm down, Em." Noah finished clearing the tea set from the table. "Maybe Lucy has somewhere else to be. She hadn't exactly planned on staying here today."

Lucy held Emma's hand and stood. "I'd love to see your room."

"My daddy painted it just like I wanted," Emma

chattered as she led Lucy away. "And then he put up this sparkly light and…"

Her voice trailed away and Noah glanced to the clock. It was almost time for him to lie down and get a few hours' sleep before going into work later tonight. The realtor had suggested a fabulous babysitter that lived only two doors down: a retired lady who was known as the town grandma and had babysat for years. Having someone dependable and trustworthy made this entire process much less stressful. Each little layer of his new life that fell into place where he needed eased his worry.

Noah wondered if he'd see Lucy at work, but then quickly pushed the thought aside. She'd been here for over an hour and if he was already looking forward to seeing her again, then he was falling down that rabbit hole he never wanted to be near again.

He wasn't ready to move on. Cara had been gone only six months. Shouldn't he wait longer before allowing that desire to creep in? Not that he'd let this happen. He looked at Lucy and…well, his thoughts, emotions and feelings had slipped from his control.

Noah rinsed out the tea set and put it away. Tea parties were a thing his wife had started with Emma and he'd wanted to keep some sense of normalcy in her life. As soon as they hit town, he took her shopping for a new tea set and they'd had a party every single day since. He didn't mind dressing up so long as it put a smile on Emma's face.

When they were gone a lengthy amount of time, Noah figured he'd better go save Lucy because Emma hadn't been around a woman, minus the sitter, since her mother passed. She was most likely craving that connection. Both of Cara's parents were gone and so was Noah's mother...he'd never known his father.

Noah reached the doorway and found Emma and Lucy on the widow seat. Emma had already draped necklaces and headbands on Lucy.

"Oh, honey. Maybe Lucy didn't want to be covered in accessories."

Lucy picked up another hair ribbon. "Actually, it's been a long time since someone pampered me. I was rather enjoying myself."

The sight of Emma with another young woman, and not his late wife, did something to him. Something he couldn't quite pinpoint. On one hand, there was that ever-pressing remorse he carried. The guilt of getting on with his life. The guilt of not having been able to save his wife.

He'd been a police officer back in Texas as well and had saved others, but ultimately he hadn't been able to save his own wife. He'd spoken to her after the storm and she'd assured him she was fine, but he should have—

He stopped himself. The blame would never end.

On the other hand, he knew his wife would've wanted him to move on, to live for their daughter.

She wouldn't like that he was feeling guilt, because that emotion robbed his happiness.

"I hate to break up this party, but it's time for you to go to Miss Mary's house."

Emma protested with a whine, but Lucy placed a hand on her knee. "It's okay. Maybe we can have another playdate."

"Really?" Emma asked, suddenly in a better mood.

Lucy glanced to Noah. "If your dad doesn't mind."

Noah weighed the options. He didn't want to let this get too routine because Emma would likely get attached. He had to watch out for her, but on the other hand, it was nice to see his daughter open up and want to play and be with another young woman.

He couldn't lie—seeing them together put his guard up. He wasn't looking for a replacement for his wife or mother for his child. At this point, he wasn't looking for anything because he was still trying to figure out this new life.

A mix of emotions swirled through him. He was attracted to Lucy and he had to assume that was normal, but that didn't mean he felt good about it. It didn't mean it was right to happen at this particular moment.

"I'm pretty busy, though." Lucy glanced to Noah and back to Emma. "I'll talk to your dad later at work and we'll see. Okay?"

Lucy took off all of her play jewelry and hair accessories. After laying them on the window seat, she bent down to Emma.

"Thank you so much for showing me your room. It is beautiful just like you. Maybe one day you could come see my horses since I know you miss yours."

Emma squealed. "Can I, Daddy? Please, please, please."

Noah laughed. "We'll see what we can work out."

Emma threw her arms around Lucy's neck and Noah had to look away. He couldn't see this, couldn't let his heart flip over in his chest. He loved Emma with everything he had in him, but Lucy was practically a stranger.

Maybe he needed distance himself, because the more he was around Lucy with her sweet smile and her easygoing nature, the more he wanted to be. And the fact she'd brought him a peace offering wasn't helping the case he was trying to make regarding staying emotionally detached.

Lucy had enjoyed a tea party, she'd played dress-up, and she'd baked him scones. And that was only in a little over an hour. What would happen if he invited her back for dinner? Or if they went to a movie or to the park? Then what? Would he grow even more intrigued?

Lucy crossed the room toward him and Noah had to shift out of the doorway so she could pass. When she got within a few inches, she paused and looked him straight in the eye.

"Thanks for sharing your day with me," she said. "That meant more than you know."

And then she was walking down the hall and out the door. That was the end of it.

Or was it? Because the sadness in her eyes when she'd thanked him had him wanting to run after her and figure out just what was hurting her. But he didn't, because he knew her angle. Yes, the attraction was there, but she wanted to cure him or make his life better. She'd mentioned her group more than once and she was the type of person who would throw herself into helping others and forgetting herself.

The unmistakable sorrow he'd glimpsed as she passed by couldn't be ignored, but it wouldn't be easy to bring up at work when he went in for his shift. There were other officers coming and going and calls she'd be taking. But he'd find a way.

Lucy may think she was going to cure him, but perhaps it wasn't he who needed the help.

Chapter Four

"You don't actually believe we're going to let you off the hook, right?"

Lucy was hoping for exactly that. She set the mugs of hot chocolate topped with whipped cream down on the coffee table and Tara and Kate each reached for theirs. This was Lucy's first night off in days and she wanted nothing more than to wear her fat sweatpants and no bra, and have some sugary drink with her friends.

The hot chocolate wasn't even spiked. Kate's parents had been killed by a drunk driver, so she didn't drink, and Tara and Lucy respected her enough to not drink in her presence.

"We'll hang around long enough and she'll be chatty. She won't be able to keep it inside."

Lucy rolled her eyes at Tara. "I'm not going to get chatty. There's nothing to tell, really."

"I heard you were at Officer Spencer's house yesterday afternoon," Kate stated as she held her moose mug with both hands.

They'd gathered at Lucy's house, in agreement they were going to stay in, binge watch romantic comedies, and have some downtime. They were all so busy with their own work lives lately that it wasn't often they could meet outside of the support group.

But here they were and Lucy was being quizzed, all because Noah lived on a street with busybody neighbors. And it wasn't like anything had happened. She'd drunk tea; she'd played for a while with Emma. End of story.

Right?

"What's that look on her face?" Kate whispered to Tara.

"I think she's trying to find a way not to answer our questions."

Lucy laughed. "Would you two knock it off? I was at Noah's house, but just to take him some scones."

"The cranberry orange ones?" Tara asked. "Those are the best things you make. You must really be interested in him."

Lucy didn't take the bait. She should've known girls' night in would turn into her best friends teaming up against her. Though, if the tables were reversed, she'd be doing the same. Still, she didn't want to talk about Noah. There wasn't really much to say. She'd seen a spark of interest, but at the same time, he'd also kept that guard up.

Even at work that evening, he'd entered with another officer coming on duty. They'd all made small talk and then the guys had been dispatched. After that, their only conversations had been emergency calls on the radio.

And now she was off for the next two nights. She wasn't sure if he was or not, but she didn't ask. She'd gotten done what she set out to do and that was apologize for making things seem unprofessional.

"So what's his story?" Kate asked. "Because the town is starting to make up their own about him. I heard he has a cute little girl."

Lucy nodded. "Emma. She's four."

Tara curled her legs to her side on the couch as she reached for her drink. "And he's a widower?"

"Yeah. His wife passed away during a storm when they lived in Texas. I heard he was a rancher and an officer, but he hasn't said any of that to me. He's pretty private."

"Yet you were in his home, with his child, for what? An hour?"

Lucy met Kate's raised brow and knowing grin. "Exactly. His child was home. We work together, for pity's sake. Nothing is happening."

"Not yet," Kate muttered around her mug.

Okay, it was time to steer the conversation away from herself because as much as she'd like for something to happen with the new officer, she wasn't holding her breath.

"Are we still on for dancing tomorrow night at Gallagher's?" Lucy asked as she licked the point off her whip cream.

Tara nodded. "Marley is with her dad, so I'm game."

Tara and her husband, Sam, hadn't been married long when they realized they didn't want the same things out of life. They'd married after a whirlwind affair and amazing chemistry, but marriages were based on so much more.

Being a single mom was difficult for Tara, but she and her ex managed to get along and put the needs of their daughter, Marley, first.

Lucy and her best friends all faced different obstacles and trials in their lives. They'd been friends since grade school when Lucy had cut off Kate's pigtails with her new sharp scissors. Kate had wanted her hair cut and her mother had kept saying no, so Kate had actually been grateful to Lucy. That same year, Tara had moved to town and the three just clicked. They'd been through it all together and always had each other's backs.

"I love going to Gray's place." Tara swiped her finger through her whip cream and licked it off. "We may be the only ones who go there just to dance. But

Gray Gallagher has taken that bar and made it even more popular than ever."

The local bar was in its third generation and currently owned by one of their good friends. Gray Gallagher was such a great guy and no doubt one of the reasons why so many women flocked to the place on ladies' night. Gray had always been that fun guy with a sexy build. When he'd come home from the Army, he'd immediately taken over Gallagher's from his father, but he'd yet to settle down.

Because isn't that what people did in this small town? They came home after college or the military and immediately met the love of their life, married, settled down and had babies. Or so the myth went. But not every life was so picture-perfect and neat and tidy.

Sometimes tragedies happened, lives were ripped apart. And sometimes something positive could stem from such tragedies. Lucy, Kate and Tara were dedicating their lives to making a change in this community. They all had their own type of heartache and voids in their lives which made them perfect to work together and comfort others.

Too often when someone suffered loss, people around them didn't know how to respond or what to say, so they just tiptoed around the delicate topic.

Lucy knew firsthand that didn't help the person suffering; it only made things more uncomfortable. Which was why she and her friends were going to start opening their doors to everyone at the meetings of their support group. Even if someone hadn't dealt with the death of a loved one, they still knew people who had, and Lucy wanted them to know how to handle those who grieved.

"I guess we should discuss the upcoming meeting since we're going to be out dancing tomorrow," Lucy stated.

"Are we done discussing your police officer?" Kate asked. "Because I don't really feel like we got much information."

"You got all the info you need." Lucy set her mug back on the tray. "We should go ahead and plan on about fifty people. That's aiming high, but I'd rather be over-prepared than under."

The more they discussed, the more their plans fell into place, and Lucy breathed a sigh of relief that they'd moved on from the topic of her personal life. She wasn't dumb enough to believe they'd dropped it for good, but at least for now she was safe.

All Lucy had to do was remember that Noah wasn't looking for anyone. And hadn't she told herself she wasn't looking, either? Yet here she was constantly thinking about him.

So what did she do? Ignore her feelings or act on them? The risk of acting and being seen as a fool put a newfound fear in her. She'd never approached a man before, but since she'd already broached that territory with him, she figured she'd have to keep riding this out.

But the ball was in his court, so to speak. The question was, would he do anything with it?

The annual fall festival was in just a few days and Noah knew he'd be working security there. Not that Stonerock was known for major crime, but security at any event was imperative.

He'd heard chatter about how amazing this festival was and how the entire town came out for it. Captain St. John had already told Noah they'd be working the same shift. Thankfully the sitter was going to bring Emma over for a little while. There would be face painting, bake sales, games, a few small rides, music, and in the evenings a big bonfire. He'd heard there was an area set up with a guy who cooked beans all day in a pot over the fire and served them up during the bonfire.

Noah was really starting to feel at home here. Nothing was the same as his ranch in Texas, but the familiarity of working on a force helped ease him into this new chapter in his life. The small town was exactly what he and Emma needed to feel like they were part of something and it wasn't just them trying to survive. She'd already made friends with some children from the sitter and he...well, he guessed he made some friends, too.

Was that what he was calling Lucy? His friend? Because he'd had female friends back in Texas and not one of them made him anxious and excited at just the mere thought of them.

Noah yawned as he grabbed his keys and started for the back door of the station. His shift was over and they'd been so slow during the night, the hours seemed to drag. And idle time was never good for someone grieving...or someone having guilt for fantasizing about another woman.

A huge part of him felt like he was cheating on his wife, but the other part of him knew he had to move on. He couldn't control his feelings and he sure as hell hadn't picked whom he was attracted to.

As he headed to his truck, he spotted Lucy in the front seat of her car. Her head was on the steering wheel. Alarm hit him first. Was she sick? Passed out?

He crossed the lot to the side of her car and gently tapped on the window. When she jerked in her seat and turned toward him, he instantly saw she was upset. Tears streamed down her face as she rolled her window down.

"What happened?" he asked, resting his hands on the door so he could lean down.

She swiped at her damp cheeks. "It's nothing. I just needed a minute."

Noah leaned down farther, resting his arm on the door. "It's obviously something, since it made you cry."

Her bright eyes seemed to sparkle even more with

unshed tears. "One of the ladies who comes to the meetings lost her dog."

A rancher at heart, Noah was an animal lover, but for Lucy to get this upset over someone else's animal was rather surprising.

"Sorry," she said with a sniff as she waved her hand as if to blow off her emotions. "It's just that Tammy bought this dog after her husband passed away last year because she wanted the company. But he got out of the house and was hit by a school bus. I just hung up with her and she's so upset."

As much as he felt terrible for this stranger, there was a stirring deep within him for the amount of sympathy Lucy had for the people in her group. Lucy cared with her whole heart. He heard it each time she came over the radio to him, he saw it in the way she was with his daughter, and now how she grieved for a widowed lady's dog.

"You going to be okay to drive home?" he asked.

Lucy nodded. "I'll be fine. I'm going to swing by her place to check on her. I don't want her to be alone right now."

Of course she wasn't going home. She'd only worked all night and had been pulling double shifts, not to mention whatever hours she logged into her schoolwork.

"It's not safe for you to be on the roads when you're this tired."

Defying him, she started her car. "I'm fine, Noah.

I'll take ten minutes to check on Tammy and then I'll go home."

Noah didn't bother backing away or even attempting to move. She glared in his direction and raised one brow as if to dare him to say another word. Whatever she did on her time off wasn't his concern, but at the same time, they were friends. Right?

"As your friend, I'm going to give you some advice."

Lucy gripped the steering wheel and stared at her hands. "A friend?" she asked, glancing back to him. "Fine. If that's how you want to play this out."

She was going to be difficult. She couldn't just let this ride out, but he wasn't taking her bait.

"Go home and rest," he advised. "When you wake up, take her some of those amazing scones or something else you bake and then you'll have time to visit and not feel rushed."

Lucy pursed her lips and he was shocked she seemed to be thinking about his suggestion instead of instantly arguing.

"Fine."

Noah stood straight up. "What?"

"Oh, don't look so surprised that I agreed," she scolded. "Your idea makes more sense. I just… I want to fix it now for her. I hate knowing people I care about are hurting. It hurts me. My heart literally aches for her."

Noah swallowed, hating the lump that formed in

his own throat. An image of Lucy going through her own grief didn't sit well with him. Who did she have? Oh, she had her friends, but what family? Because he'd never heard her discuss any. Not that they'd talked a lot, but still. In general conversation most people brought up parents or siblings. She'd only talked about her friends who helped her with the support group.

He didn't like that she gave everything to everyone and went home to a lonely house. But, again, that wasn't his business. Damn it, though, he wanted to do something. What would he do? Ask her to come over again? That wasn't smart. Having Lucy in his house was just adding another layer to this already complicated situation. His life didn't need anything else that was new and out of his comfort zone.

But Lucy didn't exactly make him uncomfortable. She made him achy, needy, wanting.

"Why don't you come over?" he asked before he could stop himself. Shoving his hands in his jacket pocket, he shrugged. "Emma would like to see you again."

Lame, Spencer. Totally lame.

"Would she?" Lucy asked, her mouth tipping up into a soft smile. "Well, I'd like to see her again."

Nodding, Noah stepped back, realizing he'd already opted to dive headfirst into this. When she continued to smile at him, he felt a stirring somewhere deep in his chest. Someplace that had been dead so long, he'd almost forgotten it existed.

"Then I'll see you later," he told her as he crossed the lot to his truck. By the time he got in and started his engine, Lucy sat in her car smiling over at him.

Whatever he'd gotten himself into was nobody's fault but his at this point. So, here he was about to have a woman to his house. A woman he'd invited under the pretense of seeing his daughter. But he was a fool and Lucy had seen right through him.

If he was going to continue on this unknown journey, he was going to have to become a stronger man, at least where Lucy was concerned, because she was quickly wearing him down.

Chapter Five

"Thanks, Captain."

Captain Cameron St. John nodded. "No need to thank me, Lucy. I'm sorry about your car."

She didn't even want to look around the captain at the sight of her car being pulled away by the wrecker. She'd just left the station and had been heading home, as she'd promised, but someone had run a red light and T-boned her car. Her car she had just paid off.

Her hands still shook and she wasn't sure she was ready to get out of the captain's patrol car yet, either. She'd never been in an accident, and she was quite certain she never wanted to be in another.

"It's a little different being on this side of the job," she stated, trying to get her heartbeat back to normal.

"I just wish we knew who hit you," Cameron muttered. "I've got some patrolmen driving around looking. Whoever it was has some massive damage to their car, so they should be easy to spot."

Lucy blew out a sigh. "I'm sorry. It all happened so fast and all I saw was a dark color fleeing the scene."

Cameron patted her shoulder. "It's all right. We take care of our own."

She loved that about her job. They were like family. Still, she wished her car weren't smashed because she had no backup. Lucy rubbed her forehead, trying to ward off a headache.

"You sure you don't want the EMTs to check you out?" he asked.

Lucy shook her head. "No. I'll be fine. I could use a lift home, though."

"No problem."

Cameron drove her home, which wasn't far considering she was only a few miles away when she was hit. During the ride she asked about his family and if they were all bringing their kids to the fall festival. Cameron had two brothers and they were all influential people in the town.

"If you need to call out tomorrow, don't think anything about it."

He pulled into her drive and Lucy grabbed her purse. "Thanks, but I'm sure I'll be all right. Besides, Carla is still out."

"I think she'll be back tomorrow," he told her.

Tugging on her handle, she smiled. "Well, I can still come to work. I wasn't injured, just shaken up and a little sore on my left side where I hit the door."

Cameron nodded. "The offer still stands."

"Thanks for the ride," she told him as she got out.

As she let herself in her back door, her cell chimed, but she was juggling her key in the lock and holding her purse. She let it go to voice mail; it wasn't like she was in the mood to talk anyway.

As soon as she stepped inside and dropped her purse to the counter, the phone started ringing again. All she wanted to do was grab a quick shower and crawl into bed. Or maybe she'd just go straight to bed.

Lucy's mind raced as she thought of getting some much-needed sleep, then getting up to bake something to take to Tammy, who'd just lost her pup.

First thing after she woke she needed to see to the horses and make sure they had enough straw and water. They should be fine, but she tended to them every single day just like Evan used to do.

Oh, yeah. Then after all of that she had an invitation to Noah's house. She may cancel that because... well, she was exhausted and sore and perhaps she shouldn't keep going around sweet, impressionable Emma. The little girl had recently lost her mother and Lucy wasn't sure of the circumstances surrounding that tragedy. But Noah had invited her over, so perhaps he wanted to grab that olive branch she'd extended. Maybe he needed a friend. But part of Lucy didn't want to just be a friend to the only man she'd felt a pull toward since her husband passed.

Though there was more time since her tragic loss than his, she knew grief couldn't be given a time frame. Everyone healed differently and everyone moved on at their own pace.

Lucy locked her back door and wondered what she'd do about wheels. On a groan, she realized she wouldn't be going anywhere with baked goods. Perhaps she could call Tammy and invite her over. Maybe getting her out of the house would be a good idea, because that's the only way Lucy was going to be able to try to comfort her in person.

And she surely wasn't about to ask Noah to give her a lift. Speaking of Noah, she'd best send him a text and tell him she couldn't make it later that day.

As she headed through her one-story house, she started stripping out of her clothes. By the time she reached her bedroom, she was ready to put on her favorite ratty nightgown, draw her room-darkening shades, and crawl into bed. She'd worked midnights for so long, she had her system down pat. Her bedroom was in the back of the house, away from any road traffic, and when her door was shut and her fan was on, it was out of earshot of the doorbell.

Lucy tossed her clothes into the basket and had just pulled her nightgown over her head when the doorbell rang. Seriously? She should've turned her fan on and shut the door right away.

She started to climb into bed, more than willing to ignore the unwanted guest. Her neighbors knew she worked midnights, so they never bothered her. But the doorbell turned to a persistent knock.

Obviously someone needed her right now. Since her nightgown was an oversize T-shirt style that hit her knees, she didn't bother with clothes. She'd get rid of this person and get into bed.

Lucy padded down the hallway and came to the small foyer. Even through the etched glass of her front door she recognized that shape. What was he doing here?

Flicking the lock on the door, she opened it and didn't get a chance to say a word as Noah stepped right up to her. His eyes raked over her, his hands falling to her shoulders.

"Why aren't you at the hospital getting checked out?"

She should've known the accident wouldn't remain quiet. Not in a small town with a small police force who knew each other's business.

"Because you told me to come straight home to bed," she countered. "Which I was trying to do."

His brows drew in. "Don't be sarcastic. Cameron said you wouldn't go get checked out."

The captain was the snitch? No, she didn't believe that for a minute. Regardless, this wasn't Noah's business. He couldn't ignore her and then suddenly show up at her door like he had a right to be concerned.

"Shouldn't you be home?" she asked, wondering when he was going to remove his hands from her shoulders. Not that she wanted him to.

The fact he rushed here and was worried spoke volumes about the feelings he went out of his way to fight off.

"I'd just gotten home and changed when I heard the call over the scanner," he replied as he eased her into her house and closed the door behind him. "A hit-and-run?"

Lucy nodded. "Yeah. Some jerk totaled my car."

"Did you get a look at the vehicle or the driver?"

Shrugging her sore shoulders, Lucy shook her head. "No. Just that the car was dark colored. It happened so fast. Thankfully I'm not hurt, just sore. My hip is a little bruised. This guy is going to have a rough time hiding with a banged-up car."

Noah raked his hand through his dark hair. "There's only going to be one dark-colored vehicle that is mangled in the front in a town this small."

Lucy noticed he kept fidgeting. Glancing her way, running his hand over his stubbled jawline and his fingers through his hair.

"You all right?" she asked.

Noah laughed as he turned his focus solely to her. "You're kidding, right? I heard you had been in an accident, a hit-and-run, and I worried. So I called the station and they said Cameron was on the scene and the EMTs had been sent away. So, no, I'm not all right because you could be hurt and not know it. Internal injuries can be well hidden."

When Lucy went to reach for him, she felt a pain in her back and she hissed.

"Damn it." Noah wrapped his arms around her and gently picked her up. "You need to be seen."

"No, I need to be in bed." Just as soon as she finished being carried like some helpless heroine in a historical novel. "I need to take some pain reliever, get some rest, and maybe soak in a hot bath later. That's all."

"Why are you so stubborn?" he muttered as he headed down the hallway. "Which one is your room?"

"As flattered as I am at your seduction, I'm afraid I'm not up to a romp right now."

Noah's glare told her he didn't find her nearly as humorous as she found herself. "Lucy, you're testing my patience."

"Last room on the left," she murmured as she laid her head against his shoulder.

Maybe just for a few minutes she'd relax and let him care for her. This wasn't anything she'd ever had before, not even with her husband. Evan had been loving, but never the type to whisk her off her feet.

Besides, Noah wasn't doing anything but trying

to get her to rest. He wasn't trying to woo her or flirt or even seduce her.

What a shame. Part of her wished they could enter into some adult agreement that an affair was the perfect way to get each other out of their systems. Because she was seriously starting to think that she was in his, too.

The devil on one shoulder told her to be the one to seduce him, but the angel on the other told her he was grieving and to put her hormones away.

Gently, Noah laid her on her bed and eased back. "Did you already take pain meds?"

"No. I haven't been home but a few minutes." She nodded in the direction of her master bath. "In there, top shelf above the vanity."

While he got her meds, she had to admit that having him here was a bit awkward. No, maybe not awkward, but definitely weird. She couldn't deny that any man in her bedroom would make her take notice, but this particular man had her aching in places that had nothing to do with the accident.

Between that thick Southern accent and the way he obviously cared, how could she prevent her heart from flipping over?

After she took the pills, all while Noah stood directly over her to make sure, he then tucked her in like a child.

"I think I can get it from here," she informed him,

feeling more and more foolish. "Go ahead and get home. Emma is probably wondering where you are."

"She's at the sitter until this afternoon."

Well, if she were feeling up to par, she may take advantage of that fact, but as it was, she was in no shape. The longer time went on, the sorer her body was becoming. Besides, she would feel even more foolish if her first attempt at seduction landed her a big fat rejection.

"I think I need to soak in the tub first." She sat up and twisted her neck from side to side. Her hip twinged in protest, but she was careful not to show pain. "And I definitely don't need you around for that. Thanks for stopping to check on me, but I can take it from here."

"Are you seriously not going to get checked out?"

She let out a laugh and came to her feet. "I'm seriously too tired, plus I'd know if something was wrong."

Lucy wasn't going to argue. She was too sore, too tired, and not about to give in. She went past Noah and closed herself in her adjoining bathroom. This was one of those times when she was so glad she'd had an old claw foot tub put in when she'd renovated the outdated bathroom. She'd gone for an old dresser-turned-vanity, kept the old tiles, found a nice mirror at a yard sale, and splurged on the tub.

Lucy quickly shed her clothes as the tub filled with hot water. She plucked a lavender bath bomb from the basket on the vanity and dropped it into the water. If she could just get ten minutes of warmth to her muscles, she knew she'd feel better and then she could rest peacefully.

With her bath pillow in place, Lucy eased herself into the hot water that would for sure turn her skin a lovely shade of red. She didn't hear anything outside her bathroom door so she assumed Noah had left. Hopefully he remembered to lock the door behind him.

Lucy twisted her hair on top of her head and secured it with a clip. As she nestled against her little inflatable pillow, she closed her eyes and let the hot water and the bath bomb work their magic.

Maybe when she got done resting she'd feel like figuring out her car situation. Right now, though, she didn't have the mental energy to worry.

As the bubbles enveloped her, she couldn't help but get all giddy as she realized something. Despite his having worked all night and despite the fact that he needed to get home to his daughter, Noah had come to her house when he'd found out about the accident. She'd seen the worry in his eyes. He hadn't simply asked how she was while standing at her door, but had picked her up and whisked her away to bed.

She made a mental note to revise her schedule for later today. First on her agenda was figuring out exactly what that all meant.

Chapter Six

She'd been behind that closed door for so long, Noah wasn't sure if he needed to knock, call her name, or barge in to see if she was still alive.

He'd notified his sitter and explained where he was and that he may be a tad late in picking up Emma. Apparently, Emma was in no hurry to get home because they were baking cupcakes and other surprises for him.

Noah stifled a yawn and stretched his arms above his head. As tired as he was, he still hadn't calmed down from hearing Lucy had been in a hit-and-run. Maybe it was the fact he'd lost his wife tragically, or perhaps he'd been so shaken because he'd actually come to care for Lucy. Regardless, he hadn't been able to get to her house fast enough.

When he'd heard she wasn't being taken to the hospital, he'd figured she was fine, but he'd needed to see for himself. He didn't care if that was crossing some unspoken professional boundary. There was something about Lucy that stirred a desire in him, a desire he'd tried to ignore, but one that was only getting stronger.

Now that he stood in her bedroom, glancing at the pictures of her and her friends that she'd placed on her dresser, he realized just how intimate this moment was. He hadn't been in a woman's bedroom since before he was married. And suddenly he found himself in Lucy's, a woman he'd only known a short time. But in that time she'd completely taken his world for a spin. She made him fantasize, desire, ache.

Since when was that okay for a grieving man? What were the rules exactly in this situation?

Noah glanced at his watch and realized she'd been in there for nearly an hour. He crossed the room, skirting around her four-poster bed and antique trunk.

Using his knuckles, he tapped on the door. "Lucy, you all right?"

No reply. He listened, but even the sound of her swishing in the water had stopped. But how long ago?

"Lucy," he called louder in case she had earbuds in. Still nothing.

He rapped his knuckles on the door harder this

time. After a minute or so of no response or noise from the other side, he didn't even think twice. Instincts kicked in and he went for the knob. She'd been in an accident and she could've had internal injuries. What if she'd passed out? What if she'd drowned in her bathwater?

He opened the door and was met with steam. Lucy lay in the tub with her arms resting on the lip of the old claw foot bath, her head tipped to the side on one of those bath pillows. All of that blond hair had been piled up on top of her head with a few random strands clinging to her damp skin.

Noah crossed the room, wondering if she was passed out from injuries or just asleep. He crouched down next to the tub and checked for a pulse. Instantly, Lucy jerked awake. Those bright green eyes met his and his worries were put to rest as his question was answered. She'd been asleep.

And now that she was awake, he felt like a fool for standing here. All of that creamy skin was on display and it took every single ounce of his willpower to keep his eyes fixed on hers.

"Noah?" she whispered, not blinking or even attempting to cover herself.

"I thought something was wrong."

That sounded so lame, but it was the honest truth.

Lucy blinked. "I must've fallen asleep."

When she shivered, he figured the water had gotten cold since she'd come in so long ago. Noah reached for a towel and extended it to her, keeping his head turned away.

"I'm sorry for just barging in here," he stated.

Water sloshed as she must have stood up, and took the towel from him. "No. Um... I just didn't realize you were still here."

Noah turned to give her privacy, but before he could step back into the bedroom, Lucy let out a hiss in pain. He spun back to her, instantly finding his arms around her.

"I'm all right," she insisted, but she clutched his arm as she leaned into his chest. "I guess I'm a bit sorer than I thought. I just stepped wrong, that's all. My hip is not cooperating."

She'd managed to wrap the towel around her body, but she hadn't dried off. Her damp skin soaked his T-shirt, her body lined up with his perfectly, and that heaviness of guilt he'd been carrying since meeting her was growing lighter. Because holding her didn't feel so wrong after all.

Without thinking twice, he lifted her in his arms once again and carried her from the bathroom.

"Noah—"

"You're fine. I know." He went into her room and set her on the edge of her bed. "What else is hurting?"

She clutched the ends of the towel between her breasts. "Just my hip. I banged it against the door when the other car plowed into me."

Rage coiled within him at the thought of someone hurting her and fleeing the scene. Noah knew the guys were out looking for the mangled car and he hoped like hell they found the culprit.

"Go home and rest," she insisted.

Her eyes held his and he couldn't pull his gaze away from just how stunning she looked with glistening skin and honey strands framing her face.

"I'm going to rest here." He hadn't thought about that before, but he could grab some shut-eye on her couch.

"Surely there is some department rule against coworkers fraternizing."

Noah crossed his arms over his chest, his gaze never wavering from her. "Are we fraternizing?"

"Well, you've seen me naked and carried me to bed." She quirked a brow as if she had him. "The closest thing I've ever done with a coworker is have breakfast with some guys after our shift. Not one has ever been in my bedroom, let alone seen me without clothes."

Noah shrugged. "We're friends. I was worried and for good reason."

Lucy came to her feet, standing only inches from him. "My friends don't come into my bathroom when I'm taking a bath."

Why did his eyes have to go to her lips? And why did she challenge him? Couldn't she just accept his help and not be so defiant? Yet something about that independent manner turned him on.

"Get dressed," he told her. "I'm going to crash on your couch."

"Why are you so adamant about keeping an eye on me?"

There went that guilt growing back to full size. His late wife had said she was fine after the storm that ripped through their tiny town. She'd come up out of the cellar with him and Emma and kept complaining of a headache after a board had hit her in the back when they all raced to shelter.

Moments after emerging when they all thought it was safe, she collapsed and died. Just because someone said they were fine didn't mean they knew what was going on inside their bodies.

"I'll be on the sofa if you need anything," he told her.

He turned and crossed the room to the door, but her words stopped him.

"I don't know the circumstances surrounding your wife's death, but I assume that's why you're so protective now."

Noah remained in the doorway, his back to her. "You don't need to know the circumstances."

No one needed to know the details of his life before coming to Stonerock. He didn't know exactly why but it seemed imperative to maintain that privacy. He just felt that if he didn't discuss the tragedy, then the hurt might ease one day. Maybe he'd be able to leave those painful memories behind and not pull them into his new life. Hell, he had no idea. This was such unknown territory, he truly didn't know how to react.

He heard Lucy shift behind him and he stilled, waiting to see what she'd do or say. "No, I don't," she whispered. "But I know that you're still reliving that moment. You probably feel like—"

He whirled around, surprised to see she'd come so close to him and still wore only the thick terrycloth towel. "You have no idea what I feel," he growled. "Our situations aren't the same and I'm not going to let you get into my head and try to fix me."

Her bright eyes held his and he hated how terrible he felt for speaking so harshly to her. But, damn it, he wanted his thoughts, his feelings to stay locked inside where they couldn't hurt.

"I don't want to fix you," she murmured. "I want you to come to the conclusion yourself that you can be happy again."

"I'm happy."

Okay, that didn't even sound convincing to him, let alone trying to sell it to Lucy. His eyes darted over her shoulder to the picture on her bedside table. A candid shot of her and who he assumed was her late husband. After two years, the fact she still had a picture of them by her bed proved that she wasn't as far removed from grief as she'd declared.

"Since we both know you're lying," she went on, "I'd say this conversation is over."

Noah shifted his attention back to her. This woman somehow managed to frustrate him and turn him on all at the same time. One minute she challenged him, and the next she tossed out that sweetness that was so uniquely her. He never knew which Lucy he'd encounter at any given moment.

"Did you have something else to say?" she asked, still clutching that damn towel between her breasts.

"I have plenty I want to say, but this isn't the time."

When he started to turn, she grabbed his arm. "Spit it out. Don't run from whatever is on your mind."

His eyes raked over her body; he couldn't help himself at this point. She smelled too damn good, looked like something from every man's fantasy. She was killing him.

And he'd rushed over here, so there was nobody to blame but himself.

But he couldn't talk. Not now.

"You're pretty much naked and we're both exhausted," he said, as if the obvious needed to be stated. "Let's just agree to revisit this another time."

Like maybe when his head was on straight and he wasn't staring temptation right in the face.

"Revisit *this*?" she questioned. "You mean the attraction and the fact you're hiding from it?"

There she went with that no-holding-back attitude. "I'm not hiding."

"But you're attracted."

Gritting his teeth, Noah fisted his hands at his
sides. There was no reason to lie about it or even
attempt to deny the truth. He knew it, she knew it.
The question was: What the hell did he do about it?

And why couldn't she just get dressed?

"You need to put clothes on and get some sleep,"
he told her.

"I plan on doing both," she informed him, tipping
her head to the side. "But you don't need to stay. My
hip is bruised, my back is sore, and my head hurts.
I'm well past the age of needing or wanting a baby-
sitter. And I don't take pity, either, so if that's the
only reason you're hanging around—"

He kissed her. Damn it all. She was ranting and
he couldn't take it another second.

Noah covered her mouth with his, but kept his
fists at his side. If he reached up now, he couldn't
guarantee that towel would stay in place. He'd seen
exactly what she had as she lay all sprawled out in
her bath and now that her body was flush against his,
he had a perfect idea of how gloriously their bodies
were lined up.

Lucy sighed into him and he felt her lean against
him as if melting into his touch. And he desperately
wanted to touch her. He hadn't kissed another woman
in years, but having his mouth on Lucy wasn't a

struggle and he sure as hell wasn't feeling guilty now. No, if anything he was more ramped up than ever.

When her hands settled on his shoulders and her fingers curled into him, the last shred of Noah's control snapped. He framed her face and shifted his stance, spreading his legs wider for her to step into him. She tasted so good, too good. He shouldn't be craving a woman he'd only known a short time, but there was no way he could ignore this tug.

Lucy's sweet body arched against him at the same time she let out a groan. Noah slid his hands down over her shoulders and between them to the knot in her towel. Just as he started to give it a tug, Lucy jerked and stepped back. She clutched that towel as she had before, but now she was panting...and looking anywhere but at him.

"This is..." She shook her head. "Noah, I can't."

Reality smacked him in the face and he wondered how the hell he'd gotten to this point. He'd been so adamant about not even admitting to the attraction, yet he was ready to take her to bed. And there was that picture just over Lucy's shoulder that mocked him, mocked them.

But there was something much larger going on here and it had nothing to do with the way they felt and everything to do with the fact that Lucy, who had pursued him, had pulled back and was now trembling.

Maybe she wasn't as healed as she thought.

Would he have been able to go through with this? Would he have been able to shove aside the guilt and all the reasons this was wrong and actually take her to bed?

She was right for stopping, but he wished like hell she wasn't trembling as if they'd done something wrong.

"I... I need to be alone," she whispered, still not looking his way.

Noah raked a hand through his hair. "For all your talk about wanting to heal people, did you ever stop to think you need to heal yourself first?"

She flinched at his words, but remained silent.

"I'll be at home if you need anything."

Not that she'd call. If she even spoke to him on their next shift it would be shocking. Well, spoke to him on a personal level. Because there was no way they could avoid each other forever. Communication was key to their working relationship.

And he'd just learned the hard way that they also had a personal relationship, whether either of them wanted to admit it or not. Because even though they hadn't taken things to the next level, they'd crossed an invisible line that neither of them could come back from.

Suddenly he found himself in a role reversal with the captivating Lucy Brooks. After all his mental battles with himself over keeping his pain inside, he knew he'd have to be the one to get Lucy to open up and heal because she was more broken than she'd let on…and perhaps more than she even knew.

Chapter Seven

"I figured you'd want to know."

Even as his captain spoke on the phone, Noah paid him no mind. He was too busy watching Emma play on the floor with her cowgirl doll and horse. She crawled all around the area rug chattering and pretending, looking happy and at ease. He marveled at how quickly she'd adapted to this home, this new life. Now if he could just take a page out of her book and do the same.

He could start by unloading some of those boxes stacked in his bedroom. He'd tried to make the rest of the house cozy and livable for Emma, but he hadn't brought himself to unpack the personal items they'd brought from Texas.

After the storm had torn through the town, he'd attempted to stay. He'd remained with the force and tried to rent a house and start over. But he couldn't. The few things they'd accumulated between the storm and now were still in boxes. They were just things, he told himself. His entire life had taken on a whole new perspective since that fateful day. So why hadn't he unpacked them?

When he heard the voice in his ear bark out his name, he focused his attention back on the call from his captain. "Why would I want to know this?"

Cameron laughed into the line. "I just had a hunch you'd want to know we picked up the driver who hit Lucy."

Damn it. Was he that transparent? Was something that he'd barely admitted to himself obvious to everyone else?

"Well, I'm glad he was caught," Noah stated. "Thanks for letting me know."

"I just spoke to Lucy, as well," Cameron went on to say. "She's taking the night off."

He'd been at her house earlier that day. The memories kept rolling through his mind and he'd barely slept since coming home. What little sleep he'd had had been filled with dreams of what would've happened had she not put the brakes on.

He'd woken restless, achy, needy, and cursing himself for letting things get out of hand.

Then he'd cursed himself for how far he'd let his feelings go. On one hand, he knew he couldn't grieve forever, but on the other, he felt like he was cheating on his wife.

And he honestly wasn't sure if he wouldn't have put the brakes on himself. Clearly he and Lucy weren't in a place to try to physically console each other—another reason he should seriously keep his distance. Which was easier said than done, he admitted.

"Is she okay?" Noah asked.

"Still sore and her hip is bothering her," Cameron told him. "Lucy is a hell of a worker and I'm going to hate losing her when she finishes her degree. But there are times I wish she had someone to check up on her."

"Are you meddling, sir?"

Again, Cameron's laugh filled the line. "Not at all. Just stating my opinion. Have a good day off, Spencer."

Noah disconnected the call and laid his cell on the table by the sofa. Like hell his boss wasn't meddling. But Noah knew he meant well. Happily married people always wanted to see single people happily married, too.

"Daddy, when will we have real horses again?" Emma asked, never taking her eyes off her toys. "I miss riding."

"Me, too, baby girl."

He may have been a police officer since he graduated college and the academy at the age of twenty-three, but ranching had always been his life. Their Texas ranch had been Noah's grandfather's, then his father had expanded it with more livestock and an extra barn, and once Noah had taken over, he'd grown the livestock even more.

Now he was starting from scratch. He couldn't help but wonder if this was how his grandfather had felt when he'd wanted to have his own spread and had gotten started.

This house they were renting was definitely going to be temporary because Noah needed space. He needed land.

The land Lucy had was exactly the type of space he was looking for. Something not too large so he could get started little by little.

As Noah stared down at Emma, he vowed their first purchase after the new house would be a horse. But that would take time and more funds than he had right now. He was keeping his eyes open for land to build or a house with acreage, but he wasn't going to rush. As much as he wanted all those things again, he knew it would take patience.

One day at a time. That had been his life motto since losing his world.

"I just want to ride," Emma stated again. "What if I forget how to do it?"

Noah sank into the floor beside her, smoothing a wayward strand of hair back from her face. "You won't forget. When you love something that much, it will live inside you forever."

Emma immediately looked to him. "Like Mommy? Because I never want to forget her."

Noah's heart clenched. The honest words of a child could absolutely gut you. Emma was so sincere as she stared with those bright blue eyes. Had she truly worried she'd forget her mother? Noah tried to keep pictures of her all around the house and especially one in Emma's bedroom. He wanted his late wife's memory to live on because Emma was so young, there was a good chance she'd forget the sound of her mother's voice or the way she'd laughed.

Swallowing the lump of grief, Noah pulled Emma onto his lap. "Mommy will always live in your heart, just like our ranch will. Those are things we love and just because we don't have them anymore doesn't mean we'll forget them. Moving away was just for us to start our new life. We'll have another ranch."

"And another mommy?"

Noah stilled. He'd never even thought about how Emma might think another woman would just step into their lives. At four years old, who knew how she truly viewed death? But he'd tried to explain it to her as best as he could.

Emma shifted in his lap and wrapped her arms

around his neck. "When can we go riding? Lucy said we could stop by anytime."

Noah pulled in a breath, ready to make an excuse for the "anytime" comment. But then something hit him. Lucy had called off work for the night, so she'd be awake. He wasn't sure if she was home, but if they casually dropped in, surely she wouldn't turn them away.

Yes, things had gotten out of hand earlier and she'd gotten spooked, but they couldn't hide from each other. He wasn't the type of guy to hide from confrontation, anyway. He believed in facing things head-on and trying to keep awkwardness at bay.

"Why don't you go put on your boots and we'll see if Lucy's home," he suggested. This whole plan could backfire, but he didn't think it would.

"What if she's not?" Emma asked as she scrambled off his lap.

"Then we'll go for ice cream. We need to get out of the house and have some fun."

Emma squealed and clapped her hands as she raced off to her bedroom.

Noah picked up her toys, setting them in the oversize basket next to the sofa. It was a beautiful afternoon and there was no reason he couldn't drop in on a friend.

Okay, that sounded like such a lame justification, even to his ears. He wanted to see Lucy again, plus he wanted Emma to be able to ride. Killing two birds with the same stone didn't always work, but he had a good feeling about this. Lucy wouldn't turn him away. And if she tried...well, he'd make sure she knew he was onto her. There was a deeper level of pain she didn't know she had. He'd seen the dawning come across her face earlier. When she'd pulled back, she'd appeared shocked, as if she didn't know why she had.

Things had gotten so intense, Noah knew it was time to dial it back a notch. But he couldn't walk away from her totally. No, keeping things light for a while may be exactly what they both needed.

But there was no doubt that they'd revisit what just happened. If nothing else, they needed to discuss what they were feeling, but Noah sure as hell wasn't ready for that conversation. And he definitely wasn't ready to act on that fantasy he had of Lucy.

One day at a time, right? Wasn't that his motto lately? He needed to remember that because he couldn't handle any more right now.

Lucy hadn't gone to Tammy's home to check on her, but she did call. Tammy had already heard about Lucy's accident, so they discussed that instead of the passing of her dog.

After their call, since Lucy was technically homebound, she opted to bake. She'd wanted to try out a new recipe anyway, so now was the perfect opportunity.

With the volume cranked up on the oldies she loved to listen to, Lucy tapped her foot as she worked the dough for the cranberry lemon bread. Anything fruity was her go-to. Most women loved chocolate, but Lucy would take a good lemon bar or pineapple upside-down cake over a brownie any day.

Oh, lemon bars sounded good. They were easy enough, so maybe she'd make those for Monday's meeting. She already had most of the ingredients out for the lemon cranberry bread anyway.

Singing along to the tunes, Lucy barely heard her doorbell ring. Kate and Tara had offered to take her anywhere and had even said they'd run over to keep her company, but Lucy had told them she'd be fine and her insurance was already getting her a rental car until she figured out what to do in regards to getting a new one.

She didn't dare mention to them about Noah being here earlier. She was still trying to grasp the fact he'd been willing to sleep with her and she'd all but freaked out. What was wrong with her? She hadn't been this attracted to another man since her husband.

But she hadn't been with another man, either.

After she'd flipped and put a halt to the intimacy, Noah had agreed it was a mistake. But part of her wondered if he wouldn't have stopped himself. Would he have pushed her away? Would he have let that guilt creep in and put doubts in his mind?

Lucy couldn't pinpoint exactly which emotion had caused her to stop. Being kissed by Noah was as glorious as she'd imagined it would be. Her entire body had craved more of his touch. But everything about the experience, as thrilling as it had been, seemed so unfamiliar to her. It had been too long since she'd been touched by a man and she'd been...well, terrified. Not of Noah, but of getting close to another man again.

Lucy wiped her hands on her yellow-and-white-striped apron and padded barefoot through the house. Well, more like she limped. Her hip was bothering her more than she'd initially thought it would and the swollen, bruised area kept rubbing against her clothes. But she was lucky. In her years as a dispatcher, she'd heard of too many hit-and-runs that had ended in tragedy.

When Lucy glanced out the front window, she recognized that black truck in her drive. She hadn't emotionally recovered from when Noah was here early this morning, but she wasn't going to ignore him. And she couldn't deny the way her heart kicked up.

As much as she'd thought she was ready to move on, clearly that had not the case. Unfortunately, she hadn't known how she'd react until she'd gotten into the moment. Now she knew and she was mortified.

Pulling in a deep breath, Lucy flicked the lock and opened the door. Noah held Emma in his arms as he met her gaze.

"We were hoping you'd be home," he said, offering a smile. "We thought we'd take you up on your offer and check out your horses."

Her horses? He'd popped in with such a simple request as if he hadn't had his hands all over her only hours ago. As if she hadn't basically shoved him out the door when her mind had overridden her feelings. He'd brought his daughter here to see the horses. Well, okay then.

"Sure. Come on in."

Lucy stepped back and let them inside. She didn't know what she expected when she saw him again, but she'd assumed it would be at work where there would be plenty of people to buffer the awkward tension between them.

As Noah passed by, Lucy inhaled that familiar deep woodsy cologne he always had on. Why did everything about this man appeal to her? Before this morning she'd relished the fact she was feeling so alive and getting to the point where she wanted to open up to those feelings of desire again.

Of course that plan had backfired because she'd rushed things, and now she probably came across as a total moron. After all, Noah was only here for Emma and the horses. There were several ranches and horse owners in Stonerock, but Noah didn't know too many people yet. Or perhaps this was his way of clearing the air and getting them back on even footing.

"Something smells good."

Lucy closed the door. "I was just mixing up some bread dough."

As she started to pass by, Noah sat Emma down and grabbed Lucy's arm. "You're limping."

That touch was so simple, yet she knew exactly how potent it was when he wanted it to be. Noah Spencer did things to her, things she hadn't experienced in years, and things she was still trying to process.

"Just sore. That's all." She wasn't about to get into all of this again, so she turned her attention to Emma who reached up to hold on to her daddy's hand. "How about you help me put the bread in the oven and then we can go check on Gunner and Hawkeye. They would love to see you."

Lucy headed down the hall to the kitchen and pulled over a chair. "Hop up here so you can see better," she told Emma. "This will go so much faster with a helper."

From the corner of her eye, Lucy noticed Noah hanging back. If he could do something else besides stare, that would be great.

Was he regretting this morning? Was he having second thoughts about kissing her and pushing toward something else? He'd been so adamant about not opening up and when he had, she'd shut him down.

She'd better be more careful about what she asked him for. Noah Spencer was one powerful man, and when he let his guard down, he was one dangerous man. Lucy could easily see herself falling for him and that was a whole other level of intimacy she truly didn't know if she was ready for.

"Can we make cookies?" Emma asked, cutting into Lucy's very adult thoughts.

Lucy laughed and reached for the greased bread pan. "Let's get this bread in the oven first and check on the horses."

"Emma," Noah chimed in, "we didn't stop by to bake."

Throwing a glance over her shoulder, Lucy met his dark gaze. "Just for the horses, right?"

Noah raised a brow as his mouth kicked up in a grin. "Right."

Every part of her tingled, from her messy hair to her pink polished toes. Perhaps it was best if they went outside. The bread could be covered and put in the oven later.

"Tell you what," she said to Emma. "Let's lay a towel over this bowl and let the bread rise awhile. That way we can enjoy the horses while it's still daylight. Once the sun goes down, we'll come back in and bake."

"Cookies, too?" Emma asked.

"Emma," Noah growled.

Lucy tapped the girl on the tip of her nose. "Cookies, too. Now let's go check out the horses. They are going to need some straw and water."

After helping Emma off the chair, Noah held the back door open and the child bounced down the steps, her curly pigtails bobbing against the sides of her head.

Lucy followed, stepping out onto the porch with Noah.

"I'll help you down the steps," he said, gripping her elbow.

Lucy didn't shrug him off, mainly because she wanted to get used to his touch. "I can hold on to the banister."

"And I can hold on to you," he claimed.

There was no need to argue. "So you're here just for the horses…or did you have a more obvious reason?"

He assisted her down the stairs, keeping that firm hold on her arm and lining his body up with hers. "I wasn't going to let this tension come between us. And I wanted to see you again. As simple and as complicated as that."

Lucy turned her gaze to his. "Is this you admitting you're interested?"

Once again his dark eyes held hers. "I think you know how much I'm interested. It was you who pushed me away this morning."

"I wasn't sure how you'd feel after I…"

Recalling the events in her mind was humiliating enough. She truly didn't want to say the words aloud.

"You think because you weren't ready that I'm suddenly not interested? I have no clue what the hell is going on here, Lucy, but I know there's an attraction I can't ignore. I can't guarantee I'm ready for more, but..."

Noah turned, one hand on each side of the bannister, blocking her from going down the steps. His eyes bore into hers.

"It took a hell of a lot of nerve for me to admit I wanted you," he finally said. "I figured if I came back with Emma, we could just start over with friendship."

Lucy nodded and realized she was still wearing her apron. She untied it and pulled it over her head, tossing it over to the porch swing.

"Friendship is a good start," she admitted, meeting his eyes once again. "You know, nothing about this is how I thought it would go when I saw you the first time."

"You thought I'd just come into your meetings and you'd fix me?" he asked.

"I thought you'd at least talk to me that first night instead of running away." Lucy opted to go for the full truth. "And I never thought I'd get closer to you and then not be able to— Never mind. The point is I was attracted to you from the second I saw you, but then you ran away."

Noah quirked that dark brow again. "Maybe I ran because you stood in the rain wearing a shirt that was plastered to your curves and I was getting away from temptation."

Stunned, Lucy didn't know what to say. She didn't get the chance to say anything, because Noah suddenly turned to his daughter. He walked up beside Emma where she stood at the fence, and pointed at the horses out into the field as he leaned in and told her something that made her laugh. Lucy had no clue what he was saying; she was still stuck on the declaration he'd just delivered to her.

From the beginning he'd been attracted to her and had been fighting it. Now their roles were reversed and she was wondering how they'd come this far, this fast. Maybe because she hadn't had someone in so long, hadn't experienced such emotions in years, she'd gotten wrapped up without thinking things through.

Watching Noah and Emma standing at the edge of the fence, Lucy swallowed that lump in her throat. When she and Evan had bought this house, this land, they'd agreed to fill it with children. That dream had died with him, or so she'd thought. Lucy wasn't jumping to the point of thinking she and Noah were going to grow old together, but seeing him and Emma here did give her hope. She could have the dream she'd once held on to. All she had to do was let go of that fear of getting too close and suffering such heartache again.

Wouldn't Evan have wanted her to find happiness?

One day she would. Lucy vowed to slowly approach this relationship with Noah. Because she simply couldn't afford for her heart to be broken again.

Chapter Eight

"My horse's name was Daisy."

Emma brushed the horse with circular strokes as she chatted with Lucy in the corral. Noah watched them from the fence. He knew she missed Daisy. Hell, they both missed the meager amount of livestock, but the ones that hadn't died in the storm, he'd had to sell to help with the move.

"She was a chestnut mare," Emma went on. "She loved apples."

Noah knew Emma missed that horse something fierce. Daisy had been so gentle and so perfect for Emma. Their daily routine of feeding her apples in the evening was no more. Soon, though, they would start new traditions in this new town. They were slowly rebuilding their lives.

"Animals are like family," Lucy added as she leaned her arm on the fence post. "These were my husband's horses and I'd thought about selling them when he passed away, but I wanted to hold on to them as a way to stay connected to him. I'm glad I decided to keep them."

Noah knew that need to hold on to any aspect of a late spouse, but everything he'd had with his wife had been taken. Except for Emma. And at the end of the day, that's all he needed.

"Daddy says Mommy will always live in my heart."

Noah glanced to Emma, who was looking back at him. He shot her a wink and she smiled. Yeah, they had each other and that's all that mattered. Memories would live on as long as he had any say about it.

"That's true," Lucy agreed. "Once you love someone, they will stay with you forever. My husband will always be in my heart as well. Being sad is okay, but we also deserve to be happy."

"I think that's solid advice," Noah stated as he turned his focus to Lucy. When she quirked a brow, he merely grinned.

"Daddy says we'll get another horse soon, but first we have to find a house that has enough land." Emma set the brush back in the bucket. "I think I'll name my new horse Daisy. I really like that name."

"Nothing wrong with that," Lucy stated with a firm nod. "But you can come over here anytime to ride or to just see these guys. They love company and I can always use help." Because of her sore hip, today was not a good day to ride.

The sun stretched an orange glow across the horizon and Noah pushed off the fence. "Maybe we should let Lucy get back to what she was doing before we came."

"I was baking, which I promised Emma could help me with." Lucy opened the gate and unhooked Gunner's reins from the post. "Let me get him put up and we'll go back inside."

"We don't need to take up your entire day," Noah argued. "I didn't expect you to have her help."

"Well, I made a promise," Lucy told him as she threw a look over her shoulder. "I never go back on a promise, especially since I've been thinking of cookies ever since Emma mentioned them."

Emma drew lines in the dirt with the toe of her boot. She didn't seem to be paying much attention and had gone to wherever her four-year-old mind journeyed from time to time.

"Are you sure?" Noah asked Lucy as she came back and closed the gate.

Resting her arm over the rung, she nodded. "Positive. If you have something else to do, go on ahead. Emma and I will get along just fine. We'll have a little girl time and you can go do…whatever it is you want."

"Is this you trying to push me away again?"

Lucy pursed her lips and tipped her head. "I'm just trying to figure all of this out. Besides, kids are honest, so I'll quiz her and we'll see just how interested in me you really are."

Noah laughed. "Fair enough. But I really don't have anything else to do."

"I'm sure you'll think of something." Lucy turned her attention to Emma. "You up for some girl time if we kick Daddy out for a few hours?"

Emma glanced up, her eyes darting to her father. "Is that okay? Lucy's fun and I really want to make cookies, Daddy."

Lucy stared at Noah as if daring him to argue with two females. He wasn't that stupid. Besides, giving Emma a little female bonding time was probably a great idea. Perhaps it would do them both good and Noah could use the time to figure out what the hell kind of emotional roller coaster he was on.

Noah threw his hands up. "Fine, but I want some of those cookies you guys keep talking about."

"Promise," Emma said as she drew an invisible X over her heart.

Noah had no idea what he'd do. Seriously. For the past six months he'd been with Emma or at work. He didn't have hobbies and there was no ranch to occupy his time, so…what the hell should he do?

"You're still here," Lucy stated. "It's difficult to have girl time when you won't go."

Emma giggled and Noah leaned down and smacked a kiss on her forehead. "I'm going. You have my cell, so if you need anything—"

"We won't," Lucy assured him. "Give us two hours."

There weren't many people he'd trust his little girl with, but he definitely trusted Lucy. Hell, he'd trusted her so much he was ready to sleep with her.

As he headed to his truck, he wondered where he should go. There weren't too many options in this small town. Maybe he'd just go to the local bar. It wasn't but a couple miles away on the main drag and he'd been meaning to swing by there. He'd heard they had really good burgers and he could use some time to himself to think.

Emma was growing pretty fond of Lucy...and Noah couldn't deny he was, too.

One day at a time. Looking too much into this or placing too much hope in one situation was just asking for heartache—something he couldn't afford.

"Need a beer?"

Yeah, he did. About six of them. "I'll just stick with soda."

The bartender turned to grab a glass and fill it with ice. "You're the new officer."

Small towns, Noah thought. Gotta love them.

"Noah Spencer," he said, offering his hand for a

shake. More than likely the bartender knew this, but it was still polite to start with introductions. "This is the first chance I've had to stop in here, but I've heard all about the burgers."

"Best in town." With his free hand he slid the glass of soda across the bar. "Gray Gallagher."

Noah gripped the glass. "The owner?"

Gray propped his hands on the bar. "Third generation."

"No kidding."

Gray nodded, resting his hands on the gleaming bar top. "My grandfather opened this bar when he returned from the war, then my father went into the Marines and he took over when he got out. I took over when I came home from the Army."

Impressed, Noah nodded. "You've got quite a family tradition."

"Minus the difference in military fields." Gray smiled. "We've had a few disagreements over which is the best."

Gray started to say something else, but glanced over Noah's shoulder. The man's lips thinned and a flash of something—jealousy maybe—came and went across his face.

Noah glanced over his shoulder to see a beautiful blonde fast-dancing with a group of guys. Harmless, flirty fun from the looks of things, but Gray didn't seem too keen on this.

"Problem?"

Gray pulled in a deep breath. "Just since high school."

Definitely jealousy. Noah didn't know what that emotion felt like, but from the looks of Gray, Noah didn't want to know.

"Hang on a second."

Gray disappeared, and Noah thought for sure he'd be heading across that wooden dance floor to interfere, but he didn't. Gray ended up at the other end of the bar, leaning over to talk to a guy who sat by himself nursing a bottle. From the looks of things, the customer was drowning his sorrows. If only life were that easy. Unfortunately, getting lost in the bottle didn't fix anything and reality was always waiting for you on the other side.

Noah glanced over the menu and quickly chose the loaded garbage burger. Anything that combined a burger with bacon, onion rings and barbecue sauce was for him. Sign him up. The messier the better.

"Sorry about that," Gray said as he came back. He nodded toward the menu. "Decide what you want?"

Noah placed his order and pulled his phone from his jacket pocket. He'd apparently had it on vibrate and had missed some texts from Lucy. Worried something was wrong, he opened the messages. Clearly there was no need to worry because his daughter was having a blast.

One picture had Emma wearing a huge apron tied in knots around her waist and neck. She was holding her hands up, palms out to show all the dough she'd been mixing. He scrolled down to see another, this time a selfie with Emma and Lucy, wide smiles across their faces.

His heart flipped in that second. There were two wounded souls bonding and living in the moment. They were virtual strangers, yet they appeared to be having the time of their lives. And Noah couldn't deny that attraction he'd initially had for Lucy grew even more. Something was happening here—nothing he was ready to put a label on quite yet, but definitely something more than just friendship.

How could that be? He wasn't ready for more... was he?

Noah scrolled on to some action shots of Emma kneading the dough and forming it in the bread pans, then the last photo of her holding up a bag of chocolate chips. Obviously cookies were next. There were many things Noah could do with Emma, but baking was definitely not his area of expertise.

The music in the bar switched from fast-paced to something slow and sultry. Noah took a drink of his soda and glanced around. The woman Gray had been eyeing earlier now danced with one guy, her arms draped lazily around his neck. Noah figured in this small town, he'd hear the gossip soon enough about that pretty blonde. Funny how her short skirt and plaid shirt tied at the waist did nothing for him, but the headstrong dispatcher who dressed on the conservative side did more than he should allow.

A waitress came with his burger and fries and set the plate next to his drink. "Can I get you anything else?"

"This will be fine. Thanks."

He sent off a text to Lucy informing her he'd be back within the hour. Maybe he'd get to sample the baked goods.

The commotion behind him caught Noah's attention. He hadn't even tasted his burger yet before he was off his stool. Gray was standing between the blonde and the guy she'd been dancing with. The blonde didn't look happy, neither did Gray, and the other guy was yelling something about Gray minding his own business.

Noah quickly crossed the scarred floor. "Problem?"

Gray kept his grip on the guy's shirt. "Just taking out the garbage."

"I can handle myself," the lady argued.

The guy in the strangle hold gripped Gray's wrists. "She shouldn't dress like that."

Gray's face literally turned red as he reared back with a closed fist. Noah jumped in just in time, but managed to take the brunt of that fist on his jaw. He shoved the other guy out of the way, someone screamed, and Noah held both of his arms out. Keeping these two guys from fighting was key, not the fact his jaw was throbbing.

"Damn, man. You all right?" Gray asked.

Noah shot him a glance. "Maybe you need to go in the back and cool off. I'll take care of things here."

Gray glared at the other guy.

"Now, Gallagher," Noah demanded.

Gray turned to the woman and she merely shook her head and went back to her table of friends. Now that Noah was close, he recognized her as one of Lucy's friends from the meeting that first night.

Whatever the story was, he was sure he'd hear it because he was going to go have a detailed get-to-know-you meeting with Gray Gallagher very shortly.

Once Gray left them, Noah turned to the other guy. "What happened?"

"He tried to punch me."

Noah wasn't in the mood. He had a burger waiting on him and he highly doubted Gray would've just sabotaged his business and threatened a patron for no reason. Yes, a woman was a valid motivation for a man to get fired up over, but Noah figured he would've heard about issues with Gallagher's if a bar fight was a normal occurrence.

"What did you do to her?" Noah asked, thumbing over his shoulder toward Lucy's friend.

Of course the guy said nothing, but kept his eyes level with Noah in an arrogant expression.

"Now would be a good time for you to go."

The guy snorted. "And who the hell are you?"

"Officer Spencer, Stonerock PD." He waited a beat. "Any more questions?"

The guy glanced to where Lucy's friend sat, then back to Noah. "She's not worth it."

"She's worth more, so get the hell out of here."

Muttering a string of curses, the guy headed out of the bar.

Once he'd left, Noah crossed to the table of ladies. "Everything all right here?"

Lucy's friend stared up at him with wide brown eyes. She flashed him a smile that no doubt had many men bowing to her commands. He felt nothing.

"I'm fine." She extended her hand. "We haven't been properly introduced. I'm Kate McCoy."

Noah shook her hand. "Noah Spencer."

"I've heard about you from Lucy."

Fantastic. Just what he wanted to be part of. Girl gossip.

"I'm Tara Bailey." Noah shifted his attention to the raven-haired beauty across the booth. He recognized her from the meeting, too. "I figured Lucy was with you since we invited her out tonight and she turned us down. She never turns us down."

They figured she was with him? Just what did that mean? No way was he about to tell them she was with his daughter. That would only add more fodder to the rumor mill. With him being new to town, he was trying like hell to stay off the radar. Plus, being an officer of the law, he prided himself on privacy. Clearly he was failing on both counts.

"I'm just here for the burgers," he replied, ready to be done here. "Have a good evening, ladies."

As he headed back to his vacated stool, he wondered if he should get his food to go so he could get back to Lucy and Emma. Then he noticed Gray standing on the other side of the counter.

"Sorry about that." The bartender gestured toward Noah's jaw. "You going to arrest me for clocking you?"

Noah shook his head. "If I thought you meant it for me, you'd already be at the station."

Gray gave a clipped nod. "The burger is on the house."

Noah laughed. "I'd rather pay for my food." He rubbed his jaw. "You have a mean hook."

Gray eyed the side of Noah's face and Noah was confident there was a bruise because he knew it was swollen. "How about some ice?"

"I'll take care of it when I get home." Noah took a seat on the stool and rested his elbows on the bar. "Care to tell me what set you off, other than that guy was a jerk?"

The muscle in Gray's jaw ticked. "I saw his hands moving toward the hem of her skirt and she shoved him. Then he grabbed her and hauled her against him and I lost it."

"Before you lost it, was she aware how you feel about her?"

Gray laughed and shook his head. "We have a history."

"Were you married?"

"Hell no," Gray declared. "We've been best friends since high school. Lucy, Tara, Kate and me. We grew apart when I went off to the Army, but since I've been back, we've reconnected. They come in here pretty often, but Tara and Lucy don't push my buttons the way Kate does. It's like she knows exactly how to irritate me."

Noah figured he may as well eat while his food was somewhat still warm. "She's taunting you," he stated as he picked up his burger. "None of my business. Just offering my unsolicited opinion."

He took a bite and nearly groaned. This was the best burger he'd ever had. No wonder the place was so popular.

"Oh, she's taunting me, all right." A waitress came to the bar with an order and Gray grabbed two frosted mugs and filled them with beer before passing them over. "She knows how I feel and it's like she thrives on it."

"Have you dated other women?" Noah asked. "I mean, maybe you should and see if that helps you get over her or makes her realize that she likes you."

Gray raked a hand through his hair. "I'm the bar

owner. I give advice and opinions to my customers. Not the other way around."

"Yeah, well, I'm sure you'll get your chance with me," Noah replied as he picked up a chip. "I'm the new guy in town and I'm sure you've heard all about my life."

"Heard you had a tough time in Texas. Sorry about your loss, man."

Noah nodded. "Thanks. It's hell trying to move on, but there's little choice when you have a child looking to you for guidance and stability."

"We all carry our own hell," Gray muttered as he glanced to the guy at the end of the bar.

"What's his story?" Noah asked.

Keeping his eyes on the guy toying with his beer bottle, Gray replied, "That's Sam Bailey."

Bailey... Bailey. "Isn't that the same last name as the lady over there with Kate?"

"Tara is Sam's ex-wife. They've been divorced for a year. That's a mess. Hell, *he's* a mess."

Obviously. "So why is he here if she's here?"

Gray grabbed a rag from beneath the counter and started wiping off the pass-through where the waitresses came for drinks. "He comes here all the time for dinner and tends to stick around to talk to me. I think he hates being home, if I'm being honest. He kept the house in the divorce. They have a five-year-old little girl. Sam just told me she's at his mom's tonight for a sleepover."

Noah glanced to the man at the end of the bar. He had no idea what the circumstances were surrounding the divorce, but Noah knew the heartache of losing your wife, the empty feeling you couldn't fill. But he had no idea what hell existed when you lost your wife but still saw her frequently.

Noah finished his meal as Gray went about filling drink orders and randomly talking to Sam. This town was proving to be more and more interesting. No doubt Gray had seen it all.

As Noah threw a tip on the bar, he called to Gray, "Stay out of trouble."

"What trouble?" Gray asked with a side grin.

Noah headed out the door and figured he'd make his way back to Lucy's, grab some cookies and Emma, then go on home to ice his jaw. In some ridiculously warped way, he almost felt like that was some male bonding experience between Gray and himself. It had been a long time since he'd been blindsided by a blow like that. But if that kept Gray from punching someone else and risking the reputation of his business, then Noah would sacrifice his face.

Noah hoped Gray got his head on straight where Kate was concerned, though. Noah didn't intend on lending the other side of his jaw next time.

Chapter Nine

Lucy was putting the cookies in a tin for Emma to take home when the back door opened. She smiled that he was so comfortable to walk in without knocking.

"Just in t—"

Anything she was about to say vanished the second she saw Noah's face. Cookies forgotten, she stepped forward. She reached out to touch his jaw, but realized he must be hurting. Her hand landed on his shoulder instead.

"What happened?"

Noah smiled. Actually smiled as he shook his head. "It's nothing. My face got in the way."

"Daddy, are you okay?"

Emma scrambled off the bar stool and came over to stand between Lucy and Noah.

"I'm fine, sweetheart," he assured her. "It smells amazing in here. I hope you made something we can take home."

Emma nodded, but Lucy couldn't take her eyes off the blue-and-purple swollen jaw. Noah threw her a glance that silently told her he'd talk about it later.

Pulling in a breath, Lucy nodded and went to finish putting bread and cookies in containers for them to take home. Her kitchen was an absolute disaster, but she didn't care.

Tara and Kate were likely at Gallagher's dancing but Lucy knew she couldn't have had more fun if she'd gone with them. It wasn't like she had ever spent the evening with a toddler, but she'd quickly found that she was having a blast staying in for a change and being silly, tossing flour at each other, cracking eggs, and having shells fall into the cookie batter. Each mishap caused Emma to laugh even louder so Lucy found herself purposely doing things wrong.

Emma spoke of her mother, she spoke of the ranch in Texas, and how she and her daddy always worked together in the evenings when he came home from the police station. She said he'd helped keep bad people off the streets in Texas and he was going to do the same here. She wished he didn't work at night, but Lucy had explained that because he was new, that was the only shift available.

It must be difficult being a single father and at the mercy of your employment, but Noah hadn't complained to her or anyone else that she'd noticed. He did his job, cared for his daughter...and managed to melt Lucy's heart in the process.

Fantastic. Now she was falling for a guy that she couldn't even bring herself to be intimate with. It had been two years since Evan passed. He would've wanted her to move on, and she truly thought she was ready. At least her body had been more than ready, but her mind and heart started battling and she'd shut down.

Lucy set the tins on the island. "Emma, would you like to go in and finish watching that movie I put on earlier?"

Emma looked to her dad. "Is it okay?"

He nodded. "You can go."

As Emma raced into the living room, Lucy explained, "I hope it was okay I started a movie while everything was baking. She said you watch it at home, so I figured it was safe."

Noah nodded. "I trust your judgment."

Lucy eyed his face, hating he'd been hurt. "Ready to tell me what happened to you?"

"I met Gray Gallagher."

Stunned, Lucy gasped. "Gray hit you? Why?"

"Your friend Kate frustrates him and she likes to push his buttons."

A sliver of jealousy speared her. Lucy knew how

Kate acted around attractive men. She was like a magnet and they seemed to gravitate toward her. No doubt Noah was just like all the other guys who found Kate irresistible.

"You were flirting with Kate?"

"What? No," he said. "She was dancing with some guy. Apparently Gray saw the guy get a little too handsy and charged after him. I tried to stop it. Well, I did stop it."

Lucy tipped her head as she reached out, barely brushing her fingertip over the bruise. "I'm sorry you got hurt. Want some ice or pain reliever?"

The muscle beneath her finger clenched and she glanced up to his eyes. His lids were lowered, but the dark eyes staring back at her held nothing but desire, want. Her heart picked up and the knots in her stomach clenched. No matter how many times she told herself to take this slow with him, some things were simply out of her control.

"It's suddenly feeling better," he rasped.

Lucy flattened her palm against his cheek, still careful not to put too much pressure on the swollen area. "Gray really is a nice guy. He and Kate… they're complicated."

"More complicated than us?"

Us. Well, he'd thrown that gauntlet down and the word solidified something…didn't it?

Kate and Gray were meant for each other, though Kate was frustrating and Gray was stubborn. The two never could see eye to eye on anything other than the fact that they both irritated each other. But anyone could see how the sparks would fly whenever they were in close proximity.

When Lucy was around Noah, they didn't so much irritate each other as confuse each other. The need, the guilt, the fear of moving forward all combined to make their situation so complex.

"Not the same," she corrected. "But just as confusing."

He nodded, then looked at her, his expression serious. "I'm sorry I let things get out of hand this morning."

Was that just this morning? The day seemed so long. So much had happened since the encounter in her bedroom.

"We're both to blame for that," she told him as she dropped her hand. "But I should apologize for freaking out. I just... I never thought that would be an issue."

"I never thought I'd want another woman," he countered. "I *can't* want another woman. It's too soon."

He seemed to be telling himself rather than her.

Lucy couldn't stop looking at those mesmerizing eyes and how they seemed to see right into her soul. How could a man be this expressive with his emotions and not be ready?

Granted she thought she could move on, but fear had her rethinking that theory.

They were at different points in their grieving and Lucy didn't want to get hurt again—and she certainly didn't want to hurt him, either.

Lucy crossed her arms over her chest so she didn't reach back out to him. "Neither of us can afford more heartache."

Noah nodded in agreement. "I have a daughter to protect."

There went more of that melting heart. "What about your needs, Noah?"

"She's my world," he said with a shrug. "There's nothing I wouldn't do for her and that includes putting all of my needs last."

Her eyes drifted to his jaw once again and she couldn't help but wonder about the details of the evening. What happened when he'd first gone into Gallagher's, how he and Gray had ended up striking up a conversation, and how Noah's face had ultimately landed between Gray's fist and some guy.

"You didn't tell anyone that we were…"

How did she ask properly without sounding like she was embarrassed?

"I mean, if my friends thought I was here with Emma, they'd think more…"

"I get it." Noah ran a hand over the uninjured side of his face, the stubble along his jawline bristling beneath his palm. "Nobody needs to know how good of friends we are. They'll only read more into it."

Good friends? Considering he'd seen her completely naked and he'd kissed her enough to spawn fantasies for days, she'd say they were extremely good friends.

"Well, Kate and Tara know a little."

Noah's mouth kicked up in a side grin. "I figured, but I just need to keep Emma protected, and for the sake of my job, I don't want any rumors circulating at work."

"You're getting nothing but praise at work lately, especially after saving that little boy."

Noah shook his head and dropped his arms. "I just happened to be the one to see him, that's all."

"You split up a would-be fight at Gallagher's and you're sporting a wound to prove it, so you may get more praise."

Noah laughed. "I think as angry and jealous as Gray was, he would've kicked that guy's ass as he shoved him out the door. It wouldn't have been much of a fight."

The television from the living room seemed to get even louder just before Emma let out a string of chuckles.

"That's her favorite part," Noah said with a laugh. "We watch that movie over and over."

"As soon as the cookies went in the oven she asked if I'd ever seen it."

Noah smiled, showcasing that dimple that drove her mad. "I think even more so now that we moved, she wants that connection. The horses in the film remind her of Daisy."

Lucy's heart ached for the precious child who had lost her mother and her beloved horse.

"In case nobody has told you, you're doing a phenomenal job."

Noah's brows drew in. "At what?"

With a shrug, Lucy replied, "Life. My husband passed away, too. I know the pain, the emptiness. I get that you don't know which way to turn for happiness or if it even exists anymore."

She didn't want to get too far into that part of her life, but she wanted him to know how much she understood, how she could offer support.

"I know after Evan passed, I went into this depression. I had survivor's guilt even though I wasn't there when he died. I was questioning why I had the opportunity to move on and be happy when he didn't. If it weren't for my friends, I'm not sure where I'd be. If you want to talk…"

He scratched the side of his jaw. "It's the hardest thing I've ever dealt with in my life," he admitted. "There are days I don't want to get out of bed. There are times, more often than not, that the survivor's guilt threatens to take over. But Emma needs her father at one hundred percent because right now, I'm mom and dad to her."

The lump in Lucy's throat seemed to grow with each raw word of honesty. "I'm here if you need a sounding board," she said. "As a friend, I know. But it's important to get that adult time and communication during your grieving process."

"I'm pretty sure my shrink in Texas gave me all the adult time I could need for the rest of my life." Noah reached over and slid the tins toward the edge of the counter. "I better get going. Thanks for having Emma over to see the horses and to bake."

"You guys are welcome here anytime." Lucy knew the night had to come to an end, but she hated for him to go. "I liked having her around. And you."

"Glad to hear it."

She opted to push a little more, testing both their comfort zones. "When we're off again, maybe you two can come back for horse riding and a picnic."

Noah eased back, his eyes holding hers. "Count on it."

"Are you sure you don't want ice for your jaw?" Lucy hated the thought of her friend losing his cool and hitting Noah.

"Nah. I've had worse," he told her. "I'll put something on it when I get home. How's the hip?"

"I've had so much fun this evening, I've forgotten about it," she admitted. "It hurts more when I walk on it, but I think that's also going to help work out the soreness."

Noah stared at her another minute and Lucy had no idea what was running through his mind. He kept his eyes on her, but said nothing. The silence stretched between them with only the faint sound of the television in the background.

"Thank you," he finally said, his voice full of emotion. "There's not much lately that really penetrates the hurt, but you have. You've not only been great for me, but to spend this time with Emma... I can't thank you enough. I know she misses having a female in her life. Her sitter is great, but someone younger and fun is what she needed for a night."

Lucy placed her hand on his. "She's precious. I can be a friend to you both."

"All while juggling work, your community service and your schoolwork?" Noah reached up with his free hand and smoothed the stray strands off her forehead. "Who takes care of you?"

"I don't need anyone to take care of me."

Though having him touch her was something she wasn't about to turn down. At least, touching when it was innocent and simple. Anything else, well, she'd have to work up to that. But Noah was the first man in so long she even wanted to explore that notion with, so she'd keep moving along and hoping something blossomed from this, because Noah Spencer was one special guy. And his daughter had captured Lucy's heart, as well.

Now she had to figure out where to put all these feelings and how to sort them.

"Maybe you could come to the next meeting?" Lucy suggested.

Noah shook his head. "I don't need meetings. I'm getting along without them."

She wished he'd just come to one, to see that it wasn't all doom and gloom. People needed a support team, and while Noah had Emma, how could the man actually grieve when he had to be so strong for a child?

"Maybe you'll reconsider," she added.

Noah's dark eyes held hers. "Don't try to get into my head, Lucy. I'm going at my own pace and it's nobody's business but mine."

He headed into the living room, clearly done with the topic. How could they move forward if he wasn't prepared to face his pain?

Lucy sank to a kitchen bar stool as her own hurt spiraled through her. Perhaps he didn't want to move forward. He'd apologized for the kiss; he'd made it clear they could be friends. He'd summed up everything neat and tidy. But Lucy didn't feel the discussion of their situation was closed. Not by a long shot.

Chapter Ten

"Why don't you put the tray of cookies over on that table against the wall?" Lucy suggested.

Tara rolled her eyes and Kate snorted. They'd both just come in the back door and Lucy was already in a panic because the community center wasn't nearly ready for the Helping Hands open house. Why were they just standing there?

"What?" Lucy asked.

"You think we can just come in here and set up for the open house and we're not going to address the fact that Noah was in Gallagher's and did some male bonding with Gray?"

"By bonding, do you mean fighting?" Lucy countered. "Because I saw his face afterward."

Kate's eyes widened. "He came to your house after? Did you make him forget all about his troubles?"

Lucy picked up the tray and crossed the room. "I'm not discussing this with you two."

"Why not?" Tara asked. "I'm sure you heard all about Gray losing his cool over Kate, and Sam nursing a beer all night."

Lucy set the tray down and turned to face her friends. "Actually, I hadn't heard about Sam at all. And I only got the abridged version of Gray."

The fact Sam was nursing a beer at Gray's bar wasn't exactly news. For the past year he'd been somewhat depressed and Gray always had his back. Lucy wished Sam and Tara would make up, for the sake of their daughter for one reason. But she knew that not every marriage was meant to be.

"Why do you two keep going there?" Lucy insisted, more than happy to turn the topic to her friends. "Why taunt those men?"

"Sam isn't always there," Tara defended. "And when he is, he hugs the same bottle all night, so I know he's not drunk. He doesn't even look my way."

But Sam knew full well his ex-wife was there dancing and having a good time. And Sam didn't look her way because it hurt to see her. Anybody could understand his logic. It wasn't just death that caused people to grieve.

"What's your excuse?" Lucy asked Kate. "You know Gray has been half in love with you for years."

Kate shrugged and smoothed her hands down her simple tunic. "He's not in love with me or halfway there. He just sees me as a challenge." She shrugged. "It's not worth damaging our friendship to let him have his thrills."

Lucy understood that logic, but at the same time, she truly believed Gray loved Kate. Maybe one of these days Kate would realize it, too.

"Let's get back to you," Tara suggested. "Noah is one hot guy. I hadn't gotten a good look at him until he came over to our table last night."

Lucy rolled her eyes. "We don't have time for adolescent girl talk. We have people coming in thirty minutes and nothing is set up the way it should be."

Kate, sarcastic as ever, pointed to the tray. "You just put those cookies in place."

Pulling in a deep breath and attempting some sort of control, Lucy addressed her friends. "Let me make this brief. Noah and I are friends. He's new on the force and is still making an impression. He has a child to look out for who just lost her mother six months ago. Rumors aren't something he can afford right now. So let's get the chairs moved out of the way so people can mingle, and get the new pamphlets on all of the tables so people don't have to hunt for them. We also need to get the music going so it's not so quiet and awkward when the first guests arrive."

Kate and Tara exchanged a look, but Lucy was done with the grilling of her social life. How could she explain it when she truly had no idea herself what was going on with Noah Spencer? And, as much as she loved her friends, she also wanted to keep Noah to herself.

Lucy ignored Tara and Kate's quizzical stares and circled around them to start setting up. They were expecting quite the crowd this evening. Their flyers had been up all over Stonerock for the past month. Their regular attendees had invited friends and family. They were hoping to spread the word that everyone could benefit from Helping Hands. If someone wasn't going through a rough patch now, it might only be a matter of time. As depressing as that sounded, it was the reality. Everyone would experience loss at least once in their lives.

The main point of tonight was to see if there was a greater need. The loss of a family member or friend wasn't the only thing that people grieved over. Sometimes it was the breakup of a marriage, the loss of a job, depression, anxiety. There was a host of problems people dealt with on a day-to-day basis, and Lucy didn't want people to feel alone in their struggles.

She'd invited Noah, but he hadn't acted like he'd make it. As much as he flirted and pretended to be fine, Lucy knew there was hurt just beneath the surface. He didn't talk about his wife's death at all, which only proved that speaking about it was too rough. And all of that was understandable because

everyone moved at the pace that was comfortable for
them. But at the same time, she truly wished he'd
quit being so strong for everyone around him. They
were friends—a little more than friends, if she were
being totally honest—and she wanted him to trust
her with his feelings.

As the first guests started to arrive, Kate, Tara,
and Lucy greeted them. With a town as small as
Stonerock, pretty much everybody knew everybody.
Still, there may be some who brought friends from
neighboring towns and Lucy wanted to make sure
nobody felt left out. Wasn't that the whole point of
this group?

With the holidays only a few months away, it was
important now more than ever to have support.

The St. John brothers came through with their
wives and children. The dynamic family was a pow-
erhouse in this town. Cameron was her boss, so she
knew him well. His brothers were known because of
their wild sides as teens and now for their involve-
ment with the town.

Eli St. John was the town doctor, having taken
over after his father retired. Their brother Drake was
the chief for Stonerock's fire department. They were
one dynamic family in the small community.

Kate and Tara greeted the crew as Lucy refilled
the coffee carafe. Lucy hoped this was a success in
bringing hope to those who were struggling with
loss, no matter how minor.

"This is wonderful."

Lucy turned to see Tammy standing there with a wide smile on her face. "Thank you. I think it's a great turnout."

"I wanted to introduce you to my nephew, Todd. He lost his fiancée a year ago."

The thirty-something man stepped closer to his aunt. "Pleasure to meet you."

"I'm glad you could come out," Lucy stated as she shook his hand. "You're not from Stonerock?"

"I'm actually moving here soon. I'm from Nashville."

Tammy patted Lucy on the arm. "I told Todd all about how you started this group and what a wonderful woman you are. I thought with him moving here soon, he may need a friend."

Lucy saw exactly where this was going. This wasn't the first time some well-meaning soul had tried to hook Lucy up with a family member.

"I'm sure you'll fit right in here," Lucy told him, dodging the obvious setup. "If you'll excuse me, I see some other guests I need to talk to."

"Maybe we can talk later," Todd added before she could escape.

Lucy merely smiled. "Thank you both for coming. Tara, Kate, and I are here if you need anything."

Okay, that kept things focused on the group. Lucy had never gone for being set up on a date. She'd been too busy with her job, her schooling and making sure

Helping Hands served its purpose. She hadn't even had the desire to date or even flirt with another man.

And then Noah Spencer had stepped into the back of the meeting with that black cowboy hat tipped low. A man with that type of presence, all menacing and mysterious, begged for attention. Her stomach knotted in a ball at the mere thought of him. That giddiness seemed to grow the more she was with him and the closer they became.

Lucy attempted to push aside her thoughts of Noah, though he always hovered near the forefront of her mind. She spoke with many people she recognized and met some new folks who were thinking of joining the group.

As the evening wore on, she couldn't help but glance around to see if Noah decided to make an appearance. He never did. She'd be lying if she didn't admit disappointment. Not that she thought he'd come for himself, but she'd hoped he'd come for her.

After all, they were friends, right?

Perhaps she was asking too much. They weren't actually a couple or anything, so there were no expectations...only hope.

After everyone had gone and Tara, Kate and Lucy had cleaned up, Lucy headed out the back door to her car. Darkness had set in, but the community center parking lot was well lit with halogen street lamps.

Movement to her right had her jumping, until she saw that it was Todd, the man she'd met earlier. He'd been sitting on the bench between the community center and the entrance to the park.

"I didn't mean to startle you," he stated.

He kept his distance, which helped because it was a little odd that he was out here waiting on her.

"It's fine." But still creepy, she silently admitted.

"My aunt obviously tried to play matchmaker and I wanted to apologize if you were uncomfortable."

Lucy relaxed a little more. "Oh, it's fine. I've been the target for many matchmakers."

"She means well," he added, shoving his hands into his pockets. "That being said, I wouldn't mind taking you out when I get into town. If you're free, that is."

Todd was a handsome man, he seemed to be polite and Lucy adored his aunt. But—there was of course a but—she just wasn't feeling anything toward him. Nothing at all in comparison to what she felt when Noah was near.

"Don't answer now," he went on when the silence stretched between them. "I'll look you up when I get into town permanently."

Lucy simply nodded and smiled as she headed on to her car. Todd turned toward the truck parked in the distance and pulled out of the lot. Even if Lucy were interested in Todd, she didn't feel right about going out with him, not with the way Noah occupied her mind so much lately.

As Lucy pulled in her driveway minutes later, her text alerts went off from Tara.

Turning down a date with another potential new guy? Sounds like Noah is more serious than you let on.

So what? Lucy wasn't even going to reply. No need to add fuel to the fire of her friend's comments. They may be true, but Lucy didn't have to acknowledge them.

Grabbing her purse and cell, she headed inside. She was due at work in a while and she wanted to go in and just relax until she had to leave again. She wasn't positive, but she thought Noah was off tonight. Sometimes those nights dragged because she'd gotten used to hearing his voice over the radio. But when he wasn't there, she could think. She could try to figure out just what she wanted and where she thought this relationship would go.

Because there was only so long she would want to stay in the friend category. And when she was ready to move forward, she hoped like hell he would be, too.

Chapter Eleven

"I'm five blocks away," Noah reported into the radio.

"I'm pulling in now," another officer responded.

Silence settled over the radio for a brief moment before Lucy's sweet voice came back. "I've informed the caller you're on the scene, McCoy."

Officer McCoy could handle it. They didn't need two officers on the scene of a woman who'd locked herself out of the house. Apparently she'd gone out for drinks with friends and forgotten to take her keys. At least she was responsible enough not to drink and drive, so that was something.

Noah turned down Pine Street and tried his best not to let his mind wander, but he failed miserably.

He'd heard about Lucy getting hit on, about some new guy asking her out after the open house. Word traveled fast in this town, especially considering Lucy's open house was only hours ago.

Maybe that's what he got for not attending, but he truly didn't think that atmosphere was for him. He was getting along just fine. The hurt was something he'd live with for the rest of his life. He just figured he'd get used to that void.

Lucy's voice came over the radio once again, this time calling him to a fender bender in the middle of the park. Chances were good that whatever he was about to encounter was more than just a fender bender. Who would be in the park at one o'clock on a Tuesday morning?

Noah soon found out there were two ladies arguing over a guy and one had ended up blocking the other car against a tree. Breaking up a catfight could be more dangerous than men throwing punches, in his opinion.

Thirty minutes later when he'd cleared the scene without incident, Noah climbed back into his patrol car and radioed the status.

"Everything all right?"

"Fine," he replied to Lucy's question.

"You didn't check in for a while," she replied.

Noah gritted his teeth. "All clear now," he told her. "Over and out."

End of conversation because he didn't want to

hear her voice right now. He didn't want to think of how that nugget of jealousy over the other guy had turned into a ball of fury that had settled low in his gut.

Honestly, Noah didn't know what had been said between Lucy and the man. And why wouldn't someone ask her out? Lucy was stunning, she was independent, she had a great career ahead of her helping so many people. She was giving, loyal and sexy as hell.

He raked a hand down his face, smarting when his palm hit his bruised jaw. What was he thinking? He needed more sleep. Maybe then he'd be thinking clearly. Because right now all he could see was Lucy with another man and he absolutely hated the image that flooded his mind.

That's precisely how he knew he was ready to try moving on. He wanted Lucy.

Did he want something more than a physical relationship and a friendship? Hell, he had no idea. All he knew was that he had an ache for her that was impossible to ignore and a jealousy that was overriding all common sense right now.

The rest of his shift went by without any excitement, which was a good thing, but the quiet made for a long night. He was slowly adjusting to working nights, though he would jump at the chance to get back on days so he could have a better schedule with Emma.

The sun beamed directly onto the blacktop as he

pulled into the station lot. He was more than ready to get home and have the next two days off. After he rested, he planned on spending some quality time with Emma, maybe have a picnic in the park or see a movie and have lunch at their favorite little diner.

When he stepped out of his patrol car, he realized he was either getting used to the weather or it was getting warmer…and considering it was inching closer to the end of fall, he knew it couldn't be the latter.

Noah passed the dispatch area and didn't see Lucy at the desk. The part-time guy who filled in as needed sat there taking a call.

He did find Lucy in the break room putting on her jacket and gathering her things. She turned to flash that megawatt smile and he wondered if that's how she'd smiled for the newcomer to her meeting.

Get over it, Noah. She's a beautiful woman and she's not going to be single forever because you can't get your head on straight.

"Everything okay?" she asked, the same way she'd asked over the radio hours ago.

Noah nodded, not trusting himself to say much else. He was too angry with himself for the jumbled-up emotions battling for prominence inside him.

Her brows drew in as she adjusted her scarf. "You've been quiet all night. What's up?"

"Nothing," he mumbled as he poured a cup of coffee to take on the road. "Just ready to head home."

He turned to get out of the tiny room.

"Did I do something to make you mad?" she asked.

Noah glanced over his shoulder and cursed beneath his breath. Damn it, he didn't want her to think she did anything wrong. Everything that he had issues with was solely on him.

"Just need to get home," he replied.

He tried to get out the back door, and succeeded, but she was right on his heels. As he reached his truck, Lucy's delicate hand settled on his arm.

"If I did something, I deserve to know," she insisted. "Look at me."

Noah spun around. "You didn't do anything, all right? I'm pissed at myself for letting the rumor mill rule my life."

"What?"

"The guy who asked you out…" Noah cursed himself once again. "Forget it. It's none of my concern if you want to go out with someone. I have no claims and I have no right to ask you not to."

Lucy stood there, her golden hair dancing around her shoulders in the wind. It almost hurt him to look at her. There was such innocence about her, but he knew she'd seen so much heartache. And he wasn't helping either of their situations.

"Forget it," he muttered. "Forget I said anything. Head on home, Lucy."

Her hold on his arm tightened. "I said no."

Noah closed his eyes and couldn't suppress the relief that swept through him. "It's not my business."

"You sure about that?" she countered, releasing him. "Because you're acting a little territorial when we haven't agreed to anything. You can't even admit you have feelings for me."

Another officer pulled into the lot just as Noah was about to grab her and show her just how much he was feeling right now.

"You don't know what you're saying," he gritted through his teeth.

"So you wouldn't care if I went out on a date with another guy?" she threw back. When he remained silent, she shook her head. "Guess not. I thought this attraction went both ways and you might actually give up the friend notion and see where we could go."

She got in her car and started the engine, not once looking his way as she pulled from the lot.

Fury bubbled within him at the way he'd handled things, not just this morning, but from the moment they'd met. It was a push-pull relationship and he was a jerk.

Damn it, he wanted her. So why was he torturing them both? The stakes weren't the same as before he was married. Now he knew full well going in exactly what to expect. They were adults who couldn't keep going on like this.

Noah turned onto Lucy's road and pulled into her driveway right behind her. As soon as she stepped from the car, she turned to face him. Her eyes were wide with surprise, but a second later, she started heading toward her back door, still ignoring him.

He hopped from his truck and mounted her steps. He managed to reach the door just before she closed it in his face.

"Will you stop for one second?" he demanded, following her inside.

"I think we've said enough." She jerked the scarf off and laid it on the kitchen island along with her purse before she turned to face him. "Unless you had something else to discuss, the topic of us is closed."

Oh, that's what she thought? Like hell. He crossed the narrow space between them and gripped her shoulders. Her body arched against his as a gasp escaped her.

"Consider the topic back open," he growled as he crushed his lips to hers.

Lucy stilled and he worried he'd pushed too far, but then her fingers threaded through his hair as she opened for him. He wrapped his arms around her waist and lifted her as he headed toward her bedroom.

"Tell me to stop if you don't want me to take you to bed," he muttered against her lips. "But I need you, Lucy. I can't keep going on like this."

Her eyes met his as she licked her lips. The subtle nod she gave was all the green light he needed.

"I want you," she murmured.

He backed her down the hall, but she put a hand on his chest as she stared up into his eyes. "Not my room."

When he wasn't in such a hurry later he'd realize just how fragile she was. The image of that picture on her nightstand mocked him, but Noah was here for physical reasons only. Nothing more would come from this because once they were out of each other's systems, they could move on.

Noah threaded his hands through her hair and backed her against the wall just outside the spare bedroom. When his mouth captured hers once again, she opened for him, arching her body and sighing into him.

Lucy's arms banded around his waist as she lined up her hips with his. Noah hadn't felt a need like this in so long, he wasn't sure how long he could hold on to his control here.

As if her thread snapped as well, Lucy reached for the front of his shirt and started frantically working his buttons loose. Pulling back from her lips, Noah pushed her hands aside and finished taking his shirt off. As soon as the uniform was on the floor, he toed off his shoes, unfastened his gun belt, and gently laid it on the floor.

Lucy immediately went for the button on his pants.

"You're wearing too many clothes," he told her, his entire body heating from anticipation.

Lucy's wide eyes met his as she bit on her lower lip. She didn't make a move to take off anything.

"Having doubts?" he asked, smoothing her hair away from her face.

She shook her head. "Just nervous."

"That makes two of us."

Noah gripped the hem of her long-sleeved tee and pulled it slowly up her body, keeping his eyes locked on hers for any sign that he needed to stop. As much as he wanted her, he wasn't about to make her more uncomfortable.

Lucy held her arms up and Noah pulled the shirt up the rest of the way. As he flung it to the side, she slipped out of her shoes and pulled her pants down, kicking them out of the way.

Standing in only her pale pink bra and panties, she set his heart beating even faster.

"You're so damn sexy."

Lucy's flash of a smile had relief spiraling through him. He picked her up and her legs wrapped around his waist as he carried her into the spare bedroom. The early-morning light cast a glow through the slit in the curtains. The beacon of sun projected directly onto the bed where he laid her and followed her down.

"I have no protection with me," he murmured against her lips. "I wasn't expecting this."

Lucy reached up, framing her face with her hands. "I'm clean and I'm on birth control. But it's your call."

"I'm clean, too." He'd had an in-depth physical before coming to SPD.

Lucy's hands slid over his shoulders and over his back. Her delicate touch spawned an even deeper desire inside him. Noah took seconds to remove the rest of his clothes and her bra and panties. When he settled back between her legs, he braced his hands on either side of her head as he stared down into her eyes. Eyes that held so much desire, so much trust.

Keeping his gaze on hers, he joined their bodies. That instant connection had him glancing away. He couldn't look into her eyes as he made love to her, couldn't allow himself to connect emotionally with her. The physical was all he could afford right now.

Lucy locked her ankles behind his back and arched against him. He risked a look back her way and noted her eyes were closed, which meant she was either in the moment or she didn't want to look too closely at him, either.

Noah pushed all speculation aside and ran his hands over the dip in her waist and up over the swell of her breasts. The slight groan that escaped her had him pumping his hips faster. Lucy gripped his biceps as she matched his pace. She felt too damn good and he didn't want this moment to end. He wanted to continue getting lost in her and never return to reality where the hurt lived.

Lucy's body tightened all around him as her short nails bit into his arms. He watched as her mouth opened wide, her eyes squeezed shut, and she twisted her head to the side as pleasure overcame her. Noah wasn't too far behind, but he didn't want to miss a second of her pleasure. He continued to watch her as his own body tightened. Only when she relaxed beneath him did he let himself go. Lucy's fingertips trailed over his chest, down over his abdomen, and back up. The pleasure he took from her overcame him and once his body came down, Noah eased to the side and gathered her into his arms.

He lay there, not quite ready for words, not ready to ruin the moment. He needed a minute to figure out what the hell had just happened, because instead of getting out of his system, Lucy Brooks had somehow wedged herself deeper into his life.

Now what was he supposed to do?

Chapter Twelve

Lucy rolled over, draping her arm across a bare, male chest. She smiled as she snuggled in closer and—

Wait. A male chest?

Her eyes flew open and everything came flooding back to her. She and Noah had… Yeah. Twice. Her body still tingled and she was sore in places she'd forgotten existed.

The bright sunshine in the room flooded through the curtains. She was used to her bedroom with the blackout curtains. She was also used to sleeping alone.

Lucy eased away from Noah and waited for the regret to settle in. There was no regret over what they'd done, but there was certainly a thin layer of guilt.

That was to be expected, right? She'd studied grief for so long, had lived with it even longer, so she knew every emotion was normal, because everyone's journey was different.

Swinging her legs over the side of the bed, Lucy tried to figure out what she'd say to him when he woke. How did they move forward? Because even before she was ever married, sex wasn't something she took lightly. She needed to have a deeper connection to someone before she went to bed with him. At this point, Lucy wasn't sure how to act with Noah. They were coworkers; they had agreed to be friends.

"I assume you're analyzing everything and trying to figure out what's next."

At the sound of his voice Lucy glanced back over her shoulder. Noah lay on his back, his hands beneath his head as he stared up at the ceiling.

"Aren't you?" she asked.

His eyes darted her way. "No. We had sex."

"Twice."

"And now we're going to be friends and go back to work."

His matter-of-fact tone sounded so cold. Why did he have to be so standoffish? That was not the man who'd touched her so lovingly hours ago.

Suddenly feeling too exposed, Lucy jerked the comforter off the bed and wrapped it around herself before she came to her feet and turned to face him. The sheet lay across his waist, exposing his chiseled abs and chest. There was nothing about Noah that didn't attract her...until now with this attitude.

"I think you need to go."

Noah sat up and raked his hands through his hair. "Don't try to get into my head, Lucy. We went into this knowing exactly what was going to happen."

True, but that didn't mean she could control how she felt.

Lucy wrapped the bulky blanket tighter around her and refused to allow that burn in her throat to turn to tears.

"I need to get in the shower," she told him. "You can lock the door behind you."

Lucy turned toward her bathroom, her heart in her throat. She just wanted to get in there before she burst into tears.

"Give me time, Lucy."

Noah's voice, full of agony, stopped her in the doorway. She gripped the frame with one hand while clutching the comforter between her breasts with the other.

"I wasn't expecting this," he went on. "Wasn't expecting you. I'm not ready."

Her heart clenched at the tortured tone of his voice. "I wasn't ready, either," she admitted. "But here we are."

Lucy shifted just enough to meet his gaze across the room. The hurt in his eyes seemed to match her own.

"You came to me," she reminded him. "You followed me home, all because you didn't like the idea of me with someone else. That should tell you that you're more ready than you thought."

Noah remained silent, his lips thinned.

"I didn't ask for you to come to my bed," she went on. "I only wanted to see where this attraction led."

"I didn't plan on being here," he told her. "I admit I was jealous. So jealous that I had to face the fact that I wanted you."

Pain squeezed her chest like a vise. "And now? You've had me. Do you feel like you've claimed me or conquered the fear you had?"

Noah jumped off the bed, crossed the room just as naked as you please, and gripped her shoulders. She twisted to try to get out of his hold, but he forced her to face him.

"I didn't claim you," he demanded. "Why do you think I left that meeting the first night I was there?"

Lucy quit struggling. "Because you didn't want to face your grief."

"That's only part of the reason," he declared, his eyes darting to her lips. "I had an instant attraction to you and it scared the hell out of me. I had to get out. Then you followed me."

He gripped her tighter as he pulled her flush with his body. "Damn it, Lucy. I'm not sorry one bit that we slept together. I just wish like hell I knew how to treat you right now."

She wanted to be angry with him for being so cold

to her, but she recognized his earlier words and actions as a defense mechanism. She could hardly blame him. They were both new to intimacy after such a tragic loss and he was standing here baring his soul to her.

"Being honest is a good start," she told him, reaching up to cup his cheek. "You don't have to pretend with me. If you need space, take it, but don't push me away and lie to me."

Noah closed his eyes and leaned his forehead against hers. "I want to leave so I can think about all of this and how fast we're moving."

"But?"

He nipped at her lips. "But I want to stay and touch you. I want to back you into that bathroom and take a shower with you."

Lucy's entire body tingled because she knew exactly what he could do to pleasure her. She opened the comforter and dropped it to a puddle at her feet.

"Follow me."

It was some warped reward system, Lucy thought. She'd completed her online final for this semester's psych class and she was so happy that it was behind her, she was actually looking forward to doing her laundry.

Granted she'd needed to do housework yesterday, but after Noah had left she'd pretty much sat in her favorite chair in the living room and stared out the window. She'd volleyed between daydreaming and analyzing. There'd been so much to take in, way too many emotional hills to climb, and she was in no better mental shape today than she was yesterday.

After scrubbing her en suite and putting her clean laundry away, Lucy still had pent-up energy she had no clue what to do with. Maybe she needed to go for a ride. She hadn't taken the time to ride for too long.

Lucy eyed her cell sitting on the end table by the love seat. Should she call Noah and invite him and Emma? Part of her wanted to reach out. The other part wanted to wait to hear from him.

What was the protocol here? She didn't want to play games, but she didn't want to push. He'd said he needed time. Honestly, so did she. But she also didn't want their relationship to lose momentum. She wanted to keep building on what they had between them because it felt so good.

She'd sworn she'd never get involved with a man who risked his life for his job ever again. And then along had come Officer Spencer. Noah was the first man to entice her in years, and ignoring such a strong ache was absolutely impossible. All she could do at this point was enjoy the ride because Noah was part of her now, no matter the red flags waving around inside her mind.

Lucy grabbed her cell and shot off a text. She kept it simple and to the point. If he answered, fine. If he didn't, that would be fine, too. As much as she wanted to see him, she also had a life to focus on. Her semester was over and she only had one more to go before she had her master's degree in psychology. Lucy figured she'd better get a start on those résumés and get them sent to potential employers.

But part of her loved the SPD and hated leaving. They'd been her family when Evan had passed. Between them and Kate and Tara, Lucy knew just how valuable a support team was in trying times.

As she headed out the back door toward the barn, she wondered who Noah's support team was. He'd left everyone he'd known back in Texas, and as lovely as it was that he and Emma were so close, Lucy knew he needed more.

Lucy readied Gunner and headed out into the field. She just wanted to ride toward the mountainside and admire the vibrant colors of fall. Autumn had always been her favorite time of year, and Stonerock, with its beautiful landscapes, showcased the season like a star. Evan had always said the same and he'd traveled all over the world. To them, Stonerock had always seemed so welcoming and relaxing.

Rocking against the saddle and the gentle trot of her horse, Lucy tipped her head back and breathed in the fresh scent of the crisp air. This perfect fall day wouldn't last. Winter would be here soon and snow would blanket the fields and mountains behind her house.

The afternoon transitioned into evening as she

tended to both horses in the barn. She brushed them, sang to them—off-key, but they didn't complain—and felt more relaxed than she had in months. Actually, she was calmer than she'd been since Evan's death.

As she shut off the barn lights and headed back toward the house, the sound of a shutting car door caught her attention. Her heart kicked up in anticipation of seeing Noah.

Instead, Tara rounded the corner of the house, holding hands with her daughter, and a sliver of disappointment coursed through Lucy. She loved seeing her friends, but all afternoon she'd been waiting on Noah to bring Emma for a riding session. Maybe he wasn't comfortable with having Emma around so much. That was understandable, but still… Lucy wanted to see him.

As Tara got closer, Lucy noticed her friend's eyes were red rimmed. Instinct had her crossing the stone path a little quicker.

"I hope you don't mind we just stopped by," Tara stated as she held on to her daughter's hand. "Marley and I were hoping we could hang here for a bit."

"Of course." Lucy bent down to Marley, who clutched her stuffed elephant. "Do you want to see the horses or go in and watch a movie?"

"A movie." Marley smiled. "Do you have ice cream?"

"You know I always have cookie dough ice cream.

Why don't you go get it from the freezer and I'll be right in to scoop it out."

Marley let go of her mother's hand and ran right up the porch steps. When the screen door slammed shut, Lucy focused back on Tara.

"What's going on?"

Tara shook her head. "I hate him. I absolutely hate Sam Bailey with everything I have in me."

Well, that didn't sound good. Lucy figured those tearstains were from rage as opposed to sadness... or an unhealthy mix of both.

"What did he do?"

Tara started pacing on the walk. She muttered under her breath, throwing her arms to the side before spinning back around. "That jackass sent me a card in the mail. A damn card with a little handwritten note like old people do."

Lucy bit the inside of her cheek to keep from smiling. Sam wanted his wife back. It was that simple. Tara kept fighting the fact, but Lucy hoped she'd realize what a great guy Sam was.

"What did he write?" Lucy asked.

Tara reached into her purse and jerked out the card that she'd shoved back into the torn envelope.

Lucy pulled the card out and opened it. The front of the card was a serene beach scene, but the inside was blank except for Sam's writing.

I still remember.

Lucy glanced back up to Tara. "This is what has you so upset?"

Tara's eyes widened. "Well, yeah. Before we were married we ran away to the beach for a weekend and didn't tell anyone what we were doing."

Lucy remembered that trip. Tara had been so in love and giddy.

"So why does this make you so mad?"

Tara ripped the card from Lucy's hand. "Because he's making things more difficult than they need to be. We're divorced now and things need to stay that way."

Lucy wished she knew what had truly broken them up. Tara had insisted that they'd married too quickly and for the wrong reasons, but Sam hadn't agreed. They'd argued, they'd said some hurtful things, and in the end they'd split up. They did manage to get along in front of Marley, so that was something.

"Maybe you need some ice cream, too." Lucy looped her arm through her friend's. "Come on in and let's see what junk food we can find."

"I'd rather have a drink at Gallagher's and dance," she muttered.

Lucy mounted the steps and held the door open for Tara. "Well, right now we're going to binge watch some kid shows and eat ice cream out of the carton."

While Tara and Marley were getting spoons and taking the ice cream to the living room, Lucy checked her phone, which had been charging in the kitchen.

She'd missed three texts from Noah, so apparently he wasn't ignoring her completely. Lucy opened the messages and was in the middle of reading them when she realized Tara was looking over her shoulder.

"So, getting closer with the new officer, are you?" Tara asked, raising her brows. "I'd much rather hear all about this development than discuss my messed-up life."

"Your life isn't messed up," Lucy stated as she clicked her phone off. "And Noah and I aren't developing."

Well, that was a blatant lie, but Lucy wasn't ready to share just how far she and Noah had gone. She wasn't ready to comprehend it all herself, let alone be analyzed by anyone else.

"From the looks of those messages I'd say you are," Tara retorted. "I saw something about his daughter. Are you sure you guys aren't getting all cozy together?"

One side of Lucy wanted to jump at this chance to potentially find happiness again. On the other hand, there was that fear and guilt that seemed to be more present now than it had been in months.

"He brought Emma out to see the horses the other day," Lucy admitted. "I simply asked if she'd like to come out and ride another time. I was heading out anyway, but apparently they were busy at a birthday party for one of her friends at the babysitters."

Tara's lips quirked as the television from the living room blared with some cartoon's explosion. "You know an awful lot about Noah and his life for someone who isn't getting closer."

The back screen door opened and slammed shut. "He's such a jerk," Kate declared as she walked into the kitchen and headed straight to the fridge.

Tara raised her brows at Lucy in an unspoken question, but Lucy shrugged.

"Problem?" Lucy asked Kate's back as her friend shifted through the shelves of food.

"Gray Gallagher can go to hell."

"Watch the language," Tara warned. "Marley is in the living room."

Kate threw a glance over her shoulder. "Sorry about that. He just pushes my buttons and infuriates me."

"We've already got the cookie dough ice cream out," Tara supplied. "We can grab an extra spoon."

Kate shut the refrigerator doors. "What are you upset about?" she asked Tara.

Tara shrugged. "A man. What else? But I was in the process of getting Lucy to spill her secrets about her and her officer when you barged in."

Kate's eyes widened as she took a seat on the stool. "That's better than any ice cream. Let's hear it."

Lucy groaned and closed the back door. "There's nothing to tell."

"Except that she's had Emma and Noah over to

see the horses," Tara added. "And he sent her three texts while she was outside."

"Really?" Kate drew the word out. "That sounds like progress. And we know he's a hero, between rescuing the boy in the creek and then stepping in to between Gray and that jerk to save the day the other night. Noah has that whole hot cowboy thing going for him, too. That accent alone is drool-worthy."

And there was nothing like hearing that accent while he whispered in her ear with their bodies joined.

"What's that face?" Kate demanded, peering closely at Lucy. "You're not sharing everything."

Lucy merely shrugged. "Not right now. Just give me time."

Those words were exactly what Noah had told her moments before he backed her into the shower and made her feel so much, too much. They both needed time, but they were in this together and they'd have to take this slowly. Lucy only prayed no one ended up hurt on the other side.

Chapter Thirteen

"Ma'am, I'd recommend not blocking the fire hydrant next time."

Noah hated giving the elderly lady a ticket, but she'd parked illegally and apparently the shop owner on the corner had warned her several times he'd call the police.

"There are no handicap spots on this street," she argued.

Noah pulled in a deep breath and glanced around. There were no designated spots, but that didn't justify breaking the law. He'd talk to the captain about the parking, but for now, Noah had to do his job.

"You're new in town," the elderly woman said. "Maybe you don't know who I am."

His pity for her instantly evaporated. Here he was, his shift over, yet he stood on the sidewalk arguing with a woman who thought she could throw her name around.

"No, I'm not sure who you are, ma'am," he informed her, shifting his stance and crossing his arms over his chest. "But I do know that nobody is above the law and Mr. Harris would like for you to not block the front of his store."

Noah had worked four hours overtime to help the captain out while he was short-staffed today. The wife of one of the other officers had gone into labor so Noah and the evening officer were splitting the extra shift. Which was how Noah found himself dealing with more traffic violations than usual.

"My husband is the retired mayor of Stonerock," she exclaimed. "Maybe you should worry about writing tickets for actual criminals."

Noah rubbed his forehead and adjusted his hat. "Ma'am, I can't pick and choose who gets to obey the law. Please, just find another place to park and I'll see what I can do about the handicap spaces."

She tipped her chin and adjusted her purse over her shoulder before snatching the ticket from his hand. Then she spun on her heel and got into her car, pulling away from the curb and running a red light.

Noah shook his head as he walked around the corner to where he'd had to park in a legal spot. Now he could head back to the station and end his shift.

He was more than ready for a day off. His schedule had been so screwed up over the past week, he'd barely had time to see Lucy other than at work. He missed her, and that was such a telling sign that she was more to him than just a friend.

Each time her voice came over his radio, he couldn't help but flash back to when he'd spent that morning in her bed, then the afternoon in her shower.

Keeping up appearances as just coworkers was becoming increasingly difficult. She'd worked last night, but had left at her regular time while he'd still been out on patrol. When the day shift dispatcher's voice came over the radio, Noah didn't like the change. He wanted his lifeline to be Lucy.

By the time he'd gone back to the station and hopped into his truck to head home, he was more than ready to make plans. He was done with trying to dodge her and pretend they were friends who'd slept together. He'd asked for time and all this past week had done was prove just how much he wanted to be with her. At least to get to know her more, to try to understand what was happening between them.

He shot off a text, knowing she'd get it when she woke up. He needed to get home and get some rest himself before getting Emma.

As he drove down the main part of town, he spotted Gray outside the bar. There was a pickup truck backed up on the sidewalk and he and Sam were unloading something.

Noah pulled into the adjoining lot and jogged up the sidewalk. "Need a hand?"

Gray had his hands full holding up one end of a long, raw edge piece of countertop. "Your timing is perfect."

"This is one heavy counter," Sam agreed from the bed of the truck. "Another pair of hands will make this so much easier."

The three of them finally got the piece into the front door and laid it across some tables that Gray had scooted together. Noah wiped his hands on his pants and propped his hands on his hips as he glanced around the bar. In the daylight with all the lights on, the place looked quite a bit larger.

"We haven't actually met," Noah stated, holding his hand out to Sam. "I'm Noah Spencer."

"Sam Bailey," he replied, giving a firm shake of his hand. "Thanks for helping. Gray is determined to get that bar set up in the back room and he's hell-bent on us doing it."

Gray ran his hand over the new piece of gleaming countertop. "Why would I pay someone when you need the distraction and I need a job done? I give you free beer, so quit complaining."

"You just getting off your shift?" Sam asked Noah.

Noah nodded, stifling a yawn. "Worked overtime this morning and I was headed home when I saw you guys. I can help if you need something."

Gray shook his head. "No. Go on home to bed. I'm sure you're exhausted. The hard part was getting it off the truck. Sam and I can take it from here."

"I'll stop in later to see if you need anything," he promised. "I'm willing to work for free beer, too."

Gray laughed. "You get free beer for not hauling my butt in when I hit you."

Noah shook his head. "Don't think anything of it. But if you hit me again, I'll hit back and put your butt in the back of the patrol car."

"I forgot about that," Sam stated. Then he turned to Gray. "You need to cool it where Kate is concerned. That woman is nothing but trouble."

"She's the kind of trouble I want to get into," Gray claimed.

Noah was not getting involved in anybody's woman troubles, not when he had his own chaos to deal with. Now was a good time to get the hell out of here.

"You've got my cell," he told Gray. "Text me if you need anything."

Gray nodded. "Thanks, man."

Noah headed back out into the morning sunshine. He wanted to go get Emma and have a fun day; he also wanted to see Lucy. And he had the perfect plan to do both. First he needed to get some sleep.

When he saw Lucy again later, he wanted to be rested up and ready to face whatever emotions came his way. He had a feeling when he saw her in her environment outside of work, all those feelings from the other morning would come flooding back and he'd want her even more.

"This is the greatest day ever," Emma declared.

Lucy held on tight as they rode on a trotting Hawkeye. With Emma in front of her, Lucy made sure the little girl was nestled perfectly against the pommel. Emma held on to the reins and steered the mare around the field. She was absolutely a natural.

"I think you are a better rider than I am," Lucy stated.

When Noah came up beside them on Gunner, it took all of Lucy's willpower not to focus on how sexy he looked on the back of her horse. She could easily see him on a ranch. With that wide black hat, his button-down shirt with the sleeves rolled up over tanned forearms, perfectly fitted jeans, and dusty boots, the man epitomized a hunky cowboy.

And the fact he'd reached out to her and wanted to come over for a ride only made her heart skip another beat. She knew they were technically sneaking around. They'd kept up the pretense at work and had remained circumspect in public. She had to admit there was something so attractive and intriguing about keeping their relationship on the down low.

Lucy loved it even more that he'd brought Emma. His daughter was absolutely the most adorable little thing and so easy to please. Give the girl some cookies and a horse and she was happy.

"Looks like it's going to rain soon," Noah commented as he stared at the sky.

"We'll go back soon," she promised. "It's such a beautiful evening with the mountains in the distance, the smell of fall in the air. I could stay out here all night."

"Do you camp?" Emma asked, still holding tightly to the reins. "Daddy took me and Mommy once and it was fun."

"I do love camping." Lucy held on to Emma's waist and glanced over to Noah. "This is the perfect time of year, too. I love being outside, but I don't like to get too hot or too cold, especially when I'm trying to sleep."

Noah's brows rose beneath his dark hat. "I imagine if the nights got too cool you could find ways to stay warm."

That heavy-lidded look he gave her sent shivers racing through her. The blatant flirting had hope filling that void she'd thought would be hollow forever. There was a light inside her, as silly as that sounded. But Noah was coming around and she found she was, too. The guilt wasn't as strong as it had been last week. The fear was still there, but overpowering that now was a beacon of hope. Lucy opted to cling to that optimism, instead of trying to find reasons to let fear rule her life.

Between her psychology classes and her partnership in Helping Hands, Lucy had talked to many people over the past couple of years about compartmentalizing all your emotions. When there were negative feelings, they needed to be put behind anything positive. And right now, Lucy was going to cling to Noah and Emma. They were here now and they were all having a great time.

"My daddy is afraid of mice," Emma said, turning to glance up at Lucy. "That one time we went camping, a mouse got in our tent. Mom screamed, I screamed, and Dad ran out of the tent."

Lucy laughed as she shifted her focus to Noah. "Is that so? A little mouse had you running for your life?"

He simply shrugged. "We all have our fears," he told her. "Those little things move so fast. I'm man enough to admit they creep me out."

"Well, if it helps, I'm terrified of spiders," Lucy confessed. "Anything with that many legs has to be created by the devil."

"You know what I don't like?" Emma asked. "Bees. I got stung once and then Daddy found out I was 'lergic. It scared me when he had to take me to the hospital."

"Scared me, too, Sweet Pea."

"That would be a good reason to not like bees," Lucy agreed. "When did you get stung?"

"Right before we moved here," Emma said. "My

arm got puffy and red and then I couldn't breathe very well."

"I'm pretty sure I lost a few years off my life then," Noah muttered.

Lucy couldn't imagine how terrified Noah must've been. He'd been a widower and had found out the hard way that his daughter was allergic to bee stings.

The first fat drop of rain his Lucy's nose. "Time to head back," she told them as she helped Emma guide Hawkeye back to the barn. "We might get a little wet."

By the time they reached the barn, they were all soaked. The rain was chilly and instantly cooled the evening down. She shivered as she dismounted and helped Emma down. She led the mare into the stable and Noah was right behind her with Gunner.

"You and Emma go on inside," he told her. "I'll tend to the horses."

"There's no reason for you to do that. You can take Emma on home and get dried off. I'll take care of the horses."

Noah stepped up to her, forcing Lucy to tip her head back. "Don't argue with me," he said in that low, commanding tone. "Take Emma inside and get warm. I've got this. Besides, I sort of miss this part of my life."

Lucy hadn't thought of things that way. He probably was missing working the ranch and tending the horses he'd always had. The void of his late wife wasn't the only hole in his heart.

"I'll make us some hot chocolate," she told him as she reached for Emma's hand. "How about we find some marshmallows to put on top?"

Emma nodded enthusiastically. "I want extra."

Noah laughed. "Of course you do."

Lucy picked up the toddler and hugged her tight. "Ready to race through the raindrops?"

"Ready!"

Lucy wrapped Emma tightly against her and tucked her beneath her chin as she ran toward the back porch. The rain came down in sheets now. By the time they got inside, Emma was trembling.

"Let's get you warmed up." Lucy eased the girl back and quickly realized she was crying. "Emma, what's wrong?"

"Is it going to storm?" she asked through tears and sniffling.

Lucy sat Emma on the bar top and smoothed her wet hair away from her face. "You know what, if it does, we will be just fine."

"But Daddy is still outside." She sniffed. Her big blue eyes were red with tears.

"Right now it's just raining," Lucy explained. "We need rain. Did you know that's what makes those beautiful trees change colors? It helps the grass to grow for the horses to eat, too. Rain isn't a scary thing."

"Have you been in a tornado?" Emma whispered. "It starts with rain. It's loud and scary."

Sweet Emma was terrified. Lucy wondered if she had flashbacks each time it rained, or what happened when it actually stormed. The poor child was suffering from a kind of PTSD brought on from the trauma of losing her mother. Did Noah realize his daughter suffered so?

"How about we stand at the window and watch your daddy?" Lucy suggested. "We can see him in the barn while he's brushing the horses and putting the gear away. Then you can see that he's okay."

Lucy hoisted the girl onto her hip and stood at the wide kitchen window. It was difficult to see through the heavy rain, but the light in the barn helped. Every now and then Lucy saw Noah walk from one stall to the next. She saw him nuzzling the horses, no doubt talking to them. She could almost feel the pain of his loss, how he ached to have that ranching life back again.

Torn between Noah's hurt and Emma's fear, Lucy figured this was the best place for her to be. Noah needed that time alone in the barn and Emma needed comforting. Lucy hugged the girl tighter.

"Did you used to help Daddy in your barns?" she asked, trying to focus on the animals and perhaps happier memories.

"He would let me stand on a stool and braid their manes," Emma told her as she continued looking out the window. "Sometimes I would brush their hair and put bows on the ends of their manes and tails.

Daddy also bought me this special paint and I got to paint the horses."

"Paint?" Lucy asked.

Emma smiled up at her. "It was supercool. I drew rainbows on the side of Daisy. Then we just gave her a bath and it came right off."

"I admit, I've never painted a horse before. That does sound supercool."

Emma's brows rose. "Can we paint your horses? Daddy can tell you what paint you need."

Lucy smiled and tapped Emma's cute little nose. "Of course we can. That sounds like a blast."

Lucy kept her sidetracked by discussing what design they'd be painting and how soon she could get the paint. Finally, Noah stepped in the back door and wiped the rain from his face. He slid off his jacket and hung it by the door. That simple gesture was like a punch of reality.

Noah was so comfortable here and no other man had hung a coat at the back door other than Evan. But here was Noah and Emma, infiltrating her life, and Lucy had a feeling this was all the start of something much bigger than she'd ever anticipated.

"Everything okay?" he asked as he took off his hat and hung it over his jacket.

"Just talking about painting the horses," Lucy stated, not wanting to bring up the bad memories for Emma again. She'd discuss that with Noah later. "We didn't get the hot chocolate started yet."

Noah waved a hand to dismiss the thought. "We can head home. You've hosted us long enough."

"It's no trouble at all," she assured him, not ready for him to leave. "Since my nights have freed up from school for a while, I could use the company."

Noah flashed her a smile. "We'd love to stay, then."

"Let me get you guys some towels."

Lucy sat Emma down and went to her bathroom. This was all so... Well, it was everything she'd dreamed of at one time. The family setting seemed all so real this evening. Lucy planned on making hot chocolate and perhaps they'd settle in to watch a movie and wait for the rain to pass.

When Lucy came out of the bathroom, Noah stepped into her bedroom. "Where's Emma?"

"I put her in the spare bath to dry off," he told her. "What happened when I was outside? Was it the rain?"

Clutching the towels to her chest, Lucy nodded. "She was worried you were still out there, but we talked and I steered the conversation elsewhere."

Noah reached for a towel and started drying off his hair, his face, and his neck. "I didn't think we'd have too much of a problem here. Storms in Texas are so common. That was another reason I moved away from that part of the country."

Lucy pulled her hair over her shoulder and squeezed the water into her own hand towel. "Anytime you're missing your ranch, you can come see the horses."

Noah's lips kicked up. He was so sexy with that stubble along his jawline and those dark eyes. The more time she spent with him, the more she realized she was falling headfirst in love with him.

Now what was she going to do? He wasn't looking for a serious relationship, and neither was she. And she'd promised herself never to get involved with a man who had a risky career.

Why did this have to be the man she fell for? It was almost like she'd ignored every single red flag waving around in her head and pushed right on forward where Noah was concerned.

But she hadn't just fallen for *him*. No, Lucy had gone and tumbled headfirst in love with a blue-eyed little girl with cockeyed pigtails.

Emma chose that moment to walk into the bedroom. "Can we still have hot chocolate?" she asked Lucy.

Lucy took the towel from Noah and tossed them both into the hamper just inside the bathroom door. "Of course we can. I say we snuggle up on the couch with hot chocolate, blankets, and whatever movie you want."

Emma let out a scream of excitement and gave Lucy a fist bump. Then she turned and ran back down the hall.

"Are you sure you don't mind us just bursting in here?"

Lucy turned her attention to Noah. "I want you

both here. I love having you guys around and I'm more than ready for a relaxing evening."

Noah took a step forward, reaching up to frame her face with his hands. "How did this happen?"

"I cracked that wall you had up."

Noah nipped at her lips. "I can't promise you anything."

Lucy's heart ached for the fear he clung to. She'd taken a huge risk and opened her heart to him. Now she only hoped he would take the leap of faith, as well.

"I'm not asking for promises," she told him, taking hold of his wrists and looking into his eyes. "I'm asking for possibilities."

"I'm doing what I can."

Lucy took a step back. "That's a great start."

Leaving him in her room, Lucy headed down the hallway. As much as she wanted to explore this conversation even further, she wanted him to think for himself. She wanted—no, needed—Noah to realize that he could open himself up again. That if she was also taking a risk, maybe they should be taking it together...and perhaps happiness could be waiting for them both.

Chapter Fourteen

Over the next two weeks, the fall air turned colder. Noah still wasn't used to this climate, but he was getting more used to the town. The people of Stonerock still considered him an outsider and a transplant, but they were welcoming and only mentioned his accent a few times a day now.

There was an opening on the day shift and he was hoping to slide into that if Captain St. John didn't give someone with seniority the position. Going back on days would be so amazing with Emma, especially when she started school next fall. Hopefully in that year's time, they'd fall into a more consistent pattern.

Of course, Lucy was almost done with schooling and in a few months she wouldn't even be at the station house anymore. As excited as he was for her, he also hated not having her on the other end of his radio.

Each night since the heavy rains, he'd seen Lucy on a personal basis. They'd fallen into an easy pattern and he'd been at her house every evening. She and Emma worked on dinner and he tended to the horses. He'd be lying if he didn't admit the horses weren't the only reason he came by.

Lucy had gotten to him. She'd shown him how easy it was to let go and open up. He hadn't realized just how easy it was to let someone else in, all while getting over such a tragic loss. Perhaps because Lucy got him. She didn't try to tell him she was sorry for his loss; she didn't try to dance around the topic. She forced him to talk about it, to keep his late wife's memory alive.

The fact that she wasn't jealous of his late wife, that she wasn't trying to replace her, was quite possibly the greatest part of this whole process. Noah wanted to be happy again; he wanted to move on and not feel like he was making a mistake. And he truly didn't believe Lucy was a mistake. He was falling for her. Each night when he left her house, he looked forward to coming back tomorrow.

Tonight, though, Emma's sitter was having a sleepover at her house. The lady was having all of her "kids" for a slumber party where they would have

movies and popcorn and games. Apparently Emma's
sitter did this quite often and the kids absolutely loved
it. So did the parents.

Noah hadn't told Lucy about this. He wanted to
surprise her by coming alone. She'd said she was
going to let Emma decide the cuisine for the night
once they arrived. But Noah had already stopped at
the diner on the edge of town and bought Lucy's favorite dish. He only knew it was her favorite because
he asked Kate. He figured that was crossing some
line, but he didn't care. He wanted to show Lucy how
much she'd come to mean to him and he wanted her
to know she didn't always have to do everything for
others. She needed to be pampered, too.

Noah pulled around to the back of her house. He
always kept his truck out of sight from anyone passing on the road. Not that he was ashamed or embarrassed, but they had agreed to keep things between
them and he wanted to be respectful to her.

He grabbed the sacks from the front seat and as
he stepped from the truck, Lucy came out onto the
back porch. This evening she wore a simple navy
dress with long sleeves and a pair of cowgirl boots.
The boots she'd often paired with her jeans when
she'd been in the barn, but he hadn't seen her in a
dress before. And he liked it.

As he headed up the stone path toward the steps,
Lucy glanced back to the truck. "Where's Emma?"

"It's just us tonight." He held up the sacks. "With

some beef and noodles, potatoes, and rolls. I decided you needed a break."

Her bright eyes widened. "Is that so? Then I guess now is a good time to tell you that I already made dessert."

Noah leaned in and slid his mouth over hers. He never tired of her touch, her taste, and he wondered if he ever would.

"Maybe I already had plans for dessert," he murmured against her lips.

She trembled against him then eased back. "Did you come here to seduce me, Officer?"

Noah's body stirred at her sultry question. "Darlin', you've been seducing me since I stepped foot into your meeting over a month ago."

She took the bags from his hands and headed into the kitchen. The sway of her hips beneath that dress had him fantasizing all sorts of delicious scenarios... none that had anything to do with the takeout he'd just brought.

Noah followed her inside and the second she set the bags on the counter, he took hold of her shoulders and spun her around. He swallowed her gasp of surprise as his mouth descended onto hers. Her fingers curled over his shoulders. He hadn't even bothered taking off his jacket. He'd taken one look at her and knew he couldn't wait to have her. It had been too long since he'd been able to touch her the way he'd wanted, the way he desired. They'd been playing it safe for the sake of Emma, and not to confuse her, but he was done being safe for the night.

"Dinner can wait," he declared as he lifted her against him.

Wrapping his arms tight around her waist, he headed for the hall.

"The spare room."

Now was not the time to question her reasoning for deterring him to the guest room once again. He wanted her now and from the way she was panting against his ear and kissing his jawline, she was just as eager. Later he would ask his questions. Right now, he had more pressing issues.

"You're so damn sexy with this dress and these boots."

Lucy's fingers threaded through his hair. "I wanted to look pretty for you."

Easing back so he could look her in the eyes, he said, "You're always pretty, Lucy. You don't even have to try."

He covered her lips once again as he tugged up the hem of her dress. Noah filled his hands with her backside and lifted her off the floor, aligning their hips.

Lucy's boots clattered to the floor as Noah trailed his lips across her jaw and down her neck. Her head tipped back giving him better access. She was all-consuming. The need to touch her everywhere all at once absolutely controlled him.

Noah lay her down on the bed, never taking his eyes off of her as he stripped his clothes. Her dress, bunched around her waist, gave him a tantalizing view of her simple white panties. Once he was bare, Noah gripped the edge of her underwear and pulled them down her legs, tossing the unwanted garment to the side.

When she started to sit up to take her dress off, Noah reached for her hands and secured her wrists in his grip. He held her arms up above her head.

"I need you now," he told her as he settled between her legs. "I'll undress you later."

Her eyes flared with desire as he joined their bodies. With Lucy wrapped all around him, Noah knew he wasn't going anywhere tonight. He wanted to stay in her bed; he wanted to be here with her in the morning. He wanted to make love to her again and again.

"Noah, I—"

Caught up in the moment, he captured her mouth with his, not ready to hear the words that she was about to say. He wasn't positive, but he thought he'd seen something more than desire in her eyes. He'd seen so much of her heart when she looked up at him. And he wasn't prepared for it, not now when his body was surging toward an earth-shattering climax.

As he surged into her again, he felt her body tighten beneath his as she arched against him. Her lips tore away from his and she cried out a throaty moan as she came. Noah held her tight as his own release hit. He kept his hold on her hips as the trembling consumed him. Lucy whispered something, but he couldn't make it out.

Once his body calmed, he pulled her close and kissed the top of her head. He wanted some answers from her. If she wanted to move forward, then he deserved some of that honesty. He deserved some of that openness she always wanted from him.

"I'm getting hungry." Lucy slid her fingertips over Noah's bare chest and down to his taut abs. "We might have to heat up dinner."

"Or we could eat it cold in bed," Noah said as he pulled her closer to his side.

"That would be fine, too." Pressing her palm to his chest, she rose up and looked down at him. "Why don't I go get it and you wait here?"

He looked at her as if he wanted to say something, but finally nodded. "Sounds good."

Lucy came to her feet and smoothed her dress down. She stepped over her underwear and boots, bypassed his clothes and headed to the kitchen, where the bags had been forgotten for a time. Her entire body still hummed. That thought was so ridiculous, but it was an accurate statement.

She pulled the boxes from the bag and sat them all out on her kitchen island. Even though everything was no doubt cold, the scents were amazing.

She figured she'd just take the boxes and some plastic forks and napkins. No need to waste plates. She had some bottles of water she'd bring in, too. A bed picnic sounded so sexy and it was something she'd never done before.

Lucy pulled a tray off the top of her fridge and stacked up all the things on there. She'd get the dessert later...probably much later.

Humming, she headed down the hall, but when she turned the corner to the spare room, Noah wasn't in there. Perhaps he went to the bathroom. She set the tray on the rumpled bed, smiling at the memories they'd created there.

She'd been so afraid at first. Afraid of her feelings, afraid of moving ahead with those emotions she didn't want. But now that she was with Noah, she'd fallen for him. She'd fallen for Emma, too, and she'd be lying if she didn't admit that she wanted that family. She wanted it here on her little ranch. She wanted more than she ever thought she'd dream of again.

For the first time in two years she had hope and she was ready to take this risk and admit her feelings to Noah. She'd started to when they were in bed together, which wasn't the best timing, but the moment had overwhelmed her and the words were on her lips before she could stop them.

Noah had stopped them. He'd kissed her as if he'd known what was going through her mind. Still, he deserved to know where she stood. He didn't need to reciprocate her feelings, but she had to tell him.

"Lucy."

Noah called her name and Lucy stepped into the hall. She went to the end where her room was and found him sitting on the edge of the bed. He'd put on his jeans, leaving them unfastened, and wore nothing else.

"What are you doing in here?" she asked, standing in the doorway.

He met her gaze from across the room. "You never bring me in here."

Lucy gripped the door frame and swallowed. What could she say? She'd never had another man in her bedroom other than her husband. After he'd passed, she'd sold their bedroom furniture and replaced it. She simply hadn't been able to sleep in the same bed they'd shared, not when she was alone.

"Lucy." Noah came to his feet. "I get loss. Believe me, it's hell at times. But you show me all these ways you're ready to move on, and yet we've never made love on your bed."

Noah kept his distance, but the pain in his eyes staring back at her might as well be a knife twisting in her heart.

Made love.

The fact he used that term had Lucy wanting to step forward, but…she couldn't.

"As long as you keep me from this room, can you

keep your past and your present in separate compartments in your heart?" he went on, hurt lacing his voice. "You wanted me to take a chance. I *did* take a chance, but if you're keeping me at a distance, we can't move forward."

Lucy let go of the door and stepped inside. "I'm not keeping you at a distance," she defended. "I've slept with you, Noah. I haven't let another man get that close to me in two years."

Noah ran a hand down his face and glanced up to the ceiling as he blew out a breath. "You trust me with your body," he told her as he brought his dark eyes back to hers. "You look at me like you want more and I can't deny that I'm starting to want more. That scares the hell out of me, because if you can't trust me in here," he said, holding his arms wide to encompass the bedroom, "then you can't trust me to form a relationship."

Tears pricked her eyes as she wrapped her arms around her midsection. The hurt seeping inside her had her shaking her head in denial.

"I do trust you," she cried. "You know I've never been this open with anyone."

Noah nodded. "I do know that," he agreed, his tone soft, heartbreaking. "I also know as long as that picture stays by your bed, nobody else will be allowed in this room, much less in your heart."

Lucy wanted to say something, to defend herself, but he was right. She honestly hadn't pushed too far into her feelings before now to see that she was indeed clinging to just a fraction of what her life was in an attempt to stay afloat emotionally.

"You've been too busy working on other people," he added. "Maybe you need to start taking care of yourself."

"I take care of myself."

Even to her own ears, the argument sounded feeble.

Noah stepped toward her, gripped her shoulders and forced her to tip her head back to look at him. "No, you haven't. I care for you, Lucy. I care more than I wanted to. You made me want things I never thought I would want again."

Lucy's heart clenched. "Why does this sound like the end?"

"We can't move forward," he stated, framing her face with his hands. "You may want to, but are you ready for me to sleep in here? Are you ready to take this public and try a real relationship?"

She was…wasn't she?

"Wait, you were the one who wanted to keep this discreet," she countered. "Why are you asking me?"

"Because you haven't dated in two years. Because you won't get in that bed with me." He kissed her softly, quickly. "And because I'm more ready than you are and I didn't think that was possible."

He let her go and took a step back. "When you're ready, let me know."

Noah maneuvered around her, leaving her to stare at the perfectly made bed and the photo on her nightstand. She was so happy in that picture. She'd had it all once—so had Noah. She'd had hopes and dreams, until they were all taken away from her.

Lucy crossed the room and sank down on the edge of the bed. She gripped the post and rested her head against it as she heard Noah in the other room. Moments later she heard her back door open and close. That final click resounded through the house. Lucy closed her eyes and bit her bottom lip, trying to keep the tears at bay.

One teardrop trailed down her cheek and she didn't even bother to swipe it away. She'd been ready for Noah to come into her life; she'd been pulling him in from day one. And all this time that she'd been trying to heal him, she hadn't recognized that she wasn't fully complete herself.

She picked up the pewter frame she'd gotten for her wedding. Evan's wide grin beamed back at her and she knew without a doubt that he would want her to put closure on her past.

Lucy's heart literally ached as she finally let the tears flow. She'd loved Evan with her whole heart. She would always love him, but she was going to have to let him go if she wanted her life back.

And Lucy was afraid she'd let the happiest part of her present life walk out the door.

Chapter Fifteen

"This isn't a sight I thought I'd see."

Noah sat on the stool next to Sam as Gray handed over two bottles of a local brew.

"I didn't plan on being here tonight," Noah confessed. "Emma is at a sleepover, though, so I don't have much else to do."

That was a total lie. He'd planned on staying in Lucy's bed all night. He'd planned on getting to know her more, opening up and explaining how much his feelings had grown. She'd shown him how it was to move on, to help others through grief. Lucy was fabulous with Emma, she was giving to him, and she was so damn sexy he ached knowing he'd never have her again.

Noah had been gone for an hour and he was already wondering if he'd made a colossal mistake. Should he have stayed and talked this out? Maybe, but knowing she didn't want him in her bed, rather than some guest bed, was hurtful. He wasn't a guest, damn it. Or maybe he was, but he thought they were so much more.

"Problems with Lucy?" Sam asked, still staring at his bottle.

"We're just friends."

A friend he could still taste on his lips. A friend who had worked her way into his heart, into his daughter's heart.

"Is that so?" Gray asked with a cocky side grin. "She just walked in with Tara and Kate."

Noah jerked his head over his shoulder, and Gray's laughter mocked him. Lucy was nowhere in sight, and neither were her friends.

"That's what I thought," Gray said, leaning over and resting his forearms on the bar. "So what's the deal?"

Noah turned back on his stool and reached for his beer. He took a hearty drink, welcoming the wheat flavor and the spices on the back end.

"We attempted more, but that didn't work out," he admitted. "That's all."

"That's all." Sam let out a low laugh. "Nothing with women is ever that simple. Even after a year apart, Tara and I still aren't simple and, according to the courts, we should be because it's over."

Noah had honestly never seen a man so devastated. "Well, Lucy and I have only known each other a short time. We just had a whirlwind...relationship. Now it's over."

"Relationship," Gray repeated. "Whatever you call it, you look like hell."

Noah picked up his bottle and did a mock salute. "Ironically, I feel like hell."

The two men tapped their beer bottles to his, then took a swallow. Before any of them could say anything, Gray got called away to a group of females at the other end of the bar. To Noah, they seemed flirty, and he already knew Gray had just enough charm to appease the group of giggling girls. From the looks of them, he surmised they were celebrating a twenty-first birthday.

Noah turned his attention back to Sam. "How long were you married?"

"Not long." Sam started to peel the label from the bottle. "A couple of years. We married right before Marley was born, which was a mistake. Marrying because of a baby is never the solution."

Noah wouldn't know. He'd fallen in love, married, then had a baby. But he would never knock someone else's life choices. Whatever worked for them.

"Not to pry, but have you told her how you feel?"

Sam laughed. "She's aware. We got married too soon, weren't really in love...at least that's what she says. I was—I am—in love with her."

Noah's heart clenched. He couldn't deny that he was feeling something rather strong for Lucy, too. Love? Hell, he wasn't sure, but what he felt was so much more than just friendship.

What should he do about it?

Did he wait on her? Did he wait around and see if she was truly ready? At what point did he move on himself?

Who the hell was he kidding? He didn't want to move on. He'd lost his wife and he'd never thought he'd crawl out from that dark hole. Then he'd met Lucy and there'd been light in his life again. The light was still there, still shining, but he was still alone.

"Fight for her."

Noah thought he heard Sam wrong. His voice was barely audible over the bass-heavy music pervading the bar.

"If you want Lucy, fight for her," Sam stated. "She's amazing. I don't know your whole story, but… Hell, who am I to give advice on relationships?"

Noah took another pull of his beer. "I lost my wife and our ranch about eight months ago. I have a four-year-old daughter. She's pretty taken with Lucy. Those two are… They're so alike and get along like they're long-lost friends. Lucy is so good with her."

"Having kids makes things so much more complicated," Sam stated. "They can also make things so clear, too."

"I can't imagine how you deal with an ex and a child." Noah finished off his beer and set the bottle on the bar. "If you want Tara back, why don't you just make her see why?"

Sam continued to toy with the label. "We're pretty complicated. I was offered a job in Nashville. Thinking about taking it and leaving Stonerock."

Noah leaned his elbows on the bar. "Does Tara know?"

"Not yet. Haven't decided what I'm doing. Marley is the major factor. I don't want to make things difficult for her, but staying here isn't good for me, either."

"I had to leave Texas, so I get where you're coming from." Noah caught Gray's attention and motioned him over for another beer. "You have to do what's best to keep moving forward."

Sam let out a laugh. "I just hang here to talk with Gray. I'm not really some sappy drunk who's lost all hope."

"Didn't think you were."

"Others do," he replied. "Not that I care. Gray is a good friend and I figure if I can hang here and give him my business, it's a win-win."

Gray slid another beer across to Noah. "You ladies done sharing life stories?"

"For now," Noah told him.

"You want to know how to get to Lucy?" Gray asked. "She's a simple person, really. Nobody has actually tried to do things for her. She's always putting herself out there for everyone else."

Noah nodded. That was the crux of the entire situation. She wanted to be the one person for everyone else, but couldn't let one person be everything for her.

"I've already figured that out," Noah replied. "Trying to get that woman to see that is like beating my head against the wall."

Gray rested his palms on the bar top. "Don't give up on her."

Noah didn't say anything. What could he say? He wasn't the one who had given up. He'd just gotten to the point where he truly wanted to try a relationship and expose his most vulnerable side and Lucy hadn't removed that steel barrier she'd had in place for the past two years.

At this point all he could do was move on with the life he'd started here with Emma. Seeing Lucy at work would hurt. Hearing her voice over the radio would be crushing. But he couldn't make her see that they could heal each other. She had to find that resolution herself.

"We have a report of an armed robbery in progress at Stonerock Bank."

He'd been right. Hearing Lucy's voice over his radio was gut-wrenching. Noah had given her a brief hello when he'd come into work; that had been the extent of their conversation. For the past week they'd been cordial, just like coworkers should be. But now they weren't even acting like coworkers. They had back-tracked to that awkward stage, almost like strangers.

They weren't strangers, though. They had been lovers. They knew each other's secrets, their fears.

Noah had to admit it. The woman had him tied up in knots. But right now, with her voice over his radio, he had a robbery to focus on.

"One report from a teller says there's only one man, but she says he's armed," Lucy went on. "She was in the bathroom when she heard him come in and demand money, so she hasn't seen a weapon. She's locked herself in and her phone is still on. I can hear the suspect, but I can't make out what he's saying."

Adrenaline pumping, Noah put on his lights and siren. If a perp was wielding a gun or any weapon, there were people in danger. Noah only hoped the perp wasn't under the influence of something, because guns and drugs made for a dangerous combo. He'd only dealt with a handful of armed robberies in Texas, but thankfully they'd all ended peacefully.

Noah pulled into the lot at the same time McCoy pulled in. This was the early bank that opened at seven to get businesses started for the day. Noah's shift only had an hour left, but he already knew this situation would take longer than sixty minutes.

"I'm on the scene," McCoy checked in through the radio.

"I'm here, too," Noah added. "The blinds are still closed."

"The teller said she thinks he forced his way in with one of the workers," Lucy informed them. "The lobby isn't open yet."

That would make sense. Get in when all of the nightly bank bags were waiting for the morning deposits.

Noah surveyed the parking lot, looking for an accomplice or a getaway car. The sun was barely on the horizon, but he didn't see any unusual cars. Just a couple parked in the employee section. Still, he scanned the street. The rest of the nearby businesses were still closed, for which he was grateful. If this robber ran out with a gun, at least the streets were still bare.

Movement in the window caught Noah's eye. "The suspect just shifted the blinds," he said in his radio. "He is holding a gun."

"I've got more units en route," Lucy informed him. "Be careful."

She'd never said those words before and Noah knew full well she was talking directly to him. He also knew McCoy and all the other units had heard her, but she'd let him know she cared. There might be hope.

Noah didn't reply. He needed to stay in this moment and make sure all those inside got out un-harmed.

While McCoy called the bank hoping to get an answer, Noah kept watch on the side of the building. From this angle he could see the back and front entrances and he'd know if either of the doors opened. No movement made him nervous. That meant the gunman was still in the bank. Hopefully the suspect wouldn't catch the teller in the bathroom. They needed her eyes on the inside. She was their only life-line between him and Lucy.

The back door eased slightly open and Noah remained behind the open door of his patrol car. His gun in hand and resting on the top of the door, he kept his eyes focused on the back. He could see McCoy get into position from the side, as well. Another unit pulled up by McCoy, instantly getting ready.

Noah knew Lucy was on the other end of that radio, but the line was completely silent. Right now, time seemed to stand still as he waited to see who had opened that door.

"Movement in the back," McCoy stated into the radio.

The door opened farther at the same time that Captain St. John pulled in beside Noah. There were several officers on the scene, but right now they were still at the mercy of the suspect.

"I've lost contact with the teller," Lucy stated.

Noah prayed whoever was on the other side of

that door was a hostage trying to escape. Just as the thought crossed his mind, he saw an arm snake around the door, then he heard shots fired…and his world went black.

Chapter Sixteen

Lucy stared at the screens ahead of her and held her breath as she listened to the radio. Gunshots were fired at the scene. Her heart stopped as she waited on the officers to check in.

"I'm sure everything is all right," Carla said as she patted Lucy's shoulder.

Lucy and the other dispatcher had worked this end of a robbery before, but Lucy had never felt more fear and helplessness than she did now. Her shift ended an hour ago. She could leave and turn it over to the day shift, but she couldn't leave. Carla wasn't leaving her, either.

Lucy gripped her hands in her lap. She willed the phone to ring from the teller; she prayed she'd hear Noah's voice over the radio. She wanted this entire situation to come to an end with Noah safe. The nerves swirling around in her stomach were so much more than she could bear.

She couldn't go through this again. She couldn't lose a man she cared about. Lucy bit on her bottom lip, willing the burn in her throat and eyes to subside. Now more than ever she needed to hold it together.

An image of Emma flashed through Lucy's mind. There was no way fate would be that cruel to steal both parents from her life.

"Officer down."

The report over the radio had Lucy gripping the mic on the desk. "Repeat," she demanded, desperately hoping she'd heard wrong.

"Officer Spencer is down. The suspect is down, too. We'll need two squads on the scene," Captain St. John confirmed. "All hostages are okay. We've secured the area, but will let the EMTs through."

"What's the status on Spencer?" Carla asked, reaching across the desk to hold Lucy's hand.

She was too stunned, almost sick to her stomach, to think, much less to speak.

"He's coming around," McCoy chimed in. "He hit his head. He needs to be checked out."

Hit his head? Lucy didn't know whether to be furious at how they'd scared her or relieved that he hadn't been shot.

"EMTs should be arriving on the scene in three minutes," Carla told them.

At least one of them was able to still do their job. Lucy wasn't sure she would've been able to do this on her own.

Time seemed to speed up a little more now that they knew what was going on and the situation had been resolved. Once the EMTs reached the scene and triaged the injured, Lucy got a report from the captain. The suspect was getting checked out after getting grazed on the arm with a bullet. He'd be accompanied to the hospital by two officers. More important, Noah would be fine, though he too was being transported to the hospital to get checked out.

He apparently had fired the shot that struck the suspect. When the suspect had fired back, Noah had ducked and lost his balance, hitting his head on the curb behind him.

Relief flooded her, yet she still had an overwhelming desire to see him for herself. She wanted to go to the hospital and be with him, then offer him a ride home. But she didn't know if he even wanted to see her. Earlier, before all this went down, she'd told him to be careful, but he hadn't replied. Not that it would've been professional, but she'd hoped he would've said something.

In the end, Lucy went home. She was too wound up to sleep, she had no schoolwork to do at the moment, and the meetings were already planned out for the next three weeks.

Which left her alone with her thoughts. Not a good place to be. She stripped from the clothes she'd worn to work and pulled on a pair of yoga pants and a sweatshirt. She'd end up at the barns tending to the horses in a bit. Since she'd gotten in late her stomach was growling, so she needed to grab a bite first.

As she sat on the bed and pulled on her socks, she glanced to the photo on her night table. There was nothing wrong with keeping pictures, and there was nothing wrong with having them on display. But Lucy completely saw where Noah was coming from. She understood his frustrations.

But Lucy had come to her own understanding earlier. She'd been right not to let Noah deeper into her world. When she'd been on the other end of that robbery, she had been close to a panic attack. She'd only known fear like that one other time. She couldn't go through that every day of her life. How was that any way to live?

Noah had been right to leave last week. He'd been right to walk away before they grew even closer with the bond they'd started. The sooner she could get out of working with him, the better off she'd be. Lucy needed to break free from Noah. She needed to not have that fear of loving someone all the while knowing he was risking his life every single day.

Leaving the picture where it was, Lucy headed to

the kitchen where her muck boots were waiting by the back door. Surely once she cared for the horses she'd be tired enough to fall into a mind-numbing sleep. She needed to do something to work off her energy and carry her away from her thoughts.

But every single thought circled back to Noah. Once upon a time her mind only held Evan. He was still there, but Noah occupied the space in the forefront now. That was how Lucy knew she'd moved on. Unfortunately, she'd moved on with yet another man who took risks.

Lucy stepped into the barn, the sunshine beaming in through the open ends. As she stepped up to pet Gunner, she couldn't help but smile at the thought of Emma painting her horse back in Texas.

The sound of a vehicle pulling up her driveway had Lucy stepping to the entrance to the stables. That black truck she'd become so familiar with pulled in like it had so many times before.

To see him perfectly fine as he stepped from his truck, still wearing his uniform, did so much to her. He was here, as if just a few hours ago his life hadn't been in danger. Noah may be able to live like that, but she simply couldn't.

Lucy stayed in the doorway, afraid if she got too close she'd crumble and go against the one rule she should've stuck to all along. The small white bandage stood out against the tanned skin of his face, looking like the perfect visual reminder that a man with a risky job was not for her. No matter how much her heart told her otherwise.

"Shouldn't you be home resting?" she asked when he got closer.

Noah stopped several feet away and shoved his hands in his pockets. "I should be here," he told her. "Carla said you were scared earlier."

Damn gossipy station house. That was the downfall of being like one big family. Everybody knew everything.

"I was worried, yes. My friends and coworkers were facing a gunman."

Noah started to take another step, but Lucy held her hands up. "What are you doing here, Noah?"

"I came to talk to you and you're going to listen."

Stunned at his abrupt attitude, she dropped her hands to her side.

"You don't have to admit to me that you were scared," he went on. "I was, too. It's natural when you're facing the unknown. But you know what I realized in those moments? I don't want to live without you, Lucy. I lost someone I loved and I sure as hell don't want to lose someone else."

Was he saying what she thought he was saying? Did he love her?

Of all the times for him to figure out his feelings.

Lucy's heart was torn in two. Part of her was elated he was finally admitting his emotions, but the other part, the realistic part, knew this could never be. She had too many fears, too many worries.

He closed the distance between them and slid his hands up her arms. "I know you're still afraid, Lucy, but I want to explore this with you. I want to help you get over your fear. I'm not ready to jump into marriage, but I'm definitely not letting you go so easily, either."

This amazing man who had just faced an armed robber after working a fourteen-hour shift stood before her ready to fight her battles. But her past and all of the doubts swirling around inside her head were keeping her from throwing herself into his arms. She had to guard her heart. She'd barely put the pieces back together and another hard blow would surely be too much to bear.

"I promised myself I'd never get involved with a man who constantly put his life on the line." It took everything in her to cross her arms and not reach for him. "Being on the other end of that call today…"

Lucy shook her head and turned her back to him, afraid he'd see too much in her eyes. She had to stay strong.

"Are you that afraid of getting involved again?" he asked. His shoes scuffed over the ground as he moved closer, now only inches from her back. She could feel his body heat permeating her. "You think this is easy for me? It's terrifying, but I'm stronger now than I was and I'm stronger since meeting you."

Lucy squeezed her eyes shut and dropped her head. With her arms banded around her waist, she willed the hurt and the temptation away. It would be so easy to turn and throw her arms around Noah, to lean into him and let him take her cares and burdens.

No. Actually that would be the hard part. Being dependent on a man who might involuntarily leave her would be the most difficult part.

Lucy squared her shoulders and turned. His eyes held hers. His tired eyes. He'd had a hard night, and had opted to come here first.

"You can't be serious," she told him. "You can't be ready to move on when you're still grieving. You just want me because you're comfortable with me and because the physical attraction is so strong."

Noah let out a bark of laughter. "You think I'm here fighting for you because of sex? Lucy, you drive me out of my mind. You make me see a future when I was positive there would never be another woman for me. I sure as hell never thought I'd find someone as soon as I got into town."

That bandage over his eyebrow and temple continued to mock her. Lucy reached up, brushing her fingertips just beneath the tape.

"Are you really all right? No concussion or anything?"

He reached up, gripping her hand in his as he turned his face into her palm. "Nothing is wrong with me," he assured her. "I care more about you and how scared you are than I do about a bump on my head."

Tears clogged her throat. "It could've so easily been a bullet."

Noah framed her face and kissed her forehead. "And you could die in a storm," he countered as he pulled back to look her in the eyes. "We can't live like that, Lucy. We have to push forward and grab happiness while we can. We're not guaranteed tomorrow and we're not guaranteed a second chance at love."

Lucy blinked back the tears, but one slipped down her cheek. "You love me."

Noah smiled as he wiped her tears with the pad of his thumb. "I've known it for a while, but I finally admitted it to myself. If you don't want to be with me because you don't feel the same, that's one thing, but if you're running because you're scared, I won't let you do this alone."

"I can't lose you," she whispered. "I can't go through that again."

"I don't want to deal with loss again, either," he told her as he pulled her against his chest. "But if I have a day of happiness with you, that's better than letting go of this second chance."

Lucy wrapped her arms around him and inhaled his familiar scent. "Why are you making sense? I'm trying to be practical. I'm trying to save us both heartache."

Noah eased her back and smoothed her hair from her face. "You're not saving either of us by pushing me away. The only thing that will save me is having you in my life."

Oh, that man had the absolute best response to everything. He was determined to save her when, from the start, she'd been trying to save him.

Lucy flattened her hands against his back and tipped her head to look at him. "You're worth the risk," she told him. "I've never met anyone who would be worth laying my heart on the line again. Until you."

Noah lifted her off the ground and captured her lips. The horses neighed and stomped behind her as if they were giving their blessing. Lucy opened to him, needing to feel him, needing to immerse herself in this moment, this man.

Finally, after so long of wondering if happiness did exist for her again, she'd discovered it. All of his emotions came pouring out into the kiss and Lucy knew this was a moment she'd remember forever.

"I think I should go inside and lay down for a while," he muttered against her lips as he sat her back on the ground.

"Is that right?"

"Unless you need help with the horses."

Lucy shook her head and threaded her fingers through his hair. "They're actually fine. I was just out here because I was too wound up to go to bed. I had nervous energy to burn off."

Noah slid his lips across her jaw and up to the sensitive spot behind her ear. "I have a better idea."

As he led her into the house, Lucy had a sense of relief, a peacefulness she hadn't felt in so long.

They'd reached the hallway and Noah turned to step into the guest room, but she stopped him, placing a hand on his chest. "Not in there," she told him, shaking her head. "From now on I want you in my bed. In my room."

His eyes sought hers, his brows drew in. "You're sure?"

Lucy pulled in a deep breath and nodded. "It's where you belong. Where *we* belong."

In one motion he scooped her up into his arms and kissed her, giving her just a taste of the pleasure that was to come.

"I love you, Noah," she said once she could breathe again.

"I love you, too, Lucy." Then he carried her into her bedroom.

Epilogue

"I love surprises."

Emma hopped out of his truck and raced ahead of Noah toward the barn. It had been almost a month since he and Lucy had agreed to start moving forward together as an official couple. Their coworkers in the department teased that they'd all seen it coming. Noah had, too, but he'd had to be cautious.

Since that time, Lucy, Emma and he had spent quite a bit of time together. They'd done picnics, horseback riding, dinners, movie nights, days at the park. There had been so many memories made already, Noah was ready to move their relationship to the next level and he'd already set the ball in motion.

As he stepped into the barn, he spotted Lucy at the other end guiding Hawkeye in. Emma ran up to her and gave her legs a hug.

"You guys are just in time," Lucy said, patting Emma's back. "I need you two to get Gunner out."

"Are we riding today?" Emma asked.

Lucy's wide smile seemed to light up her whole face. Noah figured he'd never get used to that anxious, giddy feeling each time he was with her. He hoped he didn't. Lucy was refreshing, she was loving, caring, she was the breath of air he needed in his life at just the right time.

"We may ride in a bit," Lucy said. "Why don't you go ahead and get him out and we'll take him out back. You can braid his mane."

Noah slid the stall door open and gripped Gunner's reins. As he pulled him out, he realized something was on the side of the horse. He looked closer, then gasped, his eyes darting back to Lucy.

"What does it say?" Emma asked.

Lucy stepped closer, pulling Hawkeye behind her.

Noah looked back to the horse, who had been painted in bright yellow letters: Will You Marry Me?

Swallowing the lump of emotions, Noah laughed as he turned to look at Lucy. "You're asking me?"

She shrugged. "I'm asking both of you."

"What does it say?" Emma cried, jumping up and down.

Noah focused on Emma. "Lucy wants to know if we'll marry her and be one family."

Emma's bright blue eyes widened. "Really?"

Lucy held out paint markers to Noah. "You can write your reply on Hawkeye."

Noah eyed the markers in her hand. The fact that Lucy bit down on her lip as if she were nervous was the most adorable thing he'd ever seen. Well, aside from this proposal.

He took the yellow marker and handed the pink one to Emma. They stepped to the other side of Hawkeye. Noah pulled the lid off and started writing. Emma was doing the same just below him.

Once they were done, Noah stepped back as hope flooded him.

Lucy moved around to the other side of Gunner and glanced down at his side. Noah had written a huge YES and Emma had made a large smiley face.

"This is the best day ever," Emma said as she looked up to Lucy.

Noah wasn't sure who was going to cry first, him or Lucy.

"You know, I was going to ask you this weekend," he told her as he reached out to take her hand. "I had Gray in on it and we had a whole romantic evening set up for us."

"With Gray?"

Noah shook his head. "Well, he was helping, but he wouldn't have been there for the main event."

Lucy's smile widened as her eyes sparkled with unshed tears. "You can still plan a surprise romantic evening."

"I plan on surprising you for the rest of my life," he told her. "Emma and I are the luckiest people right now."

Lucy bent down and picked up Emma, who still held on to her marker. "I'd say I'm the lucky one," Lucy stated as she kissed Emma's cheek.

"Does this mean I can get a new horse?" she asked her dad. "Daisy number two can have the stall on the end."

Noah laughed. "We can definitely look into getting you another Daisy."

"And we can save that stall just for her," Lucy added, giving the girl a smile.

"I love you, Lucy," Emma said as she threw her arms around Lucy's neck.

Lucy met Noah's eyes over his daughter's head. Nothing in the world was worth more than this moment. And no amount of fear or worry over the unknown would steal their happiness again. He'd make sure their lives were full of happily-ever-after.

* * * * *

LET'S TALK

Romance

For exclusive extracts, competitions
and special offers, find us online:

facebook.com/millsandboon

@MillsandBoon

@MillsandBoonUK

Get in touch on 01413 063232

For all the latest titles coming soon, visit
millsandboon.co.uk/nextmonth